Pogonip

POGONIP

A tale of the Old West

Book I of

The Four T Ranch Series

By O'Steve

ISBN-13: 9781493554782

ISBN-10: 1493554786

Dedication

Pogonip is dedicated to Elizabeth "Jean" Stone, my loving helpmate.

Website address: www.pogonipbook.com

Author O'Steve is the pen name of Steven P. Stone. He uses it to sign his watercolor paintings and other publications. The name was given to him by his grandchildren.

Thanks to friends Rob Wiley and Chuck Winters for their efforts in editing and preparing the manuscript for publishing.

BOOK ONE

Chapter One

Pogonip, the young man thought.

White death.

"Yep Sam, there's going to be a pogonip. I can see ice crystals forming in the air," Talon muttered, as if Sam, his blue roan, could answer.

"I really dug us a hole this time. We're trapped on this mountain trail. Jackson Slager can just wait for us at the top, where the trail crosses the ridge – an ideal ambush spot. Can't go back, with at least four of his boys trackin' us. And we'll freeze if we stay here. Yep, I really put us in a spot."

Wyoming winters had taught Talon what to expect in this kind of weather - fast dropping temperatures and, from the looks of the cloud cover, heavy snow. They were on the east side of the mountain, and the light was fading fast. He slid out of the saddle and pulled two ponchos from his saddlebags. He placed one over the saddlebags, packs, and rifle scabbard and the other over his head, pulling the draw strings tight around his waist. He replaced his hat over the poncho and slowly reviewed his situation.

The trail was at least 600 feet below the top of the butte, and it was at least 600 feet down to the valley below. They had moved above the stands of scrubby trees into the scattered stands of cedar, and the trail had narrowed considerably as it snaked around a finger in the side of the mountain. Just as the young man was ready to climb back in the saddle, Sam snorted and twitched his ears as a large mountain goat emerged from the stand of cedar growing on the mountain side of the trail. The goat stopped, glanced at Talon and Sam and quickly disappeared though the cedar.

"Well, Sam, we may have just caught us a break."

Talon walked the trail to where the goat had appeared and pushed his way into the thick stand of cedar. He stopped at the base of an overhang and visually followed the game trail that ran along the side of the mountain, up and over a small ridge that was covered from view from the main trail by the cedar. His eyes continued to the ridge top and saw where the path extended through a notch in the side of the mountain, the top of which was an overhang. The notch looked just large enough to walk Sam through. Talon returned to the trail where Sam patiently waited.

"I think we've found a place to get out of the weather," he whispered.

He grabbed Sam's bridle, turned the big horse around and backed him up the trail where it would be a level walk into the cedar. Getting Sam past the thick cedar branches was the hard part. He left him on the game trail while he returned to remove any signs of their leaving the main trail. Talon carefully brushed away any tracks from the soft areas on the main path, starting a hundred paces back and working up to the point where they entered the line of cedars. He then checked the cedars for signs of their entry, moving twisted branches back in place and picking up any broken branches. Satisfied that their detour from the main path would escape all but the best tracker, he returned to Sam and led him over the ridge and into the notch.

The path flared into a small alcove a few yards up, protected from the weather by an overhang large enough for man and horse to comfortably walk under. He noted a small patch of grass at the base of the opposite ridge and a good-sized basin where the ridge met the overhang. The path continued along the side of the mountain to another overhang before it switched and climbed the reverse side of the ridge supporting the cedar stand. He followed it no further because it was doubtful Sam could use the trail. At least they had found a secure hiding place protected from the bad weather he knew was coming.

Talon returned to the alcove, realizing there wasn't much time to prepare for the deep freeze of the pogonip. A light dusting of ice crystals already covered Sam's poncho, and weather happened quickly at these heights. He started gathering as much dead cedar as he could, stacking it at the back of the overhang. Fortunately, dead cedar snags were everywhere and in a short time he had built quite a pile of fuel—about three days' worth, he guessed. Then he pulled a few of the larger rocks to a level area under the overhang close to the basin, since it seemed this area would be protected from the wind and snow. Just as he thought the word, heavy snow flakes began to fall. He noted that the exposed trail had glazed with ice and the cedars were shrouded with crystals. There wasn't time to lose. He recovered a flint and steel from the saddlebags and sparked a fire within the circle of rocks.

He built a fire reflector by draping the poncho he had been wearing over two large dead cedar skeletons. Gradually, the fire began to grow, and its heat was welcome. Next, he filled his canteens and placed them between the fire and the poncho to keep them from freezing during the night. He quickly unsaddled Sam and placed his gear along the back wall of the overhang. He found the currycomb and started to give Sam a thorough combing. He then replaced the poncho on Sam's back, tying it on with a rope. He pulled a feedbag full of dry oats over the stallion's head and watched silently as the big roan ate his fill. The bag was almost empty when Sam started nodding his head, and Talon removed the bag with care.

"That will help some, old boy," Talon whispered as he stroked Sam's sturdy neck.

Talon rummaged through his packs and found a small coffee pot which he filled at the basin. He took some coffee grounds from the food pack, dumped them into the pot and sat it in the fire. He knew a cup of hot coffee would shake the cold from his hands and body. Then he retrieved two small cooking pots, one packed inside the other. He unrolled an oilcloth package that contained a small hunk of bacon, from which he carved two slices. He dropped the bacon into one of the pots and placed it on the fire, then filled the other pot with water. Talon then pulled out a handful of chili beans from a small cotton pouch. After the bacon had started to render, he dumped the beans and water in on top, thinking, *that will be a good dinner in an hour or so.*

He hacked the small limbs off two of the dead cedars with his hunting knife, walked over to the basin, and placed one from one edge of the basin to the other. He used the first limb as a fulcrum and placed the other pole over it into the water.

If the water freezes, I'll be able to lift the pole to break the surface ice on the basin without making a lot of noise.

With dinner on the way, he turned to his sidearm and rifles. Talon carried four Colt 45 pistols - two 5 1/2 -inch barrel Colts, one holstered on his right hip and the other in front on his left side in easy reach of his right hand; one 7 1/2-inch barrel Colt holstered across the small of his back, also in easy reach of his right hand; and a 43/4-inch Colt in a shoulder holster under his left arm. For long shooting, he carried a Winchester 73 and a Sharps 50 with a 34-inch barrel. He cleaned each one of the guns thoroughly, leaned the Winchester against the gear within easy reach and replaced the Sharps in its scabbard.

Carefully, he wrapped his three long-barrel pistols in an oil cloth sheet. He decided to stay with his custom of wearing the shoulder holster only when in camp, although he didn't expect unwanted visitors in the deepening winter storm.

Wonder where we are? He pondered as he refashioned the fire. *How did Jackson Slager alert those hombres? I sure didn't see any signs of him meeting them. Did I miss a lookout or message drop along the way?*

Deep in thought, Talon walked to the edge of the overhang and stuck his spoon into the falling snow. He waited until the spoon was full of flakes, returned to the fire, opened the coffee pot and deposited the snow.

That should settle the grounds. He poured a cup and let it warm his hands before taking a big sip. *Not bad for basin water and snow. Bet those hombres down below are searching for someplace warm to stay and I sure wouldn't want to be on top of this mountain unprotected.*

He stirred his dinner, dropping in a pinch of salt and a few small slices of jerky.

His feet were almost numb in the cold, wet boots, so he pulled them off, pulled on a dry pair of wool socks, and covered those with a pair of soft rawhide moccasins that covered the calves of his legs. He was awfully fond of those wool socks, mainly because they never failed to keep his feet warm but also because T. T. had knitted them especially for him.

Wonder how T. T. is doing? I sure miss her, he thought as he placed his wet boots next to the canteens to dry. The thin mountain air was filled with the largest snowflakes he could remember, and the cold was encroaching into his shelter. He unrolled a groundcover and positioned it between the fire and the back of the overhang. Then he wrapped his blanket around his shoulders, sat with legs crossed and enjoyed another cup of coffee and his dinner.

I think I have figured it out. I saw signs of several horses going into the water where we crossed the Canadian River, and the same horses tracked out at the same place. Four went north, and we followed the other one west. We were following Slager's horse from the time we started, and we're still following it. I bet he swapped his horse mid-stream and we're following a decoy. He fooled us again.

The warm fire and the woolen socks did their work, and it wasn't long before Talon began to doze, stirring only to pour more water into the bean pot and place it on the fire. *Breakfast*, he thought as he slowly fell into a deep sleep full of dreams about the eventful two years that had led him to this spot.

"Talon, Uncle Jim wants to see you right away."

'What does he want now, Gary?" Talon asked in a tone that didn't quite meet with Gary Ogdalh's approval.

"Well, there has been a change of plans and he needs to see you at the corral right away, and I suggest you hop to it," Gary returned.

Talon knew he had stepped a bit too far out of the way when Gary abruptly turned and rode away without another word. Gary grew up with Talon and T. T. and adored Uncle Jim. He was completely loyal to him.

Talon climbed into his saddle and spurred his horse toward the corral. He could see Jim at the corral gate talking with a U.S. cavalry lieutenant. The lieutenant rode off just before Talon reined his horse at the corral gate.

"What's up, Uncle Jim?" he asked while sliding out of the saddle.

"The army wants us to take our horses to Fort Concho, which is somewhere south of the Texas panhandle."

"Why?" Talon asked.

"They're worried the horses are not properly trained and want us there to train them if they are not. So you are going to move the horses to Concho."

"Who's goin' with me?"

"From our group, you alone are going."

"Uncle Jim, how can I move 200 horses alone?"

"The army has sent a detail to Fort Dodge to be the wranglers, and being from Texas, I suspect they know something about horses. That's the bad news. The good news is that they are going to give two dollars a head extra when satisfied they are trained and delivered to Fort Concho. I thought you could take the money and make a trip to see T. T."

"Jim, you know these horses are trained."

"Yep," Jim nodded with a grin. "But the Army has 400 dollars they don't need."

Talon chuckled.

"When do I meet the wranglers?"

"I thought we would mosey over there now and I would introduce you. Think up a plan of action on the way."

They both mounted up and headed toward the post. They saw two officers standing on the porch of the headquarters building when they arrived, and Jim recognized the officers as the leaders of the detail.

"Howdy, gentlemen," he said.

"Mister Finley," nodded the first lieutenant.

"I want to introduce you to Talon Finley," Jim said. "He will be going with you to Fort Concho. He is our best trainer and will be able to handle any problem with the horses."

"My gosh, Mister Finley, how old is he?"

"I'm 16," Talon said, "and you can talk directly to me. May I ask your plans for moving the herd?"

"As of now, we're going to move out as soon as possible because we feel it will take over a month to get the herd to Concho."

"How far is it to Concho?" Talon asked.

"Around 500 miles straight south from here," replied the lieutenant.

"Let me introduce you to the lieutenants, Talon," said Jim. "This is First Lieutenant Jason Carter, and the other officer is Second Lieutenant Mathew Coleman. Gentlemen, Talon knows these horses and has a couple of ideas on how to move them. I suggest you listen to him."

"Okay, let's hear them, Mr. Finley," barked Carter, directly addressing Talon.

"Well, first let me ask, how many men do you have?"

"We have 26, broken down into two officers, four Tonkawa scouts, and 20 Buffalo soldiers, which includes one sergeant, 15 mounted troopers, and four drivers for the two wagons. We also have eight mules to pull the wagons."

"We'll make the trip in two weeks or less, but we'll need to change your unit," Talon said.

Carter stiffened and appeared both startled and annoyed at Talon's confidence, which to the career cavalry officer bordered on arrogance.

"That's pretty bold talk," he said, staring at the young man. "What's *your* plan?

Talon grinned.

"First you'll need to drop the wagons and split the supplies among the troopers. Second, we'll go over to the corral and cut out 31 mounts, so that everyone has two mounts to ride. We'll take them to the smithy for shoeing. Third, you'll need to send your scouts forward to mark a path for us around any major hazards. That way, we can run the horses without break 35 to 50 miles a day. Fourth, after any major river crossing or at noon every day, we'll switch mounts; any horse carrying 200 pounds of rider and gear will tire quicker than a horse running on its own. We keep the men freshly mounted and we'll tire out the herd every day. They'll settle down at night and be easier to control. Since your men are from Texas, I'm sure they can handle this type of move, and it will also prove to you the soundness of the herd. Lieutenant Carter, these are great horses, and they'll do everything we ask of them."

Carter had visibly relaxed as Talon described his plan, and was smiling broadly as he finished.

"Sounds like a plan that will work," he said. "Lieutenant Coleman, assemble the men and move them over to the corral for new mount selection. Send word to the smithy we're bringing him 31 horses to shoe. We'll walk the horses over from the corral as they're selected. Mr. Finley, we'll be at the corral shortly."

Talon and Jim climbed into their saddles, wheeled, and started for the corral. Gary was waiting for them to return, and when he saw their approach, he knew there was work to be done.

"Gary, let's cut out the two mahogany bay stallions, and as many close to their color as possible for a total of 30 mounts, and Sally, the strawberry roan for me," Talon said.

"Great choice," replied Gary.

Jim stationed himself at the gate leading to a smaller loading corral. The smaller corral featured a shoot that would allow the troopers to remove the horses one at a time, halter their new mounts and move to the smithy without interference from the others. The two stallions put up a spirited small fuss, but soon moved to the small corral. The other horses quickly followed the stallions' lead. The troopers arrived soon thereafter, and Talon explained how they were to select their mounts.

"Lieutenant Carter, we have your mount ready for halter," said Talon. "I hope you like him."

Carter's face filled with gratitude when he saw the stallion Talon had picked for him.

"What a magnificent animal! That dark bay color just glistens in the sunlight," he said.

"Lieutenant, he's one of the leaders of the herd and with you riding him out front, they'll follow you anywhere," replied Talon.

Soon there was a steady progression of mounts led by troopers walking to the smithy. The Army blacksmiths knew their work; it wasn't long before all the horses were shoed. The next test came when the troopers mounted them for the first time. The horses hadn't been ridden for a time, and at first some were antsy. The Texans, however, handled them with ease, and most were riding comfortably within minutes. Carter then assembled the troop for a drill and had them push their new mounts hard. He approached Talon when he returned.

"This is the sharpest looking unit in the U.S. cavalry, thanks to you and your selections," he said. "I apologize for doubting you before."

"Well, you know dark bay horses are hard to see at night," replied Talon. "I figured that would be a good thing for a cavalry officer."

"Lieutenant Coleman, have the men move their new mounts to the stables," commanded Carter.

Two or three troopers lagged behind as the main group began to leave and moved toward Talon and Gary.

"We're just wondering if you really knew how to use those sidearms you're carrying," one of them said. "We thought you could show us after mess, when we test fire our weapons at the range."

"Sure, why not? We've been invited to dine with you and after you finish testing, Gary and I will be happy to show you what we can do."

"There are a lot of good gun throwers in Texas, and we just want to see what you can do," The trooper said.

"Have you ever used them in a fight? Have you ever killed any-one?" asked another.

"Yep, I've used them in a fight," said Talon. "Not counting Indi-ans, I killed two. That was about a year ago.

"Face up?"

"Yep, face up. Only one was with my knife and the other with my snub forty-five. Killing is no fun, but it ain't a stranger to me. You kill if it's required," replied Talon.

Jim, Gary and Talon walked up the steps to the mess hall, where they were greeted by the sergeant. He escorted them to the back of the room where a rail separated the officers' mess from the enlisted men's mess. Both Carter and Coleman were waiting for them. When they were seated, an orderly brought the evening meal that included slabs of beef, beans and sourdough bread, along with plenty of hot coffee. The meal was enjoyable. A hot meal after trail food for the last couple of weeks settled their longing for anything different to eat. And, Talon noted with approval, the enlisted men ate pretty much the same meal. They would all be riding the same trail and would need the same energy to complete the drive.

After a brief period of the usual banter, the conversation turned to the show Gary and Talon had planned for the troopers.

"Our troops will fire their weapons and clean them for inspection before we retire for the night," said Carter. "Now after they fire, I understand you will demonstrate your gun-throwing skills. Is that correct?"

"Sure is," replied Gary.

"I hope you are impressive," said Coleman. "If you know the history of our Buffalo Soldiers, you will understand they have been through a lot. They are not easily impressed, but if you do impress them, it will get this drive off to a good start."

"Well, they'd better be paying attention, because we're so fast they may miss the show," declared Talon.

"We'll see," replied Carter.

The sergeant assembled the troopers after mess and marched them to the firing range for their final preparation before moving out in the morning. It didn't take very long for the troopers to fire their weapons at the designated targets, which were six-inch fence posts positioned about 10 steps down range.

Talon saw the opportunity and spoke up.

"How about putting some of these playing cards on the posts where we can show our marksmanship?"

The sergeant detailed two troopers to attach a card on top of two posts. As soon as the troopers returned to the firing line, there were two flashes followed by several more along with the sounds of Gary's and Talon's arms being discharged. They had each fired five shots so quickly that none of the troopers witnessed the action.

"Wow, Gary, you have been practicing; that was quick," said Talon.

"Yep, I'm trying to get to where you are," he answered.

"Wait a minute," cried the sergeant. "We didn't see that."

"Check the cards," said Talon.

The two who had placed the cards returned to the posts to check them for hits. Their report was a simple. "Five hits, both cards."

"We didn't see it," complained one of the troopers. "Do it again."

Two more cards were placed on the posts, and again Gary and Talon drew their pistols and fired five times, grouping five more in each card.

"Wooiee, you can sure throw them guns," one of the troopers shouted. "That's good shootin'."

"Satisfied," asked Talon?

Lieutenant Coleman had a wry smile on his face. He knew Talon had gained respect from the troops. They now knew he understood horses and could shoot, and that went a long way in settling their doubts that he would stand up in bad times. In their eyes, this kid had sand.

Talon and Gary ambled off, knowing they had passed muster with these soldiers. Talon knew he could count on them to back him when and if necessary, as they could count on him. He noticed Carter watching from the far end of the headquarters building and walked over to him.

"Lieutenant, the townsfolk over to Dodge City tell me the best way to cross the Arkansas is by the old Santa Fe cutoff trail. It takes us across two islands in the middle of the river and keeps us away from the deep sands on either side.

"The Tonkawa scouts have already confirmed that crossing, and have marked a path to the Cimarron, plus the next large creek beyond," replied Carter.

"Good, I'll see you sunup tomorrow," said Talon.

Chapter Two

A loud snap jarred Talon awake. Gradually, he came to his senses and immediately looked at Sam. Sam seemed peaceful and didn't appear to be disturbed. The only motion Talon detected was the flickering shadows of his dying fire. He sat up and pulled two limbs from the fuel stash, snapped them into smaller sticks, and placed them in the fire. It began to rekindle, as the warmth fought against the encroaching cold. The snow had continued to cascade into the surrounding cedars, its weight bending their tops— changing them from the shape of trees to hoary ghosts parading in the dark cold night. He reached across the fire, grabbed one of the canteens, and quenched his thirst. Adding water to his breakfast soup, he stirred it and repositioned it in the fire. He pulled the blanket around his shoulders, leaned against the saddle, and fell asleep. His last thought was how could a Texas Ranger, already seasoned at 16, get into this mess?

The early spring dawn broke cool at Fort Dodge. The cavalry were ready, and in quick order they started nudging the horses out of the corral. Talon was impressed at the order of the day. Carter was riding his new mount, and half of the unit was riding new mounts. The other half was riding regular mounts. Immediately, Carter took the point position of leading the horses. Talon on Sam, pulling Sally, joined him at the front.

"Good idea to split the mounts as you did," Talon commented as he approached the lieutenant.

"My thought was Coleman could lead on his new mount the second half of the day. That way, if you are right about the horses following these stallions, we will have a fresh leader when we change mounts at noon," replied Carter.

"Oh, they'll follow."

The move to the Arkansas didn't take that long. Carter's new mount was the first to splash the water. The spray reflected the golden morning sky as the herd launched into the Arkansas River, following the old Santa Fe cutoff to the first of two islands in the middle of the river. Talon turned Sam and headed to the drag. There he found Jim and Gary watching the procession. With a tear in his eye he said his goodbyes to them. And, for the first time in his life, he was venturing alone— away from family and friends. At 16, Talon was going to Texas.

The water was colder than it looked. Sam took it gracefully as did Sally, the strawberry roan mare Talon had picked for his second mount. The cavalry was doing a good job moving the horses through the water. Each rider pulled his extra mount while pushing the horses forward. The Tonkawa scouts had marked the chosen path and soon the crossing of the Arkansas was history.

The herd climbed gradually from the river's edge to the top of a low bluff overlooking the river. The grass was green from recent spring rains and still damp from the morning dew, so the herd threw very little dust. From the top of the bluff, looking south away from the river, the riders could see that the trail selected by the scouts followed a low mesa top between two small creeks merging with the Arkansas. Soon, the breaks surrounding the creeks fell by the wayside as the herd passed onto the prairie. The troopers nudged the herd into a fast canter and Carter lead the way on the slightly undulating terrain. The trek to the Cimarron was about 35 miles and would be a good test for the plan of running the herd to Concho. The scouts had reported there were one or two spots along the way where the terrain would have to be negotiated more slowly, the last of which was the path off the high ground to the Cimarron river basin.

Carter halted the procession at half past noon and gave the order to change mounts. During the change, the troopers also ate a cold meal of beef and biscuits. Talon, used to trail drives, chowed down on beef jerky and water. He was ready to move out 30 minutes before the order was given. As planned, Lieutenant Coleman assumed the lead of the formation on the second bay stallion. The herd responded to the urging of the Texans.

It was a sweet, new grass-smelling spring day with the tempera-ture just right for a spirited run for the herd. They were moving along effortlessly through the short grass at a pace not usually seen in the U.S. cavalry, but the Texans adapted quickly and kept a steady hold on the herd. The scouts were right, as later in the day the course turned more serpentine around hazards and outcroppings of higher hills. The trail became more sandy and dusty as it broke off the mesa to a downward course to the Cimarron river basin. The brown winding stream was much smaller than the Arkansas, and the horses barely slowed when hitting the water. The scouts had picked a spot to cross with very little sand to impede the herd. On the other side there was a grassy area, low to the river, surrounded by higher terrain, which offered a makeshift corral for the night. There was plenty of water on one side, grass in the middle, with an elevated bank carved by some ancient flood forming the corral.

The cavalry set up camp on the bank overlooking the corral, with the troopers riding new mounts drawing first watch. Their tugged-along mounts were hobbled and left to roam the grassy area. The remaining troopers set to work combing their mounts, after which they were also hobbled and set free to graze. When the watch changed, the oncoming watch would saddle their new mounts, while the retiring watch would take care of their animals. This group drew the short straw because their work would be done in the early morning by the light of campfires.

It didn't take long for the drivers and the cooks to unpack the supply mules and have a campfire dinner on the way for the troopers. They started by setting up a lean-to with a large porch fly to cover the makeshift cooking area. The four drivers compensated for the dropped supply wagons by packing the mules, which they tugged along with the herd. The first day had been an excellent demonstration of a well-executed plan. Talon was impressed by the way Lieutenants Carter and Coleman checked on each of the men, praising them for a job well done, and how they took care of their own horses and gear. Although tired, the men had high morale.

It wasn't long before all four of the Tonkawa scouts appeared in camp to brief the officers. They had mapped the route for tomorrow's run and were explaining to the officers how the route was marked for them to follow. Gibson, the scout leader, and Go Paw changed their mounts and left the camp. They would ride far into the night before making a dry camp, and early in the morning they would start to scout the third day's move. Big Jim was assigned the task of watching the back trail for any approaching strangers. He saddled, and headed across the Cimarron to explore the approach the herd had taken to the river. Tommy was to scout south of the river for any possible interposers. It seemed to Talon they were over-taxed on their duties, but

Carter assured him they would sleep. Any sounds would alert them to any intruders trying to approach the herd.

The dinner bell rang about dark, and the troopers drifted in to claim their meals. The pickets were relieved one at a time, picked up a meal and headed back to his position so the next in line could break for a meal.

Talon noticed quickly the easy respect the troopers gave Coleman. Obviously, as green as he was, they held him in high regard, most likely because of previous actions Talon didn't know about. In fact, Coleman had spent the last few months on patrol and had proven himself several times to the men. They knew firsthand of his solid judgment and that he could hold his own in a fight. The night was peaceful.

Chapter Three

Again, Talon was jarred awake, this time by the cold stealing into his domain. It was early dawn and the area was enshrouded with a fine mist. He realized a cloud bank had settled into the area. With little wind to blow it away, it appeared he was in place for a few hours more. The snow had accumulated about six to eight inches, covering the alcove except near the cedars next to the second ridge. Their cover protected a small area of grass, and Sam had moved in to take advantage of an opportunity to munch on it. The tank was frozen and after Talon rekindled his fire he used his makeshift lever to break the surface ice. The idea worked with very little sound coming from his effort. He refilled his coffee pot with water and started another brew. He added a little more water to the soup and in a short time he was enjoying a warm morning meal.

What should I do next? He figured he needed to establish a concealed outpost overlooking the mountain trail, so he started preparing the items he would need to endure the cold away from the campsite. He would need the oilcloth ground cover to place over the snow and a blanket upon which to sit. He could use the poncho to cover himself. Even with this, he wouldn't be able to sit in the cold for very long. That meant he needed a spot with easy access. His best guess was up the game trail to the ridge, then up the spine on this side to a higher vantage point. After gaining height, he could slip over the ridge into the cedars on the other side.

He cleaned his pots and cut a couple of small strips of bacon. He threw the bacon into one of the pots and placed it on the fire. Then he grabbed a cotton sack from his food supply along with a can of peaches. Fishing the bacon out of one pot, he put it in the other, along with beans, salt, chili spices and water. He added slices of beef jerky before placing the pot on the fire. Then he opened the small sack and dusted the bacon grease in the first pot with flour. With a new-fangled can opener bought in Brownsville, he went to work opening the can of peaches. He cut halfway around the lid and bent it up to pour the peaches in the pot on top of the flour. He dusted the top of the peaches with flour, put the lid on it and placed it in the embers. Slowly, he raked the embers around and on top of the pot.

"That should really warm me up when I get back," he muttered.

Talon rolled up the blanket inside of his ground cover, retrieved the poncho from the cedar skeletons and proceeded toward the ridge. He was carrying all his guns. He didn't need them in camp, but while out on the ridge, he might. The trail wasn't easy. Negotiating the back side of the ridge was risky because of the snow-covered ice. Slowly, he managed the climb to a high vantage point and slipped over the spine of the ridge into the cedars. With the spine of the ridge at his back and the cedars in front, at least he would be protected from the wind if the weather changed. The trail was covered in a blanket of mist, giving the whole area an eerie silence. An occasional small avalanche created by the snow falling from the top of a cedar tree was the only movement detected, and after a few hours he abandoned his outpost and returned to camp, where he knew a hot meal would be waiting.

He didn't venture from camp that afternoon because the weather conditions had not changed. There was no need to freeze himself on the side of a mountain, he thought, because it took him most of the afternoon to warm up from the morning foray to the outpost. He kept busy around the campsite, taking care of the little details needed to survive, and as the sky darkened, he fell into a fretful sleep.

"Mister Finley," Lieutenant Carter barked as he approached Talon who was finishing the act of saddling Sam. "Our plan for the day is to cross a small creek not very far south of here. To do this effectively, we'll need to veer to the southeast to make our approach to the crossing. If we were to head straight south we would have to make two crossings because two creeks merge into one. Then for a few miles we'll head southwest. The scouts have marked a route that will turn due west leading us between two low ridges, where they have found an oasis of grass for the horses. There we'll dry camp for the night. This area of the panhandle is known for large gangs of rustlers and whiskey runners such as the Conleys, and we are going to try to avoid them. By making dry camp, we'll hopefully stay undisclosed to any of the gangs— any one of which would outnumber us. Tomorrow, we'll cross the Canadian River just north of the settlement of Canadian. This should be about midday. We'll rest, water the herd, change mounts and spend the rest of the day moving as far south of the Canadian river as possible. Once we've crossed the Canadian, every outlaw in the panhandle will know where we are."

"Thanks for the briefing," acknowledged Talon.

"We'll move out as soon as Big Jim reports."

"I'm ready."

"By the way," Carter added, "the garrison at Fort Supply will detach a small force to be our rear guard. I've sent Tommy to lead the way for them. They'll cross the Canadian a few hours behind us and camp just south of the river. If any large bands of riders move south out of the old buffalo hunting camp at the river, they'll continue to trail us. If not they'll be on their way back to Fort Supply. Other Army posts south of us will pick up the rear guard duties. Not expecting any trouble, but no need to take a chance."

The day went as planned. The herd settled down on the secluded oasis of grass. The Tonkawa scouts were now in Texas, their home territory, and the need for scouting ahead fell to Gibson. Since the route was known, he only had to worry about detecting any human deterrence to the moving of the herd. Big Jim and Go Paw handled the flanks. Tommy brought the rear guard. The old camp at the Canadian River was the first civilized settlement of any size they'd seen since Dodge City. The crossing north of there was through a tributary basin that cut through the bluff overlooking the Canadian River. And the herd's arrival raised some heads among the population. Only two riders were detected leaving the community to the north, and it was assumed they were riding to alert others to the herd's movement. After a couple of hours, the troopers moved the herd out of the river basin and across a serpentine path south from the river settlement. In late afternoon, after the second creek crossing, the order was given to make camp. The scouts had found another natural enclosure in which to corral the herd. It had water, grass and elevation on three sides.

Just after dark, Big Jim rode into the camp and approached Lieutenant Carter. He reported three riders were approaching the herd from the northwest and felt they were on a scouting mission with a sinister motive.

"Sergeant," Carter bellowed. "Alert Lieutenant Coleman we have visitors approaching from the northwest. Let them pass and have Big Jim guide them to our camp."

"Yes, sir."

Talon had just finished combing Sam and Sally and was standing in the shadows away from the flickering campfires when the riders were escorted into camp. At first, he didn't think much about their arrival, but suddenly he thought he recognized one the riders. Remaining in the shadows, he moved closer for a better look and confirmed he was right. It was Rags McLeod, a hard case who had battered Gary Ogdalh's mother and sister before hightailing it out of Wyoming. Gary had sworn to kill him if he ever found him, and Talon had taken the same oath. *Well… there he is.*

"You the captain in charge?" asked the spokesman for the three.

"You're correct, but I'm a lieutenant," replied Carter. "What can I do for you?"

"Well, since you are crossing our land, eating our grass and drinking our water, we thought you would want to pay us a tribute for our services."

Talon stepped closer to the three and was yet to be noticed. He crossed into the light to the left of the three riders as they dismounted.

"Now, we figured about five dollars per head would do the trick."

"We don't carry money for such transactions," replied Carter.

"Well, then, we'll just cut the herd by a few head for payment, or maybe we'll just take them all. Since we see you're understaffed."

Talon stepped into the light. "Hello Rags."

Rags turned toward him, "Do I know you?"

"Yep, I'm Talon Finley, Gary Ogdalh's friend from Medicine Bow. Remember me?"

"Sure, I remember you. What are you doing in these parts?"

"Moving my horses. And there seems to be a problem as to who owns Texas. But we're going to settle which part you own tonight. Aren't we?"

"What do you mean?"

"There's that little matter of battering Ogdalh's mother and sister before you left Wyoming. You *do* remember that, don't you? Tonight you are going to buy six feet of Texas, and if your friends back your play, from what I've seen of Texas there's room for them, too."

"Who's this hombre, Rags?"

"He's Talon Finley, a gun thrower from Wyoming."

"Why he's not even dry behind the ears yet, he ain't goin' to make no play."

"Are you hard cases in or out because I wouldn't want to make a mistake?"

"Well, since there are just three of us and you have the Army surrounding you, I'm sayin' we're not in the scrape."

"I may go ahead and kill you anyway for being stupid enough to ride with this yellow hard case."

The leader shifted his weight from one foot to the other and surveyed the surrounding troopers holding their firearms.

"This is between you and Rags. I think we'll leave."

"Wrong, you'll leave when we let you leave," broke in Carter.

"You can't just let him brace someone while you just look on."

"It's my command and I'll do what I want."

Talon took a step closer and the flash of his gun illuminated the night. Rag's pistol hadn't cleared leather. He had bought six feet of Texas just as Talon had promised. The other riders were quiet and afraid to move as they realized if they had backed Rags they would have died, too.

"Sergeant, get two shovels for these hombres to dig a grave, and after they're finished shackle them. We'll hang them when we get where we are going."

"Talon you could have spooked the horses with gun play," Carter said as he watched the two riders pick up Rags.

"They're tired, they weren't going anywhere."

"What would have happened if the others had drawn?"

"I guess I would have been burying three hard cases because I suppose you would have said 'you shot 'em, you bury 'em.'"

Carter shook his head turned and walked away. The troopers in camp now knew Talon could throw a gun when it came time to kill.

A fine mist began to cover the herd just after the change in pickets. Occasionally, the mist turn into a steady rain and after a few minutes would return to a mist. The gray morning saw the Texans scurrying to protect their gear from the wet and to prepare for the day's mission. The two prisoners were soaked as two wet birds flying alone at night. Rags McLeod's grave was unmarked and forgotten. The order was given and the herd began to move onto the rain-soaked prairie.

"We are going to try and make the Sweetwater Creek by noon," Lieutenant Coleman told Talon as he approached.

"How far is that?" asked Talon.

"Ten to 15 miles south of here," replied Coleman. "That's where we'll pick up support from the Sweetwater Garrison to screen and protect us as we move south. Major Biddle's men will join us after we cross the creek, and escort us 60 miles south, before returning to their fort west of here."

"How many men do you think, and how do they know where to meet us," asked Talon?

"About 12, and they will be our rear guard. Go Paw is bringing them to us." Coleman spurred his animal and left Talon sitting alone with his thoughts in another flurry of rain.

The Army has this move planned more than I expected, he thought. *How naïve I've been throughout the last few days. They knew about the gangs and how they would operate, and had planned for a superior show of force to discourage any attacks. So far, the only contact has been the hard cases that rode in with Rags. Their demands had been whopping but not unexpected. Taking them as prisoners had obviously been part of the plan.* He rejoined the herd with even more respect for the men in soldier blue.

The path to the Sweetwater was broken by several crossings of small creeks with an abundance of scrub trees lining their banks. The creek also meandered through rough terrain, and even with the rain the movement was slow. They finally crossed the Sweetwater in midafternoon. There was a surprising amount of scrub trees lining both sides of the creek. Pushing the herd across became a challenge because they didn't want to fight through the hazard. Also, the water level was higher than expected, which made entering and exiting the creek basin more challenging.

Go Paw was waiting on the south side with a detachment from Major Biddle's command. The detachment of 14 men included two Tonkawa scouts, with orders to protect the rear of the unit as it moved south. Carter ordered Go Paw south to find Gibson and alert him to their progress for the day. He had made a decision to stay close to the Sweetwater for the night. The weather made it difficult for the cooks to put together their cooking fires, but somehow they managed to supply hot coffee. The weather was breaking, but remained cooler than normal, and the troopers appreciated the cooks' efforts to supply a warm meal even though it was meager.

"Talon," called Carter. "Join us for a discussion of our plans for the next few days."

Talon walked over to the officers' campfire and was immediately introduced to Second Lieutenant Grayson Tull.

"Gentlemen, this is going to be our plan of action for the next two days. We are going to negotiate the North Fork and the Salt Fork of the Red River tomorrow. We'll camp after the second crossing. The next day we'll cross the Prairie Dog Fork and camp between two ridges that run north and south about four miles apart. Along the bottom of the eastern ridge, there is a creek that has better water than the

Prairie Dog. Mister Tull, you will set your pickets at the north entrance of this valley. We are going to change direction at the exit of the valley and go east to a little north around the finger of another north-south running ridge. This will put us moving south under the cover of this ridge. Because of the outlaws, I've decided to follow a more eastern route than first planned. When Mister Tull reforms his command and slowly moves through the valley, he will continue south until such time he feels necessary to return to the Sweetwater Garrison on a route to the west. Anyone following will see his command moving south and hopefully will assume we have continued to move south, too. Are there any questions?"

"Sergeant Flowers, you have the first watch tonight. I'll take the second," Tull informed his sergeant.

"Why are you taking the second watch?" asked Talon.

"Generally, if there is an attack, it comes early morning and I want to be in command of the guard if that happens," replied Tull.

Talon suddenly realized that Carter organized his camps the same way.

He always took the second watch. I really have to give the cavalry credit. They expected trouble and planned for it. We've had rear guards since we crossed the Canadian.

He would remember that lesson well.

Chapter Four

Something jolted Talon awake. It was dark and the fire was almost out. He lay still for a while, trying to hear what had disturbed his sleep. Satisfied that the sound had been natural, he rekindled the fire. Although not as cold as it had been, he felt the chill because of the dying fire. He checked the pot of peaches and found it still warm.

Wonder where the hazers are? They should be trying the trail by now. I guess by noon tomorrow I could have some company.

He finished the peaches and poured a lukewarm cup of coffee to wash them down. He poured out the balance of the pot and started a new brew. A quick check of his fuel stock indicated that he needed to restock soon. Only snags protected from the snow would be dry enough to use. Securing fuel would take time, but it would have to wait until morning— about the time when he expected company. Taking a spoonful of snow, he settled grounds in the coffee pot, then poured a cup and sat back to warm his hands and sip the warm brew.

Here I am, 16 years old, a seasoned Texas Ranger, and I'm trapped on a frozen mountain. I should just kick myself.

The coffee didn't keep him awake for very long as he fell into another fretful sleep.

The morning broke in a fog that disappeared when the herd moved onto the mesa above the Sweetwater. Carter led the way across the still soggy grass, through outcroppings of scrub trees that outlined small creeks of the area. The rear guard took up their positions and gradually followed the herd. They also took charge of the prisoners, a task they seemed to enjoy. The run for the first four hours seemed a never ending dodging of scrub patches steadily moving south. Finally, they came to the bluff overlooking the North Fork of the Red River. After an uneventful crossing, Carter stopped the unit and gave the order to change mounts.

The weather had warmed, and the horses were ready to run. Again, they climbed the gradual ascent from a river basin to the mesa above and started their trek southward in a steady canter. Gibson veered from the route to the southwest for a few miles before turning southeast. The terrain ahead gave an outcropping of the closest thing to a mountain Talon had seen since being in Texas. The herd slowed to negotiate the obstacles and the path was up and down through several shallow hollows. They broke clear of one hollow and came to a dead stop. The herd really didn't want to stop and the Texans spent some time corralling them. There, in the middle of the path was a small herd of buffalo. As they swung the herd to the east, four or five Indian braves broke to the west on their ponies. In short fashion they were over the next hill and gone from sight.

"Send for Tommy," ordered Carter.

"Tell Lieutenant Coleman to get this herd moving, and I'll handle the Indians," he barked.

Coleman had anticipated the move and already had the herd moving to the east.

Tommy rode in to meet with Carter, and Talon could see that Carter was giving him instructions. Tommy jerked his mount away and moved out at a smart run to the west, following the Indians.

Talon approached Carter as the herd regained its canter.

"Chance encounter," yelled Carter. "I've sent Tommy to investigate. Hopefully, it's just a small hunting party. These Indians are supposed to be on the reservation, and you can see they are not.

"We're going to start a campaign to rid the Llano Estacado of all Indians this summer," he continued. "That's why we need these horses. Under our rules of engagement in this Red River War, we are ordered to kill all Indian ponies when captured. I bet we killed at least a thousand ponies that we could have used. What a waste."

Talon nodded in agreement, his stomach sickened by the revelation of the slaughter.

The herd continued to set a blazing pace over slightly rolling terrain with very little to deter its progress. Occasionally, they ran across a dry creek bed to negotiate, and a few patches of rock outcroppings to serpentine through. Then the terrain would return to a gradual rolling plain. By afternoon, they had crossed the Salt Fork of the Red

River without incident. The herd settled into a natural corral selected and marked by Gibson. In true fashion, the troopers organized their duties and all were satisfied with the move for the day. With Gibson on advanced scouting duties and Tommy missing from the formation, Big Jim and Go Paw were in charge of the group's security. Right at dusk, Tommy made it back from his chase of the Indians. He gathered the officers to share information.

"I believe they were Kiowa off the reservation," he said. "My best guess is that they were following the Buffalo herd for a larger group hidden further west of where we were. On my way back, I had to avoid a large group of riders that were shadowing our path. They do not know they were detected and are camping northwest of here on the Salt Fork."

"That's good scouting. Thanks for a job well done, Tommy," said Carter. "Tull, when you break to the west, stay alert to both the out-laws and the Kiowa that may be in your path home," suggested Carter. "What are your orders of engagement?"

"Not to engage if possible. Biddle only wanted movement intelli-gence of outlaws and Indians, if there were any. I plan not to engage if we can move around them," he replied.

"Well, as it looks now, we should have an easy run to the Prairie Dog tomorrow. Then the next day, our move should lose them. Since you have the outlaw prisoners with you, I expect they'll try to find you," said Carter.

"Don't mind fighting them, but we'll get by them without one. The Tonkawa scouts will see to it," Tull said.

Carter had the herd moving before dawn, and as it burst from the Sweetwater Basin, the sun was peeking through the eastern cloud cover. The day was overcast to the west. The wind was up— an omen of storms approaching. The pace was torrid, but the course void of obstacles. The mounts were changed at noon, and by late afternoon the herd made the bluff overlooking the Prairie Dog. This was the highest bluff to date, and it overlooked a wide expanse of sand dunes with two narrow ribbons of the river, breaking the trek across into three parts.

Coleman turned the herd west to a break on the bluff which allowed the herd to approach from a gradual decline running parallel to the river. Then he turned and took the herd down a fast breaking rocky slope into the soft sand. Slowly, the horses followed, struggling to move in the sand. It was a relief to hit the shallow water of the first channel, as exiting the sand took its toll. Finally, the hard rocky surface island sitting between the channels gave their legs a small chance to recover. Another wider ribbon of water awaited. The soft sand on the other side of the island was more of a struggle. It was deeper. The second channel was three times wider than the first, and the packed sand of the river was enough to give the herd a surge to climb out of the river basin. About the time the horses cleared the basin, shots rang out from the north down in the basin. Talon turned his mount and started to move toward the action. Carter stopped him.

"We lost three horses in the approach to the river. One horse stepped into a hole between two boulders and two other horses tumbled over him. They had to be put down," Carter told Talon.

Talon turned his mount south to follow the herd. "That was a hard crossing. I guess we've been lucky so far with only losing three," he said.

They were at the southern end of the valley, which was running through north to south ridges and contained plenty grass and water.

"This is where we make our break in the morning, to lose our followers," said Carter as Talon approached him.

Talon nodded, "Are there any more crossings like this one for tomorrow?"

"Only one, late tomorrow. It has a steep approach down and a steep climb out. Make sure you carry plenty of water. It's going to be drier from here on out," Carter answered.

Chapter Five

Talon awakened to a damp cold permeating his protected domain. He listened briefly for any sounds of movement and checked Sam for any alert to approaching unwanted visitors. The area appeared to be enshrouded in clouds with a fine mist.

No one in his right mind would be on the mountain in this kind of weather. This means my stay is going to be extended and I have to gather more fuel for the fire.

Begrudgingly, he moved from his blanket and rekindled the fire using a severely depleted fuel supply. Drinking a lukewarm cup of coffee, he rinsed the pot and started another brew. It seemed early dawn, and if it was going to rain he needed to act quickly to find the driest fuel available.

He removed the poncho from the two cedar skeletons and cannibalized them to replenish his fuel supply. He fed the fire and left the alcove. He followed the trail beyond the second overhang to a slide of dead cedars on the backside of the second ridge. He selected a large cedar carcass that would replace the two he used for a fire reflector. The skeleton came out of the snow and ice easily, but returning to his camp became a struggle because of its size. He placed it in position and draped the poncho over it. Briefly, he rewarded his effort with a hot cup of brew. Returning to the slide for more wood, he began to form a plan on how to dry the dampness from the new fuel. He selected two short, sturdy trunks and hacked off the protruding limbs to build a rack in front of the reflector.

"Might as well dry the wood while staying warm," he muttered aloud, knowing Sam likes to hear his voice occasionally.

For the next few hours he stacked the new fuel in front of the reflector. Finally, he took some time to feast on the pot of beans he had started the day before. *I can't wait to taste a good slice of beef.* With the new fuel supply drying, he took time to attend to Sam and his weapons. As expected, it began to rain.

If it's warm enough to rain, the trail will be washed of snow and ice and I should be able to leave this place on the first good day to ride. With time on his hands, his thoughts turned to his Ranger years.

How did I ever get to be a Texas Ranger? When did that start? He sat back and smiled. It was in Concho. The memories came in a flood as he gently stoked the sizzling fire.

Concho was a bustling Army outpost supporting the Tenth cavalry. For the last two days, the herd had been escorted by additional troops, and the drive was a breeze compared to the days surrounding the Prairie Dog crossing. As the horses entered the holding corral, the U.S. Army went to work putting its seal of approval on the hip of each mount. The soldiers wanted to brand Sam and Sally, but only treated Sally since Sam already wore a brand.

"We'll give you a bill of sale for Sally," Carter spoke up as Talon was about to make a fuss. "That way you have official ownership if any prying Texas official wants to question you on the matter. People in Texas don't treat horse thieves gently, but they won't bother you if you have solid proof of ownership."

"Okay, then, brand Sam, too, and I'll take two bills of sale," retuned Talon.

"Good thinking, Mister Talon," the lieutenant grinned.

Carter and Coleman nudged closer and extended their hands in gratitude for a job well done.

"I would salute you, but it's against army regulations," Carter said. "I need to report to the commanding officer, and I want you to go with me, Talon. Coleman, see to the men and make sure our new mounts get their seals. We're going to keep the new mounts."

"Yes sir," came the quick reply.

Coleman wheeled his mount and joined the men at the corral.

Talon noticed something interesting. All the troops were riding their new mounts and their old ones were in the corral with the herd. He smiled at the thought.

"Follow me," said Carter.

Talon joined Carter in riding over to the headquarters building.

They dismounted, tied their mounts and entered the long wooden building. Carter marched directly to the big office at the south end of the building, closed to the public by a big oak door with the rank and name of its current occupant— Colonel William R. "Pecos Bill" Shafter. They were greeted by an orderly wearing corporal stripes. The orderly knocked gently on the big door, slipped his head through a narrow opening and announced their presence to the colonel. The colonel's voice boomed through the hallway as he invited them into his office, where he greeting them warmly. It took a few minutes for Carter to give his verbal report and he turned over his written journal to the orderly for the colonel to review at later time. Talon took the time to scan the room, noting the West Point insignia and diploma displayed on the colonel's desk, along with various weapons obviously from Civil War and other military campaigns.

When Carter finished his report, the colonel thanked him and turned to the younger man. "So, Mister Finley, what did you think of the way Mister Carter handled the move from Fort Dodge?"

"Very impressed, Colonel Shafter," answered Talon.

"As you can see, Mister Finley, we have a large contingency of Buffalo Soldiers, both infantry and cavalry. We needed these mounts to complete our mission into the Llano Estacado this summer. We are to rid the area of Indians, mark roads and build telegraph lines for expansion into the area. Listening to Mister Carter's report, we may have to chase a few outlaws, too. What do you think?"

"I think that is going to be a tough job, sir."

"What are your plans now, Mister Finley?"

"I'm heading east to a port city, to catch a ship going to the northeast to see my sister, T. T."

"Well, you're in luck," said the colonel.

"How's that?" asked Talon.

"It so happens that Captain L.H. McNelly of the Texas Rangers has requested that the army supply a Black Seminole Indian scout by the name Night Stalking Cat to reconnoiter for the Rangers south of the Nueces River. He is due from patrol day after tomorrow. Since you don't know the state of Texas as well as he, I'll have him take you east in the safest fashion. While you wait, we'll check to see if your horses are broken for riding."

Carter didn't mention that the horses were well-trained, figuring the colonel would find that out soon enough.

"I'll take the offer of a guide and protection," replied Talon. "One thing: I picked a stallion for you out of the herd. He's a nice dark red with a lot of spirit. Maybe tomorrow I can show you what he can do."

"Corporal, what does my schedule look like for tomorrow?" asked the colonel.

"You have nothing scheduled after two, sir."

"I'll see you after two, Mister Finley. Mister Carter, find a spot in the OQ for Mister Finley."

"Yes, sir."

Carter smartly saluted the colonel, wheeled and left the room with Talon in tow.

"Carter, I've never seen this many Negroes at one time. What is this?" asked Talon?

"This is the Tenth cavalry, which has six companies of Buffalo Soldiers, four of them garrisoned here at Concho. We moved here from Kansas, where the officers of other units treated them poorly. Many of these soldiers fought for the Union in the Civil War, and many others drifted out here from the South when they couldn't find work.

"While the officer ranks are all white men, all the non-commissioned officers are Negroes. We've trained these men, and they are honed to do any job asked of them. I would stack them up against any soldiers in the army. Their next challenge will be to rid the Llano Estacado of all Indians."

"Why are they called Buffalo Soldiers?"

"Story goes the Comanche started calling them that because their hair reminded them of a buffalo's coat, and because they are damn fine fighting men," Carter said. "One thing the Comanche recognize is a fellow warrior."

"Well, they did a good job getting the horses here," Talon said. They'll do a good job out there, too."

Talon spent the next morning helping the troops hackamore the mounts and move them to the smiths. The Tonkawa watched, and when they had a chance to approach Talon, they did.

Gibson spoke first, "Talon, we want to thank you for the horses. They're beautiful and well-trained."

"Thank you, Gibson, and you, too, Tommy, Go Paw, and Big Jim."

"We hear they're sending you east with Night Stalking Cat."

"Yep."

"He's the best of the best. Gain his respect with a gift of one of these horses— and let him select it."

"Don't know that I can."

"Ask the colonel to let you have one more horse for Night Stalking Cat."

"Will do."

The colonel arrived at two o'clock, eager to see his new mount. The smiths had shod the horse first thing that morning. He was standing saddled and ready to meet his new master.

"I have a request, colonel. Would the army allow Night Stalking Cat to have one of the remaining horses?" asked Talon.

"Granted. We'll work out the details with the quartermaster for Cat to get a bill of sale. Let's see what this stunning animal can do."

"That was easy," Talon muttered to himself.

"Yes it was," Carter's voice came from behind. "He can see how you treated his troops with the horses you selected for them to ride. Believe me, he is grateful. I thought you would like to see the town of San Angela, if you are up to it."

"Let's go."

Together, they rode from the fort's corrals to the village. San Angela sat at the convergence of two main branches of the Concho River. It was naturally fortified by the river on the north, east, and south. The fort lay on the western approach.

"We're going to Molly's for southern fried chicken that will melt in your mouth."

They tied their horses to the hitch post outside a large freestanding shack and walked up the open plank steps to the porch that ran across the front of the building. It had been weeks since Talon had been in such a place: Miss Moore's back in Wyoming. They moved away from the door to the end of the room and sat down at a table. A young girl, about Talon's age, came over to the table with a slate and sat it in front of them. She had long dark-brown hair and eyes to match along with a girl's body coming of age.

Carter looked up and greeted her. "Sophia, this is my friend, Talon Finley, and we're here to eat anything other than army food."

"Mamma has outdone herself tonight on the southern side, and we have plenty of her Texas favorites, if you like it hot."

"I think we are going with the southern. Let's see, the slate says you have southern fried chicken or beef steak. What comes with that?"

"Well, we have white beans, squash, boiled new potatoes and turnips — with or without greens — and cornbread. And for after, apple or peach deep pan pie."

"What do you think, Talon?" asked Carter.

"I think I've died and gone to Heaven. I'll take the chicken along with those other things you listed because I've never eaten them before."

"Same for me, Sophia."

The front door opened and two men entered. *Hard cases*, Talon immediately thought. They continued walking toward the table at which Carter and Talon were sitting.

"Who's riding that blue roan hitched out front?" the leader asked.

"My horse," replied Talon.

"You stole it."

"Better look at the brand," Carter spoke up.

"I'm taking him."

"You can try," returned Talon.

A third hard case entered, and walked up behind the first two. Other bystanders sensed trouble and started to move away from the action. The third came forward and pointed a finger at Talon, who recognized one of the outlaws that had rode into camp with Rags. Either he escaped or Tull had found trouble.

"You ain't got the army around you today, kid."

"What's that mean?" asked Talon.

Three locals entered at the front with their pistols drawn and stood behind the outlaws.

"It's time to leave, gents," one said. "And keep your hands off the hardware."

Talon spoke, "Before you leave, let it be known to every man here that I didn't need the army's help with the likes of you. You came in here and braced me without any intention of making a move. I could see yellow in your eyes. Besides that horse of mine wouldn't let you ride him. He has good taste. I'm going to eat my dinner and laugh about Rags' buddies who were too yellow to draw when I braced the three of them. You *did* tell them the whole story, didn't you, hard case? Three of you now and you pick inside this nice lady's business. We'll do it after I eat."

They turned toward the door.

"Wait a minute, sit down over there at that table and wait till I finish. Then we'll go outside together and get it done."

The leader shifted his weight and spoke, "Next time, kid."

"Next time you're dead."

The three turned and walked through the door, with the locals still covering their move with drawn pistols.

Carter spoke first, "Well, you build friendships fast, Talon. Where did you learn to talk so tough?"

"I was 12 before I figured out Uncle Jim and Aunt Bertha bluffed with their talk."

Sophia started filling the table with plates of fried chicken and bowls of beans, turnip greens with roots and squash. Next, she poured the hot coffee and served the cornbread.

"This is my first time ever for turnip greens and cornbread."

"What kind of bread did you eat at home?" asked Sophia.

"Sourdough biscuits and rolls, most of the time, along with pan-fried hotcakes."

"Didn't know if you wanted gravy or not, so I brought you a bowl to try so you'll know next time," said Sophia.

Carter thanked her and he and Talon started their feast.

After the apple pie, Sophia brought another pot of coffee.

"Sure hope Tull and his men are safe," said Talon. "Those outlaws sure traveled fast to get here for that meeting."

"I'm sure they are safe," replied Carter as he paid the bill. "If you don't mind, I need to check the men to see if everything is getting done. I have guard duty tonight."

"Thank you for dinner. I'll have to hit this place again before moving on east," said Talon.

"You know, they could shoot you in the back. They're not obligated to brace you openly."

"What, between here and the fort? They're working on something else right now. They need to stay around without being bothered and it's more important than killing me. I'm leaving in a couple days, and will never see them again," replied Talon.

"Talon, let me tell you something about Texans. Every family has an outlaw. And family comes first. Brothers and sisters want to get even with anyone killing a family member. It doesn't make any difference how bad or outside the law they are, so watch your back."

Talon and Carter parted company at the fort's front gate, Carter turning right toward the enlisted barracks to check his men and Talon heading the other direction toward the officer quarters. He delivered Sam to the post livery and left instructions for his care and feeding before finding his way to the small room in the OQ.

Talon had just washed his face and checked in the mirror to see if he needed to shave when he heard a knock on his door

"Come on, Talon," Coleman shouted through the door. "I need to escort you to the quartermaster pronto."

I guess my beard can wait, Talon thought with a wry smile as he opened the door and greeted Coleman. They proceeded to the quartermaster's office, where they were announced by an orderly.

"Come on in Mister Finley, and have a seat. I'm Major Sullivan."

They shook hands and Talon took a seat in a chair to the left of the major's desk.

"We ended with 190 horses," the major said. "One you selected for yourself, for which you are going to pay $26, three that were put down, and six that were lost in the drive. Let's see… 190 times $2, less $26 settles to $354. How do you want to be paid?"

Talon thought a minute and requested payment of $300 in gold coins and the balance in silver.

The major agreed, counted out the coins and had Talon sign a receipt for the money. Then he gave Talon the bills of sale for Sam and Sally.

"It was nice meeting you, Mister Finley. I think you are to be escorted over to the colonel's from here. Orderly, show Mister Finley to the colonel's office."

That's a good way to start the day, Talon thought. Although the Finleys had prospered in Wyoming, this was the largest amount of cash he had ever handled. He put the small sack of gold coins in a pouch belt worn under his shirt. The silver sack went into the button-down pocket on the inside of his vest. T. T. had designed it to conceal a small sack of money when she made the vest from a lamb fleece. A few silver coins he kept in his right pocket to keep from having to fumble around with the pocket every time he wanted to pay for something.

The colonel was on the porch of the headquarters building when Coleman and Talon arrived. Coleman gave the normal military address, to which the colonel replied.

"Mister Finley, I would like to personally thank you for the mount you selected. Now come with me and I'll introduce to you the escort I selected for you. Join us, Mister Coleman."

They left the porch and walked toward the barracks that housed the Indian scouts. Gibson was in front, rubbing down his new mount.

"Gibson," barked the colonel, "Find Night Stalking Cat for me, and bring him to the front porch."

Gibson whirled and disappeared through the front door of the barracks. Soon, from around the side of the building and up on the porch came Night Stalking Cat. He was a Black Seminole Indian of sturdy build, known for his strength of character and willingness to go to extremes to win in a fight. Night Stalking Cat gave the usual military greeting as he approached, which was returned by the colonel.

"Night Stalking Cat, it has been requested by your old friend Captain McNelly of the Texas Rangers that we transfer you to him. The Army has agreed to the request and you are to leave immediately to comply. In doing so, you are first to see the paymaster and draw the pay you are owed. The army is also giving you a new mount, at the request of one Mister Talon Finley. The army has also granted that request. Mister Finley, step forward, this is your escort east. Night Stalking Cat, you are to lead Mister Finley east as far as you can without interfering with your duties for Captain McNelly. Mister Finley's gift of a new horse is for your kindness of leading him to the east"

"Mister Finley, where do you go?"

"Somewhere east to catch a ship to the northeast," replied Talon.

"Where's my new horse?"

The Indian scouts started to gather around the steps of the porch, and shortly they opened a lane for Gibson to bring the new horse. The scout led a painted stallion forward and handed the reins to Night Stalking Cat. His actions at the appearance of his new steed showed his deep appreciation of the mount selected by Talon.

"When do I have time to train a new horse?"

"This horse is trained better than you could ever train him," replied Gibson.

"Mister Finley, I leave you and Night Stalking Cat to start your journey," the colonel said. "Good luck to you and thank you for a job well done for the army."

The colonel and Coleman left the porch.

Night Stalking Cat looked at Finley and said, "Thank you for honoring me with such a gift."

"Don't mention it."

"We leave after I get paid; are you ready to go?"

"I've been waiting on you for two days. I'll go and get my gear and we can be on our way."

"Meet back here in one hour."

Talon left Night Stalking Cat rubbing his new horse while the other Indian scouts gathered around him. It didn't take long to gather his gear and ready Sam and Sally for the trek. Returning to the scout's barracks, he could see a saddled steed and a pack horse hitched to the post in front of the porch. It wasn't long before Night Stalking Cat returned.

"I'm ready, are you?"

"Yep, let's go, but I'm not going to call you Night Stalking Cat. From now on I'm calling you Cat."

"I'll call you Kid."

"Cat and Kid… sounds good to me."

"Tonkawa scouts tell me you are one brave hombre filled with sand. They tell me why you fight when you have to, why you love horses. I can tell we'll be great friends and become blood brothers."

"Lead the way, Cat."

Chapter Six

Wonder where you are now, Cat, Talon thought as a hard rain pounded the ground around the overhang. *Somewhere in southeast Texas looking for gangs would be my guess.*

The driving rain had driven Sam to cover. Talon reached over, poured a cup of coffee and sat staring into sheets of rain. Every now and then the wind would change the direction of the drops, and dampness would blow under the overhang just enough to make it uncomfortable.

If I'm right about the way they decoyed me back in Texas and led me into this trap, then my guess is that the most recently stolen cattle were not taken to Mexico by their regular routine, but instead moved west and assembled for a trail drive north. They couldn't drive them to Kansas, because the law at Fort Dodge would know the cattle were stolen by who was driving them. More likely, they would take a more western trail to move north, either to Santa Fe or into Colorado. So it's not so bad to be this far north and west. Since they failed in their ambush, why wait for me? The weather has me trapped. They probable have pulled out and joined the herd somewhere on a far western trail. I'm guessing it shouldn't be too hard to find. People notice a couple thousand head of cattle being moved. Find the trail, find Jackson. Ole Cat, you night phantom, where would you start?

The wind shifted again and the rain was being blown away from the overhang. The basin had filled to extend closer to the camp site.

When the weather clears, I'll double back on my trail looking for signs of a cattle trail or civilization. If civilization, I'll find my bearings and then find the trail.

Another cup of coffee brought him back to thinking about an earlier trail, the one that led to his becoming a Ranger.

With their pack horses in tow, Cat and Talon crossed the river south of the fort and headed to the southeast. The country wasn't difficult. It was a flat, slightly undulating plain leading Talon to believe the whole state would be the same. This area seemed more arid because the plant growth was short and stubby, and a paler green than the area north of Concho.

"We ride until after sunset and make dry camp tonight," Cat said. "Gibson tells me outlaws want you dead. Dry camp, no fire. Fire can be seen for miles out here. We'll camp high and look for their fire. If we see one, we'll lose them tomorrow when we move into hill country. Where we are going, San Antonio, isn't far. You go to Houston to catch ship. Another two-day ride for the way you like to travel."

"You're the leader, and I'll do what you say, and when you say it."

"Kid, you gave me the best horse ever."

Cat chose to camp behind a small rise about half a mile north of the trail. They took the gear off the horses and hobbled them, and slowly crept to the top of the ridge. They put down the ground covers, weighting them down with the saddles, pulled the blankets over their shoulders, and looked out over the plain toward the back trail.

"You take first watch Kid, and wake me when the moon gets about half way to the horizon."

Then they saw the flickering in the distance near the area where they had crossed a dry wash. Cat nudged Talon's shoulder and pointed, and he silently acknowledged the touch and the light with a nod. Cat smiled, rolled over and went to sleep.

Was someone trailing us or was it just a coincidence? Maybe we'll find out tomorrow, Talon thought.

The moon finally reached Cat's position in the sky and with a small nudge he was wide awake. It didn't take long for Talon to crash into a sound slumber.

Early morning light was barely crawling above the ridge to the east when Cat signaled for Talon to get up. His horses were still hobbled but saddled and ready to go. After taking the hobbles off, Talon signaled Cat and he ran down the hill to mount his horse. They rode at a fast clip, staying behind the ridge until there was a gap to the south through which they could rejoin the trail. The sun was directly in their eyes when they hit the highs of the wavelike terrain.

"You think they'll follow us, Cat?"

"It doesn't make any difference because we will lose them in the hill country ahead."

By noon, they began to see outcroppings of taller ridges to the north of the trail. They looked like toes protruding from under the plain. As they crossed the high spots of the trail, Cat hesitated and watched the back trail for signs of any followers. He spurred his steed and they resumed a fast canter down a long, gradual slope where the trail crossed a small river. In midstream Cat turned south leading Talon through the break-lined stream, avoiding any islands where their tracks could easily be spotted. After several turns in the channel, he turned east behind a solid flat rock and climbed the bank of the river through the break, following a small wash where a tributary drained into the river. The channel had a dry, sandy bottom, and was completely covered by the foliage of scrub brush making up the breaks. He led up the wash around the first bend.

"We need to cover our tracks out of the river," Cat whispered as he slid out of his saddle.

He grabbed his Winchester, motioning for Talon to follow him. Talon reacted as promised, without question. There was plenty of room for a man to walk under the canopy of the break. When they got to the river, Cat took a small cutting of brush and wiped out the hoof marks that had been left in the sand. Then he turned north through the break, climbing the bank of the river to a point from which he could see the river crossing.

In a whisper, he said, "We'll watch to see if they are looking for us or have something else in mind."

"How did you know they were so close?"

"Morning sun reflecting off the dust they were throwing in the air. Could tell they were close from the last ridge we crossed."

Sure enough, it wasn't long before they hit the crossing. They didn't appear to be searching for any sign while negotiating the river. Quickly, they vanished over the next ridge. Cat nudged Talon and pointed to the sand at their feet, where with his finger he wrote a nine.

After nodding yes, Talon and Cat retreated though the break to the wash to claim their horses.

"Something's not right," Cat said.

He held the reins of his horse and they continued walking the wash to the east. It wasn't long before the break cover was gone, and they were completely exposed except for an occasional patch of scrub brush growing next to the wash. Then they heard the shots. Again, they tied up the horses and went to investigate. They climbed the ridge to the north to a vantage point above the main trail, and took shelter under the brush. They could see nothing from that position but didn't want to take the risk of traversing to the next ridge without cover. So they waited. It seemed forever, but finally they got their answer. The outlaws were driving about a hundred head of cattle toward the river crossing.

"They'll camp at the river tonight, and water the cattle and horses," Cat whispered.

Talon nodded.

They quickly returned to their horses and continued to move east through the wash.

"We will find the trail around the next turn in the wash, and see what has happened," Cat said.

The wash had followed the backside of an east to west ridge overlooking the trail, and turned north to cross the trail and disappear. They moved at a fast pace along the trail to the east. Over the next ridge they found the bodies of the slain family. Altogether, they counted seven dead, including a woman.

"We have to leave them here," said Cat.

Talon's heart sank, but he didn't question the scout's wisdom.

Cat pulled the reins of his steed, and they were off at a fast canter, moving east on the trail. The terrain continued arid and hostile. Late afternoon, they crossed a ridge that served as a bluff to a small river. The trail stayed on the ridge and continued to move east. Just at dusk they moved into a small community straddling the river. Crossing the bridge to the south, they found the local livery. A youngster greeted them and took their animals to be watered and fed.

"Where can we find a good meal?" Talon asked.

The boy replied, "You can eat at the inn, but the man you're traveling with can't."

"Why not?"

Cat spoke, "My skin color."

"What's that got to do with it?"

"You'll see."

They walked down to the inn. When they entered, they were greeted by the owner, a short, stocky man wearing an apron tied around his waist.

"What can I do for you?'

"We need to eat."

"We don't serve darkies here."

"We are Texas Rangers, and we will be fed."

"Come with me."

He led them through batwing doors to the kitchen.

"Please, sit at my personal kitchen table and I'll feed you."

"Do you have local law?"

"A sheriff."

"Get him for us."

A youngster left the back door.

"Where's he going?'

"To get the sheriff."

Cat took a seat at the table and poured coffee for both of them. The owner served them beef stew and sourdough rolls, and they waited.

The sheriff entered the back door behind the youngster.

"What's going on?" he asked.

He was an older man and looked like he could handle himself if braced.

Talon spoke, "We just left a dead family out on the prairie about a day's ride west of here. They were killed for their cattle."

"It must have been that outfit that pushed through here three days ago. They were driving the herd to San Angela. Nothing I can do for them."

"Can you send someone out to bury them?"

"Nope, no way."

"We have someone trailing us from San Angela. Can you warn us if anyone asks questions about us?"

"Now, I can do that."

"If we are braced, you need to stay out of it, understand?"

"How old are you?"

"16."

"Aren't you a little young for the job?"

"How old do you have to be?"

"Well, I'm thinking older. Who is this, uh… Negro, you're running with?"

"Since I'm not from Texas, Captain McNelly thought I needed a guide to show me around, he's my guide and a scout for the Texas Rangers and the Tenth U.S. cavalry. He is a Black Seminole. And he is also my friend, so I'd be careful with your use of words in his presence," Talon said, barely controlling his anger.

"Sure, sure, kid. I'll stay clear, and let you two handle it. I'll be happy to warn you, too. And I apologize if I've offended you or your friend."

"You have outlaw spies in your town, hard cases for sure; do you have any idea who they might be?"

"Yep, there were three fitting that description over at the saloon. I've been watching them the last few days. One did leave, heading west the day the cattle moved through here. And I noticed one leaving just a few minutes ago headed west."

"Why are they trailing Texas Rangers?"

"While I was working for the cavalry, I killed one of them on the trail just south of the Canadian, and they didn't like it. We're staying the night and will be out of here before dawn."

Talon and Cat finished their meal, slipped out the kitchen door and headed back to the livery.

"Kid, you're not a Texas Ranger."

"So, I lied"

Cat chuckled and for the first time Talon caught a spirit of appreciation in Cat's eye. As they rounded the last building on the alley and started across to the livery they came face to face with two strangers. They appeared to be the hard cases the sheriff was talking about.

"Are you the Kid from Wyoming?" asked the closest one?

"Who wants to know?"

"You killed a friend of mind."

"Who might that be?"

"Rags McLeod."

"I didn't know that yellow batterer of women had any friends. The two with him didn't seem to care what happened to him. They just froze while I killed him. Do you want part of me?"

The two split apart and faced Talon.

"Well, that's okay with me."

Talon started walking toward them, closing the distance. The townspeople began to figure what was about to happen and they started scurrying for cover.

Talon kept closing the distance. Cat couldn't believe his eyes.

Finally, the closest outlaw went for his gun and before he cleared leather Talon's first shot hammered his gun hand elbow knocking him to his right. Talon was still closing the distance when he fired his second shot into the other outlaw, as he was lifting his gun to fire. The shot caught him high in the gun hand arm. The next shot caught him right above his right knee. He went down unable to move. Talon's fourth shot hit the first outlaw in the back of his left thigh and down he went. He walked over to the first outlaw and kicked his gun away, reached down and untied his gun belt and jerked it off. By this time, Cat had disarmed the second outlaw and the sheriff was on the scene.

Talon returned to the first and kicked him over on his back and stepped on the wounded elbow.

"Who's responsible for killing those settlers on the trail?" he asked, his blood and face hot from the short battle.

"I don't know."

Talon grazed him with a shot to the right knee. "Tell me or the next one will be in the gut."

"Okay, okay, I'll tell. I'll tell"

Pulling the hammer back Talon asked, "Well?"

"Jackson Slager's gang out of Mexico."

Talon started toward the second outlaw.

"Don't shoot, please don't shoot. I'll talk."

"Well?"

"Jackson Slager's gang."

"Hear that, sheriff?" Talon asked. He glanced around the street, now filled with people. "Anyone here know if these men have horses?

One of the townspeople spoke up, "They're hitched in front of the saloon."

"Get 'em for me, will ya?"

The horses were brought to the scene. Cat and Talon lifted the wounded outlaws, tied them in their saddles, and wrapped the reins around their good wrists.

"Now, when you get to ole Jackson, tell him the Wyoming Kid is looking for him," Talon said as he slapped their horses to a run to the western trail.

Chapter Seven

A strong wind gust drew Talon's attention to the ridge line where the cedars were shedding their ghostly shroud of ice. Every time the wind blew or changed direction, more ice would cascade from their limbs and crash to the ground. With the rain, the freshets running down the side of the ridge looked like miniature ice flows, the grand-daddies of which flowed out of the rivers of Colorado during the spring break. His wood dryer was working so well that the limbs closest to the fire could be used for fuel. He saved the old stash and used the new. After, he would replace the wood at the back of the stack closer to the fire. This process continued throughout the day. He had repacked most of his supplies, keeping the coffee pot available along with the beef jerky. His plan was to ride as soon as the weather broke and to retrace his trail to signs of a herd passing or to civilization. He would grab his bearings and get to a telegraph. Drinking his coffee and leaning against the grounded saddle, he started to recall the last year as a Texas Ranger.

Cat led them southeast through the Texas hill country, and they made San Antonio in about three days.

"Cat, I've never seen so many snakes in my life as we saw going through that scrub brush, rocky country."

Cat laughed. "You only saw a few compared to the ones you didn't see."

That unnerved Talon enough to keep him quiet as Cat led him to the Texas Ranger's camp on the outskirts of town.

"We'll spend the night here in camp, and I will report to Captain McNelly."

They found a soft spot close to one of the cooking fires where they unsaddled and unpacked their horses. Talon took the four over to a metal watering tank and let them water. After hobbling, he let them loose on the green pasture next to the camp. Cat was gone when he finished, so he unrolled his ground cover and weighed it down on the end with the saddle. He pulled his gear to one side and laid down to rest for a minute before searching for a meal. One of the Rangers came over to investigate and to get a read on this new hombre in camp.

"Howdy, stranger, are you a Ranger?

"Are you?" Talon retorted.

"Yep, I joined today for $20-a-month, food and a horse. My name is Lowry Cook."

"Well, Lowry, you can call me the Wyoming Kid— from Medicine Bow, Wyoming."

"I'm from Corinth, Mississippi. Nothing doing there, so I moved out here to make my fortune. We're getting ready to chow down, want to join us?"

"I sure would, let me grab my cup and plate."

Talon followed Lowry over to the cooking fire where the cook in charge was starting to serve the evening meal.

"Hey Cookie, this is a new Ranger that wants to get fed."

"We'll fix him up."

Talon, having only eaten trail jerky for the last three days, sat down and feasted on fresh beef and potatoes, plenty of hot coffee, and a peach pie of some kind.

"Cookie, will you tell me how you made that peach pie?" asked Talon.

"Why, sure I will."

Lowry spoke, "Cookie, this is the Wyoming Kid."

"Don't mind at all, Kid. I'll write it down where you won't forget anything. I'll have it in the morning right after breakfast"

"Thanks, Cookie, and thank you, Lowry"

Lowry introduced Talon to several of the newly-recruited Rangers. They came from everywhere but Texas, and most were young and had limited experience in the west. From their looks, Talon figured none could handle a firearm sufficient to stay alive in a face-to-face fight. *Seeking their fortunes?*

Cat returned and motioned for Talon to come over to him.

"McNelly wants to meet you."

Moving into the largest tent he had ever seen, Talon noticed two desks at the far end. Cat approached the larger of the two, and Captain McNelly rose from his chair.

"Captain, this is Talon Finley, sometimes known as the Wyoming Kid."

"Talon, it's good to meet you. Night Stalking Cat speaks highly of your gun skills."

"It's good to meet you, Captain."

"Would you consider becoming a Ranger?"

"Yes, I would, if it means I can legally go after those cattle-rustling, women-killing outlaws run by one Jackson Slager. You can count on me."

Cat smiled and looked at McNelly, "Told you."

"I need something done before I can turn you lose to chase outlaws. I'm sending Night Stalking Cat to Brownsville to search out Jackson Slager's gang. I will send you in 10 days to join him there. This will give him enough time to get an idea of what we are up against. When you get there, you will need to follow his lead. Can you do that?"

"I got here following Cat, and he knows I obey."

"Let me tell you about Jackson Slager," McNelly continued. "He showed up in Mexico around Nuecestown about five years ago, and won the ear of Juan Cortina. Now, Juan Cortina was a wealthy land owner in Old Mexico, and when Texas won independence from Mexico he held large tracks of land on both sides of the Rio Grande, as well as others. He had a large army to protect his interests in both countries. He formed an army to support the revolution in Mexico, while at the same time warring with the Texans over their expansion into Brownsville. After the Civil War, his gangs were ruthless in their pursuit of taking over Brownsville. After the Brownsville War, the president of Mexico, who he supported, had him arrested and moved to Mexico City, and held without trial in the early 1870s—and he's still there. In his absence, this Jackson Slager has taken over the Cortina gang. He raids into Texas from across the Rio Grande, robbing, killing and rustling cattle. We know he has some kind of connection with a Northeastern United States cattle shipping combine, because he takes the stolen cattle into Mexico and loads them onto clippers bound for Cuba. That we know, and as of right now, everything south of the Nueces River to the Rio Grande is in his killing zone. And the Governor has charged us to bring law and order to the region.

"Here's what I want you to do for me before you join Night Stalking Cat. You see these new recruits? I want you to spend the next 10 days teaching them how to shoot. I don't need fast draws, just straight shooters who can hit an enemy. If they want the other, they'll learn on their own. Will you do that for me?"

"Most of these recruits are not from Texas. What's that all about," asked Talon?

"Well, if I hire Texans, most will have family on the outside of the law, and that may cause them to hesitate pursuing the other outlaws that their kin ride with. It may also get other Rangers killed. So, if you are not from Texas, you probably don't have any family riding with outlaws in Texas. The newspapers call them 'New McNellies' because they are new to Texas. I guess, Kid, you are now a New McNelly."

"I don't care what I'm called as long as I get a shot at Jackson Slager. I'll do your training. "

"How old are you Kid?"

"16."

"You have aged before your time. You'll be the youngest in the Rangers. Since you have your own gear, horses, and experience, I'm going to pay you 40 dollars a month. Anything else you need?"

"Yes, a Sharps 50 with a 34-inch barrel and ammo."

"I'll see what I can do. See you in the morning after breakfast."

When the Kid made it back to the cook fire, Cat had turned in and was under his cover looking up at the stars. Talon plopped down on his own ground cover and pulled the blanket over the lower part of his body. He slept only with a shoulder pistol— with his other guns close by— and a rifle across his saddle.

"Don't think you need them tonight, Kid," said Cat.

"When do you leave, Cat?"

"Early in the morning."

"I'll be doing pistol training for new recruits after breakfast, how do you think I should start with these pilgrims?" Talon asked.

"Give them a show of your fast draw and accuracy. They'll pay attention once they see that."

"After I train them for 10 days, I'm to join you in Brownsville, so wake me up when you get up."

The sun poked in and out through the clouds late in the day, but too late to move to the trail. It meant another night in his hideout, which gave him time to again clean his gear.

"Sure wish we had Sally with us, Sam."

Talon spent a good while rubbing Sam down and getting him ready for the trail. He ate a final evening meal, then cleaned and packed his cooking gear. Coffee and jerky would be the morning fare. He rekindled the fire and started another brew as his thoughts returned to San Antonio.

"Wake up, Kid."

Talon reacted quickly to Cat's prod. He rolled out of the blanket and bounced to his feet.

"You leavin'?"

"Yep."

"See you in Brownsville in about two weeks. Keep safe."

"Will do. See ya, Kid."

The morning started with Cookie serving something called grits, bacon and biscuits, with plenty of steaming coffee. The recruits staggered in one and two at a time to get their morning fare. Talon banged on his coffee cup with a stick he had been whittling.

"Listen up," he yelled to be heard over the clamor. "Starting tomorrow if you want to eat breakfast you'll be here by seven. If you are late you'll not eat. Immediately at eight, we'll start your training. Second in command in this training unit will be Lowry Cook. Any questions?"

"Yeah, who elected you to lead?" one of the recruits asked.

"That would be Captain McNelly. Form here at nine and we'll start our day."

"How old are you?" asked another.

"Old enough."

I'm tired of that question, Talon told himself as he went back to his gear to arm for the day.

At nine o'clock, the men had formed and were ready for their first day of training, or at least to see what the brash young man could show them. Talon marched them over to where the Rangers had set up a firing range. It consisted of a line of posts placed in front of a fast rising ridge as a back drop. Talon gathered them around him in a semicircle facing the posts.

"This is about 30 feet away from the posts. I want to show you what we are training to do with our sidearms."

He turned, crouching, and drawing at the same time, and fired five shots into the post he was facing. It splintered with the impact of the lead drilling through at dead center. The effect on the men was evident. Most didn't see the action, as it was so quick and they were not expecting it.

"Now I'm going to teach you to shoot. We're not about fast draws like I just showed you. We are about steadfast aiming and firing as a unit to be effective against a large force. We're going after outlaw gangs that will shoot back and we have to be more accurate. Lowry, assign each of the men a firing position."

The men complied quickly.

"Each of you fire five rounds in the post you are facing. Remember, the post is an outlaw."

The firing started with rounds peppering the bank beyond the posts. When it was over, Talon asked, "Did anyone hit a post?"

No one claimed a hit, and Talon went to work on instructing the men on the proper use of their Colts. The morning went slowly, but by noon the recruits had made progress, some more than others.

"We're going to break for a while to eat something, if you are hungry, and to clean your weapons, which will be inspected before we return to the range this afternoon. You must remember to take care of your weapon, so it will be ready to take care of you when you need it."

In three days, he had them hitting the posts consistently at 30 feet. In six days the men were firing five shots into the posts while advancing on foot toward them. The next four days dealt with shooting while mounted. By the tenth, Lowry could handle the drills, and Captain McNelly was impressed.

"Captain, if these men have sand they'll do in a fight," Talon told McNelly.

"We're moving out in the morning, and we'll escort you south of the Nueces, where we'll break off to Corpus Christi," said the captain. "I'm going to give you a message for George Patterson that will sidetrack you for a day on your trip to Brownsville. He has a large ranch southwest of where we'll leave you. It's important you get the message to him without being intercepted on the trail by anyone. So take your time and stay aware of your surroundings. Do the same going to Brownsville. Our intelligence indicates that Jackson Slager has put a price on the head of a Texas Ranger by the name of the Wyoming Kid. For the money, a shot in the back is better than bracing you."

"Got it," Talon answered.

The unit left as planned, with seven additional Rangers along with the new recruits. The pace was torrid across arid, scrubby land. Undulations in the terrain were a constant reminder that just over the next hill could be the best place in the world for an ambush. The course led to the east of southeast, and the Rangers were at a dead run. Finally, at dark, McNelly made camp at a small creek holding water.

"We'll stop here for the night," he said, and he called to three of the Rangers Talon didn't know. They had a short meeting after which the three left the unit, moving to the southwest.

Early the next morning, McNelly had the unit on the move before sunup. Again, the pace was fast over the same type of terrain. Late in the afternoon, they crossed a rise to see a river. As they approached, Talon could see a ferry crossing the water to greet them at the river's edge.

"Can't take all of you— only half," said the ferryman.

McNelly led his horse on first, followed by the seasoned Rangers and a few of the new recruits. After about an hour, Talon and the others led their horses onto the ferry. On the south side of the river, there was a small settlement surrounding a general store. The owner met McNelly in the middle of the street, wishing to talk to him about something. One of the Greaser Gangs — so named by inhabitants on both sides of the Rio Grande because of the bandits' slovenly appearance and to distinguish them from the hard-working field-hands and cowhands on both sides of the border — had robbed his store and taken most of the new saddles he had on hand, along with other supplies.

McNelly immediately dispatched his remaining experienced Rangers on their missions. All left together toward the southwest. He had ordered his scouts into the field. Shortly, they would be riding alone in different areas south of the Nueces, and Talon understood that he would be riding alone to Brownsville.

Morning broke cooler than the day before, an omen of bad weather on the way. The unit moved to the south, everyone riding as if this were their last day to live. McNelly halted the column around noon and summoned Talon to the front.

"Talon, this is where we leave you. We'll move east from here to Corpus Christi, and I want you to ride to the Patterson ranch with this message."

McNelly handed him the handwritten message. "Make sure you hand it to George Patterson only. Understand?"

Talon nodded in reply.

"Remember to keep out of sight as much as possible and travel just to the west of south to find the ranch. You should run into some cotton fields, Follow them to the ranch headquarters."

With that, McNelly jerked his reins and was off, with the recruits following. Several yelled "adios Kid" as they passed. In a short time, the silence of the plain turned Talon's attention to the task at hand: for him to move across this scrub wasteland without being seen. Sam and Sally looked exhausted from the fast-paced run they had endured for the last three days, and Talon thought it wise to slow the pace. It stayed windy and overcast throughout the day, but no rain.

At dusk, Talon found a small hollow off a dry creek bed to dry camp for the night. He hobbled, groomed and fed the horses before dining on jerky and water, daring not to light even the smallest of fires. He walked to the top of the highest ridge around and surveyed the area. He quickly saw he wasn't alone; a flicker of light to the west proved that fact. Chances of the people in the camp being friendly were remote; it had to be the outlaws, as only they would light a fire without fear. The size of the gang offered protection, and their willingness to kill deterred even the bravest of souls. They were not to be tackled alone, and Talon was as alone as he could be. Cat had taught him how to follow the dust scurrying to meet the sky as a way to track where a group of riders would be during the day. Only problem was, if it rained there would be no dust.

Leaving his protected area before sunrise, Talon kept a steady pace to the south, trying to stay off ridges and always checking his back trail for signs of discovery. He managed to make progress through the scrubby land, and by noon, he crossed a ridge overlooking a large expanse of a shallow valley. At the other end was what appeared to be a ranch headquarters, with a two story ranch house along with three separate barns, several corrals, and livestock abounding. Breaking from the scrub tree line, he set a fast pace toward the buildings while trying to keep his line of sight behind the barns. This didn't work for very long, as several riders came into the valley from the east on a course to head off the stranger. At this point, he knew he had to keep his cool when questioned by the riders, and only indicate that he was delivering a message to George Patterson before moving on his way. He slowed his pace.

There were four men and a girl facing off with Talon.

"Howdy, stranger," said their lead rider. "What can we do for you?"

"I have a message from Captain McNelly for George Patterson. Is this his ranch?"

"Yep, but we'll take the message to him."

"Have instructions to hand it to him personally."

"Are you a Ranger?" the girl spoke.

"Yes ma'am, I am."

"Luke, let's take him to daddy."

"Since it looks like it's going to rain any minute, may I seek shelter in one of the barns for the night?"

The clouds to the west had built during the day and glimmers of lightning could be seen in the distance. The cowboys surrounded Talon and escorted him to the headquarters. Just as they entered the yard surrounding the main house, the wind started kicking up swirls of dust and in the distance you could see the rain was a downpour. All the riders headed to the barn nearest to the house and escaped the early drops of rain. From the barn, they dashed to the back porch of the house. Still surrounding Talon, they entered the home into the kitchen. The aroma smelled like Martha Moore's kitchen in Medicine Bow. The smell of biscuits and the aroma of a hearty stew filled Talon with precious memories. He was led into a hall between the kitchen and the main house.

"Mister Patterson," the leader addressed a man sitting in a rocking chair, viewing the falling rain.

"What is it, Luke?"

"This here so-called Ranger says he has to deliver a message to you personally from Captain McNelly."

Patterson twisted his chair around to get a better view of Talon. "Well, let's have it, son."

Talon produced the message and handed it to him. Patterson opened it and took a minute or two to read the note.

"What's your name, lad?"

"Talon Finley, and before you ask, yes, I'm old enough to be a Ranger."

Patterson chuckled. "That was my next question. Since you have come out of your way to deliver this message, we welcome you into our home for the evening. And I expect you to join us for dinner here in the main house."

"Thank you, sir."

"Have a seat, Talon, and tell me how a kid like you ended up being a Ranger."

"Well, I ran into a little outlaw trouble in the hill country northwest of San Antonio."

"You're him, ain't you?" asked Luke.

"What do you mean?"

"You're *that* Wyoming Kid— the one Greasers have a bounty out for, right?"

"Where did you hear that?"

"From the Greasers. They spread the word and want you bad."

"What did you do, Talon?" asked Patterson.

"I'll tell you what he did. He shot and wounded two of the Slager gang, tortured one by stepping on his wounded knee, strapped them both to their horses and ran them out of town."

"Well, Talon?"

"I reckon it was sort of like that."

"Did you shoot them from ambush?" the older man probed.

"No, sir, they braced me, and I shot them eyeball to eyeball."

"Where are you going from here?"

"Brownsville."

"I'm going to send company with you to the end of our range, then you'll be on your own."

"Thanks, Mister Patterson. I'll be obliged to you."

"Now, I want you to eat with us and we'll make room for you here in the house tonight."

"If it's just the same to you, I'll sleep in the barn loft. I need to work on my horses and redistribute their loads."

"That was an unusual stallion you rode in on. How did you come by him?"

"Captured him two years ago out of the herd he was running in as a young colt. Trained him and we have been companions since."

Luke spoke, "Why is he wearing an army brand on his hip?"

"I delivered two hundred horses to Fort Concho and the Quarter-master there said that they would brand them and give me a bill-of-sale. That way there would be no question of ownership."

"Luke," Patterson turned facing him, "who gave you permission to take Mimi riding out past the cotton fields?"

"I did, daddy," said the girl.

"Luke knows better. How many others were with you?"

"The five best riders you have, daddy."

"Don't give me this daddy stuff. You know I'm not happy about you being beyond the fields with these Greaser gangs roaming around."

"Luke, you can't let this girl tug your heart to doing everything she wants you to do. Start standing up to her. Do you understand?"

"Y-y-y-yes, sir," Luke stammered, looking at the tips of his boots.

Talon took a glancing look at Mimi and knew he would be just like Luke. He would give in, too. The rain was steady and the lightning was flickering in the clouds to the east. It looked like it had settled in for the night.

"We finished planting the cotton yesterday, and the rain should kick our crop off to a good start," Patterson said.

"If you say so, sir. We don't grow much cotton up in Wyoming," said Talon.

The conversation died as they sat on the porch and watched the nature's distant light show as the evening sky turned into darkness.

After dinner, the rain had slacked and Talon dashed to the barn. He lit an oil lamp and started working on his horses. He found an empty stall, pitched some hay, and moved Sam and Sally into it. They had been combed and fed. He took his bedroll and climbed the ladder to the hay loft. He prepared his place of rest. When his feet hit the ground to douse the lamp, he was startled by Mimi entering the barn.

"Wyoming," she said. "I have a good and dear friend in Brownsville, would you consider taking her a letter?"

"Sure."

There you go, he thought. The first innocent request from this dark auburn-haired beauty, with the bluest eyes he had ever seen, and the skin of a porcelain doll. Her build reminded him of Sally Moore.

She broke the silence, "How old are you?"

Talon melted and replied, "16."

"I'm 16, and my daddy won't face it."

"Yes, he is, by telling you he loves you in the most, manly way he knows how."

"What do you mean?"

"Restrictions."

"Are you taking his side?"

"Yes."

"I'll give you the letter in the morning." She turned and slipped out the barn door.

Talon killed the lamp and climbed into the loft. He didn't know which girl to dream about: Mimi Patterson or Sally Moore.

The roosters were up early, and from the loft, Talon could see a low-clinging mist over the fields of this shallow valley. Riders were moving into the yard after their nightly watch. He strolled over to the bunkhouse and washed his face in the washbasin outside the rear door. Then he took a gander in the mirror hanging on the wall next to the basin. *I'll never get a beard*, he thought. *That's why I look like a baby.* As he turned, Luke motioned to follow him.

"They want you over to the main house for breakfast."

"Sounds good."

"Afterwards, some of the boys and me will escort you to the end of our range."

"That really sounds good. About how far is it to Brownsville?"

"Two days easy ride, but since you need to stay hidden, I would suggest you take your time during the day and ride straight through the night. Just past full moon, there should be plenty of light. Avoid any sparkles of light, man-made, and you should be safe."

Mimi greeted Talon as he walked up the steps and handed him a letter.

"This is to my dearest friend, Billie Jo Wise. Her daddy owns the largest mercantile store in Brownsville, so she'll be easy to find."

"That will be my first stop reaching Brownsville."

After breakfast Patterson came over to say his farewell.

"Well, son, I've been watching and she has you running an errand already, am I right or wrong?"

"Yes sir, it's a letter to her friend Billie Jo Wise."

"That's all? Looks innocent doesn't it, but I know her, she's trying to get her hooks in you."

"She's a pretty filly, Mister Patterson, and I think there are several who would like to have her hooks in them. I told her you loved her and she could tell by the restrictions you put on her."

"Thanks for telling me that. Good luck."

Talon checked his gear, climbed into the saddle and led Sally out of the barn toward the south gate of the yard. Luke and four other cowpokes met him there and they were off at a fast canter. A little after noon Luke halted the group.

"I see a small herd of cattle to our right," he said. "We are almost to the end of our acreage, so we are going to cut you loose and see why these cattle are so bunched. Something doesn't look right. We're going to leave you on your own and drive these cattle back to head-quarters."

"Thanks for the escort," Talon offered.

"Good luck, Talon."

Patterson's riders turned to the west to gather the cattle and start their move home. They had moved over a small rise and out of sight when a lone rider approached Talon out of the scrub trees to the east. When the rider got closer he could see it was Mimi. *What bad luck*, he thought. Then he heard gunfire from over the rise. He spurred Sam into a run into the scrub trees to the south and turned up the rise to get a view of what was happening. Mimi was right behind him. When they got to the top, they could see the Patterson riders being fired on from the next rise by a Greaser gang. They were closing in on the cowboys, who were out of their saddles and on the ground firing back. Talon slipped his saddle and tied his horses to the largest of the scrub trees. He pulled out the Winchester and went to Sally's pack and pulled the Sharps, too.

"What are you doing here?" he whispered to Mimi.

"Disobeying."

"Can you handle this Winchester?"

"Yes."

"Good. Get over there behind those trees and if anyone circles and comes at my back, kill him."

"I've never shot anyone before."

"It will be either him or me, your choice."

Talon turned and ran up the rise to a better vantage point. From a prone position behind the trees, he surveyed the action. He used a low fork of one the trees to steady the Sharps. He took a bead at the trail-ing outlaw, who had stopped to get a better aim. He noticed the Greasers were not very good in hitting what they were aiming at. He fired. The 50 caliber shot hit the outlaw dead center in the chest, and collapsed it. One was down. None of the other outlaws paid any attention to his firing or the fact that their companion was dead. He took aim at the second Greaser and fired. The rider's horse pull into the line of fire and the bullet went through its neck, but still hit the Greaser below the stomach. The horse fell like a rock and pinned the wounded Greaser under him. There was still no indication from the other Greasers that they knew they were under fire.

The cowboys were putting up a good fight. Although two were hit, they managed to hammer three of the Greasers. The Greasers were now outnumbered. Talon had just dropped his third when he heard the familiar bark of his Winchester from behind. He rolled down the hill to his right, drawing his long-barreled Colt, when he heard the second shot. Mimi had shot one Greaser and missed the second. It left the second exposed and Talon hammered him with three quick shots. The first hit the Greaser in the chest, the second hit him in the leg, and the third missed. He rolled back to his original position, grabbed the Sharps and continued the fight. In a matter of a few minutes all the Greasers were killed or wounded.

Talon moved from his firing position and checked the two Greasers on the ground behind him. They were both dead. He called for Mimi to join him.

He replaced the rifles, and they went to check on the cowboys. There were seven dead Greasers, and two wounded, including the one pinned and dying. Three of the cowboys were wounded. Two had shoulder wounds and the other had been shot in the arm, but nothing serious. Talon took his time in bandaging the three, and then he went to work on the Greaser.

"Who do you ride for?" he asked.

The Greaser pretended not to understand English. One of the cowboys repeated in Spanish just as Talon stepped on his wound.

"Slager," he yelled in agony.

"Luke, use Mimi's horse and round up your horses."

It didn't take long to gather theirs and the outlaws'. Talon jerked the wounded Greaser off the ground and strapped him to the saddle of one of the horses.

Grabbing the Greaser by his throat, Talon looked at him and said, "Tell Slager the Wyoming Kid is south of the Nueces looking for him." He slapped the horse, and yelled, "Tell him, you hear?"

Mimi collapsed to her hands and knees when she realized that she had killed a man.

"Talon, I did what you said to do. It was either you or him." she said.

Her color had turned a ghostly white.

"Luke, you have your work cut out for you. You need to get Mimi back home as quick as you can. If the wounded can't keep up, you'll need to leave them to fend for themselves, got it?"

He nodded and helped the wounded get in their saddles while Talon helped Mimi.

"I owe you my life," he said.

She tearfully looked at him and nodded. He kissed her hand, and slapped her horse. He watched her until she was out of sight then climbed into the saddle, jerking the reins south. He stopped in the tree line at a vantage point overlooking the dead Greasers. At sundown, another group rode over the western rise, surveyed the corpses, and started driving the cattle to the west. One of the Greasers rode over to the obvious leader of this band and pointed to the north. They disappeared to the west.

The night was clear and the recent rain softened the sounds of the horses' hoofs as they traveled across a road that led south. Talon could see the flickering of lights along the way. Every so often, to avoid riding too close to such a fire he left the road and traveled across the scrubby land of south Texas. The detours took time because of the hazards of uneven ground. He always set a fast pace after rejoining the road. Early in the morning, he crossed a rise and found himself on the outskirts of a small settlement. He retreated to a dry wash the road had just crossed, plunged through the scrub brush lining it and followed it to the east. He estimated how far he had come and turned out of the wash to the south. He still wasn't very far from the settlement, but continued on at the fastest pace he could manage safely. Sam and Sally showed their big hearts during the night, as they never seemed to tire.

As dawn was breaking, Talon found a tree-infested outcropping of rock that stretched a great distance following a parallel path on the west side of the road. The trees in this area were larger than those he had traveled past during the night.

There must be water in the area to grow the larger trees, he thought. He turned west off the road and lost himself in the trees. There he found water dispersed in small potholes throughout the area. These natural basins obviously held rain water, allowing the growth around them to prosper. He found a place well-hidden from the road from which he could keep track of the road's activity.

He watered and hobbled the horses. There seemed to be enough grass for them to graze on. He checked diligently for snakes before crawling under the trees to a spot where he could watch the road. It wasn't very long before two empty wagons heading north passed. A while later four cowboys passed heading south. During the day, there was no single person traffic. An omen: *was this road safe for lone travelers?* After the short rest, he started southward through this rough terrain. Every once in a while, he would cross a sand dune, and by late afternoon he had come to the end of this area. He decided to wait for nightfall before venturing back to the road. Again, he set a brisk pace.

The road had been kind to him. He had traveled a great distance without interference, and at dawn he was approaching a small settlement. The small town was wide awake when he passed through. There was an old gentleman repairing the corral fence next to the livery. Talon stopped to get his bearings. The old man confirmed that Brownsville was about a half day's ride down the road he was following. The old man noticed the brand on Talon's horses, and asked if he were in the army. Talon confirmed he was, thanked him for the information, and continued on his journey. *Well, I guess I broke the not being seen rule,* he thought.

Talon looked like a tough-enough stranger to be traveling this road in south Texas. More and more, the population had turned to brown-skinned Mexicans. As the old man had said, Talon hit the outskirts of Brownsville about noon.

He entered the main plaza from the north and found a livery sitting off to the west. He pulled up to the hitching rail and slid out of the saddle. A youngster bounced out of the barn.

"Señor, may I help you?" he asked.

"Yes, how much to groom and oat my horses, and store my gear for a while?

"One dollar for regular feed, but for the best feed it will be two dollars."

"What's the best feed?"

"Crimped oats, cracked corn held together with sorghum molasses. Really makes their coats shine."

"I'll take the best, then," Talon said.

Talon reached into his vest for his poke and gave the youngster two dollars.

"Do you know Billie Jo Wise?"

"Sure, I do. Her daddy owns the mercantile store on the north side of the plaza street. You can walk over to it." He pointed to it across the street.

"It has three doors you can enter."

All of a sudden, there was a scurrying of people running into stores along the street heading east from the livery.

"What's going on?" asked Talon.

"See that cantina across the street from the mercantile? Seven outlaws are bracing the Black Seminole Indian standing on the corner of the boardwalk next to the mercantile hitching and watering corral. One has just left the cantina and moved off the porch to the east of where the Indian is standing. People feel there is going to be a fight and they are getting out the way."

"Thanks." Talon turned and started across the street to the mercantile to deliver Mimi's letter.

He walked up the steps to the boardwalk and entered the door on the west side of the building out of sight of the cantina. An older woman approached him and asked how she could help.

"I have a letter to deliver to Billie Jo Wise."

"Come, this way young man. Billie Jo?" she called.

A blond, blue-eyed Texas beauty, Billie Jo came bouncing from the back of the store. Talon felt he had fallen into a pail of cold buttermilk on a hot day.

"Are you Billie Jo?" he asked.

"Why yes, I am."

He handed her the letter from Mimi. She opened it and read it. The she looked at him, and started to giggle.

"Thank you so much for bringing this to me. It's word I've been waiting on for weeks."

"You're welcome. How do I get to the door closest to that corner of the building?" Talon asked as he pointed.

"Oh, you don't want to go out that door. There's going to be trouble, we think, and it wouldn't be safe."

"My friend Cat's being braced and I need to back him."

"Go to the end of this aisle and you'll see the door from there."

Talon slowly walked toward the door, checking his guns as he went. He knew Cat was really feeling lonely, having to face several Greasers alone. He walked through the door as Mister Wise was shutting it. Slowly, he walked down the steps from the boardwalk and started to approach Cat.

"Cat, what have you gotten into?"

Cat turned toward the voice and smiled when he recognized Talon. Another Greaser left the cantina and slowly walked to the east corner of the porch. Then the batwings open again and another stepped out on the porch in front of the door.

"Had a run in with some Greasers south of the Nueces. They don't shoot very well and they die crying. We need to get closer. You take the one on the left. I'll get the one in front of the batwings. Then we'll both hammer the one in the middle."

Cat didn't say a word, he wasn't afraid because he knew the Kid would fight. Talon reached into his vest pocket and retrieved his fake Ranger badge and pinned it on his vest pocket. He started to close the distance— a move that was totally unexpected by the Greasers out front.

"Hey, outlaws, you can come along peaceful like or suffer."

They were about 30 feet away when Talon's target started to draw. The other two, not seeing his action, were late to the party. Talon's first shot hit his target below the right knee, as he had misjudged the height of the porch, but his second shot hammered in the middle of the chest, about the time his target fired his first shot into the ground in front of the steps. Talon and Cat both hammered the middle target, killing him before he could level his gun. Then the unexpected, another Greaser burst through the bat wings firing on the run; his first shot hit Talon in the right leg above the knee, knocking him down and to his right and likely saving his life as the second shot hit him on the left side of the head knocking him backwards. Talon dropped his first gun and drew the second returning fire into the belly of the Greaser. In a daze of blurred vision, he emptied his gun firing at the batwings, tearing out two of the slats. Another Greaser dead man walked through the wings and stumbled down the steps of the porch.

Cat wasn't finished either, as another Greaser had come around the east side of the building in full charge, firing as he came. He nailed Cat in the left arm before Cat knew he was there. Cat paid him back in full with two hits in the chest.

Talon rolled to his left to get the long Colt from behind his back. He drew it in time to return the fire from two new Greasers moving down the porch from the batwings to the west. He tried to raise his hand to shoot and did get a shot off, killing one of the horses at the west side hitching rail, but missed the Greasers. Cat wounded one as they made their escape.

Talon was still trying to fight. He would try to point the Colt, but couldn't lift his head or arm off the ground. Blood was pouring into his left eye, closing it. His head was spinning, rendering all his valiant efforts to continue the fight useless. He could hear stirrings around him, not making any sense of them. He blacked out in a fog of pain.

Chapter Eight

Talon stirred the embers of his fire, as the evening shade had covered the alcove. Sam was munching grass across the way, undisturbed by any intruders, human or otherwise. He poured the last cup of coffee and started another pot. He resisted the urge to cook another meal, settling for the jerky for his evening fare. He chuckled to himself about the aftermath of the gunfight in Brownsville. His thoughts strayed back to the hours following the Brownsville fight, especially when he woke up and faced one of the most embarrassing moments of his life.

It seemed as if rays of light were trying to pry open his eyes. They were painful in their efforts. Finally, he succeeded in opening his eyes, and he remembered the fight. He lifted himself up on his elbows, raising the covers to view his naked body.

"It's still there."

Talon turned and saw Billie Jo and Mimi smiling at him.

"What's still there?" he asked.

"Your love handle," replied Mimi.

"All men waking up after being wounded look to see if they're still together," said Billie Jo.

Talon could feel his face begin to burn. *How could she know that?* he thought.

"Still works, too," said Mimi.

And how could she know THAT?

Talon laid back and pulled the cover over his head. He could hear the girls giggling at his fate. His thoughts — and their giggles — were worse than his wounds.

"Bet you're hungry. We'll be back with something for you to eat. Don't move around too much, or you will pass out again," said Billie Jo.

Then reality struck: *I hurt all over.* He had bandages on his head, the left side in the middle of his rib cage and around his right leg above the knee. He could remember the leg being hit, and maybe his head, but not his left side. *When did that happen? How long have I been out? I must have been out for a while, because Mimi's here and that ranch is a good 3 or 4-day ride. How long?* It wasn't long before two ladies walked into the room. Talon recognized Mrs. Patterson.

"How you doing, sweetie?" she asked.

"Not so well," Talon replied.

"Hazel, let me introduce you to Texas Ranger Talon Finley."

"We've been introduced, but not formally. You hungry, darlin'? We've been spoon feeding you, but you haven't taken much."

"Thank you, I am more thirsty than hungry."

"Understandably so, you've been running a fever," said Hazel Wise.

"How did I get here?"

"Grateful townsfolk brought you."

"Cat?"

"Who?'

"My friend, Night Stalking Cat, how is he?"

"Oh, he's out on the front porch nursing his sore arm."

With that, Talon relaxed into his pillow.

"Have you been taking care of me?"

"Some, but Billie Jo and Mimi have done most of the care giving."

Talon could feel his face burning.

"Look here, Annie Patterson, our Ranger is turning red. Darlin' there's no need to turn red. These girls of ours have grown up with brothers and all sorts of injuries. "

"Hazel, have the girls bathed him today?"

The thought of Mimi and Billie Jo bathing him was too much.

"Oh, please tell me you didn't let them bathe me."

"Sweetie, a girl in south Texas can handle anything, including bathing you," retorted Annie.

Cat walked into the room.

"Cat, you got to save me."

"From what?"

"They've turned those two girls loose on me."

"You have bigger problems, Kid."

"Like what?"

"Getting over your wounds is going to take some time."

Billie Jo and Mimi entered the room, carrying a tray and a pitcher. They sat them on the table next to the head of the bed.

"Want to sit up to eat?" asked Mimi.

"Mimi?"

"Yes, Mama."

"You and Billie Jo need to leave. We'll handle the feeding."

"Oh Mama, why?"

"Because! Want me to call your Daddy?"

The girls left the room.

"Thank you, Mrs. Patterson."

"Sweetie, you have to get over this being embarrassed, the girls have been cleaning you up for the last two days."

"But I didn't know it."

"Honey, you do now."

"I should have died."

Hazel, Annie and Cat laughed at him. The ladies left the room and Cat pulled up a chair next to the bed. He poured a glass of water, and helped Talon sit up with his legs over the side of the bed. He propped a pillow behind his back to help him stay put. Then he pulled the table in front of him. Handing him a spoon, he pushed a bowl of beef broth over to him. Although feeble, Talon responded by feeding himself.

"How long have I been here, Cat?" Talon asked.

"Five days, but they've managed to feed you. And the ladies were right. The girls have been taking care of all your needs. They're like those little hummingbirds in and out."

"Cat, how do I face the girls?"

"Kid, they're not Greasers with guns. Look at it this way. You must have something that interests them."

"They said... 'It worked'."

Cat fell out giggling.

Four days later, Cat rejoined McNelly, and Talon was up and about working the soreness out of his leg, when Joe Wise approached him.

"Talon, the livery tells me you are running up a bill."

"How much do I owe them?"

"They say two dollars."

"Two dollars a day, that's 20 dollars."

"No just two dollars. Things have been calmer around here after your party and they appreciated what you did. So do a lot of other folks. I told McNelly he could have his Ranger back in five days. Do you agree?"

"Well the headaches are gone, and I can live with a limp for a while. Yes, I think so."

"He's making a big push against the Greaser gang that raids through Rio Grande City. He says he really needs you along for the ride."

"Mister Wise, would you mind if Billie Jo helped me exercise my horses?"

"Talon, my friends call me Joe. If you feel up to it, okay."

"Thanks, Joe."

"We all suffer our own fates."

Talon went looking for Billie Jo and found her on the west porch. He approached with an exaggerated limp.

"Billie Jo, I asked your Dad if it would be all right if you helped me exercise Sam and Sally. He said it would be okay. Would you help me do that now?"

"Get one of my brothers to do it," she replied.

"I thought you would like to ride Sally."

"Ride, oh you mean by exercise to go for a ride?"

"Yes."

"What would Mimi think?"

"What do you mean?" Talon asked.

"She's my best friend and she has her eyes on you, and it could hurt her feelings."

"This sure got complicated! Do you want to go for a ride or not?"

"Let's go," she said.

Talon and Billie Jo spent the next four days riding together in the guise of exercising the horses. On the morning of the fifth day, Talon paid his livery bill. He walked Sally over to the Wise's stable and placed her in their corral. He stored the gear he didn't need in the back of the tack room. He mounted his horse and rode to the west side of the building, where he found Billie Jo.

"Billie Jo, I have left Sally in your corral. Will you take care of her for me while I'm gone?"

"Where are you going?" Billie Jo asked.

"Call of duty."

A tear fell from Billie Jo's left eye. Talon unsaddled and climbed the porch steps. He looked down into her face and put his arms around her in a soft hug. Then he kissed her.

"I'll be back," he said.

She kissed him. He turned and vanished from the porch, and for the first time in his life, Talon feared not making it back.

Chapter Nine

Talon knew he had to make his break in the morning. His plan was to back track the trail to get his bearings. He planned to proceed slowly to the scrub trees below the cedar line to find a different path off the mountain. It would be harder to trail him through dense growth, which offered a more secluded path than the trail he had ridden onto the mountain. Once off the mountain, he would search for civilization. Mentally, he checked every detail of his gear and how it was to be stowed. Pouring a cup of coffee, he settled into a resting posture before the fire. *The last night,* he thought. *It's like leaving home. Someday I'm coming back and spend a night or two to see if I can find that mountain goat that saved our lives.* His eyes filled with tears when he thought of the last time he saw Billie Jo, when he had kissed her and she had hurried through the doors of the Mercantile. Then he pounded his fist on his leg when he remembered the cause.

When Talon made the ranger camp, the men of the force were saddling the ponies and checking their gear. He rode straight to the captain's tent, slid out of his saddle and announced himself at the open tent flap.

"Come on in, Kid."

McNelly was sitting at his makeshift desk, staring at a map hand-drawn by the two scouts in his tent.

"I want you to join Cook's squad for this mission. He knows the details and the terrain we'll be traveling tonight. He can explain our plan of attack. Also, you need to know our new rules of engagement with regard to prisoners. They will be tied to their horses, hands to the saddle and feet to the stirrups. Their horses will be tied to each other in single file, by the saddle strap under their bellies. If any attempt is made to escape or if their friends make any attempt to rescue them, it will be met with instant execution. The Greasers call it, *la ley de fuga.* This seems to be working among the prisoners, and we've had very little trouble out of them since we started this. It helps us because it only takes one or two Rangers to control several prisoners. Any other new regulations you need to know about, I'm sure Cook can catch you up on them."

"Thanks, Captain. Where's Cook?"

"Out of the tent to the right, about a hundred yards. You'll find him," McNelly gestured.

When he found Lowry, he and his men had just finished getting ready. Lowry turned and smiled when he saw Talon.

"You look good for a man with a growing legend," Lowry greeted him.

"What are you talking about?" asked Talon.

"Cat told us how you saved his butter in Brownsville. He thought he was dead for sure before he heard your voice. He said you killed two Greasers without seeing them while you were on your back with blood in your eyes."

"I could hear and smell them," Talon said with a slight smile.

"That's what he said… and that *he* taught you were the smelling part." Lowry said with a bigger smile.

"As Uncle Jim says, 'it ain't bragging if it's true'. What are we doing tonight?" Talon asked.

"We're going after Juan Salinas' gang north of Rio Grande City early in the morning. Our scouts tell us they are crossing the Rio Grande and heading north into the Nueces strip. Our plan is to fall in behind them and block the river crossing, where they'll have to scramble to make it back to Mexico. Talon, we will shoot to kill. No messin' around with trying to take prisoners. Our scouts are giving us good information and we don't need any misinformation from prisoners to confuse us."

"What about this new regulation in handling prisoners?" he asked Lowry.

"It works. No need for you to risk rescuing a prisoner if the prisoner is dead when you get there. It took a couple of executions for them to get the message, but we haven't had any problems since. Let's get you ready. You need rations and water. By the way, the training you gave us has saved lives," Lowry reported.

The sky didn't have a cloud, allowing the stars to show their majesty and to light the Rangers' way westward. When dawn broke, they were hidden in a dry wash awaiting the passage of the Greaser gang heading north. This gang had been raiding the ranches all along the border, as far north as the Nueces. They were after cattle and horses, stealing 300 to 400 head a trip. They would drive them across the Rio Grande and move east to a secluded barge-loading spot. The cattle were being sold to the same combine that the Juan Cortina gangs were using.

Hours passed, letting the heat build to levels Talon had never experienced. Finally, the gang meandered past to the west of their position in the dry wash. Lowry led his men in behind the gang. They charged the Greasers with guns drawn and blazing. McNelly popped onto the scene to the northwest of the gang's position, turning them to the east. The remaining Rangers greeted them from the northeast, opening fire as they charged. The Greasers were trapped. None chose to surrender. They dropped from their horses to fight on foot, from the small pits in the terrain using the small grubby vegetation as cover. But it was too late; the Rangers were upon them. The fight was over in a matter of minutes, with all 17 gang members dead or dying of wounds. The ambush had been a success. Four of the Rangers had suffered minor wounds.

"Gather their horses, sidearms, rifles, money and any other items worth keeping," yelled McNelly.

After the orders were carried out, he led the Rangers to the north at a torrid pace. By late afternoon, the Rangers were approaching a ranch headquarters. It seemed to Talon that this homestead was in the middle of nowhere. Four vaqueros, sitting their ponies, were in the yard when the Rangers arrived. An older gentleman walked onto the porch and greeted them.

"Señor Olvera, we have brought you a gift from the outlaws that have been raiding your ranch," said McNelly. "We have several horses, arms, and a little gold and silver to give to you."

"Thank you, Captain. I'm happy you're here because my vaqueros have just informed me a band of outlaws are stealing a small herd of mine off my southwestern range. There are about 10 or 11 of them pushing fast toward the Rio Grande, west of Rio Grande City. Can you help me?"

"Sure we can help. I'll leave a third of the unit to go with your vaqueros," replied McNelly.

He turned and looked at Cook, "Lowry, this is a job for your men."

"Yes sir."

"We're going east. When you finish, work your way back toward Brownsville and we'll meet you there."

"Yes sir."

McNelly led most of the column east toward Brownsville as Lowry asked Señor Olvera if he would lead the way to the herd.

"I'm unable to ride, but my trusted vaquero Jose Cortez can lead the way."

"If we leave now, we can have them rounded up by morning."

Olvera introduced Cortez to Lowry Cook and they were off for another night ride at the usual scorching pace to the southwest. Two days of all out running was beginning to tell on Sam. His breathing was labored and his coat was lathered. Talon could tell he was running on his heart. One of the Mexican scouts met them before dawn and pointed to a wide wash still holding water. This was where the raiders had bedded down for the night. In their usual no-fear fashion, the raiders were asleep with two guards riding the perimeter. Talon suggested to Lowry that Cat should scout the lay of the camp before taking any action. Lowry nodded to Cat and he was gone. After about an hour, Cat returned.

"This is worse than we thought," he reported. They're not moving the herd. They're are killing it and taking the hides. They also have three captives tied to the wheels of one of their wagons. They have three wagons. Two are loaded with stolen goods from earlier raids, and they're piling the other with cow hides."

"Cat, you and Wilson handle the perimeter riders. We'll give you 30 minutes. Then the rest of us will quietly walk in on them. We'll try to capture them to keep the captives safe. But orders are orders and any sudden moves, we shoot them all," said Lowry.

Cat and Wilson left to carry out their tasks, and Lowry took the time to position his men, instructing them which areas of the camp they were to cover. At 30 minutes they moved on the camp and with surprise working in their favor, took seven Greaser prisoners. This raiding party had come to an end.

"What do we do with them now?" asked Talon.

"We tie them to their stirrups for you and Cat to take to Browns-ville," Lowry stated.

"We can do that," Talon agreed.

"We'll take the captives and wagons into Rio Grande City along with the two guards that were killed. Your job will be to get the pris-oners to Brownsville while scouting for other raiding parties along the way. I'll have our scout following your path after we finish in Rio Grande. Good luck to you," Lowry promised

Olvera's vaqueros took charge of what remained of the herd, along with the extra horses, and started driving them back to their range. Lowry kept the firearms they had taken from the raiders. The herd had been recovered without a shot— not exactly the way the Rangers had been doing it over the last few weeks. The orders were to shoot first, then bury. Lowry took his eight-man squad and left Cat and Talon to move the prisoners to Brownsville.

The Nueces strip was a boiling pot for the Rangers. Cortina's raiders over the last few months had invaded the area, robbing, kill-ing, rustling horses and cattle, taking captives and battering women. To counter this activity, many of the white-skinned residents had set up vigilante organizations to track down the raiders and kill them. The vigilantes often didn't distinguish between "good" Mexicans and bad ones.

Any Mexican rider with a new saddle was shot on sight. The Mexican rancheros who legally owned their land were murdered and their buildings were burned to the ground. Many Mexican land owners fled for their lives to Mexico. Olvera was an exception. He had enough vaqueros to withstand the raiders and the vigilantes. One of the tasks of the Rangers was to disband the vigilante groups by making it certain to them they would be shot just like the raiders from Mexico. Further complicating the issue, some of the large white ranch owners frequently raided into Mexico and rustled Mexican cattle and horses. To battle the resulting anarchy, the Rangers implemented a simple policy that covered vigilantes, Greasers and raiders on either side of the Rio Grande— if caught, law breakers would be shot.

The poor Mexican inhabitants on either side of the river could only look on with bewilderment at the killing of some of their family members who happened to get caught in the middle— the wrong place at the wrong time.

Cat and Talon's journey to Brownsville with the prisoners took them through several Mexican communities that were established north of the Rio Grande before the area had become Texas. The Rangers couldn't help but see the hatred in their dark eyes for both their prisoners and themselves. The going was slow because of the horses being tied together single file. Occasionally, they would cross the path of a raiding party that had moved through the area, and their progress slowed even more. Following Cook's orders to check out any sign of other raiders, Cat would leave and scout the area for leads on where the groups might be or where they had crossed the Rio Grande. This left Talon alone to guard the prisoners. Talon carried his Winchester across the pommel of his saddle when left alone. Camping for the night was a chore, so they didn't take the time or trouble, except to water, feed and rest their horses. They slowly moved through the two nights they were on the trail. They arrived at the Ranger camp in Brownsville around midmorning on the third day, exhausted from the three-day trek.

They could see right off that something wasn't right. The usually boisterous camp was quiet and subdued, as though the men had suffered a disastrous loss. No one would meet their eyes, so they quickly surrendered their prisoners to the duty guard, dropped their tired mounts at the camp livery with directions on feeding and grooming them, and rushed to Captain McNelly's tent.

Talon pushed through the tent flaps first and saw the captain seated at his desk, his head down and cradled in both hands.

"What's happened, captain?" Talon cried as he approached the desk. "Did you get ambushed?"

McNelly looked up briefly, then quickly turned away from the young man's probing eyes.

"Son, you need to see Mr. Wise in Brownsville— now."

"Captain?" Talon's voice dropped as fear clutched at his heart.

"Just go, son. Just go. Take my horse."

Talon rushed through the tent flaps and jumped atop the captain's big stallion. He spurred the big horse through the camp and quickly rode into the main plaza, his fatigue forgotten as he noticed that part of the mercantile store was scorched and still smoking. He slid out of the saddle and raced up the steps to the main door facing the south. Joe Wise was standing there, staring at his feet as though he could will them to move. He knew it was Talon without looking.

"Talon, I don't have the right words, so I'll just spit it right out. One of Jackson Slager's Greaser gangs hit us two nights ago and cleaned us out. They singled us out because we helped you and Cat."

"And?"

"They killed Billie Jo, son. They gunned down my little girl."

Talon wept.

Chapter Ten

The raw pain never left, even months after the young woman's death. Talon's sobs echoed under the enclosed overhang and brought him back to the present— in front of a small campfire, hiding out from dangerous pursuers. He carefully checked each of his firearms and moved to where Sam stood munching grass. It had been a restful few days for Sam, and Talon felt a good rub would be just the thing to ready the big horse for what was coming. Tending to his horse quelled the pain of his memories and gave him a chance to review the vendetta he had started against Jackson Slager's gang. He returned to feed his fire, and his thoughts turned to his friends Cat and Lowry. They stood with him and backed every play he made during the deadly actions in Mexico.

"Kid," Cat nudged Talon. "Kid, you been asleep for over 10 hours." He nudged him again finally getting a response. "Kid, you need to get up."

"Cat, they killed Billie Jo," Talon said.

"I know."

"I'm going after them."

"I know that, too. And Lowry and I are going with you," promised Cat.

"Can we find out who they were?"

"Already working on who, and where, they are now."

Cat began outlining a plan.

"My home — where my family is now — is about 15 miles south of Matamoros. My ancestors migrated there to escape oppression in the United States. I know the area and have family and friends that will help us. They hate these Greaser gangs as much as we do because of the way they treat us. You will need to go in a disguise to keep from tipping off the local informants that you're in Mexico. Change your clothes and carry only two pistols, not your usual four. Leave the Sharps and Sam here because everyone knows you ride a blue roan. And try to look a little older.

"We'll go across into Mexico on the ferry between Brownsville and Matamoros in the early evening and pay the operator to meet us on the Mexico side late in the evening. In the next few days, I'll find the gang and where they are staying. Then we raid them and blow them away. The three of us — you, me and Lowry — should be more than enough to get the job done."

"Good plan. When do we start?" asked Talon.

"Now," Cat turned and left the tent. "I'll see you in two days. Be ready."

Talon left the tent in search of a new horse and different clothes to change his looks. His first stop was Joe Wise's mercantile, where he found Joe still despondent, but at least trying to stay busy.

"I'm going after them, Joe. And I'm going to make them pay." Talon predicted.

Joe looked at him, his face ravaged with grief and loss. "Thank you, Talon. Hazel and I need the closure it would bring. What do you plan to do?"

"I'm going after them, and I'm not bringing them back alive."

"Be careful, son."

He changed his clothes for some worn by Billie Jo's younger brother, and got Joe's dark red horse from the stable. He slid the holster of his long-barreled Colt to the left side on his gun belt, and dropped the other two holsters. He felt naked without the other two Colts, but he trusted Cat's judgment and followed the plan to the letter. Cat's plan was excellent, and he was going to work it. He returned to the Ranger camp to find Lowry.

"Lowry, have you talked to Cat?"

"Yes, and I'm ready. I see you are, too. Where did you get the horse?"

"Joe Wise," Talon answered.

"We should hear from Cat sometime this afternoon."

It took three days instead of two, but Cat finally made it back.

"I found 'em," he said. They're holed up in a small cantina a few miles south of Matamoros. They show up every evening to gamble and drink until the early hours of the morning. The place is crowded early, but thins out after midnight to mostly the Greaser gang we're after."

"Good. When do we go?" Talon asked.

"We go now. I've got something for you and Lowry." Cat handed each a double-barrel shotgun. "We'll get the hombres that killed Billie Jo, and a few of their friends. These scatterguns are really good for close-in work, and we'll mess them up real good before using our Colts. Killing a few of their friends along the way will send a message that they are not safe in Mexico, that we'll come and get 'em wherever they run."

Talon looked at his friends without speaking. The looks he got back spoke louder than any voice could. They were united in this quest for justice and wouldn't stop until they got it.

The western sky had turned its dying deep orange as they rode up to the ferry. Talon recognized the ferry operator as a customer at the mercantile and a friend of Joe's. If he recognized Talon, he didn't show it. The ferry pulled across to the Mexican side and with gentle handling, hit the off ramp exactly where it needed to. As they walked their horses off the ferry, Cat hesitated for a moment to exchange a few quiet words with the operator. He quickly joined Lowry and Talon, giving them a nod of approval.

"What did you tell him?" asked Talon.

"I told him to stay awake until we get back and to remember if he sees anyone while he's waiting."

"Did you tell him it may be all night?"

"He knows and is willing to stay."

They mounted up, nudging their horses to a slow canter following Cat's lead. They looked like Texas hard cases making their way through the Mexican community, and their passing didn't draw any undue attention. The night covered their passage for the last few miles to the cantina where the gang usually spent the evening hours. This night was no different. They showed, as Cat had promised. By early morning, most of the regular patrons had left, and only hardcore gang members and the cantina's señoritas remained. Although smaller, this group made more noise than the full cantina. Lowry and Talon realized that innocent people were going to be in their line of fire, but to the Rangers, on this night, they were no more innocent than Billie Jo.

Cat gave the word: "Let's do it."

The band and the señoritas had filed out the back into the cool of the night for a short break. The break in routine was the signal Cat wanted, so he motioned that it was time to move. Lowry entered the cantina first and moved straight to the bar. The gang's members had gathered around several tables at the rear of the room and didn't give the disguised Ranger a second glance. Lowry held his shotgun in his left hand, close to his body where the gang couldn't see it. When he reached the corner of the bar, he slowly switched the shotgun to his right hand, keeping his left elbow on the bar— looking like a drifter who needed a drink. The shotgun was still out of sight.

Talon came in next, followed closely by Cat. When they got halfway across to the bar, all raised their shotguns and gave the cantina six barrels of buckshot that covered the whole room. The sound was deafening and the next sounds to follow were the groans of the wounded and dying. Lowry had wiped out the three standing at the bar with his blast. Talon wasn't as lucky with the four at a table in the center of the room. The one with his back to him had just leaned over to say something to the Greaser on the right as the Rangers raised their scatterguns, and his buddies blocked most of the shotgun blast. As the others at that table fell, the survivor drew his Colt and fired at the only target he could see, Lowry. Cat wasn't lucky, either, with his the four targets. The blast totally missed the one leaning back in his chair toward the window, and he managed to draw his Colt as he fell backwards to the floor. He snapped off a shot at the only target he could see, Talon.

Lowry pulled his Colts and pumped three shots into the Greaser that had just wounded him. Cat was shooting at the same Greaser and hit him twice. The Greaser firing at Talon was almost on the floor, and his shot hit Talon's right leg. This Greaser was Talon's target. He hit him three times, once in the left arm and the other two times in the right gun arm. Although surprised, the Greasers managed to get a few shots off at their attackers. Lowry received a burn high on his left shoulder, and Talon caught one on his right leg just above where he had been wounded before. The shootout lasted less than five minutes. Talon walked over to the wounded Greaser, while Cat and Lowry made sure the others were dead. They stripped their guns and found them flush with money. They had been recently paid in gold coins.

Talon looked down, pointed his Colt at the wounded Greaser and asked, "Where is Jackson Slager?"

"He's moved west, big doings and a change of plans because of the Ranger pressure."

"Where to the west?"

"West of Rio Grande City."

Talon had wounded him, and took his weapon and gold. Their injuries weren't serious, and the Rangers calmly walked through the front door and rounded up the Greasers' horses. When outside, Talon found the wounded hombre to be a gringo.

"What do they call you?" he asked.

"Tex-Mex."

Then they crossed the small plaza pulling the prisoner along to retrieve their own mounts. With Cat again leading the way, they made it to the ferry in quick time and walked the horses aboard.

Talon tied a scarf around his leg. Then he helped Lowry place a folded scarf on his shoulder wound. The ferry operator didn't say a word or even acknowledge that they were on his ferry. On the Texas side, the three were off at a gallop, and the ferry operator closed his operation for the night as if nothing had happened.

The raid caught the six gang members who raided Brownsville and killed Billie Jo, and the Rangers doled out Ranger justice to them and five other unknown gang members who happened to pick the wrong cantina on that night for their gambling and drinking. They had not, however, found Jackson Slager.

Talon glanced at his friends and acknowledged their efforts with a simple "Thanks, Cat. Thanks, Lowry."

Cook nodded and said, "That went well, didn't it? Those Greasers won't be killing any more innocent young girls."

"Lowry," Talon was looking at him. "We could really keep these Greaser gangs on edge if we were to raid them now and then. Do you think McNelly would object if we tried another raid or two? Cat, what do you think?"

"We can't use the ferry again, as it would put the operator in danger. But the strategy is sound. We could go west a ways and swim the Rio Grande. Raid and make our way back, never crossing at the same location, or maybe just staying in Mexico for more than a day."

"What do you think about giving the gold to Joe Wise and his family?" Talon asked. "Its small compensation for his loss, but it would help repair the mercantile. We'll keep the horses and the Colts and rifles we found for the Ranger arsenal, and we'll give Joe the saddles to make up for the ones stolen from him."

"It's fine with us," was their reply.

Talon grinned in the darkness. *I've selected my friends well this time around. These are good people to ride with.*

Dawn was breaking through the darkness in the east when Talon and Lowry dismounted in front of Doc Stone's office. Brownsville's only doctor's living quarters were above the office, and the two Rangers slowly climbed up the outside steps to the doctor's living quarters and rapped gently on the weathered wooden door, trying not to wake all of Brownsville. Doc Stone, who had been doctoring Brownsville neighbors and Rangers for 20 years, quickly appeared, carrying a lamp in one hand and his bag in the other. His practiced eye quickly determined that both Rangers were wounded, and without a word ushered them to the small back room where he treated more sensitive cases.

"Been talking to Joe Wise," he said as he pulled the old bandages off the two Rangers' wounds. "Told me you boys were off doing a little hunting. Where did you two get these hunting wounds? Didn't know the animals could shoot back."

He looked at Lowry first, cleaning the shoulder wound and carefully covering it with clean bandages to protect the wound. He shook his head when he turned to Talon's leg. Next he handled the prisoner.

"You were hit almost in the same place as last time, but not as serious. You'll limp a day or two but that's about all," he said. "You know, I delivered all of Joe's kids, but I always thought Billie Jo was special. Was your huntin' trip successful?"

"Yes sir, very."

Doc Stone smiled and finished dressing Talon's leg wound. When he finished, he walked with them down the stairs to open his office for the normal weekday traffic. He watched with admiration as the Rangers joined Cat and the prisoner and mounted.

"Thanks, Doc. Sorry we had to get you up so early," said Lowry.

Talon nodded in agreement.

"No problem, men, no problem at all. No offense, but I hope you don't show up here again for a good long while." He smiled again as the four rode away.

"Tex-Mex, I think you were in the wrong place at the wrong time. I'm letting you go, but if I ever find you in Mexico or Texas again I'll kill you. Do you understand?"

Tex-Mex nodded his head.

"Now, git!"

They were back in Ranger camp before the sun was up. Cat, Lowry and Talon made their way to McNelly's quarters. He was up and busy, coffee mug in hand, reviewing scouting reports delivered to him that morning. They recounted their invasion of Mexico, including the results.

"That wasn't a bad idea, as long as you didn't get caught by the Mexican authorities," the captain said. "They can be a mite touchy about our operating in their territory. Cat, do you think you can pull off that kind of raid again?"

"We can't use the ferry, but with good scouting and careful planning we can do it regularly if we pick our targets carefully," Cat answered.

"Okay, I'm authorizing you to continue raiding the gangs in Mexico. Make sure you plan each raid carefully and recruit good men from our troop here to help you."

"Captain McNelly," Talon said. "Jackson Slager is working on something big west of Rio Grande City. I want to go that way if you would let me."

"Slager will run into King Fisher out that way, and that wouldn't be pleasant for him. Fisher raids into Mexico and rustles the cattle taken from the Texans, along with any other cattle he can find. In fact, we have been ordered to stop his activities. I was planning something for him later in the summer. I want you to raid into Mexico for a couple more times, then we'll all move west. With Slager gone and Cortina in house arrest in Mexico City, we'll have these local gangs broken in a short time. Will you do that for me?" asked McNelly

Despite Talon's growing obsession to get Jackson Slager, he gave the response Captain McNelly expected from any good Ranger: "Yes sir," The young Ranger said. "I'll follow your orders."

Talon, Lowry and Cat walked over to the mercantile where they unsaddled the Greasers' horses. They placed the saddles on the south porch. Joe Wise greeted them as they walked into the store.

"Joe, we brought you some saddles and this sack of gold coins to help you with your repairs."

"Where did you get the gold?"

"You could say some of our closest friends took up a collection for you."

"How much is it?"

"We don't know; we didn't count it. You know, you don't look a gift horse in the mouth. Just don't tell anyone where you got it."

"Thanks, and I won't. Talon, she loved you, and so do we," Joe said.

"Thanks, Joe, for letting me know."

The Rangers then moved the captured horses to the livery.

"Feed and water these horses for us," Lowry told the boy.

"Looks like we have to find us more men to raid Mexico," said Talon.

"I have a couple in mind who would work really well with us. They're fearless," replied Lowry.

"Fearless is always good," Cat grinned.

Chapter Eleven

Talon stirred the fire. *This will be the last night here*, he thought, since the weather had moderated and the paths, although muddy, were clear of ice and snow. Sam seemed to be enjoying the grass on the far side of the alcove, and his slow ambling through the clearing was the only movement other than the flickering fire. Talon poured another cup of coffee and leaned on his gear, remembering the audacious raids into Mexico.

I have to admit they were fun to pull off and have to admire the captain for making the decision to let us loose, he thought. It disrupted the Greasers so much that they complained to the Mexican government. The Mexicans didn't know what to do because they benefitted from the raids into Texas. So they did nothing. Nothing was good for us Rangers because we went after the worst hard cases we could find, and the Mexican police wouldn't protect the outlaws unless they actually saw us crossing into Mexico. Turned out the Mexican police didn't like the hard cases much, either.

He chuckled as he stirred the fire and sipped his hot coffee.

We could get pretty hard to see when we crossed that river.

It was late summer, with sweltering heat, dust devils, and long days of chasing Greasers back to Mexico. The Rangers enjoyed the havoc they created among the Cortina gangs. Sure, the gangs could raid into Texas, but the price they paid was taking a toll. Their leader, Jackson Slager, had disappeared with no leads to where he had escaped.

A lone rider approached the Ranger camp. As he got closer, they could see it was a dispatch rider from Captain McNelly. Lowry met him in his usual southern fashion. The rider dismounted and handed the message to him. Lowry read it quickly and sent him on his way.

"Well, Kid, it looks like you have caught a break on the trail of Jackson Slager. It seems as if he and his men have raided Olvera's ranch. The Captain wants you to gather your gear and winter clothing and get on his trail. He has determined the names of the others with him and is getting the necessary paperwork together for you to chase them into any other state or territory, with orders to capture or kill. "

A broad smile crossed Talon's face. "I'm on my way. One against how many would you say?"

"He didn't say, but I'm guessing seven to nine."

"That should be about even," Talon replied.

He wasted little time on the ride to Brownsville for his gear. Trails grew cold quickly, even in the Texas heat. Talon grabbed his gear, loaded Sally, exchanged the old red for Sam, and lit out for Olvera's ranch. He headed north to the Patterson Ranch to say his goodbyes to Mimi. The instructions he received at Brownsville were to proceed to the Ranger camp at Austin to obtain the warrants, and Patterson's place was on the route. The ranch was a hard day's ride and Sam and Sally were up to the task. When he came over the last southern ridge before reaching the ranch headquarters, he was greeted by Mr. Patterson's cotton fields in full bloom. This was the first time he had seen cotton growing, and could understand Patterson's strategy for using his land for cattle, cotton, sheep and goats. The wintertime forage on the cotton fields brought the herds in close to the headquarters for protection. It wasn't long before three hands approached him.

"Howdy, Wyoming," they greeted him with all smiles.

"How have things been going?" Talon asked.

"We haven't had any trouble since you had the shootout."

"That's good to hear."

As they made the yard, Mimi came out on the porch of the main ranch house. Before she could speak, Talon addressed her.

"Mimi, will you do something for me?"

She nodded yes.

"I've got a line on Slager and I'm going after him. Will you take care of Sally until I get back?"

She nodded yes again as a tear came to her eye.

"I'm leaving here to go to Austin to get the warrants."

"Warrants?" she asked.

"Yes, he has others with him and I'm going after them."

"Alone?" Her expression showed concern.

"Believe me, if I can find him, he won't ever have enough men to stop me."

Slowly, he rearranged his gear on Sam. "Where can I stow this extra gear?" he asked.

Mimi left the porch and took Sally's bridle and started walking toward the barn where she stabled her horse. Talon followed like a lost sheep. He pulled the pack from Sally's back and stacked it where Mimi pointed. When he turned, she kissed him.

"Come back to me, Ranger, you hear?"

He kissed her back. "I hear."

Sam had cooled from the long ride and Talon took him over to the water tank and let him drink. When Sam finished, Talon mounted, leaned over and touched Mimi on her tear-stained cheek, pulled the reins around, and rode out of the yard. He wasn't going to waste time for any reason. His heart ached to leave in this fashion, but it had to be done. Ranger duty called.

From the time he first received his orders until his approach to Olvera's ranch. Six days had passed. It was going to be a cold trail, at best. The vaqueros followed him into the main ranch house. They remembered him from the earlier trouble and welcomed him as a trusted ally and compadre. Olvera greeted him while standing on his front veranda.

"Wyoming, they sent you. This is good, and you are in luck."

"How so?" Talon wanted to know.

"Slager wounded Arnado and stole his horse."

"That doesn't sound too lucky for Arnado."

"Arnado is okay. It's lucky, because he had just shoed his horse and the left front shoe has a slash mark on the right side. It's easy to follow. The vaqueros will show you."

"It's been six days?"

"Sí, but they stole some of my cattle and my vaqueros have been trailing the herd." Olvera answered. "They can take you to where they last saw the herd."

"Can we start now?" Talon asked.

"Sí. Salvador, Pablo, show Wyoming the way."

The two vaqueros led the way west at a brisk pace, wasting no time telling Talon where they were going. At dusk, they made a permanent camp on Olvera's western range, where the cattle were stolen and their friend was wounded.

"We'll camp here tonight, and in the morning we show you the trail," directed Salvador.

The night took forever to pass, as Talon was eager to start the chase. Dawn broke, and after a cup of coffee and some jerky, the three started to look for the trail of the stolen horse. At midmorning they found it meandering along with the stolen herd to the west.

"Good luck, Señor," Pablo said. Salvador nodded his head in agreement.

"Thanks," Talon replied. "Vaya con dios, amigos."

He was now on his own, and at first he followed the trail carefully and slowly. By midafternoon he picked up the pace to a faster clip. The herd was easy to follow; the stolen horse stayed on the northern flank, making the tracking easy, but Talon had to watch for outriders and traps along the way. Although the trail was several days old, the dry conditions kept the tracks clear and easy to follow. Weather conditions could change quickly to windy or rainy and make his task harder, but Talon pushed to gain ground on the herd while the conditions were favorable. He knew he could cover ground faster than the outlaws, who had a big cattle herd to handle.

Then, suddenly, he lost the sign of the stolen horse. Overconfidence led him to a mistake. He had lost the trail.

Doubling back on the herd's trail and staying wider to the northern flank, he guessed if the horse had left the herd moving north he would cross the break somewhere. It took most of the day but he finally found where four riders had left the herd moving to the north, as he figured. He followed at a much slower pace now, not wanting to lose the trail again in the harsh terrain. The trail continued north through the hill country that saw small ranches tucked into hidden valleys where sheep, goats and cattle thrived on the same ground. Evidence of logging also dotted the landscape the further north he went. Finally, he hit a road, and the outlaws had obviously used it to quicken their pace to the northwest. He wondered where the road led. A few miles riding along the road answered his question, at least for the short term; he was riding on the main street of the western hill country settlement of Kerrville.

Talon glanced at the darkening sky as he debated with himself on the wisdom of continuing along the well-used road in the darkness. *Don't know if I can tell just how long they stay on this road if I can't see the tracks*, he thought. *Sam is almost tuckered out, and I need rest, too. They likely will not keep traveling at night, and I don't believe they know I'm on their trail. I think I will stay the night in Kerrville.*

He found the livery stables easy enough, and bought Sam a good meal, a better brushing and a clean stall for the standard two dollars. It had been awhile since he had slept on a bed, and the two dollars for his room seemed like a bargain. He ate a huge meal at the eatery across the street. Returning to his room, he sat in the plush chair, pulled his boots off and opened the leather pouch containing the warrants. "Let's see just *who* I'm chasin'." he said.

He untied the ribbon around the warrants and looked at the one on top of the stack.

Jackson Slager: Ringleader of the notorious Cortina gang of northern Mexico. Is about six foot-three inches tall, and weighs about

240 pounds. Wanted for killing men, women, children, robbery, and cattle rustling.

Bulldog: real name unknown. Wanted for murder. Is about five foot-ten inches tall, and weighs about 170 pounds. He is Jackson Slager's right-hand man.

Harry Simpson: Wanted for cattle rustling and robbery. Is about five foot-seven inches tall, and weighs about 160 pounds.

Max Kelly: Wanted for Murder, rape, robbery and cattle rustling. Is about five foot-ten inches tall, and weighs about 200 pounds. Speaks with a heavy southern accent.

Lightfoot Labo: Wanted for murder, rape and robbery. Six foot tall, and weighs about 220 pounds. He is a half breed.

Tex Ham: Wanted for murder. Six foot tall and weighs about 160 pounds.

Clyde Hood: Wanted for murder, rape, robbery and cattle rustling. No good description.

To Texas Ranger Talon T. Finley, you are ordered by the Governor of Texas, Richard Coke, in accordance with the laws of the State of Texas, to capture or kill these men and any other outlaw abetting them.

Wonder which of the seven I'm following? Talon wondered. *Guess time will tell.*

Talon retrieved his horse from the livery at dawn and asked the livery boy if any strangers had passed through town in the last couple of days. He remembered four men two days earlier staying the night and asking the owner for directions to San Angela. He had pointed them northwest through the hill country. Then he directed them northward after they left Fort McKavett.

"Did they follow the road?" asked Talon.

"Yes, through Fort McKavett all the way to San Angela there's a good trail," the boy answered.

"Well, Sam, I need some extra from you."

Armed with the new information on where Slager and his men were going, Talon picked up his pace and didn't bother looking for the trail of the stolen horse. Sam responded as they rode through the day and most of the night. Finally, in the early morning Talon stopped to take a rest. He found a creek that was still maintaining water flow. It was late summer and most of the creeks they had crossed were dry, with widely spaced pools of water. One with moving water was the place to stop.

He unloaded Sam and hobbled him to let him forage on the grass surrounding the creek. He moved higher on the creek bank and found a place to secure a resting spot. His excitement kept him from a sound sleep. After a short nap, he built a small, smokeless fire to make a cup of coffee. The coffee, along with jerky, made his morning meal. It went quickly, and once again, he was on the trail to San Angela.

The one or two hours of rest was enough to regenerate Sam's ability to maintain a fast pace. They made Fort McKavett late in the day. Talon pushed through without stopping, knowing he was now a good day's ride from his goal. If he stopped late in the night, he would be able to make San Angela by late afternoon tomorrow. Having pushed through the hill country, he found himself on a ridge overlooking the flat terrain to the north. He stopped, secured Sam for the night and climbed to the top of the ridge to search for campfires to the north. None were to be seen, which suggested the outlaws had made it to San Angela. If they hadn't made it, they were taking no chances with a fire.

Do they know I am on their trail? Have I guessed wrong about the direction they headed based on the information of a livery boy? When will I know?

The questions swirled around in his head.

Around midafternoon, Talon crossed the river ford into San Angela. He headed straight to Fort Concho, knowing he would be able to get good information there. Go Paw and Gibson were on the porch of the scout barracks when he rode into the plaza. He guided Sam over to them. They greeted him with big smiles and were happy to see him.

"What happened to your trip east?" asked Gibson.

"It didn't happen, I got sidetracked."

Talon explained what he was doing and the help he needed in finding the outlaws. They remembered four riders moving through about noon yesterday. The leader they described had to be Jackson Slager.

"Which way did they go?" Talon queried.

"We'll ask around for you," Gibson offered. "That way, no one will know you're looking for them and tip them off. You go visit Carter and Coleman while we check. They're at the headquarters building."

Talon nodded in agreement and turned Sam to move across the plaza. When he stepped out of the saddle, he saw four or five scouts leaving on a mission. He walked up the steps and through the doors into the main hall. There was Coleman, sitting at an entry desk.

"Well, I see you advanced to first lieutenant." Talon declared.

Coleman looked to see who was talking and when he recognized Talon his face broke into a broad smile. "Have you already been east?" he asked.

"No, got sidetracked. How have you been doing?"

"Indian war gave me a promotion. At my age, that is good."

"How's Carter?" asked Talon.

"He's great. He is now Captain Carter, and commands a company of Buffalo soldiers. I'm one of his platoon leaders. What have you been doing?"

"I've been Texas Rangering along with Cat. That's what brings me this way. I'm on the trail of four hard cases. Have seven warrants to serve."

"That's long odds, Talon." Coleman observed.

"I say about even."

Coleman chuckled while nodding his head in agreement. Then he stood.

"Let's go over to the mess and get a cup of coffee and some apple pie."

"That really sounds good."

"Sergeant Bilsky, you are in charge of this post 'til I return."

"Yes, sir." the sergeant replied.

Coleman and Talon strolled to the mess hall, which hadn't changed. The coffee was good and hot and the pie was a real treat. Talon noticed through the window that the Scouts were gathering on the porch of their barracks.

"Hate to cut this short, but I've got outlaws to trail. Thanks for the coffee and pie." Talon said.

"You are welcome."

They returned to the headquarters building, where Talon climbed into the saddle and said his goodbyes to Coleman. Then he turned Sam toward the Scouts.

Gibson explained to Talon what they did.

"Two of us asked around about the four riders, and three of us watched to see if it produced a response. It did. Two riders left right after we asked at the livery. They rode toward the north. We found out the four you were interested in were going to Canadian River from here. They're a day ahead of you."

"Thanks, Gibson." Talon appreciated the information.

"Let us show you the tracks of the two heading north."

"No, remember how we came in here on the trail drive from the northeast? There'll be less of a chance of being ambushed if I go to Canadian River from the southeast," Talon proposed.

"Let us show you the tracks anyway. It may come in handy."

"Okay."

Talon was determined to use his plan, but it didn't hurt to have all the information.

Chapter Twelve

Talon's last night in the alcove didn't go well. He slept fretfully, his muscles twitching and his body tossing all over the small bed he had made. Awake well before dawn, he rekindled the fire to boil a last pot of coffee in his small hideaway. Even Sam could feel the tension as reflected in his pawing and snorting. Talon finished the last of the coffee just as first light crept into the alcove. Sunlight reflecting off the naked rock face above the encampment and piercing the cedar tops along the eastern ridge told him it was time to try the trail.

He saddled Sam slowly and methodically, not knowing just how much hard riding lay ahead. After placing each part of his gear in the most advantageous position, he tugged the bridle, and Sam fell in behind him on the game trail over the first ridge, through the hole to the spot where they had crossed from the trail through the cedars. Talon left him there while he crossed through the cedar to survey the trail. There were no unusual sounds, and the only motion came from the light breeze blowing through the valley. With caution, he pulled Sam through the cedars, and led him down the trail while scanning the terrain in front and back. It took some time to gain the tree line of the lower trail, since there was no reason to be in a hurry. Talon even took time to erase some of the signs Sam and he were leaving on the trail.

The first finger ridge leaving the side of the mountain extended in a gradual slope covered in an aspen, cedar and pine mix all the way to the valley floor. He left the trail to the north of the east to west-running ridge to stay in the shadows as long as he could. Only on occasion did he risk the south side, where the ridge line flattened and offered little protection from the sunlight. He took extreme caution in crossing those open areas. As soon as he got past the open area, he would spend several minutes observing his back trail and the trail forward.

No need to be aggressive, he told himself, since he had already lost Slager's trail. *Can I find a cattle herd moving north? Would it be the right herd? Wonder where the closest telegraph is?*'

His thoughts tumbled through his mind like melting snow falling from the cedars.

He took the full day to get halfway down the slope. He built a small fire late in the afternoon, using dry branches to cut the smoke. His menu items, coffee and jerky, had to be eaten before dark. No fires after dark. He hobbled Sam in a small grassy area, and climbed to the top of the ridge. He wrapped in a poncho to keep the cold wind gusts at bay, and watched the setting sun dive below the mesa, leaving the area in twilight. He watched the night grow. He was high enough to still catch the flickering of careless campfires across the valley.

Would early fires be friendly or bad? What if they burn all night? Mimi kissed me. Oh, Sally, what am I to do?

His thoughts bounced from the practicality of staying alive in a hostile world to the two girls he loved. For now, practicality won out.

He saw some lights flicker looking northeast through his field glasses. They were a great distance away and probably a settlement or a desert ranch, but comforting in that they may be friendly. Then he turned his attention to the next ridge, running east off the trail. As he scanned, he picked up several flickering of campfires. Someone had also camped on the north side, but the ridge was lower and Talon could see the whole backside. Then he noticed lights flickering along the trail. *They must have spotted me somehow, but how?*

Again, he turned to the eastern extremity of the ridge where it melted into the valley floor. He saw more lights there swinging around scrubby growth and heading toward the south to intercept the ridge on which he was hiding.

How did they find me so easily? he wondered. Then he realized he had made another error. *Here I am, a seasoned Texas Ranger, making such a stupid mistake. Building a fire in the shadows of the ridge is like building a fire at night. It pinpointed exactly where my hiding place was. Now they're closing in on me.*

He scurried to where Sam was hidden. Thinking quickly and realizing he need to change his appearance, he replaced his hat with an old stocking cap Aunt Bertha had knitted for him for the Wyoming winters. He didn't wear it much because of the ear flaps. Just maybe, in the dark, the flaps would like the long hair of an Indian. Then he changed into his moccasins. He took stock of his ammo: 20 shots loaded in his pistols plus 24 in his belt. He pulled out a cotton pouch with jerky and put two boxes of ammo for the Sharps and two for the Winchester, plus seven loose shells in it. Grabbing the Indian scabbard that was home to his Sharps, and bow with 12 arrows, he put its sling over his shoulder. *My only chance is to make them think they're closing in on a pack of Indians.*

He backtracked the trail to the last break in the ridge. The area was flat for several yards, and supported only grassy vegetation. He hid among the trees in the middle of the ridge. They gave him protection from all angles and plenty of room to use the bow. At night, using the bow, his enemy would have to be close. But in an ambush, they wouldn't know how close he really was until he used a firearm. With luck, hitting one or two with arrows would change their thinking about whom they were attacking.

That's why they have been so careless about the lamps. They think they're tracking one Ranger. Well, this Ranger has some stingers.

The night wore on, with little movement except for an occasional gust of wind swirling through the trees. The quiet night and the cold surrounded Talon as he noted hoarfrost dusting the bare outcroppings of rock and on the lower, larger limbs of some of the trees. Then, out of the darkness came a clatter of motion down the game trail. A large buck and several doe scampered by in a mad dash. He counted at least seven. *Where did they come from? I didn't see one deer when traversing the ridge earlier today. Something must have spooked them pretty good.*

Their hasty movement down the trail alerted Talon to the Greasers closing in on him. They would be expecting him to be further down the ridge where he had built the fire. They wouldn't be moving too cautiously as yet, giving him a decent chance of springing a surprise ambush. If the first ambush worked, he could slip back, get Sam and head straight down the slope to the canyon floor and try moving past the Greasers, through the canyon to the valley. Once in the valley he would head toward to the northeastern lights.

Well, that's my plan. Forgot to bring a canteen, dang it, another mistake. Might not make it to 17, after all.

It wasn't long before he heard the Greasers walking up both sides of the ridge. Confident in their numbers, they weren't hiding their approach. They merged toward the center as they broke into the open area. Talon saw five about five feet apart walking abreast across the clearing. He couldn't see them clearly with less than a quarter moon, but he could darn well follow their silhouettes. It had been awhile since he had practiced with his bow, but he figured he could still shoot. Maximum range for the bow was 15 to 20 yards, and if he were discovered, five men could overrun him in a few seconds. Talon had earlier paced the distances to different land marks, so he knew where his boundaries were.

He wanted to work the oncoming line like a turkey shoot, picking off the last one in line and working forward, but only the straggler was to his right. Sam was hidden on that side of the ridge, and Talon couldn't afford to take a chance on getting cut off from his mount. He got lucky; the Greaser on Talon's right trailed the others by about five yards. He pulled the bow and let the first arrow fly at the straggler, stringing the second arrow before the first found its target. He fired the second arrow just as the first hit its target low and hard, penetrating the Greaser's poncho just above the gun belt through to his left side. The arrow was solidly in its target, and the Greaser let out a wild scream. It froze the other targets in mid step, and the second arrow also hit home, lower than the first but in the meaty part of the second Greaser's right leg. Talon adjusted a bit too much on the third arrow and missed high, but he got the effect he wanted. Two Greasers were down and screaming, "Indians! Indians!" He pulled out his Winchester and snapped off three quick shots while throwing out what he felt were real Indian whoops. The muzzle flashes disclosed his position, but it was too late for the other three to react. He hit all three but didn't hang around to see where the shots struck. He knew he had hit them, and that was good enough for now.

Talon was convinced the Greasers felt like they had been ambushed by Indians. He made his way back to Sam, grabbed his bridle and started leading him down the steep slope to the canyon floor below. He took his time weaving through rock outcroppings and dead tree falls. It was still dark when he reached his goal. He looked forward into the canyon for careless lights and saw none. He continued to walk toward the mouth of the canyon. He exited it just as the coral-colored clouds appeared above the distant mesa to the east. He climbed into the saddle and gave Sam a pat on the neck and whispered, "It's going to be an all-out run to the next high ground where we can set up another ambush, are you ready?" As always, Sam responded to his urging, and they were off.

Talon took the straightest path he could see, which called for circumventing several obstacles. When he looked over his shoulder, he could see the other Greasers organizing to follow. If he could make the next high ground about three miles away, he could slow them down again with the Sharps. If they still thought he was an Indian, they might get careless enough to get within range of the Sharps, and he could cut down the odds even more.

The Greasers on the west made a mistake by attacking at night. He wondered if their plan was to close in on him at first light of day. It was about time someone made a mistake other than him. He had a good head start. Judging by their slow reaction to his break, he knew he would have time to prepare. He had no idea where he was, but he felt the settlement to the northeast would shed light on his location and where he needed to go from there. He also knew the hunted – him – was now the hunter.

He rounded the finger where the ridge met the valley and rode up the ridge on the east side where the following Greasers couldn't see him. The slope was gentle to about 100 feet above the valley floor. He slid out of the saddle, grabbing the Sharps and ammo bag before he hit the ground. He made his way to the ridge line a few feet from where Sam was standing. Glancing back, he could see that Sam was well protected from any stray round that might make it to the ridge, which eased his mind considerably. He found a spot on a level rock out cropping sandwiched between two stands of trees. *This place looks as good as any for a few shots*. With the sun at his back, it was going to be hard for the Greasers to spot his firing position. They would be looking directly into the sun. With any luck, he could drop most of them before they got close enough to find him.

They were riding toward him in a tight bunch, with stragglers strung out behind. He had practiced with the Sharps at 400 yards, close but far enough to deter even brave men when their comrades start to fall. Talon wasn't sure just how brave this pack of Greasers was, but he aimed to find out. From his vantage point, he decided to start firing at what he thought to be about half a mile. At that range, a horse killed is as good as a man, and with them bunched they made easy targets. He felt he could shoot two or three times before they were aware they were being shot at. As packed as they were, if he hit a lead rider, others could fall over him. That is, if he were lucky. Not knowing how much to lead the first rider he aimed his first shot well in front of him and fired. He absorbed the big gun's power and looked for a hit. No one was down, so that shot was just a range finder. He shortened the lead and again fired. This time he took out a horse two behind the leader, and two others barreled over him. It didn't appear as if they knew they were being shot at yet. The sound was too far away to be heard over the noise of the horses. This was going to be fun and maybe sell a lot of dime novels back east. They were still closing. Taking his time, he started to eliminate his pursuers. He couldn't really tell if he hit any Greasers, but their horses were falling. Finally, they realized they were being engaged. There were only shallow washes in which to hide, and the Sharps round would penetrate the soft lip of the wash making it risky to stay in one place after being seen. Horses had no cover and were easier targets than men. Talon marked his target as the canteen on the horse's saddle. The Greasers mostly used bags draped across the front of the saddle to the front of the horse. Hit the canteen, you get two for one. Talon took no delight in shooting the horses, but this was life and death – their deaths prolonged his life.

After three more horses dropped, the Ranger saw the stragglers pulling up well back of their fallen comrades. He figured he had won this round and it was time to move. He crawled from his perch, put away the big Sharps, mounted Sam and rode away to the northeast.

Distance can deceive at night. Talon didn't reach the settlement until the second day. The farming community didn't have a name, but they directed him to another settlement further to the east. After another day, Sam was feeling the pace. Talon kept moving toward the northeast, which seemed a never-ending uphill trek. Finally, he crossed a ridge and there lay a U.S. Army fort in his path. Continuing into the open courtyard of the fort, he was greeted by the sentry on duty.

"Where am I?" Talon asked.

"Fort Union, New Mexico, stranger," was the reply.

"Do you have a telegraph?"

"Coming next year, we hear."

"Where's the closest one?" Talon asked.

"I'd say up the Santa Fe Trail through the Raton Pass to Colorado. At Trinidad, take the Santa Fe Trail to La Junta, Colorado. The railroad has big doings there and they'll have a telegraph," the sentry said.

"Thanks. Where can I buy some provisions?"

"Down to the left, you can't miss it."

"Thanks. How do I get to the Raton Pass?" asked Talon.

"Leave here to the north and follow the ruts, you can't miss the trail. Be careful going it alone, 'cause there are lots of spots for an ambush, and be careful in Trinidad."

Talon stocked himself with light provisions and got back on the trail. He didn't have time to waste.

"What is the date?" he asked the storekeeper.

"Twenty-first of September," was the reply.

Provisioned and watered, he started north. The trail was easy to follow, although the terrain was rugged. He didn't see another soul the first day but mid-day the second, he ran into a train moving south along the trail. He gathered as much information from the folks as he could. They had not seen a herd of cattle on the trail, but they had run into one east of La Junta, moving north. Rough-looking wranglers pushing a thousand head or so. The ramrod was a tall man with light-colored hair. It sounded like Slager. He had pushed north with the herd— further east than Talon expected. Slager had duped him into following a false trail into a trap. Payback would be coming soon.

The trail into Trinidad crossed a small river south of the main town. Several buildings extended away from the river crossing. *Where do I find this Santa Fe Trail?* he thought as he tied up at the hitching rail in front of the general store. He climbed the steps to the board-walk fronting the business on the west side of the street.

As Talon entered the store, a young man approached him and spoke. "How can I help you?"

"Do you have any canned peaches?" Talon asked the man.

"Why yes, we do." Directing Talon to the other side of the store, he led the way.

"Is there a good place to stay here?"

"Yes. The best is down the street on the right. Good rooms, food, and baths are available. How many cans do you need?"

"Two."

"Anything else I can get for you? If not, that's 50 cents."

Talon reached into his vest pocket and retrieved the coins needed to pay.

"Is there a livery there, too?" he asked.

"Further up the street on the same side, you'll find the livery. Thanks for coming in." the young man replied.

Talon left the store. Before unhitching Sam, he packed the two cans of peaches into his stores bag. He led Sam down the street to the hotel.

Walking into the lobby, he asked the clerk, "how much for a room?"

"One dollar," replied the clerk.

"And the charge for a bath?"

"You'll have to ask the barber about the bath. He has all kinds of deals."

Talon placed the dollar on the counter and the clerk answered by turning the registry book around for him to sign. He signed in T. T. Finley. When he finished, the clerk handed him a key.

"The room is up the stairs, to the right. It has a window overlooking the main street. There's a water bucket is at the end of the hall. Use it to fill up the room's pitcher. Take a left there, and go to the back stairs; the facility's out back."

"Thanks."

Talon retrieved his gear from Sam, hitched him in front and carried everything up the stairs. He filled his water pitcher, locked the door and stepped outside to find the livery for Sam. Grabbing Sam's bridle, he led him across a side street to the next corner and into the livery.

"How much for feeding and staying the night?" he asked the livery boy.

"One dollar and I'll rub him down if you want."

"Sounds good, here's the dollar." He flipped it to the youngster and left the livery. He wanted to look up the barber. He couldn't remember his last full bath and he could feel the smell. The barbershop was on the east side of the hotel on the ground floor.

He opened the door, stepped inside and asked, "How much do you charge for a soaker?"

The barber looked and answered, "One dollar plus six bits for a shave and a haircut."

Talon thought to himself, *I've never had a shave*. He looked over at a mirror and decided it was time for the first one.

"I'll have all three. Go ahead and set up the bath. It will take me a minute to get some clean duds."

"Ready for when you get back."

The bath was relaxing, but with the haircut he got questions.

"Say youngster, this is quite a scar you have at the scalp line."

"Yep," Talon answered.

"Couldn't help but notice your right knee has really been shot up. Are you some kind of gunfighter?"

"Nope, Indians about a year back. I'm lucky to be alive. They got me in the side, too. Never want to do that again."

"How old are you?"

"16, close to 17. Have never shaved, can you tell?"

"Good that you waited, and truthfully, you needed one. Now, if you are not a gunfighter then why are you wearing four pistols?"

"I promised myself after the Indian fight that I would never borrow another gun in my life. A borrowed gun will get you killed. Right now, I just train horses."

Too many questions Talon thought, but he had endured.

"Where's a good place for chow?"

"The best in town is across the street at Sophie's place."

He paid the barber and headed to get something to eat. He could feel his long johns protecting his body from the late September coolness. He entered Sophie's and selected a table with his back to the wall and a view of the main street. A young girl approached and handed him a menu. He loaded up on the vegetables to go along with his fried steak.

Returning to his room, he noticed it had been searched. Knowing this could happen, he had made sure not to leave any information as to who he was in his gear. He went to work cleaning his guns while eating one of the cans of peaches. When he finished, he turned his lamp to low and leaned back in his chair, foregoing the bed. They'll try again after I turn out the light. Might as well make them wait for the chance. He took a short nap. When he awoke it was about 11 P.M., according to the mantel clock in his room. He turned off the light.

Chapter Thirteen

Talon was wrong about another visit. It didn't happen. Trinidad had stayed awake until about four when the girls turned out their lights. As dawn broke, several wagons pulled by oxen rumbled down the street to the river crossing. Obviously, another train headed into the Raton Pass bound for Santa Fe. He wrapped his dirty duds in a poncho, gathered his gear, and made his way out of the hotel. He carried his gear to the livery where he found Sam in one of the stables. It looked like the youngster had done a good job on the rubdown. He thought for a minute, looking at Sam. Then he pulled his left hind leg up to look at his shoe. On the right front he noticed there had been a slash filed into the shoe. He bridled Sam and walked him around the corral in the back of the livery. Walking over to the area just outside the barn door he squatted and found the sign. How many people does Slager have working for him? Or is there someone else I need to fear? Well I was warned about Trinidad, and I do look too young to take care of myself. He led Sam into the barn where the smithy was standing at his forge preparing for the day's work.

"How much to shoe my horse?" he asked.

Seeing Talon, the smithy answered, "One dollar a shoe."

"Can you do it now?"

"I can start right now."

"How long will it take?"

"About an hour."

"Okay, but make sure there are no telltale marks on them."

The smithy started on Sam's front right hoof as Talon walked out the barn door.

Talon walked over to Sophie's for breakfast. A different girl greeted him as he came through the door and escorted him to a table. She turned over the cup on the table and poured the coffee.

"What can I get you?"

"How about ham and eggs?" he asked.

"No ham, how about bacon?"

"Okay bacon."

"Over medium good on the eggs?" she continued.

"Yep."

Not like home, but close on the breakfast, and the coffee was hot and black. Talon returned to the livery and watched the smithy finish the work. He inspected every hoof, looking for any signs that the shoes were marked. He found none and was happy with the job. He paid the four dollars and asked to see the livery boy. The smithy called him. He came bouncing in as if someone had lit his shirttail.

"Thanks for rubbing down Sam."

"I didn't mind at all, he's the best looking horse I've ever seen."

Talon flipped him a dollar, and said, "You did a good job, Thanks."

He saddled Sam and turned to the smithy and asked, "Which way to Denver?"

"Take the trail that heads north out of here, and go due north along the eastern flank of the mountain range to the west of town. You can't miss it."

"Thanks."

With all his gear situated exactly where he wanted it, he climbed into the saddle. Just a slight urge bounced Sam to a gallop headed north down the street. He rode out of sight of town and swung off the trail to the east. *Have I gone far enough to throw my followers off the trail? Will the Santa Fe Trail be hard to find? If the trail was like the one in the Raton Pass, the wagon ruts will give it away. Wonder why they use oxen?* The questions filled his mind. He gave it some thought and decided the Indians didn't like the oxen because they needed horses. It didn't take long before he found a spot on high ground from which he could watch his back trail. After a good length of time with

no movement, he continued east. He came upon the trail while crossing through a dry wash. Wagon ruts — four abreast — carved in the
arid landscape. He turned northeast and galloped on. No need to wait
around on the slightly undulating terrain where there wasn't a place to
hide. If he was being followed, he needed to run.

Sam showed his heart and kept the strong pace throughout the
day. At dusk, Talon could see campfires on the trail ahead. How far
away he couldn't guess. He continued riding toward the fires. By early morning he was closing in on their position. He veered from the
trail to the east and walked Sam around the train at a good distance.
They never knew he passed them during the night. Any followers asking about a lone rider heading up the trail would get an honest answer.
No one would have seen him. Sam enjoyed the breather of the walk
around. Immediately, he returned to his trail-burning pace. Following
the ruts was easy. They were step-by-step markers leading all the way
to La Junta.

It was late in the day when he met another train. They told him he
would make his goal by early evening. La Junta was a railroad town,
and most of the residents worked for the railroad. A large mainte-
nance shop with a roundhouse next to the depot was the town's main
industry. It made the depot easy to find.

Talon walked to the telegraph window. The operator greeted him
with the usual, "How can I help you?"

"I need to send a message."

"It is a dollar plus 10 cents a word."

"Would it be the same for a Texas Ranger?"

"*That* would be free. Write it out for me on this pad."

To Captain McNelly of the Texas Rangers, Austin, Texas.

In La Junta, Colorado. Following Slager gang's stolen herd of cattle. They're heading north. Will continue to follow unless there are
other orders. Waiting here for reply. Talon Finley

He handed the operator the message.

"How long before he gets this?" Talon asked.

"They'll have this in Austin tomorrow morning. Let me see your badge."

Talon reached inside his vest pocket and produced his fake badge.

"I guess you're for real."

"Is there a hotel here?"

"It's down the street, to the left. No livery. Their stables are in the back, and you'll need to take care of your own horse."

The lobby of the hotel was well-lit and full of activity. Talon walked over to the front desk.

"Nice place you have here. Can I get a room?"

"Only rooms I have left are on the front, overlooking the rail yard. I'm telling you up front, they're noisy over there at night. It could keep you awake."

"Where I've been, noisy would be good." Talon smiled.

He signed the register. The eatery across the street caught his eye as he was unloading his gear. *Wonder why they're never on the same side of the street,* he mused. He carried his gear up to his room, found the water pitcher, and started searching for the water. He found it on the back balcony, overlooking a corral and the barn. He returned with water to his room, and went to take care of Sam.

Grabbing Sam's bridle, he walked him around to the barn in back. There were several empty stables, cleaned and ready for use. He spent the next hour taking care of Sam. He returned to his room, using the back stairs, and washed up for dinner. La Junta seemed to be a happy little town. He walked into the eatery and found a table facing the front door, with a view on the main street. About the time the girl was pouring the hot coffee, an older gentleman entered the room. He was well heeled and wearing a star. He surveyed the room and walked over to Talon's table.

"Okay to sit?" He asked.

"Yes, sir."

"Sweetie, bring me a cup of that coffee please," the man said to the waitress. "I'm Bart Starns, sheriff of La Junta. I heard you were in town. Anything I can do for you while you're here?"

"Need some information, if you could help," said Talon.

"Glad to," the sheriff replied.

"I've been trying to follow an outlaw gang that's moving a herd of stolen cattle north. One of the trains on the Santa Fe told me they had run into a herd east of here. Have you heard of such a herd moving north?"

"Seems like I have. Their leader, a tall fellow, used the telegraph here and waited for a reply."

"What name did he use?"

"Lester Jackson."

"I have warrants for Jackson Slager and six others I think are traveling with him."

"I didn't see the others," the sheriff continued.

"You saw the one that counted. Do you think the telegraph operator will let me look at the messages?"

"Sure he will."

The sheriff joined Talon in the evening meal, which they topped off with a fried apple pie. Then they paid the checks and walked over to the telegraph office. The operator was finishing his day when they walked in the door. He listened to the sheriff, and then went to his files and came out with two messages.

"Here's a wire to a James Kincade of Laramie, Wyoming," the clerk offered.

Talon read the wire.

WILL HAVE HERD INTO WYOMING IN 3 WEEKS, BUT THEN WHAT? STOP. AWAITING REPLY IN LA JUNTA, COLORADO. STOP.

"This is the answer he got."

Talon read the answer.

WHEN YOU GET TO WYOMING, HEAD WEST PAST FIRST RIDGE OF MOUNTAINS. STOP. FIRST VALLEY, HEAD NORTH TO MEDICINE BOW. STOP. CATTLE RANGING THERE CAN MINGLE ALONG THE WAY. STOP. MEET ME IN LARAMIE AFTER YOU GET NORTH OF MEDICINE BOW. STOP.

"Well that's the idea. I didn't see it until now. Course the herd through outskirts of cattle ranches, mingling their cattle along the way, growing the herd. By the time a rancher finds he's missing cattle, they're long gone."

Talon handed the messages back to the operator.

"Why drive stolen cattle to Wyoming," asked the sheriff.

"A lot of free range and a direct rail route to move the stolen cattle east right away. Any unbranded stock stays on the range to build their herd. All paid for by someone else," Talon replied.

Talon took the wire pad and filled in a message.

TO JIM FINLEY, MEDICINE BOW, WYOMING:

JIM MOVE CATTLE OUT OF OUR EASTERN RANGE TO THE WESTERN RANGE. STOP. MOVE SHEEP WEST TO EAST AND BE QUICK. STOP. RUSTLERS ON THEIR WAY, SHOULD BE THERE IN ABOUT TWO WEEKS. STOP.

T. T.

Talon produced four dollars and paid the operator. The operator collected the money and left to send the message. After he had finished, he closed the office.

"Thanks for the help," Talon addressed the operator. "Join the sheriff and me in a cup of coffee at the eatery."

"I will. Thanks."

They spent an hour or so with Talon outlining the hard cases he was after. As they broke up, Talon asked the operator, "If they come back while I'm here, will you let me know?"

"Sure, Ranger; how old are you, anyway?"

"17," Talon lied.

"But you're up against eight or more men?" he asked.

"As a Texas Ranger, that makes it about even." Talon smiled.

They parted.

Still waiting a reply to his wire, Talon sat in the lobby of the hotel reading the old newspapers left on the tables. It was getting cooler by the day, and he had selected a chair out of the sunlight where he could view the street without the glare in his eyes. A rider came to the hitching post of the hotel. Slowly, he moved out of the saddle, taking in everything around him as he did. For sure, he was looking over his shoulder for any omen of alert or danger. His horse was a beautiful grulla, a gray with a dark mane and a streak running down his back deep into his tail. He also had dark stockings of the same color. Talon had not seen many horses with this color combination in his life, but this one was stunning. The rider came through the front door and looked around, but saw nothing that disturbed him. It would take a few seconds for his eyes to adjust to the darkness of the lobby. He walked up to the desk.

"I'm looking for the owner of the bluish gray in the corral out back."

Talon eased his paper higher in front of his face. Before the clerk could answer, he noticed five more riders approaching the hitching rail. They hitched their horses and walked over to the grulla. One lifted his left hind leg, and nodded to the others. They slowly approached the door.

"Well, did you hear me?" asked the stranger.

The clerk looked up and replied, "I don't know who owns the horse, because I never look at them."

Another voice spoke from inside the door. "Who owns the grulla?"

The first rider turned and with a slight sneer said, "I do."

The grulla owner was about 5'10" tall and about 170 pounds. It dawned on Talon this must be Bulldog.

"We want to discuss a little matter of cattle rustling with you."

"Don't know what you're talking about," he answered in a hateful slur. "If you are calling me a thief, you didn't bring enough guns to the party."

"Just a minute, boys," Talon spoke.

"This man belongs to me."

"Yeah, and who are you?"

"I'm a Texas Ranger, the Wyoming Kid."

Bulldog's face tightened with the surprise announcement.

"I have a warrant for him, dead or alive, and I would appreciate you letting me do my job. You can back me, of course."

Talon was only about 15 feet from Bulldog.

"Now, Bulldog, this is how I see it. You can drop your firearm, and I'll turn you over to these cowpokes or I'll kill you."

"Why, they'll kill me as soon as they get out of your sight."

"So, then, you want *me* to kill you, right?"

Bulldog could see where this was going, and drew. His first shot exploded, hammering the floor about four feet in front of Talon, showering the area with splinters. A split second later Talon's first shot struck Bulldog about six inches above his gun belt. Bulldog managed to get a second shot off, but like the first, it struck the floor in front of Talon. By this time, Talon had hit Bulldog three times— like buttoning his shirt. Talon's second shot penetrated Bulldog's chest six inches above the first. The last one hit him at the neck. Bulldog's body fell straight back into the front desk. He tried to muster a third shot, but couldn't raise his gun, which he dropped as he expired.

"Sorry, gentlemen, to interfere with your play, but one or two of you would have died. I didn't think that was necessary. Now, I know it doesn't pay for the cattle they stole from you but you can have his horse."

"You're right, Ranger; he would have gotten one or two of us. Thanks for stepping in when you did. Did he know you?" asked one of the cow men.

"He knew of me, but we had never met. He knew I was fast and I knew he would fight. That's why I got so close. I figured if he got me, you would finish him."

"I've never heard of a fight so close," the man said.

"It unnerves these black-hearted hard cases to fight close. They want to shoot you from behind."

The sheriff pushed his way through the bystanders. "Is this one of them, Talon?"

"This is Bulldog, and Jackson's right hand man." Talon pointed to the dead man.

A youngster from the telegraph office pushed through the crowd looking for Talon.

"Mr. Hanks told me to tell you that two of the men you were looking for were in town."

Then he handed Talon a message. Talon gave him a nickel for bringing him the news. He turned to the rancher and asked, "Did you see anyone else before you rode in here?"

"Why no, we had just found Bulldog's trail and thought we were lucky in finding it."

"Sheriff, Bulldog's horse goes to these men for partial payment for stolen cattle. The town will have to make due with what's left for burial."

"You fellows take the horse and go home and leave these men to me. Understand?" said the sheriff.

He opened the message from McNelly

STAY IN LA JUNTA. STOP. COOK AND CAT ON THEIR WAY TO MEET YOU. STOP THEY'LL BE ON A TRAIN FROM DODGE CITY. STOP. THEY HAVE YOUR ORDERS. STOP. GOOD LUCK. STOP

MCNELLY.

"Ranger, thanks again for saving our bacon. He outdrew you."

"He won the drawing part, I won the shooting part," Talon replied with a slight smile. "I'll take those results every time."

BOOK TWO

Chapter One

Phsssssh!

Phsssssh, chug, chug, chug.

Phsssssh, chug, chug, chug,

An even louder echoing sound of a blast of steam than the others was coming from the Union Pacific eastbound engine.

The great steam engine continued to tell the world that it was in place and needed to be moving. The passenger depot was a bustle of movement. The morning arrival of the eastbound train usually heralded the start of the day at Medicine Bow. For some unknown reason, the train was generally on schedule to Medicine Bow, which had a 7:30 A.M. arrival time, but the next few miles to Laramie could take hours. It had something to do with the dedicated freight trains moving in and out of the sidings between Medicine Bow and Cheyenne. Whatever the reason, Martha Moore made a living supplying the morning fare to the passengers. If they didn't eat at Medicine Bow it may be hours before they would have a chance to do so later. This eastbound stop was famous along the Union Pacific because of Martha's tasty treats. Those treats included breakfast biscuits, doughnuts, tarts, fried pies, along with ham, sausage, bacon, and slabs of beef and mutton. Coffee was the best and hottest on the line. Ladies and children could get milk and tea to their satisfaction, too. The summertime water had a nasty taste at Medicine Bow, so Martha had kegs brought in on a daily basis from the mountain springs south of town to ensure the quality of her coffee. This employed several of the youngsters of the town during the season, which included her daughter Sally.

Today was a red letter day.

T. T. Finley was waiting with her Aunt Bertha to board the train. Bertha had agreed to travel with Mary Barton to Chicago, Illinois. Mary, the wife of Lieutenant Jim Barton of the U. S. cavalry, was going to her family home for the birth of their first child. The lieutenant was moving her out of harm's way because of increased Indian problems in the area. All the signs looked toward severe problems for the spring of 1875, about the time predicted for the birth.

Bertha and T. T. would then continue on to the Finley family home in Philadelphia. The plan was to enroll T. T. in a girl's finishing school for the next two years. T. T. was dancing with excitement as all her friends gathered to see her off. She was tall for her age, a beautiful budding blond; vivacious, smart and an extremely hard worker. The commotion of her leaving was a witness to her big heart. There wasn't a soul in Medicine Bow that hadn't been a recipient of an act of kindness from T. T. If one needed help, she was there to help— a wonderful trait for a 15-year-old. She had a dark side, of course. Everyone does. She was competitive— extremely competitive. Among her peers she was as good a wrangler and horse trainer as any of them. Also, she could handle a .38 Colt pistol better than anyone in town. The two fastest draws in the area were T. T., followed closely by her twin brother, Talon. This had been proven on several occasions. Her kind heart didn't extend to bullies and braggarts; she had no use for either, and didn't back down when confronted with bad behavior. She had no fears when pushing the right issue. Ms. Lucy, the town's teacher, told Bertha that beyond a doubt T. T. was the smartest child she had ever taught, which prompted the decision to take her east to school.

Talon, Running Wolf, Gary Ogdalh, Clair Ogdalh and Sally Moore circled T. T., each clamoring to say their final goodbyes. She gave each one of them a goodbye kiss, as the engineer signaled to board. The conductor was yelling, "All aboard."

The passengers filed onto the train with their morning meals wrapped in thin butcher paper. Sally had a stream of tears running down her cheeks because she was losing her closest companion in life. She adored T. T. as T. T. did her.

"Write me, please, T. T." begged Sally and T. T. nodded with a tearful face.

The young girl then then turned to her twin, Talon, and gave him an embrace and kiss. "We've never been apart, Too," she said.

"It'll work out, Two," he replied.

They both laughed at the infrequent yet familiar use of their middle names.

"If you need me, sis, just call and I'll come running."

"Same to you," she replied.

She hugged and kissed him again before climbing the steps onto the train.

Mary, Bertha and T. T. found seats facing each other on the depot side of the car. Being late summer, the windows were open where they could lean out for a last parting touch and wave as the train lurched into motion. The sounds of the engine's struggle to put the train in motion drowned out the last goodbyes. They were on their way.

It didn't take long before the windows closed at the bottom and were opened at the top. Cinders would blow in their eyes through the lower windows. Not only was T. T. experiencing her first trip on a train, but she was also wearing a dress, an uncommon situation for this girl of the West. She felt uncomfortable without her denim pants. *How's a girl to ride a horse in this thing?* she wondered. *Will there even be horses to ride where she was going?* Aunt Berta hadn't said. Then she noticed Mary squirming in her seat.

"Mary, can I help make you feel more at ease?" T. T. asked.

"Why, yes. Riding backwards like this is making me sick. Would you swap seats with me?"

T. T. got up and moved so that Mary could take her place by Bertha.

"Would you two like some coffee or tea?" T. T. offered.

"Where are you going to get coffee or tea?" Bertha asked.

"Sally and Martha supplied us with a jar of coffee and a jar of tea. They should be okay as long as we keep them from turning over," she replied.

"Girl, I do believe you think of everything, and I'll gladly have some tea," said Mary.

The tea worked. It settled Mary's stomach and made her more comfortable. The constant rocking of the train soon put her sound asleep, resting on Bertha's shoulder. Today was unusual. The trip to Cheyenne only took three hours rather than the eight that occurred regularly. The fellow passengers were of all types, but most were businessmen. Few locals actually used the train. So when at a small stop east of Cheyenne two hard cases boarded, T. T. was the only one to notice. For the first time, she was glad that she and Sally had taken the time to design a hidden pocket for her short-barreled Colt .38. She was also carrying a two-shot derringer. She intently watched every move the two men made. The train was making good time— no rails pulled by Indians or attacks of any kind that trains were often subjected to while crossing the prairie.

About two hours later, the engine pulled into a siding to take on water. T. T. could see the only existence for this town was to water and fuel trains. Her window was toward the mainline side of the train. Looking backward from the train, she could see four horses hitched to a rail in front of the only watering hole in town. Then she saw two men walk out on the porch of the saloon. *Ah*, she thought, *we are about to be robbed.* The two men on the train were in her sight, at the end of the car. One got up and moved to the door, with his sidearm drawn and held close to his leg down low.

Both Bertha and Mary were asleep and unaware of what was about to happen. *Just as well,* thought T. T. *They might not approve of what I'm about to do.* She removed her Colt from the hidden pocket with her right hand. She was holding her two-shot derringer in the left. The first hard case had his back turned, looking toward the following car. The men approaching the train were beginning to cross tracks to the train. No one else was aware they were about to be robbed.

The second hard case started to rise from his seat, and T. T. could see his gun was already drawn. Her only hope was surprise.

The second hard case turned toward T. T., who standing in the isle. He said, "This here is a stickup."

Just as he muttered his last word, T. T.'s shot hit him in the middle of the chest. Her second shot two inches lower knocked him down, as she closed in on the two outlaws. The first outlaw turned in time to catch the third shot in his right shoulder, which dropped his gun hand to his side, and he fired a shot into the floor. T. T.'s next shot sent him to join his partner. T. T. had only killed once before in a gunfight, but just a horse she shot out from under its rider. These were men — bad men, to be sure — but still men. Now she knew how it felt to kill a man. She was surprised at the lack of remorse; these outlaws were willing to kill innocent people, and she found that she was willing to kill to save those people.

The gunplay inside their train car alerted everyone on the train that they were under attack, and she could see the other outlaws retreating quickly to their horses. Several railroad men gave chase. The bandits made it to the horses, but no further.

"T. T. what have you done?" cried Bertha. "Where did you get that gun? You can't be carrying a gun. Young ladies don't do that."

"Well, Ma'am, you know I always carry."

"But not when you're traveling. You're a young lady you need to start acting like one. This would be unacceptable in the east — a 15-year-old carrying a gun. Hand it over to me!"

T. T. slid the derringer into the left pocket of her dress as she handed Bertha the Colt.

"Aunt Bertha, I need to clean it. Can I do that tonight in case I need it later?"

"I can't think about that right now. Let's sort out what has just happened."

A gentleman stepped forward. "Ma'am, this little lady saved us from being robbed and maybe worse by these outlaws. For the life of me, no one else picked up on the fact that we were being robbed."

A second man spoke, "How did you know, little lady?"

"Local cowpokes don't ride trains, they ride horses. That's what tipped me off. When we pulled into the siding, I noticed four horses hitched to the rail in front of the saloon. When two men started walking from there to the train and one on the train got up with a pistol at his side, I knew it was time to act."

The conductor entered the car from the rear, stepping over the dead men.

"Is everyone all right in here?" he queried.

There was a resounding 'yes' from the passengers.

"Who did the shooting?"

They all looked at T. T.

"You mean to tell me that *she* shot these men?"

Heads were nodding and yeses were muttered.

"Where did you learn to shoot like that, young lady?," asked the conductor.

"Medicine Bow, Wyoming, sir," answered T. T.

Other railroaders entered the car. The conductor motioned to them to remove the bodies of the dead outlaws.

"Get us a bucket of water and start cleaning this mess up. You folks want to step off the train while we take care of this?" he asked.

Gradually, all got off and mingled around the siding, discussing what had happened. In a way, T. T. felt bad about delaying the trip but decided it was better than being robbed. In a few minutes, they were allowed to board the train. With the usual sounds of struggle, they were off. Several passengers entered from the trailing cars, and moved toward T. T.

Their leader said, "We want to thank you, Miss, for your bravery."

"You're welcome," she returned.

At sundown, the conductor came through, announcing the next stop would be a dinner stop. With all the excitement, T. T. had forgotten all about eating. She was hungry, but didn't feel like eating. The train started to slow, coming to a full stop in an easy, gradual way. Then the engine struggle noises began again as it pulled its load onto the siding. It seemed like it took forever to position the passenger cars alongside the depot boardwalk. Passengers filed out onto the boardwalk and headed to the eastern end of the building. The conductor stopped Bertha. He asked her to follow him. Mary and T. T. fell in line, moving into the depot's small waiting room. From there, they moved into a larger baggage room where a table had been set for dinner. They were met by a tall Negro finely dressed in all black except for a sun-white shirt.

"My name is Charles, and I'm to serve your meals as long as I remain with you." T. T. noticed a slight Southern drawl to his otherwise precise words.

Bertha looking at the conductor asked, "What is this?"

"The railroad has arranged a special thank you for the rest of your trip for T. T.'s bravery in stopping the robbery," replied the conductor.

"What does that mean?" asked Mary.

"The railroad is refunding your fares, and has arranged special transportation throughout your trip. One of the owners has sent his private car for your use. Also, one of the men killed was a known outlaw, a robber of trains who generally worked with a gang in Iowa and Missouri. To ensure your safety, the railroad is surrounding you with six of their best inspectors to act as guards."

"My goodness," muttered Bertha.

"When you finish your meal, we will escort you to your car."

The meal was served on fine china, the likes of which T. T. had never seen, and consisted of fried chicken, summer squash and lady peas. The bread was sourdough rolls with butter and strawberry jam. The ladies drank tea, while T. T. drank coffee. Sugar was served in lumps. Charles attended to their every need.

After the dinner, the conductor escorted the three to the mainline side of the depot. Across the boardwalk, T. T. could see several men loading their luggage in the baggage car. She also noticed Charles and two women entering the next car with the dirty linens and dishes from their meal. Not only did they have a special car, they had their own engine. The conductor said his farewell as they entered the car. The engine announced its departure with two whistle blasts. With a fair amount of jumping and grinding, the train began to move.

The ladies were sitting in their own car, not knowing what to expect. Charles appeared with the two women at his side.

"Let me introduce to your two sleeping room attendants," he said. "This is Ruby."

Ruby stepped forward and gave a slight bow.

"This is Angel."

Angel bowed also.

"If you have any questions or needs throughout your trip, please ask one of us to help. We also have a cook. His name is Harold. It's our job to make you comfortable and we are here to serve."

"Thank you, Charles," said Mary.

T. T. spoke, "What does a sleeping room attendant do?"

"Would you like to show her, Ruby?"

"Yes, Mister Charles. Come with me, sweetie, and I'll show you where you are going to sleep tonight."

T. T. popped out of her seat and followed Ruby and Angel to the back of the car. There, Ruby showed her four sleeping rooms, all quite spacious in design.

"You mean we each have our own bed?" T. T. asked.

"Yes, Ma'am, you do."

"Where's the cook?"

Ruby answered, "In the next car forward, toward the engine."

"Show me, please. Does he know how to make doughnuts?" T. T. was excited, now.

Ruby guided T. T. through the car to the dining car ahead, while Angel stayed to prepare the sleeping rooms for the evening. Charles was still in conversation with Bertha and Mary.

Through one door, then another, the two entered the dining car. The train seemed to hit an uneven patch of track, resulting in the cars swaying from side to side while they were walking through the dining area. They entered the cooking area and Ruby introduced T. T. to Harold, the cook.

"Do you know how to make doughnuts?" she asked.

T. T.'s first words startled Harold. "Why yes, Ma'am, I do," he answered.

"When are you going to start on them for in the morning?" she asked.

"I have already started."

"Let me see."

Harold pulled a shallow baking tray from his prep area and moved it around to the counter between them. The dough was a large glob with evidence of rising. A smile broke out on T. T.'s face.

"Miss Ruby, will you be kind enough to wake me when Harold starts in the kitchen in the morning," she asked. "Oh, oh I forgot, is it all right if I help you in the morning, Mister Harold?"

"Why, Ma'am, you don't need to get up that early, I can handle it."

"Oh, you don't understand, Mister Harold. For the last three years, Sally Moore and I have helped her mother prepare breakfast for the train passengers at Medicine Bow stop. I'm used to getting up."

"Medicine Bow? Miss, are you telling me that you made the doughnuts for the Medicine Bow breakfast stop?"

"Yes. I helped make them every morning, along with biscuits and fried pies. I can do pancakes, too, but we never served them to the passengers. They were too messy for travelers."

"Glory, child, it'll be a pleasure to share a kitchen with you. On the mornings we went through Medicine Bow, we always stopped to get your doughnuts, and fried pies. Maybe you'll share your secrets with me."

"Sure, why not," she replied.

T. T. skipped with delight to the special car to let Bertha and Mary know that she was going to help Harold in the kitchen in the morning. With the day's events being so exhausting, the ladies turned in early.

Chapter Two

The train had made good time moving across the prairie because it was not required to stop at every little station. On two occasions they did have to move onto a siding to let westbound traffic pass. Every time the train jerked into motion, it awoke T. T. She would peer out the window to see what was happening. It was too dark to tell. True to her word, Ruby nudged her at 5:30 A.M. for her to join Harold in the dining car. She was up and dressed in a flash, and tiptoed by Bertha and Mary to avoid waking them. Harold was all smiles when he saw her.

"What am I to call you, child?" he asked.

"You can call me T. T."

He was busy rolling the doughnut dough on the baking table.

"You go ahead and make your doughnuts and I'll take the scraps and make something special for the staff."

Harold took an old condensed milk can and started pressing circles into his flattened dough. Then he took the screw off lid to a whiskey bottle and pressed out the doughnut holes. He ended up with two dozen raw doughnuts.

T. T. started in on the scraps by adding more flour to help in the process. She rolled a thin rope of dough. Every few inches she would cut the dough. She would start a circle by mashing down the first inch and coiling the remainder around the flattened center. She had enough scraps to make eight of her coils, which she placed on a flat baking pan. While the cooks waited for their creations to rise, Harold started heating a large Dutch oven filled with lard.

"This will be just right to cook in when the dough finishes rising," he said.

T. T. nodded in agreement.

Harold started to slice some bacon. T. T. sat and watched as he prepared several slices. Then he placed a large cast iron skillet on his wood-burning stove and placed several slices of bacon on to fry. He took the lid off one of the large cooking pots and placed it on the bacon, finger loop up. He reached into a cabinet and pulled out a wooden mixing bowl. He sifted flour into the bowl without the use of any measure. He added the necessary amount of whole eggs to the flour and some butter and cream along with one or two other ingredients. She couldn't tell what they were. He stirred until it was mixed. It wasn't long before he had a baking pan full of biscuits. He reached over with a toweled hand and removed the lid from the bacon. Next he took a large cotton-rag swab and dipped into the bacon grease and coated each biscuit. When finished, he placed them into the oven. Then, he started a new round of bacon slices in the skillet, placing the lid on top as before.

"T. T. is the grease ready for the doughnuts?"

"It looks right to me," she said.

"Start the doughnuts, then."

She jumped into action. One raw doughnut at a time went into the Dutch oven. She made sure the ones cooking were not too crowded. It looked to Harold as if this child really knew what she was doing. He started the sugar glaze. He placed a footed, wire rack on the table with a baking pan beneath. T. T. had just turned her first doughnuts. They were timed to perfection, golden brown in color. She used a small wire basket to pull the doughnuts from the grease. The process continued with her frying the doughnuts and Harold glazing them. Then came her special-designed doughnut swirls. There was just barely enough room on the glazing rack to hold them all.

"Where's the strawberry jam?" she asked.

Harold reached into the cabinet and handed her the jam. She took a large spoon and placed the jam in the flattened center of the swirls.

"Now you can glaze. These are for staff only," T. T. said.

"Lord a mercy, child, these look great," Harold observed.

Harold opened the oven and changed the position of the biscuits to a higher shelf to brown their tops. He sent Ruby to alert the guards that their breakfast was ready except on the eggs, which the cooks would prepare as ordered. Three guards came in for breakfast, leaving three on duty. All wanted their eggs over medium.

Harold removed the second batch of bacon from the skillet and plopped in six eggs. In a short time, he turned the eggs. T. T. was amazed. He didn't break a single yoke. He placed two eggs, two slices of bacon, two biscuits, and a doughnut on each of three plates. T. T. had already served three mugs of coffee when Harold placed the plates in front of them. Then he placed another plate on the table with a mound of doughnuts on it.

"Ruby, get Angel and Charles. Your breakfast is ready," Harold said.

They joined the three guards at the table, and T. T. served them. One of the guards noticed the swirl.

"What is that?" he asked, pointing to the swirl. "How come I didn't get one like that?"

"I made those for the staff, not realizing I didn't have enough to go around. Please forgive me, and I'll make you one tomorrow."

"As good as those look, I'm wishing my life away for tomorrow."

They all laughed. T. T. unthinkingly had served the Negro staff ahead of the guards. She had never been around such troubles, and didn't realize the implications. People were people to her and to many in the West; skin color was just skin color. What it covered mattered more than how it looked on the outside. It was already bad enough the guards had to eat at the same table. But her attitude, asking for forgiveness, and promising to make swirls for the guards saved the situation. T. T. was a server and all could see that she was innocent and meant no harm.

Harold ate his swirl standing in front of the stove, washing it down with his special brew of coffee. He poured T. T. a cup, which she used to dunk a doughnut.

"Mercy, child, young ladies are not supposed to dunk doughnuts," said Harold.

"Why not?" she asked.

"It's not ladylike in fashionable quarters," he replied.

"Mister Harold, I may be headin' to finishing school, but I'm not finished yet, and until I am, I'm dunkin'."

They all laughed.

It was past 7:00 A.M., and dawn brought a rainy day. The staff had finished eating and Angel was already heating water to wash the dishes. Ruby had gone to the sleeping car to await signs of life from Mary and Bertha. The remaining three guards gathered at the table. T. T. served their coffee and breakfast as the plates became available. They were on their third mug of coffee when the last doughnut disappeared.

Darnel Heston looked at T. T. while she was pouring his coffee and asked, "Are you the one that shot the outlaws?"

With a little tear in her eye she answered with a nod. Truly, she didn't want to think about her actions. It was something she hoped would never happen again.

Realizing he had upset her, he dropped the subject. "Did you make the doughnuts?"

"I only fried them. Harold made the dough before we got on the train last night. So, I guess you can say it was a joint effort. I plan to make something special for you tomorrow, and I'm not telling you what it is. It'll be something special— for the railroad inspectors, only."

T. T. had noticed a can of Dutch chocolate in the galley storage area.

"Harold, I need to make the inspectors something in the morning, are you going to make doughnuts again?"

"Yes," he answered, realizing what she was doing.

"Good. Then tomorrow, we'll make a dozen chocolate glazed doughnuts— for them only."

"When do the engineers eat?" she asked.

"We get something up to them whenever we stop. Early this morning, when we were on a siding, I took them hot coffee, ham, biscuits and doughnuts."

"I didn't see you do it."

"Oh, child, you have to be quick to keep up with me."

"What's for dinner tonight?" she asked.

"Well, we're going to fix a venison roast, cooked in the Dutch oven with carrots, turnips, apples and onions."

"I've never heard of such a mix. We have apples?"

"Why, yes, child," Harold answered

"Sounds like tomorrow evening we can have fried apple pies."

"If you want fried apple pies, sweetie, you can have them."

The train lurched as it slowed to enter another siding to make room for a westbound train. This siding was in the middle of nowhere, on the prairie. The rain made the landscape into a miserable gray mass without a horizon. At times, the rain fell in sheets.

"What are you going to feed the guards for a noon meal, Harold?"

"Oh, I've got a bean soup with toasted bread and cheese, and lots of hot coffee. I've got to have something ready all the time, because they eat when they find time to eat. That's why I make doughnuts as a ready treat."

An hour after hitting the siding, the westbound traffic finally passed. The fireman threw the switch and they moved onto the main line. Afterwards, one of the inspectors threw the switch to the main line and locked it. Soon, the inspector came through, soaking wet, heading to his quarters to change shirts. When he came through again, he stopped and got a cup of coffee and some toasted bread and cheese. He passed on the soup, saying he would come back later.

The rain made everyone sleepy. Mary and Bertha were curled up in their seats, taking advantage of the steady rocking and sounds of the train. Soon, T. T. joined them.

When she awoke, it was still raining and all she could see on either side of the train were boxcars. They were placed in the middle of a freight yard. Mary and Bertha were in the dining car, drinking tea and eating fresh-baked cookies. She joined them, but had coffee instead.

"What time is it?" she asked. "It has rained on us all day."

Mary looked at her, "That's because we are traveling with the rain. It's moving west to east, as we are."

T. T. responded, "I didn't think of that."

One of the inspectors came through and T. T. stopped him. "Where are we?"

"We're in a freight yard in Omaha, waiting for an engine from the Chicago, Rock Island and Pacific to pick us up. They're attaching us to an eastbound freight leaving here early evening. Hopefully we'll slip through Omaha unseen by any prying eyes. The newspapers are full of your exploits and we are trying to avoid their reporters. For your sake, we are hoping the story will die."

Charles entered and announced dinner. Dinner was always served at 7:00 P.M. The ladies sat at the table as Charles served the meal. The venison roast was displayed on a carving platter, the vegetables in a large bowl and the cooking broth in another. He laid two slices of venison on each plate and placed them in front of the ladies. They passed the vegetables and broth between themselves. The bread of the evening was again sourdough rolls. The ladies drank tea while T. T. stuck with coffee. The train lurched with a loud bang and moved backward a few feet.

"What was that, Charles?" asked Mary.

"The engine we have been expecting just hooked us onto the end of a string of cars."

The guards moved through the dining area, pulling all the blinds of the windows lower where you couldn't see into the car.

"We'll raise them when we get rolling," one stopped to say.

They started to move slowly and in a few minutes they stopped. They resumed moving, only this time it was backward. In a second or two there was another jolt and bang, more cars were picked up. Then, with a struggle, they were being pulled forward and gained speed.

Dinner finished with slices of yellow cake with fresh strawberries. T. T. wondered where Harold got the fresh berries, because she hadn't seen any earlier in the day. By the motion of the train, the ladies could tell they were entering a main line, and beginning a climb. T. T., cup of coffee in hand, started toward the kitchen to ask about the strawberries, when she was met by Charles.

"Miss T. T., young ladies do not leave dinner tables carrying coffee."

She handed him the cup.

"I wanted to find Harold and ask about the strawberries."

"Yes, Ma'am. But you don't leave the dinner table carrying anything with you and remain a young lady with standing."

"I understand."

He escorted her back to the table.

Mary and Bertha looked at her and laughed.

T. T. said, "I ran afoul of the finishing police."

The guards returned and raised the blinds and they could see the bluff line on the other side of the river they were crossing.

"What river is this?" they asked.

"The Missouri," he replied.

After crossing, the guards lowered the blinds.

"We're going to be dropped onto a siding, awaiting our ride. We don't want prying eyes to know who we're carrying," one of the guards explained to the group.

The ladies returned to their sitting room. T. T. went on to her sleeping room, where Angel had just finished preparing the beds for the evening. She wasn't quite asleep when she felt the bump of the engine as they connected more cars.

As promised, Angel wakened her early. She bounced out of bed, dressed and made her way to the kitchen. Harold was in the middle of his morning routine when she walked into the galley area.

"Harold, I promised them something special. We are going to glaze their doughnuts with a chocolate glaze, made with the Dutch chocolate you have in the cabinet."

She prepared two dozen doughnuts with her chocolate glaze concoction. The guards thought they had gone to heaven.

Moving across Iowa was like the prairie, but with more trees and farms of corn. The freight being pulled was cattle, bound for the Chicago market. Because of the live load, the train was making good time without having to stop for other traffic. They were the traffic being stopped for now. Every now and then they would get a whiff of the smell of cattle. The rain had outraced them and the day was sunny and a touch cool. Finally, the engine had to pull into a siding to take on water and fuel. This was going to take some time. The stop was isolated, but judging by the piles of fuel, well-used. The guards summoned T. T.

"They tell us you are a crack shot. Is that true?" one of them asked.

"It depends on what you mean by being a crack shot, but I think I can outshoot you six."

They laughed as one got off the back platform of the sitting car. He went over and placed a few pieces of ballast rock atop the brick barrier that was retaining the cutout bank of the right of way.

"What do you want me to shoot those with? Not much of a challenge; they're only about 30 feet away," T. T. smiled.

They laughed again.

"Tell me which weapon you want me to use," she said.

She turned and disappeared, leaving them to wonder what had just happened. In a few minutes, she returned with her .38 Colt pistol. She sat a box of shells on the back rail of the car, and proceeded to load her gun.

"How far is it to the targets, say 30 feet?" she asked.

She fired five shots, hitting five rocks without hitting the brick upon which they were sitting. The guards looked at each other and shook their heads.

"You really can shoot," one said.

The noise attracted some other railroad workers at the stop and they wanted to know what all the shooting was about. The guards told them they were practicing and that they were through now. T. T. took her Colt and shells and returned them to Bertha.

Chapter Three

The Chicago, Rock Island and Pacific dropped the four dedicated cars onto a siding in a switching yard in Chicago. A carriage met them to take Mary to meet her parents at the main passenger depot in the city. T. T. and Bertha went along with Mary, with the plan to do some shopping after leaving her. Two of the inspectors went along to escort them around the city. They took a circular route that led by the lakefront before moving to the depot. After saying their goodbyes, they were driven to State Street and the largest dry goods store in town, Field, Leiter and Company, where they spent the afternoon buying clothes for T. T. First, Bertha bought her a pair of ladies' shoes. They were simple brown leather slippers with wooden heels the height of those on her riding boots. They had two straps that buttoned on the outside, and had an embroidered silk patch on the toe. Very stylish for this year, they were told. Then they purchased undergarments, stockings and dresses. Stylish riding boots were bought as a late decision before leaving the store. On the way back to their cars, the inspectors took them on a sightseeing tour of Chicago. The city was still recovering from the fire of 1871. They enjoyed seeing Lake Michigan for a second time, along with the grand hotels that lined the lakefront.

The most interesting place they visited was a warehouse manufacturing ice. Blocks of ice in such large quantities were unheard of in Wyoming. The ice primarily went to refrigerated rail cars serving the meat industry. Cattle were no longer shipped to the east for processing, but processed right in Chicago and then shipped east. The refrigerated cars were also used for fruits and vegetables.

With their busy day winding to a close, they made it back to the siding. The lead inspector gave them some good news. The Pennsylvania Railroad, known in railroad circles as the Pennsy, was going to pick them up early in the evening for their trip to Philadelphia. They would miss seeing most or all of Indiana, but would get to see Cleveland before turning south to Pittsburg. T. T. had been bored by the trip through Iowa and Illinois and she was looking forward to something other than corn fields and sawmills. The crew had been telling her how beautiful the Pennsylvania countryside was.

T. T. had made a solid impact on Charles. He realized she had a large, loving heart, and was willing to help anyone, even with the most daunting of tasks. The guards were impressed also how she handled herself when around them. Her gun play didn't hurt, either. To all the crew, she was someone special. They adopted her favorite saying, 'If you can do it, it ain't bragging'.

As if by magic, the switch engine arrived when scheduled, and pulled them to the Pennsy yards south and east of Chicago. *What type of train are they going to latch us to this time?* T. T. wondered. *Would it be freight or passenger? Would it be on the back or next to the engine?* Secretly, she hoped for the back of the train, where she could stand on the rear platform and watch the scenery fly by. She knew the guards wanted to be next to the engine, where it would be difficult for an intruder to uncouple the cars from the train. End cars opened opportunities to disconnect anywhere along the train. She was right. Late in the evening they attached, next to the engine of a freight train.

At daybreak, they were in Ohio, and it looked like Illinois to her. The fields of corn stretched for miles. Late in the day, on their approach to Cleveland, they got to see Lake Erie. Early evening found them moving onto a siding somewhere near Cleveland. T. T. was asleep when they resumed moving. With Mary gone, T. T. spent more time with Bertha and less with Harold. Charles continued to school her on the things a young lady needed to know about setting tables and serving in high society. She was an avid student, knowing he was trying to eliminate future embarrassing moments due to her lack of knowledge.

The closer the train got to Pittsburg, the hillier the terrain became. On several occasions, it seemed as if the engine was struggling with its load. The turns were sharper, and they could see the end of the train out the side window. The surrounding area had more tree growth and less cropland. The trees were beginning to change to their fall colors. She knew of the large oaks, the maples and the sycamores, but there seemed to be a thousand others she didn't know.

They were hours on a siding at Youngstown, waiting to be connected to yet another train. This time, T. T. got her wish and they were added to the tail of a passenger train that would take them to Philadelphia. Unbeknownst to T. T., the Pennsy was the largest corporation in the world. The company maintained more than 6,000 miles of track and shipped twice as much tonnage as its nearest rival. Pennsy employees had successfully engineered a railroad that crossed the

Appalachian Mountains, connecting the east with the west. It played a huge role in opening the frontier to the eastern markets for food and it helped Pennsylvania develop its coal and steel industries, while being the leader in innovation for railroading during one of the worst recessions the country had yet seen.

The Pennsy didn't know T.T. but treated her as royalty because of her heroic actions during a train robbery. Their train made the Youngstown to Pittsburg run during the night, and it took all night. Bertha and T.T., even with the luxury of the dedicated cars, were beginning to get travel weary, but the daylight move out of Pittsburg renewed their energy. The steady climb into the Appalachians gave a breathtaking panorama of scenery with something new to look at around every turn. The terrain changed often from small patches of farm land to deep and densely covered forests. From the high vantage points, the enthralled Westerners could see large valleys of forests full of strange trees. And on the industrial side, they marked man's progress across the state, with its filth from burning coal and the rusting iron left to waste along the railway. The towns grew larger as their train crept closer to its destination. They agreed the trip across Pennsylvania had amazing sights, although they did miss some of the scenery because of the night travel.

T. T. spent at least an hour saying goodbyes to her new-found friends. She tearfully parted with the cooking crew and especially Charles, wondering *what will my new life out East bring and just what is a finishing school, anyway?*

Uncle Jim's sister, Mary Grace Bolton, was waiting for Bertha and T. T. in the ornate and new Tamaqua Station, where Pennsy dropped its passengers. The eastern Finleys were a wealthy family and Mary Grace had married into another wealthy family. Uncle Jim and Aunt Bertha had moved west to acquire land for the families and had managed to do quite well with their endeavors. It had been several years since Bertha had seen Mary Grace. They had been best friends in childhood.

"Mary Grace, I want you to meet your niece Talon Two Finley," said Bertha.

"Please call me T. T., Aunt Mary," said T. T.

Mary Grace hugged Bertha and then T. T.

"Okay, I'll call you T. T." she replied.

The carriage ride through the streets was a lot different than through the streets of Chicago. The buildings were taller, and there were more people. At a distance, it reminded T. T. of bees around a hive. The smells were different— dirtier and musty. Dust swirled, noise was everywhere. *How could these people live in such a place?* she wondered. The Bolton household was on the outskirts of the city, and the environment was quieter, cleaner and cooler than the main part. John Bolton came from wealth, but had been very successful in the shipping industry on his own. One could tell from the way his home was maintained that he was industrious.

John Bolton arrived a few minutes later. He was thrilled to see his sister-in-law and to meet his niece.

"Well, T. T., what do you think of our home and Philadelphia?" asked Uncle John.

"From what I've seen of Philadelphia, it's big and crowded. It reminded me of bees around a hive. Your home is beautiful, and as they appeared from the carriage, the grounds are peaceful and relaxing. Do you have riding horses?" T. T. asked.

"Why, yes, I bet you do like to ride, being from Wyoming. I tell you what we'll do. I'll have Leroy saddle two horses for us tomorrow morning and we'll ride the grounds. We sit on 20 acres, but we don't have to stay confined to the grounds, it just depends on how you feel. Now the earlier we ride, the better, because of the heat. We'll shoot for 9 A.M."

"That will be great, Uncle John."

After being introduced, Tammy, the maid, showed Bertha and T. T. to their bedrooms. They decided they would take a little time to settle in before four o'clock tea. T. T. fell on her bed and found it to be very soft and comfortable. She dozed, her last thought again: *what is a finishing school?*

Tammy knocked on her door to waken her for the tea. She opened her door and with a sleepy look, asked if she could drink coffee instead of tea. .

Tammy giggled. "No, Ma'am, tea is tea."

"Can you take me to the kitchen?"

Tammy took her as requested. When they got there, Tammy introduced her to Meg, the cook.

"May I use one of your knives?" T.T asked.

"Sure, child, what size do you need?"

"The big one will do." T. T. replied. She pulled a thin peppermint stick from a small sack as Meg was handing her the knife. She proceeded to slice the stick into small half-inch pieces, and dropped them back into the sack.

"Thanks, Meg. Do you make doughnuts?"

"I can, but not very often."

"Why not?"

"The boys are grown and not around very much for breakfast, Mister Bolton is usually up early and gone to work. Miss Mary prefers toast and jam."

"Do you like doughnuts yourself?" asked T. T. "If you do, we'll make them for us."

Tammy interrupted, "You need to go to tea; you're having guests."

T. T. put her sack into the concealed pocket and followed Tammy into the tearoom overlooking the flower garden. She was the last one there and was immediately introduced to the guests.

"T. T., this is Margaret MacDowell, and her daughter Elizabeth. They are our neighbors and Elizabeth will be attending Mrs. McIntosh's school with you," said Mary Grace.

"Nice to meet you," said T.T. as she stuck out her hand in greeting.

"Young ladies don't extend their hands to older ladies, T. T." said Mary Grace.

"I'm so sorry, Aunt Mary, please forgive me."

The five sat around the table and Tammy served the tea. The ladies, in turn, used the cream and sugar except T. T. She skillfully removed a peppermint from her sack and dropped it into her tea. The ladies didn't see her do it, but Elizabeth did, and slid her cup toward her. T. T. dropped one into her cup, too. They both looked at each other and smiled. The peppermint was the only way T. T. could endure the tea. The only problem was, the peppermint didn't dissolve very quickly and emitted an aroma not found around teas of fashionable ladies.

Aunt Bertha picked up on the caper rather quickly, and looked T. T. straight in the eye. When T. T. dropped her eyes to her cup, Bertha leaned over and looked.

"T. T., what did you put in you tea?"

"A piece of peppermint candy, to change the taste," she replied.

Aunt Mary and Margaret laughed, but that didn't change Bertha's demeanor.

"May I try one?" asked Margaret.

T. T. pulled one from her sack and placed it into Margaret's cup.

"Wouldn't you like one Elizabeth?" asked Margaret.

"No mother, I don't think so."

Then, Aunt Mary pushed her cup forward and eyed Bertha sternly. Reluctantly Bertha offered her cup, also.

"You know this would be a good idea for a Christmas tea. It tastes rather good. What do you think, Elizabeth?"

"I liked it," Elizabeth responded.

Caught in a trap, Elizabeth dropped her eyes to the ground.

"Just as I thought, you got one earlier, didn't you?"

Elizabeth nodded that she had.

"T.T, are you a good influence on my Elizabeth?"

"Why, yes Ma'am, I am."

"I think you will be, too"

From that point on Elizabeth and T. T. were fast friends.

"Next week, we'll take you girls to introduce you to Mrs. Ledbetter, the Lead Scholar at Mrs. McIntosh's School for Young Women."

T. T. asked Elizabeth if she would like to see the garden and the ladies excused them from the tea.

"Do you go by Elizabeth or another name?" asked T. T.

"Call me Beth," she said.

"How old are you?" T. T. continued the questions.

"I'm 15. And you?"

Beth was about T. T.'s height, maybe slightly taller, with golden red hair that was thick and curly. Her skin was light in color, with the appearance of freckles at the hairline. *The cowboys at home would line up to be with such a beauty, and when they got to the head of the line, none would know what to say*, T. T. observed.

"Same. Do you ride horses, or what do you like to do for fun?"

"I have a horse, but don't get to ride him very often. My parents don't feel it's safe for me to ride alone, and I don't know much about horses. Do you ride?" Beth asked.

"I love to ride. Uncle John is taking me riding tomorrow. As soon as we can, you and I will go riding. I know a lot about horses. At home, I helped to train most of the horses on Uncle Jim's ranch, and also helped in catching them. How far is it to your home? "

"We're the next home down the lane— about two miles," Beth answered.

The girls finished their time together, wondering about their futures at Mrs. McIntosh's.

The next morning, as promised, Uncle John took T. T. riding. He walked with her to the stable area where two saddled horses patiently waited. The horses matched in color— a dark bay. As T. T. got closer to the animals, she noticed there was something different about the saddle on one of the horses.

"Uncle John, what kind of saddle is on this horse?"

"That's an eastern lady's saddle, a side saddle."

"I never used a side saddle."

"It's good that I am going with you this morning since you don't know how to ride. Sissy is a good steady horse she won't throw you."

She looked around the stable area and found another saddle to replace the lady's saddle. She walked over to Sissy and in her normal charm began to woe the horse. She rubbed her nose and ears in a gentle fashion. Then she moved to her neck and slowly reached down and rubbed the inside of her leg. Next she removed the saddle followed by rubbing her ears.

"What are you doing, T. T.?" asked Uncle John.

"I'm changing saddles. How old is Sissy?"

"She's seven."

"She's beautiful, Uncle John. I love her."

"Let me get..." Uncle John started to say.

But T. T. interrupted him. "I'll saddle her, it won't take long."

With the saddling finished, she went through her rubbing routine and while asking Uncle John if he was ready, she grabbed Sissy's mane and bridle in her left hand put her toe in the stirrup, and mounted. Sissy didn't move and again received a massage around her ears.

"You ready, Uncle John? I am," T. T. said.

Uncle John slowly led the way out of the stable area into the open field behind the barn. On the other side of the barn, was a closed pasture of maybe an acre or two for the horses to roam. *Real confining*, thought T. T.

"Uncle John, are we riding or walking? Show me what you can do, Sissy."

She was off, but not at as fast a pace as she wished. It did leave John standing in her dust, and startled him. Soon she found that riding on a 20 acre estate was like riding on a postage stamp. At best, it was a small circle. When she figured out where the gate to freedom was, she made a beeline toward it. She rode up to it, lifted the latch and swung the gate open. She held it open until John got there.

"Where're you going?" he asked.

"I'm going to let Sissy roam," she replied.

John rode through the gate and T. T. closed and latched it. After seeing her ride, he no longer feared for her safety. She could out ride him and he hoped he could keep up. Down the estate drive and to the public lane, T. T. led the way. She turned right and gave Sissy a gentle urge to move faster. She responded with a nice, steady canter. John was keeping up and enjoying the romp. In a short time, they were at the estate drive of the MacDowell's and T. T. turned and started up the drive. John followed. When they got to the front of the estate, T. T. swung down in one motion, dropped the reins and bounded up the front steps to the front door. John rode up and grabbed Sissy's reins for fear she might run off.

A servant answered the front door, and while giving T. T. the once over, asked if she could be of service. T. T. told her she was here to see Beth. The servant closed the door and left T. T. standing, not knowing what to do. Soon the door opened and Beth popped out.

"Oh, T. T. what are you doing here?" she asked.

"I'm seeing if you would like to go for a ride," T. T. answered.

About that time, Henry MacDowell walked through the door.

"How are you, John?"

"Trapped, I am." Uncle John replied.

"What's going on here?" Henry asked.

"Well, Mister MacDowell, I'm here to see if Beth could go riding with me and Uncle John."

"You must be T. T.! I've heard a lot about you. I tell you what: John, you know the way to the stables. Beth and I will meet you there after we change clothes."

T. T. bounded off the porch and onto Sissy in one, fluid motion. John led the way to the MacDowell stables. It wasn't long before Beth and her dad were there.

"Show me your horse, Beth." T. T. urged.

Beth pointed to the stall next to the window on the right. T. T. moved over to take a look. Beth had a stunning animal for a horse. She unlatched the door and stepped into the stall.

"Watch out, T. T. she'll kick you."

T. T. heeded the warning and gave her a couple of kiss sounds. The horse turned and looked at her. T. T. turned her back on her and moved to the far corner of a spacious stall.

"What's her name, Beth?"

"Amanda."

A couple more kisses and T. T. slowly approached her. She backed off and T. T. returned to her corner. Then she tried again, starting with her kiss sounds. This time, Amanda let her touch her nose. Then the rubbing routine began with the nose then the ears and soon Amanda seemed under her spell.

"Where's your bridle, Beth?"

Beth handed it to her.

"Don't you have a single bit one?"

"She's trained to the double bit," responded Henry. The stableman handed her a different bridle.

She gently placed it on her. The stableman brought in the saddle. It was an eastern lady's saddle.

"Beth, can you ride using this kind of saddle?"

"Yes, it's the only kind I've ever used.

She threw the blanket on and then the saddle. She made sure all the straps were tight. She returned to her rubbing with the nose, around the eyes, and ears.

"Let's go for a ride." She walked Amanda out of her stall, and handed Beth the reins.

"What do I do with her?" Beth asked.

"Walk her out of the barn; rub her neck as you go," said T. T.

"John you have an impressive little lady on your hands," said Henry.

T. T. held Amanda steady while the stableman helped Beth into the saddle. With Beth ready to go, T. T. swung into her own saddle in one quick motion. They gradually moved out into the open area of the estate at a very gentle canter. Again, to T. T. it was like riding on a postage stamp, but she could tell it was a challenge for Beth. *This could be corrected*, she thought. The rest of the morning went well as the two girls were left to roam while John and Henry watched.

Finally, Beth grew tired and the ride was over. At the barn, the stableman helped Beth off Amanda and started to walk away with her.

"Stop," cried T. T. "Beth, take the reins and rub Amanda's nose."

She did and in no time T. T. had her petting her all over. All could see Amanda loved it.

"Now, Beth, remove the saddle," directed T. T.

She did and handed it to the stableman.

"Rub her neck and go back to the ears. Lead her back to her stall," T. T. advised.

Beth did as instructed.

"Now take the bridle from her, rubbing her nose while you doing it."

She did, and as Amanda stood there for more attention, Beth continued to rub and pet her. Beth left the stall and looked at T. T., "I've never done that before."

"If you do, Amanda will love you, and she wants to love you. Later I'll show you how to groom her."

The morning was satisfying, and gave John and Henry time for a good look at this girl from Wyoming.

Chapter Four

The day was clear, and warmer than usual. The girls were in the MacDowell carriage on their way to meet Mrs. Ledbetter, the Head Scholar at Mrs. McIntosh's School for Girls. They rode in the front seat of the carriage, facing backward, while their escorts sat in the back. Margaret, Mary, and Bertha were enjoying the ride. It was the first time Bertha had been out in about a week. The school was about a 30-minute ride through the outskirts of Philadelphia through picturesque estates. The approach to the school was a long circular drive with enough space to enable several coaches to come and go at the same time. Their carriage stopped in front of the steps of the front porch. The ladies were helped from the coach by the attending doorman.

They were escorted into a large study where several other girls with family were awaiting the start of the meeting. From what T. T. could see, there were at least six other girls. It wasn't very long before Mrs. Ledbetter made her way onto the podium and approached the lectern. It got so quiet, the drop of a pin would have sounded like an avalanche.

"Parents and young ladies, I am the Head Scholar, Mrs. Ledbetter. I want to welcome you to your first meeting at our school. Your school days will be from 9 A.M. to 3 P.M., Monday through Friday. This is a small school and the classes are small. Today's greeting is only half of our new entering class. The eight young ladies in this room will be instructed in the same classes throughout the day by the same instructors. The other half will have a different schedule, and will also remain together. Your subjects will be English, with focus on Literature and Writing; History, with European History this year and American next; Math; Latin and Science. Throughout your entire time with us, you will be guided in the social graces, including public speaking. We already know you young ladies are smart. Our job is to polish you into spectacular social gems. Some of you will be ahead of others in that area, and our plan is for those of you needing instruction to gracefully catch up with the others. We are here to instruct, not to punish. Our methods have received accolades from parents, students, and halls of higher education. We want you to enjoy yourselves while you're here."

"Now, let me introduce you to your instructors. Before leaving, I want each of you to introduce yourself to them, and parents, that includes you. Teachers, please stand when I call your name. Mrs. Burton, Math; Mrs. Davis, Latin; Mrs. Newport, English; Mrs. Lamond, History; and Mrs. Wise, Science. You can see they are positioned around the room at different tables. I also expect you to introduce yourself to me. I'll be at this table in the front."

Beth and T. T. started with the instructor closest to them, Mrs. Wise. After a brief chat, they moved to the next closest, Mrs. Lamond. Then they got to Mrs. Newport, and she gave them an assignment for the first day of class. Then came Mrs. Ledbetter, and they had to wait for the politicians to finish before having their turn.

"Hello Margaret and Beth, it's so good to see you, and this little Lady with you is...?"

"Oh, Mrs. Ledbetter this is Talon Two, and her Aunts, Mary Grace and Bertha," said Beth.

"Well done, Beth. Mary Grace, it's so good to see you again and this is your younger sister?"

"Yes, this is Bertha Finley."

"Bertha, it's so nice to meet you."

"Mrs. Lucy referred to you as T. T. in her letters of introduction. I want you to know you are our first young lady from Wyoming. I'm hoping you will be able to share with your fellow students the beauty of the West."

"Oh yes, Ma'am, I will. Mrs. Newport said we would start the first day sharing with each other," T. T. promised.

They finished with Mrs. Ledbetter and continued to the other instructors, after which they were escorted into another parlor for tea.

While in their meeting, the day had grown warmer, and their return trip was met with windy and dusty conditions. The MacDowells agreed to take T. T. to and from school with Beth. The girls were shocked to have an assignment before classes began. They spent the next few days together, learning how to ride and how to take care of a horse. Each day Beth grew in confidence, and riding became a great part of her being. The MacDowells could see a change in Beth, just from being around T. T. Not that she wasn't a free spirit on her own, but her curiosity for practical matters had picked up. And, in fact, she was taking care of her horse and was wearing a pair of her brother's denim pants to ride. No longer was she a rider in a lady's saddle. They would spend all afternoon giving Amanda and Sissy baths before grooming them. Their horses were the best kept of any around.

Monday morning came. T. T. entered the MacDowell's carriage and sat alongside Beth. They were the only passengers, so they took the back seat. The ride was pleasant. The valet helped them from the carriage in front of the steps, which they bounded up with enthusiasm.

The two English instructors met the girls and moved them to a great parlor. The room had four tables facing a lectern in the middle of the room. Mrs. Newport approached the lectern and asked for their attention.

"It is our tradition for each of our new pupils to read their first assignment to their fellow students on the first day of classes. If you are not prepared, you will be sorry. As we call your name, you will approach the lectern with your work and read it to the class. This will be one of the few times your class will meet together. The purpose is for you to know your other schoolmates. We will begin."

Mrs. Ledbetter entered the room about midway through the session and sat with the teachers. The essays so far had been predictable and a bit boring, with nothing earth-shattering being revealed. Most of the students got their names from other family members, which made for short essays. Finally, T. T. was called to the lectern. She walked to the lectern with several pages of an essay in her hand, which she placed on the lectern as she scanned the room with curious, alert eyes.

"My friends and family: I hope all of you will call me T. T. Finley. T. T. is short for Talon Two. How did I get the claw of a hawk and a number for a name? It was early spring in 1859 when my parents joined a small wagon train moving to the Oregon Trail. Somewhere on the prairie of eastern Kansas, the train was raided by who knows. The horses were stolen and the people were all killed. The wagons were looted of valuables and set ablaze. We had been hidden in our family's wagon. Oh I forgot to tell you I have a twin brother. His name is Talon Too, that's spelled T-O-O for also."

The class giggled.

T. T. waited for the giggles to die down before resuming her story. "How did we get such different names? Uncle Jim and Aunt Bertha's wagon train came upon the scene later that afternoon. They were moving west to fulfill a contract with the Union Pacific Railroad, and had a much larger force with them than our train had. After we were raided and our wagon set ablaze, one of those quick and violent spring rainstorms blew in and dowsed the flames— and saved our lives. The fire sat there smoldering, waiting for the prairie winds to dry us out before rekindling. The part of the wagon destroyed was where our parents kept their records and books, including the family Bible, so our real identities went up in flames. About the time Uncle Jim climbed up on the back of the wagon, Talon, my brother, began to cry. I've always teased him about it being a good time to wet his diaper."

More giggles erupted.

"Uncle Jim picked him up, and that started *me* to crying. He placed Talon on the tailgate of the wagon and picked me up. And my introduction was to scratch him on the nose. His comment, so I've been told, was, 'This baby has talons.' He climbed out of the wagon with me in his arms and reached back to get Talon. Immediately, my brother scratched him. 'So you have talons, too' he was heard to say. He carried us over to his wagon and handed us to Aunt Bertha. 'Oh, Jim,' she said. 'This one is a little girl.'

'She was the second baby and attacked me like an angry eagle. I'm naming her Talon Two, and her brother followed her in the attack. I'm naming him Talon Too.' We couldn't have been found by any better people. When they got to Wyoming, they adopted us and named the ranch the Four T after the initials of our names. We call Talon, Talon, and me, T. T. I hope in the future to share with you how my brother and I grew up under the nurturing of Uncle Jim and Aunt Bertha," T. T. finished.

Mrs. Ledbetter left the room immediately after T. T.'s presentation. All the other essays were completed and the students moved to the dining room for lunch, which consisted of a fruit bowl and soup. Tea was served and T. T. asked for coffee, but ended up with drinking water. Beth giggled at her asking for coffee. Then, T. T. pulled a sack from her satchel, which contained a bacon biscuit sandwich and a doughnut. This didn't go unnoticed by Mrs. Ledbetter. One of the instructors came over to T. T. and told her Mrs. Ledbetter wanted to see her when they were finished with lunch. She was instructed by Mrs. Ledbetter not to bring food from home. It was a school rule.

It was back to the parlor, where the afternoon was spent with the other instructors giving their first assignments to the class. The new English essay — titled: *What is the worst feeling you have ever experienced?* — was to be read, starting tomorrow.

As they were riding on the way home, T. T. looked at Beth and said, "I'll starve to death in that place."

Beth laughed at her.

The next day, T. T. was ready for her classes, which took some help from her Aunts. At first, there seemed to be a lot of reading, and it was time consuming and took time away from Sissy and other things T. T. liked to do. *This finishing thing is going to be a chore*, she thought.

Since there were only eight girls in the class, the next essay was read over a two-day period. It was also explained that the essays would be read on a rotating basis regarding who goes first, so T. T. went last.

"These are the two worst feelings in my life. The first is as follows: It's a hot summer day and you have just finished your morning chores, and you have time to do what you want to do until late afternoon chores. You decide it would be a good day to go to the swimming hole and you head out the front door in a scamper, and you're barefoot. You take maybe a dozen steps through the grass and it happens. It oozes up through your toes and you know what has happened. You have stepped into chicken poop. It adheres and you can't wipe it off. You find a stick, but by then the dirt of the path has made it worse. You scrape, but it doesn't do the job. By the time you reach the river to wash you are dreading what you have to do."

The class was laughing at the description. Mrs. Newport was trying to gain control of the situation, when Mrs. Ledbetter walked into the room. One of her classmates spoke up. "T. T., rest assured that has never happened to any of us." Mrs. Ledbetter asked Mrs. Newport to join her in the next room. She explained what T. T. had written about and they both laughed silently. Mrs. Newport entered the room and instructed T. T. to continue.

"The second feeling is as follows and is much more serious than what you just heard. I wish all of you could experience the first and none of you should experience the second."

You could hear a pin drop.

"One of the passions my brother and I shared with our running mates was the use of firearms. The West can sometimes be a dangerous and unpredictable place, so this skill is a practical one to learn. We practiced drawing and firing pistols every day. At 12, I won my first Fourth of July shooting contest in Medicine Bow. Talon was second. We could outdraw anyone. Talon could never outdraw me, but it was always close. He used a Colt .45 and I used a .38. I won again in 1873 and '74. At 13, all the kids of our age could ride and shoot. All of us were competitive and could handle ourselves with firearms. Early summer of this year, the older kids were helping the younger kids with their times tables, when Gary Ogdalh saw a hard case ride by the school house. Then he saw a second. He alerted us to the fact that it looked like there was going to be a robbery. We looked down the main street and saw two more approaching from the other direction. Gary, Running Wolf, Talon, and I jumped into action. We armed ourselves and walked four abreast down the street. It was late afternoon and the sun was at our back and it was hard for the outlaws to see us.

They had just completed the robbery and were saddled and ready to ride when we braced them. The leader went for his pistol and I beat him to the draw. My aim was right on target, but when he drew, he jerked his horse and my shot hit his horse over the right eye and it went down in a flash. His shot went into the ground about five feet ahead of us. The other outlaws didn't attempt to draw. When the horse fell it slammed the rider's head into the boardwalk in front of the store, breaking his neck. He died on the spot. His death was the worst experience I have ever felt, but so it goes in the West. You must be ready to protect yourself at all times and when a neighbor is in need, you must be ready to help. I hope none of you ever have to experience killing a fellow human being."

You could hear a pin drop and Mrs. Newport didn't make any comments. One of the girls asked T. T. if she expected them to believe such a story. T. T. replied, "Uncle Jim always says 'if it's true, it ain't bragging'." She sat down. By that afternoon, the whole school knew that T. T. claimed to be in a dime store western novel shootout with outlaws.

The result was Aunt Bertha being asked to the school for a meeting with Mrs. Ledbetter and Mrs. McIntosh. In the meeting, she confirmed T. T.'s version of her story, and it was agreed for Mrs. Newport to review her essays before she reads them aloud to the class. Mrs. McIntosh realized she had a real gem in T. T., but she needed to protect the other students from some of her worldly experiences. She handled all complaints from concerned parents, explaining that a 15-year old in the West was like a 21-year old in the east. And that T. T.'s shared experiences were good for the other children to hear.

Chapter Five

All of T. T.'s instructors had to review her work before she presented it to her class. She didn't let this bother her. They loved to hear her yarns of the work she had done while growing up in Wyoming, and would tease her about the truth of some matters, to which she always replied with her Uncle's favorite caveat 'if I can do it, it ain't bragging'.

Her next essay for Mrs. Newport — titled *What I Did Last Summer* — positioned her for acclaim throughout the school. She wrote about one of her favorite subjects: the training of horses. Mrs. Newport approved her essay and it was her turn to take the lectern.

"What I Did Last Summer. The Four T ranch received a contract from the U. S. cavalry for 300 trained horses in the early spring of 1874 for delivery in the summer of 1875. This gave us a year to catch the horses we needed from the wild herds in our area and train them for cavalry use. Cavalry horses had to be specially trained because they were used hard, even in their daily routine. They also had to be trained by what the cavalry called the 'belly button method'— the horse has to know which way to go by where your belly button points. It may sound silly, but it makes perfect sense when you realize that riding and firing a carbine often meant that the rider's hands were not on the reins. Basically, pointing your belly button one way or the other changed the pressure in the legs on the sides of the horse. This change of pressure guides the horse on which way to go. To get the best out of the horse, you had to train him by whispering in his ear. Calling Eagle and his son Running Wolf had taught us the method several years before and our horses were sought after by wranglers all over the plains. When the order came in, we already had several horses trained, some being trained and a few ready to start the process. We also needed to capture several more to make sure we had enough to deliver. During the roundup, Talon found Sam and Sally, the two horses that became the loves of his life."

"Uncle Jim had given us kids the task of rounding up the horses we needed and promised to pay each of us for the horses we caught and trained. We put our heads together and decided we would deliver as many as we could. It was our usual running crew; Talon, Gary, Running Wolf, Sally Moore and me. Running Wolf had spotted a herd several miles to the west of Medicine Bow. We had watched that particular herd for years and we knew it well. It contained a good crop of three-year-old stallions and mares. If thinned properly, the herd would continue to thrive, and could be harvested again in two or three years."

"Now, we had a fair idea of where the dominant mare would lead the herd. It was a watering hole of a natural spring, in the middle of a ridge of mountains on the western Four T range. Wolf felt it would take a couple of weeks for the herd to arrive, and if we needed it sooner, all we had to do was to start them running then back off, and they would find their way to where we wanted them. Our job was to build a fence across the mouth of the canyon, using natural brush, with an area wide enough for the herd to enter without suspecting anything was wrong. We would close the fence after the herd entered the canyon. It took us six days to build the fence, and then all we had to do was to wait. That summer had been drier than usual and the creeks on the plains were reeking of bad, sour-tasting water. This forced the mare to find cooler and better-tasting water, and her routine was the canyon. She led the herd though the gap in the fence and into the box canyon. The canyon extended about five miles to the pool of spring fed water. We closed the gap, and they were ours."

"Trying not to spook them, we took a trail to the top of the canyon to get a count of the herd size. We only needed about a fourth of the herd to meet and exceed our needs. This is where Calling Eagle's training helped us capture the horses we needed. The mare would oust some of the younger members for bad behavior. They were usually male, which should tell us girls something about boys."

The class giggled.

"We had also built several holding corrals close to the mouth of the canyon. We took the rails down between two solid posts at the first corral to allow the horses to enter. We slowly walked our horses up the canyon to where these troublemakers had been banished. They didn't even know we were there, because they were awaiting the herd's signal for them to water. Slowly, we circled them and gently urged them to move toward the mouth of the canyon. The herd was busy watering and they didn't notice us, either. We picked off 12 horses on our first pass, of which seven were of the type we needed. After opening the second corral, and freeing the unwanted horses from the first, we repeated our actions. This time, we had to move into the herd to cut out the horses we wanted. This meant they would put up a fight by running away, but they were trapped and couldn't go far. It also meant we had to cut the horses out of the herd and then lasso them, or lasso them first and pull them from the herd. The trick was to let them run until they got tired. Once exhausted, they were easier to separate. It took us the rest of the day to gather and cull down to 37 horses, plus Talon's first love, Sam."

"We let the herd rest and water overnight. Early the next day, we opened the fence to allow the herd to escape. And, when we gently urged them to move, they bolted for their freedom. Then, we closed the fence and started training the horses we had corralled. The boys had learned from past years, proving boys *can* be trained, and that Sally and I could train the males faster than they could. Girls, it's easy: flirt with them and they'll follow you anywhere."

Another giggle.

"We built five training pens. We opened the pens and moved the two males into mine and Sally's pen. Talon took the most dominant, Sam, to his corral. At first, we thought Sam was a dark grey, but upon closer inspection we found him to be a blue roan. His mane and tail were a dark blue-black grey that reflected an intense blue in the right sunlight. This blue hair mingled with a light grey to white hair making up his coat. For all intents and purposes he was a blue roan. This was the first one we had ever seen. Sam was about three or four years old near as we could figure, and massive for a mustang. His strength and confirmation pointed to him as an heir to being the dominant stallion of the herd. Gary and Running Wolf also took horses. The training began.

"Sally and I could do in three days what it took the boys six, when it came to training the males. We would have them following us around like lost puppy dogs. Talon took Sam, while Sally and I trained the other males, and the females went to Gary and Wolf. To train a horse, you must gain its confidence. The horse lets you know when this has happened. One sure sign is when he drops is head in front of you. If he holds his head high he is leery and not relaxed. When the head comes down, that's when the real training begins."

Beth spoke up, "That's true. When my horse, Amanda, dropped *her* head, we became great friends."

The class tittered at Beth's proclamation.

"Once their heads dropped and we could get a hackamore on them, we would lead them to water. After watering, we would take them to a much larger corral containing a pasture and let them graze. Now, I'm not going to bore you with every little detail of training a horse, but if you have an unruly one that you would like trained, I would be happy to do it for you."

"When we started moving the newly trained horses to join our herd, we came across another wild herd. Talon spied within this herd the second love of his life, Sally. She was a stunning strawberry roan mare. She looked like she was three or four years of age and slightly smaller than Sam. He told us he was going to put Sam to the test and cut out this mare for training. We watched from a hillside while he and Sam closed in on the herd. Once they noticed him they began to move, but they had not reacted fast enough. Talon had moved among them, and started chasing the strawberry. She finally broke free from the herd with Talon giving a steady chase. Gary and Wolf stayed with the new horses while Sally and I followed Talon. They ran for six hours straight. Our ponies were worn out, but Sam never faltered. We could see in the distance the strawberry finally gave up, allowing Talon to get a lasso on her. After catching up with him, we held Sam while Talon quickly fashioned a hackamore from another rope and got it on her. He led her with the hackamore back to Sam, climbed into the saddle, and we were off at a much slower pace to rejoin Gary and Wolf. Talon spent the next three weeks training Sally and Sam. Guess why he named her Sally? She was the prettiest horse he had ever seen and it reminded him of the prettiest girl he had ever seen, Sally Moore. Brothers can be so embarrassing, but they can't help it, they're male," T. T. finished.

The class broke out in laughter and applause.

Margie Braun spoke up, "T. T., my dad owns a horse that you can't train. So I challenge you to train him. We call him Deacon, and if you can train him, I'll stand up in front of the class and say, she did it, so she ain't bragging."

More giggling and laughter erupted, with a gasp here and there at the direct challenge.

"We always have a Fourth of July fox hunt and shooting contest at our estate in Maryland, and I am inviting you and Beth to join me there the third week in June. That will give you about three weeks to try to train Deacon."

"I don't know about Beth, but I'll ask if I can come," replied T. T. "And I'll train your horse. You can count on it."

The evening dinner bell reminded T. T. that she was starving. She put her schoolbooks away and hurried to the dining room. Uncle John was already seated when she entered the room. They were soon joined by Mary and Bertha.

"Uncle John, may I ask permission to do something?"

All ears perked up.

"Why, yes, sweetie."

"Margie Braun has invited Beth and me to her family's estate in Maryland for three weeks starting the third week in June through the Fourth of July week. May I go?"

"T. T., do you know who Margie Braun's father is?" asked Aunt Mary.

"No, Ma'am."

Uncle John spoke, "I'll talk to Clarence Braun to see what this would entail."

"John, if this is truly an invitation, we would certainly have to let her go. That is, if the invitation is for real."

"T. T., the answer is yes, we would let you go and I'll check out the invitation for you."

"Thank you, Uncle John. Aunt Bertha, they have horses to ride and on the afternoon of the Fourth they have a shooting contest, would you let me take my .38?"

"Let me check that for you, too," said Uncle John.

Aunt Bertha said, "If it checks out okay, I'll leave the .38 with Uncle John for you to have."

"What do you mean you'll leave it with Uncle John?"

"I've finished the business I was sent to the east to do, and I'm leaving to go home tomorrow."

"Oh, Aunt Bertha, I'll miss you so much," T. T. said tearfully. "What business did you complete?"

"I bought 120 Merino sheep from Spain, and 25 Rambouillet sheep, five rams and 20 ewes, shipped from France to Canada. The Merinos will be shipped to Medicine Bow from California by rail, and the Rambouillets will be shipped from Canada to Chicago by boat and on to Medicine Bow by rail. I'm hoping they'll beat me home. We're going to breed them to our Churros ewes and make wethers out of the male Churros. The only males we'll have will be the new breeds. All others born will be used for mutton. We are going to make an effort to produce finer wool and more of it, giving the Four T ranch another source of income. You're almost 16 now, and well on your way to being a very sought after young lady. The whole family is proud of you. Your big heart and willingness to work has already had an influence on your schoolmates, and particularly with Beth. I cannot tell you how thankful the MacDowells are for your influence on their daughter. Besides, when Uncle Jim and the boys drive the horses to Fort Dodge in the spring, someone has to stay home to watch after things."

T. T. really sobbed, bringing cascades of tears running down her cheeks. This would be the first time in her life that she would be apart from Aunt Bertha. Aunt Bertha held her close and kissed her checks.

"I've got more news for you," Aunt Bertha said.

T. T. perked up.

"According to the school's information, you will be attending a Christmas dance, and I have made arrangements for you to get dance instructions. Also, I thought it would be nice for you to give each one of your instructors a pair of lambskin mittens from Wyoming for a

Christmas gift. There is a pair of winter riding boots like yours coming for Beth, as a gift for her. Aunt Mary Grace is going to take you
shopping for your dress. That should take care of your needs for the
year at school. Uncle John said he would take care of the .38 for you."

Another kiss.

After Bertha's departure, the demands of schoolwork became the
routine. Home from school and two hours of study preparing for
school the next day became the norm. There was very little time to
socialize with Beth or the others. When the weather started to turn to
ice and snow, along with the days getting shorter, the work became
drudgery. The only things of fun were the dance instructions and the
thoughts of the upcoming dance. The Thanksgiving holiday gave a
brief respite from the routine. In two weeks, there would be a dance
and the start of the Christmas holiday. At last, there would be a
chance to rest. Even with the busy schedule, T. T. did manage to ride
on Saturdays, but often times Beth was unable to join her.

The dance included parents and siblings of the students. The last
few days there was intense instruction on how to perform socially.
They practiced daily on how to accept an invitation to dance and how
to carry on a conversation, by concentrating on the person to whom
they were talking. Finally, the day of the dance had arrived.

Uncle John and Aunt Mary Grace took their niece to her first
dance. The weather was cold but clear, making it a night to see with
all the stars aglow. The ballroom was decorated in the Christmas fashion, including an evergreen tree with sparkling ornaments. The
Christmas candles on the tables circling the dance floor made the
room seem very relaxing. Uncle John and Aunt Mary knew several of
the parents and were engaged in several conversations at once. Suddenly, Beth appeared at T. T.'s side. They hugged.

"Oh, Beth, you look so beautiful," T. T. gushed.

"Thank you, and so do you," said Beth.

"Oh Beth, I'm so scared. This is the first time I've worn these silk
slippers in public, and I don't know if they'll stay on my feet while
I'm dancing."

"Oh my, look at all the boys, T. T."

"Just remember to flirt — just a little — and they'll flock to you like honey."

They laughed.

Margie Braun entered the Ballroom with her parents and her older brother Jonathan. He was tall and slender, and very good looking. As expected, Margie was elegant. T. T. could see that Margie's dad and mother had made their way over to the MacDowells and her Aunt and Uncle. They seemed to be engaged in conversation and from the outward appearance they knew each other very well. The tables were round and sat 10. Guests were assigned their seats, and by chance, T. T.'s family sat with the Brauns and the MacDowells. T. T. spoke to Margie and gave her a gentle hug. So did Beth. In turn, she introduced them to her mother, dad and brother. Mrs. McIntosh approached the lectern. She gave a little ring of a bell. When the room fell quiet, she welcomed everyone. She also announced that dinner was being served, and wished everyone a good time. Mrs. Lamond came by the table and asked to speak to T. T. She excused herself and followed Mrs. Lamond.

"T. T., I want to thank you for the authentic, Indian-made lamb-skin mittens. They are so warm and I'll get a lot of use out of them," Mrs. Lamond said, smiling.

"You're welcome. They were made on the Four T ranch by Little Bear. She has made our winter coats, boots and mittens all my life." T.T said

"Again, thank you."

The servers came to each table with glasses of water and asked each person what they wanted to drink with dinner. Little attention was being paid on what was being ordered and so T. T. ordered coffee. The musicians started playing a wonderful melody, providing a soft background to the clamor of the ballroom. The servers began serving the meal and the hubbub changed to that of clanging silverware against china. It was in the middle of the meal when Mary noticed T. T. was drinking coffee. She shook her head, and you could read in her eyes, *will this child ever learn?*

Soon, the tables were cleared and the Christmas dessert arrived, along with a parade of young men visiting their table to complete their dance cards. The parents sat with pleasure, watching their blossoms handling the pressure of the attention. The boys would fumble, and Beth and Margie would giggle making the situation worse. T. T.'s approach was different. She would reach out and touch her suitor. This seemed to calm the awkward moment, allowing them to carry on with their request. She would also ask a question or two which seemed to relax them. The parents sat and admired how adroitly she handled each and every request.

Jonathan Braun was first on her list. As he escorted her to the dance floor, he explained he was a little out of practice and asked that she be kind to him with her assessment. She looked at him with a funny expression on her face and said, "You do know, this is the first dance that I have ever attended, and I'm wearing silk slippers that may not stay on my feet. It's so kind of you to worry about *my* assessment of *you*."

The music began to play. Jonathan put her at ease, guiding across the floor. She did well, and the parade began. Uncle John danced with her for the Father and Daughter Dance and later told Mary she danced extremely well, considering she had never danced. The night was a wonderful experience.

Mrs. McIntosh stopped by the table and addressed the parents.

"Has T. T. told you about what she did this week?"

"Why no," was Mary's response, expecting the worst.

"She saved us from a horrible accident one morning. As a group of students were arriving, one of the carriage drivers began to lose control of his horses. T. T. dropped her books on the porch, bounded down the steps and grabbed them just as they were beginning to run away with the carriage. There were several students in their path. If she had not acted so quickly, we would have had a terrible accident. I would say what she tells us about how she can handle horses is true, and in her words, 'if she can do it, it ain't bragging'."

T. T. turned several shades of red. The parents were still laughing as Jonathan took to the floor for another dance.

On the way home, Uncle John told her about his discussion with Clarence Braun.

"It seems it's true. You will be invited, along with Beth and others, to join them at their estate in June. It will be okay to bring your gun for their shooting contest. He did feel you would be out of place shooting, but at times the ladies do participate. He didn't know anything about your retraining Deacon. He said the horse was impossible to deal with, but he would have the stableman let you look at him. They have several other horses you can ride, and he said knows you'll have a good time."

The wait for the summer break seemed to take forever.

Chapter Six

Jonathan Braun was assigned the task of escorting Beth and T. T. to the Maryland estate. The estate was on the western side of the Susquehanna, just south of the Pennsylvania state line in Maryland. The trip would take most of the day, and if things didn't go well, maybe part of a second day. For Jonathan, what generally would have been a chore was going to be a pleasure, because he couldn't think of two prettier girls to be seen with. As they climbed into the carriage, he hoped there would be delays, giving him more time to be alone with them. The first half of the day went well, but as was common in train travel of the time, delays slowed their progress. It was the middle of the night when they arrived at the closest depot to the estate. The servants sent to meet them were already waiting, and soon they were off to the estate. The ride was pleasant. They arrived just as the staff was starting their day. They were escorted to their room. Beth immediately went to sleep, but T. T. wasn't tired. She made her way to the kitchen. Entering, she spotted a coffee pot and availed herself of a cup of the freshly brewed coffee. The servants looked at each other with quizzing eyes. *Who is this creature invading our space?* they wondered.

"Hi, I'm T. T. and this coffee is really good. When is breakfast?"

An older lady approached T. T. and said, "I'm Lara, the kitchen manager."

"Nice meeting you, Lara."

"Miss, our routine is to open the kitchen at 5:30 A.M. and to start serving the servants at 6 A.M. James, the valet, and Gibbs, the stable manager, is usually the first ones to eat. The servant dining room is through the door on the right. The door on the left is to the back porch of the kitchen and the area immediately behind the porch is the gardens and chicken yard. Past them is the lane to the stables. We grow most of our own fresh food here on the estate. The Brauns and their guests usually have their breakfast at 9:30 A.M."

"Oh, that's way too late for me," responded T. T.

"Would you like something now?" asked Lara.

"Do you have doughnuts?"

"No sweetie, I don't, but the biscuits will be ready shortly."

T. T. finished her coffee, and said, "I'm going to change my clothes and I'll be back for breakfast."

She scampered off to her room, and quickly changed into her work clothes. They looked like rags, compared to the clothes the servants were wearing, but these were horse-handing clothes and comfortable to wear. She reentered the kitchen, grabbed her cup and poured another cup of coffee. The biscuits were being placed on a serving platter for the servants. There were other platters with bacon and sausages already on the servants' table. Butter, strawberry jam, cream and sugar were there, too. T. T. grabbed a plate and fork and helped herself to a biscuit. James and Gibbs were sitting at the table and T. T. took a seat across from Gibbs. She introduced herself to them.

"Mister Gibbs, Miss Lara tells me you are the stable manager."

"Why, yes I am."

"When do you start your day at the stables? T.T inquired.

"Usually around 7 A.M," he replied.

"Will you show me this morning please?" she asked.

"Yes," he agreed, while giving her a puzzled look.

"I want to see the outlaw Deacon," she continued.

"Well, he's there to be seen."

"Do you have any western saddles?"

"I think I can find one or two," Mr. Gibbs smiled.

"Good."

"What are you going to do with a western saddle?" he asked

"I'm going to retrain the Deacon."

"That'll be the day."

"You're right, and that day is today," T. T. announced, confident-ly.

"Does Mister Braun know about this?"

"Yes, that's why I'm here, to train the Deacon."

"Has anyone told you that he hasn't been ridden the last two years?" asked Gibbs.

"So they say, but that's not a problem with me. Just point me to him."

"Well, I can do that."

T. T. finished her sausage and biscuit and had started on her third cup of coffee before Gibbs finally was ready to move to the barns. *I can tell these folks never lived on a real ranch,* she thought.

The stable manager stood and asked T. T. to follow. The morning was beautiful and the sound of the barnyard was music to T. T.'s ears. Roosters starting their day, cow bells chiming their morning arrival to the pasture, pigs squealing at Gibbs' approach and the birds singing sounded like the home she really missed.

"How many hands do you have working here?" she asked.

"I have eight working this summer."

"This estate is not at all what I thought it would be. There is more forest and it's much hillier than I expected. There is a sizable amount of open land, but it is back away from the river."

"There is a dense forest and a sharp drop to the river. The bluff is rolling on top and easier to clear. Any land cleared to the river has a tendency to erode over time so to control that, we've kept the forest. There are several riding trails through the forest to enjoy while you're here. The Fourth of July fox hunt will take place on top of the bluff and extend to the far western edge of the estate."

"Do you have a round training ring?" T. T. wanted to know.

"Yes we do, it is quite large— about forty feet across."

"That'll be just right. Do you have a long rope?"

"How long does it need to be?"

"Oh, I would like one at least 25 feet," T. T. answered.

"We have one, what else do you need?"

"Do you have a western saddle and a halter?" she asked.

"We can fix you up. You *do* know this horse is the meanest animal in the state, don't you?"

They walked into a barn larger than any barn T. T. had ever seen, and it was cleaner than any she had ever worked in. You could tell Gibbs took pride in his work.

"How many horses do you have here?"

"About 20, mostly thoroughbreds we have converted from the track to hunter jumpers. Deacon is a large black thoroughbred with one small white patch and a cowlick just above, between his eyes. Here he is in this stall," Gibbs told her.

He was a stunning animal. He was much larger than T. T. was expecting.

"Please put him in the ring for me," she stated.

Gibbs went to the far end of the barn to open the door to the path leading to the large pasture. He continued to the first pen on the right and opened its gate. Returning into the barn, he picked up a lead rope off a peg by the door and proceeded to open Deacon's stall door. He put the rope through a ring on the halter Deacon was wearing and led him from the stall to the ring. He placed him in the ring and closed the gate.

"He didn't act mean." T. T. observed.

"He knows me," Gibbs explained. "When I didn't enter the stall with a saddle, he felt safe. Now, what are *you* going to do?"

"Stay and watch," she said.

"I think I'd better," he answered.

T. T. picked up the 25-foot rope, opened the gate and walked into the ring. The Deacon just stared at her, his head held high. She walked to the center of the ring and gave a couple of kissing sounds, then turned her back and walked to the rails opposite of where he was standing. She slowly turned to see what he was doing. He hadn't moved. She returned to the center of the ring and tossed the coiled rope at his hind legs while holding on to one end. The Deacon scampered away from the rope and followed the ring around to the right. She recoiled the rope and threw it at his hind legs a second time. This kept him moving around the ring. After several tosses, driving him several circuits around the ring, he finally stopped and looked at her. She turned her back and walked to the opposite side of the ring. When she turned, he hadn't moved. He just stood there, staring at her. She repeated the process.

Gibbs had never witnessed such as this before in training horses. He wondered how long she would be able to keep this going.

The sun was getting high in the morning sky, and then T. T. got the response she wanted. When she turned her back, Deacon moved toward her and followed her as she moved to the side of the ring. He continued to follow her as she moved around the ring. Slowly, she turned and moved closer to him while giving him kissing sounds. He didn't run from her and she reached and touched him on his nose giving it a very soft gentle rub. Then she moved away again and he followed. Again, she rubbed his nose, only this time she rubbed the side of his face, too. Deacon was enjoying the conversation. He was moving his jaws like he was eating, and she knew he was depending on her for protection and was telling her that. Even at a closer distance, she gently rubbed his neck and the back of his ears and then moved to his eyes. He loved every gentle caress. Without him realizing, she had put the rope around his neck and tied a bowline knot to secure the loop. Gently she pulled the rope toward her as she backed away from him. He followed and she put her hand on his nose and stopped him. Gently she went through the rubbing routine. In less than three hours she had Deacon following her around like a little lost puppy. She led him out of the ring and back to his stall, where she released him.

Gibbs couldn't believe his eyes.

"Let's go get a cup of coffee and a cold biscuit or two and talk about what I'm going to do this afternoon," T.T proposed.

On the way back to the kitchen, Gibbs thought to himself, *she's got me following her, too.* When he entered the kitchen, he winked at Lara.

"She's for real. It took her about three hours to put Deacon under a spell."

The staff laughed.

For the next three days, T. T. was up early and in the kitchen to help with breakfast for the staff. Her doughnuts were a hit. She shared the preparation work like she was one of them, and soon had them under her wiles. The training of Deacon changed his demeanor. The hands commented on how well behaved he had become. One of the hands reported seeing T. T. in the creek with him, giving him a cool bath. They had never seen anyone treat horses as she did. Her morning work ethic changed to an afternoon social façade, around the other invited guests. With a few afternoon rides, she was able to determine the riding abilities of the guests and match them to a horse. She never rode Deacon in their presence.

One morning, Clarence Braun entered the kitchen to find T. T. and the staff finishing their breakfasts. T. T., in her usual manner, was dunking a doughnut in her coffee. He sat down across from her at the table, and asked for a cup of coffee. Lara poured it for him. He was there to eat breakfast and ordered what he wanted. Janie started to prepare his meal.

"What are these?" he asked, pointing to a platter of doughnuts.

"They're doughnuts that Miss T. T. fixed for us," replied Lara. "She cooks them fresh every morning."

Clarence reached over, picked one up and bit into it. The expression on his face, after the taste, was priceless.

"Why, Lara, has she showed you how to cook these?"

Lara answered him with a question, "Do you like them?"

"Why yes, I do."

"Want to try one of her fried pies, left over from yesterday?" she asked.

She placed one in front of him. He cut it with a fork and took a bite. Again, a classic expression formed on his face.

"Gibbs, has she looked at the Deacon?" Mr. Braun queried.

T. T. was sitting there, all ears, not knowing what to expect.

"Well, Mister Braun, she has been working on him all week. She's in the barn no later than 7 A.M., and generally works with him three to four hours before joining your other guests in the afternoon."

"How is the Deacon treating her? You know, I told her he was mean and to be careful."

"Well they got in at about 5:30 A. M. and while the others went to bed, she came to the kitchen. She insisted that I take her to meet Deacon. And I did. And I stayed and watched. In three hours she had Deacon under her spell. You won't believe the change"

"You mean she's trained him?"

"Yes, to the extent of giving a cool bath in the creek one morning this week."

Clarence looked at T. T. and chuckled. "Well what other surprises will you show us while you're here?"

"I can't think of any right now. I really love your estate. Please don't tell anyone about the Deacon, because I want it to be a surprise for the Fourth."

"Little lady, they won't hear it from me. Have you looked at any of the other horses?" Clarence asked.

"That I have. You have a wonderful stable of well cared for horses. Are you planning to breed any to Deacon? On that, I could make some recommendations," T.T answered.

"When I first bought him that was my intention, but he had such a bad demeanor, I didn't want to risk it."

"His attitude was from the poor training he had received. The Indians believe in talking to the wild things to bring them into harmony with all the creatures around them. Our Indian friends have shared with us the whispering way of training horses. It's a loving, gentle method that makes up part of the herd. If you watch wild horses, the herd moves together. If they are running from danger, it's all together, never running into each other. When turning, it's together as one body. It's beautiful to watch. When training, you have to gain their confidence that you'll protect them. Would you like to go for a ride with me this morning and I'll show you what the Deacon is doing? I'll also show you which mares I think you should breed."

"Gibbs, saddle us a couple of horses. Let's go for a ride." said Clarence.

"Yes, sir," Gibbs said with a smile.

The three left the kitchen for the barn. Clarence watched as T. T. pulled Deacon from his stall and saddled him. Gibbs brought forward two more mounts and they left the stables for a romp around the holding pasture. T. T. pointed to six mares, explaining why she picked them. Clarence and Gibbs were impressed she knew so much about the herd. She also pointed out several horses she would sell and replace, if they wanted. Her explanations showed a deep understanding of what was happening within the herd.

The fact that T. T. was riding without putting pressure on the reins impressed Clarence and Gibbs. They noticed that when she moved her body, Deacon would respond.

"T. T., do you think Deacon would be a good match for these mares?"

"For the ones I pointed out to you, but not for the others."

"What do you think about our oldest mare, Babs?"

"You keep her. She controls the herd for you. She's also a good role model for the younger mares. Watch, they look to her for leadership. It's the same in the wild. Every herd is controlled by a dominant female."

Clarence and Gibbs had never heard such candid talk from a young lady before. After hearing her reasoning, they knew she knew more than they did. The morning romp around the estate brought a great feeling to Clarence. He couldn't remember the last time he felt so relaxed. Entering the barn, he looked at T. T. and invited her to walk with him back to the house. She refused, saying she needed to spend time with Deacon rubbing him down after the ride. She explained it was bonding time.

Chapter Seven

At Friday afternoon tea, Margie looked at T. T., "How have you enjoyed your visit?"

T. T. replied. "It's been so wonderful. It's a beautiful estate."

"Sunday is your day, are you going to be able to ride Deacon?"

Laughing, T. T. responded, "Are you ready to say 'she did it, so she wasn't bragging'?"

"Everyone I have asked says they don't know if you can ride the Deacon."

"You'll see soon enough. My big worry is my shooting. I haven't practiced in months. But I guess it's like riding a horse. Once you learn how, you never forget."

Early Sunday morning, people started to arrive for the brunch and the fox hunt. T. T. was in the kitchen helping with the preparations by frying doughnuts and other breakfast foods. The table looked fabulous. About 8 A.M., she left the kitchen to dress for the fox hunt. She was going to ride with the western saddle. She and Beth were the only two females wearing equestrian pants for ladies— mostly worn in jumping competitions. The kennel master had brought the dogs. They were eager to start the hunt. The hunt master sounded a starting warning and T. T. left the stables riding Deacon. She had his mane and tail braided, and his legs were fitted with white stockings. He looked fit for a king. She easily guided him to where the riders were gathered to start the hunt. When Margie and the others saw T. T., their jaws drooped. Other riders that didn't know T. T. but knew Deacon, couldn't believe Clarence would let a young lady ride him. The hunt master signaled the release of the dogs. Off they ran, signaling their break to freedom with choruses of yelps.

T. T. joined Beth, riding alongside her in a custodial fashion. She reminded Beth that these horses were trained to jump over obstacles. The first was a dead tree trunk and Beth negotiated it without any problems. The hunt was progressing into a more hazardous part of the estate. T. T. was watching her friends in a parental fashion, fearing for their safety. She noticed that Margie had dropped her reins over the last jump and she closed in to help her. To get to where she needed to be to help, Deacon had to make a tremendous, breathtaking leap over a huge fallen tree, only to cross a deep gully a few feet beyond. Those seeing the jump were petrified until he safely landed on the other side of the gully. T. T. was closing in on Margie and was beside her over the next hazard. She grabbed the horse's halter, pulling her to a stop. Then, she gathered the reins, tying them in a knot so they wouldn't fall to the side of the horse if she dropped them again.

"Let's join the hunt," she shouted to Margie.

Margie nodded and off they went. The hunt lasted for about an hour and a half. T. T. thoroughly enjoyed the ride. She hadn't had an occasion to ride at such a thrilling pace since leaving Wyoming. The ride back to the staging yard was a quiet walk compared to the hunt. Margie moved over to where Beth and T. T. were.

"Thank you for saving me," she said to T. T.

"You're welcome. You did great to be riding side saddle like you were. You need to drop that and really start to ride. I think I can talk your father into letting you do it," T. T. said.

"Would you?" she asked.

"Yes."

"It's the only way to ride, Margie," said Beth, who nodded at the gentleman who had just joined their little group.

"Well, young lady, I saw that jump you took Deacon over," the newcomer said. "There's not another horse or rider out here that could have made that jump."

"Thank you, sir."

"That was one of dad's greatest friends. Mister Charles Harrison. He'll probably tell dad I dropped my reins."

"Yeah, what is it with dropping the reins?" T. T. asked Margie.

"I didn't think about tying them. One more jump and I'm afraid I would have been off the horse."

"You did a good job of hanging on," T. T. observed.

"Thanks again, T. T."

Gibbs took the reins from T. T. when she got closer.

"I saw the jump," said Gibbs. "I'll take the Deacon and give him a gentle rub down cool him off. He earned it today. Enjoy yourself. I'll take care of him."

"Thanks, Mr. Gibbs."

More of the guests started to gather around T. T., expressing their disbelief of that jump ever being made. Mister Braun came over and gave her a big hug.

"Mister Braun, we need to get Margie off the sidesaddle."

"I think we can do that if you teach her how to ride."

"I would love to teach her."

"Margie, your dad said you could leave the sidesaddle."

"Oh T. T., you are so wonderful. I can't believe he agreed."

"Have you practiced your speech?"

"Not only have I practiced, but I can't wait to give it."

Jonathan Braun came over and told T. T. that his dad had her gun for the shooting contest. The noon meal was finished, and Clarence announced the shooting contest would begin in a few minutes. He urged those wanting to participate in the shooting to join him at the judges' tent. The brackets were formed. Pistols, rifles, and shotguns were the sections and lots were drawn to place the shooting order.

T. T. asked if she could borrow a rifle and a shotgun. Jonathan made the weapons available to her. The first round with the pistol would be at 40 feet. Three shots were to be fired in the initial round, and the best 10 would move forward. The firing line was at the base of a natural knoll, which allowed viewers to use blankets to sit on the grass and picnic while watching. There were 10 shooting positions.

For the pistol competition, there were 34 entrants, with T. T. being the only female.

The first 10 participants went to the line, with instructions to fire three shots within five minutes. Of the first shooters, three had all center hits on the target. The second group did better, with five moving on in the competition. The third group had none. Four shooters were trying to fill the final two spots. T. T. was among the four. She fired three shots with her .38 Colt in less than a minute and retired from the line. She had centered all three and was one of the two to move to the next round. Same rules for the second round: three shots within five minutes and five would move to the next round. Eventually they made it to the last five, and T. T. was still shooting.

The five took their positions on the firing line. Again T. T. fired three shots in less than a minute— all three centered. One of the shooters only got two in the center and was disqualified from the contest. The next round saw the target moved back another five feet. The four approached, with all hitting the center three times. Again, the target was moved back. This time, two were disqualified. It came down to T. T. and another guest.

The rules changed and the targets were brought to the original position. The challenge was for each to shoot and if both centered all three the winner would be determined by the shooter taking the least time. They were to shoot separately so as not to present any confusion on the timing. T. T. drew the short straw and elected to go first. She approached the firing line. The first shot started the timing. She aimed and fired three shots in eleven seconds— all hitting the center. The other competitor shot in nine seconds, but had only one center. T. T. had won the pistol contest.

The rules for the rifles were different, in that it was match shooting. Two would compete at a time and one had to be eliminated. This brought five pairs to the line at a time. Each pair had a deciding judge, who would determine the closest three shots to the center. The targets were set at 60 feet. For the rifles, they had an odd entrant, T. T. It was decided that the last three entrants would shoot against each other. The eliminations went smoothly. The last three, including T. T., were at the firing line. T. T. fired her three shots. They hit center but high and to the right on the center circle. She moved through, while the other two had failed to place three in the center.

The targets were moved to 90 feet. T. T. moved through again, shooting against two others. T. T., seeing where her first shots were falling, changed her aim for the second round and placed three in the center and moved through to the next round. There were only 10 shooters remaining. The heads up match would draw the competition down to five. Again T. T. made it through. They drew lots to see which of the shooters would be in the group of three. The targets remained at a 90 feet. T. T. got the honor. She failed to place three center shots, and was eliminated.

The shotguns competition was about shooting thrown clay targets. T. T. took the firing line first, with her pistol holstered. The target was thrown and she drew, fired and hit the target. She was firing birdshot pistol ammo. The crowd didn't know it and thought she was hitting the targets with one piece of lead. They were "oohing and aahing" at her success. She lost in the second round because the pistol shot couldn't carry the distance needed to hit the targets. But, winning the pistol contest made it a good range day.

Clarence called for T. T. to come forward. She came to the front. Then he announced that she would give a western-style draw and shoot demonstration. They moved five targets to about 20 feet of the firing line. She took her position on the line. One of the judges of the contest placed five playing cards in the center of each target, standing 20 feet away, and two feet apart. She checked her pistol to make sure how many rounds were loaded. There were five, and they were regular rounds. She looked at the judge and said, "When you say draw, start the watch, and I'll start my draw."

He nodded in agreement. She was poised and ready.

"Draw," he yelled.

She drew her pistol and fired five shots in a slow eleven seconds. Being out of practice, she didn't try to hurry. The judge walked forward and replaced the cards, while collecting the ones that she had used.

"Five hits in eleven seconds. Anyone want to challenge?"

A guest held up his hand while approaching the firing line.

"What is your name?" he asked.

"My name is Ben Iverson. Mister James Talbot brought me along for the festivities today as his guest. If you will remember, I won the rifle contest."

"Oh yes, so you did," said Clarence. "The cards are set. So, take your position on the firing line and await the signal."

When Iverson signaled he was ready, the judge gave the signal. He drew and fired, hitting all the targets in nine seconds.

"All hit in nine seconds," announced the judge.

"Miss T. T., would you like to try and better that score?"

She nodded that she would. Again, on the firing line, she checked her loads while taking her position. At the signal, she drew and fired hitting all targets in eight seconds.

The judge announced the score. He looked at Iverson, who wanted another try to beat her score. Before he took his position, T. T. spoke up, "you know I can do it in five seconds, can you?"

He looked at her. "Can't be done," he said.

"If I can do it, it ain't bragging."

"I can't do it, so go ahead and show us you can."

She checked her loads and took the position on the firing line. At the signal she pulled and fired five shots.

"She fired in five seconds," yelled the judge. "Now let's see if she hit the targets." "She did, she did hit all five!"

Iverson looked at her. "I'm from Dodge City, Kansas, and I have never seen anyone draw that fast. Was the fight on the train a fair fight?"

T. T. turned white. "What do you mean?" she asked.

"Did you give them a warning before you drew on my cousin?" Iverson asked.

"Why, no, I didn't. I didn't think I had to since their guns were already drawn. My only advantage was they didn't expect anyone to put up a fight," T. T. replied.

"You mean to stand there and tell me their guns were already drawn?" Iverson asked.

"Well, if you mean by being drawn and pointed at me, why yes they were. They were lined up like ducks in a row. Neither got off a shot, they were so surprised."

"How do you think you would do against me?" he asked.

"If you can't do five in five, you would be dead before you fired a shot. You know I'm sorry about your cousin, but he was robbing innocent folks, including women and children. He just didn't give a care about those he was robbing, and there was no way to tell if he would hurt someone or not. I figured he would and took action. If you have a grudge, we can settle it now. We even have a judge that can declare it fair. One rule though, we stand 10 feet apart. I want to see your buttons clearly. I think I can hit three before you drop. What do you say?" T. T. challenged.

"You're bluffing."

T. T. reloaded her pistol. Sliding it into her holster, she stepped back two steps. "Take your time, and when you're ready, draw."

About this time, the judge was waving for Clarence to come over. Guests close to the conversation started to move away in panic. It looked as if there was going to be a real gunfight at the party. James Talbot got there at the same time as Clarence.

"What's going on, Iverson?" asked Talbot.

"You know that I was searching for the person who killed my cousin in Nebraska. Well, I found her. She's standing right before your eyes. She's bracing me."

"What's going on T. T.?" asked Clarence.

"It's true. I did kill two men in Nebraska while they were trying to rob the train passengers. Which one was his cousin I don't know, but in the West, it's a tradition for family members to go after the person who killed their kin. He's thinking I don't have the nerve to face him. 'He was wrong' will read on his tombstone. And if he succeeds, I have a Texas Ranger brother, the Wyoming Kid, he'll have to deal with."

Iverson shifted his weight. T. T. looked him in his eyes and she could tell he wasn't ready to die. The closeness was making him uncomfortable. She could tell he hadn't counted on his prey being this good with a gun. He had planned on shooting fish in a barrel.

"What are you thinking about Iverson? You have already have broken several local laws by approaching this girl with the idea of killing her. Hell, man, in the East, killing a robber in the act of a crime is not condemnable. Besides, you have ruined my reputation among my friends for bringing you."

Iverson looked at T. T. "I'll be seeing you, missy."

"No you won't. Besides, I'm going to have my brother look you up the next time he comes through Dodge City. You had your chance, you yellow piece of crap."

Talbot grabbed Iverson by the arm and pulled him away. Two of the men listening followed behind, to make sure they left.

Clarence looked at T. T. "Would you have tried to shoot him?"

"No sir, I would have killed him. Mister Braun, I thought something was up when he challenged me in the contest. When I showed him five in five, it rattled him. Then he got courage to brace me. He didn't plan on a fight. When he confirmed I had killed his cousin, he knew I would kill and that I was faster than he. When I laid down the ground rule of 10 feet apart, he knew he would die. I could look into his eyes and tell he had lost his nerve. I can tell you he is truly thankful his friend stepped into the fray."

"Mercy, is there anything you haven't done?" Clarence asked.

"I've never been married," she retorted, smiling.

"You're never going to be, if you keep killing people," he observed.

"Truly, Mister Braun, I'm so sorry I brought this to your party. I'm so sorry. Believe me, it brings no joy to my heart to know that I've killed someone."

A little tear came in her eye. Clarence reached out and put his arm around her. "Sweetie, you're welcome here anytime. I can't think of a finer person to have in my home."

"Who is Talbot, Mister Braun?"

"He's involved with a company he calls The Combine. Up until last year, they were shipping cattle from western Kansas to the east. Now they are moving their operation to Wyoming to start raising their own cattle, rather than buying them. That's all I know. Other than they used our schooners out of Mexico to Cuba for cattle, and rum and molasses from Cuba to the east coast."

The picnicking continued into early Sunday evening. Just at sundown, the guests started leaving. T. T. pitched in with the staff to clear the trash from the yard. She had been up early to help the staff prepare the Sunday brunch, and they insisted she leave the cleanup to them. She thanked them for a wonderful day.

Margie and Beth came over to her and Beth said, "I asked my daddy to tell your folks you were staying another week. Was that okay? That means we'll get to ride together for another week."

Tired as T. T. was, she just nodded.

"We'll start training you tomorrow, Margie," Beth said. They all laughed.

Clarence entered the kitchen early and sat down across the table from Gibbs and T. T. As tired as she was from yesterday, she had managed to gather enough strength to make it to the kitchen early to help the staff prepare breakfast. She was sort of leaning on one elbow to keep her head up while she dunked her doughnut in her coffee.

"Child, didn't anyone tell you at finishing school not to dunk doughnuts in your coffee?" asked Clarence.

"Yes, they have, but I thought that rule applied only *after* they finished me."

Everyone in the kitchen laughed.

"Sweetie, when I get to Philly I'll get in touch with your parents to let them know you'll be staying a little longer. I want to deeply thank you for helping Margie during the hunt. She could have been seriously hurt, and you prevented it. By the way, Gibbs tells me two of the mares you pointed out are coming into season. Do you think he'll have any trouble handling Deacon?" Clarence asked.

"Why no, he should be okay," T. T. answered.

"You'll need to ride a different horse this week, then."

"That's okay, you have plenty of horses from which to pick."

"About yesterday, are you okay?" Clarence asked.

"Yes, sir," T. T. replied.

"Good. I truly want you to be."

The last day, she did get to ride Deacon. She finished her time with him with an extensive rub down and said her goodbyes.

In Philly, the girls started a riding circle, which included Margie, as well as three other girls in the class. They would get together and travel from one home to another. One of the rules of the club was: no eastern ladies' saddles allowed. This helped them pass the dog days of summer. School was about to start.

Chapter Eight

It was the first assembly of classes and the first speaker, by request, was Margie. "When we left school last spring, I had given T. T. a public challenge. It was because some of her stories were hard to believe. So I challenged her to come to our estate in Maryland and train Deacon, the meanest horse in the area. I am now reporting on the outcome of that challenge. She did it, which means …"

"She ain't bragging," was chanted by the whole class. The assembly broke out into laughter, including Mrs. Ledbetter and Mrs. McIntosh. There seemed to be a lot of pressure lifted from the instructors and the students. Miss Talon Two Finley was the real deal when it came to horses and firearms. The feat was witnessed by four others in the class. The school year started with a bang.

Mrs. Newport's first assignment was for them to bring a letter to class for whom they were the addressee. They were going to read the letters aloud and discuss letter writing. The timing couldn't have been better for T. T. She had received a letter from her brother at the end of August. It was really interesting and something the class would enjoy hearing. She was sure if it was just the letter there would be doubts about the content. The letter supplied the answer to any doubts, because it included a newspaper article describing the scene from an unbiased point of view. T. T.'s turn came quickly, and she approached the lectern. Taking the letter from the envelope, she unfolded and placed it on the lectern.

"This is a letter that I received before school started from my twin brother. He lives in Brownsville, Texas, and is the youngest Texas Ranger ever. His letter is his own account of the actions he engaged in while on assignment. This letter is interesting because there is a newspaper article enclosed describing the same event. So we get to hear it in his words and the words of a reporter— so we can compare the two."

Dearest Two,

I cannot tell you how much I miss you. I never dreamed we would be apart so long without seeing each other. I miss you and love you. To catch you up on what happened this spring and summer, we started the drive to

Fort Dodge, Kansas, and found the army wanted us to move the herd to Fort Concho, Texas. They paid an extra $2 a head for me to help with the move. Uncle Jim wanted me to take the money and come see you this summer, but I got sidetracked.

While I was being escorted to Galveston to catch a boat to the northeast, I ran into trouble with some outlaws. This was over shooting Rags McLeod. You know, I promised Gary I would kill McLeod if I ever ran across him— for what he did to Gary's family. And I did. Anyway, my guide to Galveston, an army Indian scout being reassigned to the Texas Rangers, helped me dodge them on the trail. When they couldn't find me, they settled on killing an entire family for their 200 head of cattle. When I saw what they did to this family, I knew I needed to join the Rangers and search for these killers. Believe it or not, the Rangers let me join, and the first two weeks I spent training other new recruits how to shoot, and some to ride.

My first assignment was to meet Cat the Indian scout in Brownsville, with orders to apprehend as many outlaws as we could until the main force of Rangers got there. Before going to Brownsville, I was sent to deliver a message to a large rancher by the name of Patterson. His daughter Mimi gave me a letter for her friend in Brownsville. Her name was Billie Jo Wise. When I got there, I noticed a fight brewing in the middle of the plaza, Cat on one side and three outlaws on the other. They were bracing him, and I knew I needed to help him. To get there unnoticed, I went through the mercantile store the Wises owned. While walking through, I delivered the letter. Then I joined Cat. I told him I would take the hombre on the right, standing on the cantina's steps. Since there were three, I told him he could have the one on the left and we would meet in the middle and both shoot the third man. He said that sounded good to him.

On my first day of a first real assignment, I found myself closing the distance on these Greasers. My target went for his gun. As he did, two more Greasers burst through the bat wing doors of the cantina. My first two shots dropped the first Greaser. The two coming down the steps behind him both fired at me. One hit me in the right leg, saving my life because the shot staggered me and caused the shot of the second to hit me under the brim of my hat giving me a wound across the top of my head. The bullet thumped me pretty good. About that time, another shot sizzled around my left ribcage. The three had knocked me to the ground. I was trying to return fire while on my back. I put three shots in the second Greaser, and drew my belly gun. Blood was flooding my eyes from the scalp wound, but I managed to fire five shots at the third man, and then I drew my long barrel and fired at the bat wings just above where I could see the legs of another Greaser coming out. He staggered forward through the doors firing his pistol into the porch before he fell. Another one burst through the doors and headed for his horse, which was tied up at the end on the porch to my right. My head was pounding and my eyes were blurred. I don't know if I hit him or not. I did kill one of the horses at the hitching rail. Then I passed out for I don't know how long. Then I rallied and tried to get up but went down again. They tell me that I would come and go out of this fog just long enough to take some liquid to eat.

When I finally woke up, I rose up on my elbows and looked under the covers at my body. My head felt like someone had driven a railroad spike into it and they were still pounding it. Then I heard giggles. It was Billie Jo and Mimi. I asked them what they were laughing about and they told me that all wounded cowboys check to see if they still had a love handle when they first woke up. I tell you, Two, I wished I hadn't asked. I could feel my face burning. Mrs. Wise came in and ran them out. When they were leaving, Billy Jo yelled out 'It still works.' My face turned red again I could feel it. Mrs. Wise told me to pay them no attention. I asked her who undressed me and she said the doctor and she, but the girls had been feeding, bathing and other things that needed to be done. My face turned red again.

It took several weeks to fully recover, and in that time I fell in love with Billie Jo. While Cat and I were on patrol toward Rio Grande City, a Greaser gang led by a killer named Jackson Slager raided Brownsville. He burned the store and killed Billie Jo.

Cat, another Ranger named Lowry and I found the gang in Mexico, gambling and drinking at a cantina. We stepped in and killed or wounded the whole gang, but

Slager wasn't there. We took their belongings back to Texas with us. I think we accounted for 10 of the gang that night, and I picked up another wound in the right leg—about the same spot as the first. It wasn't as bad, though. Since then, we have made several raids into Mexico, killing any suspected gang member we could find. This action did help to cut down on the raids the gangs were making into Texas. Now I'm on the trail of Slager, who seems to be heading north to continue his work for something called The Combine.

His crew trapped me in the mountains of New Mexico, but I fought my way out. Worked my way back on his trail and found myself in La Junta, Colorado. I was waiting there for Cat and Lowry to join me when Slager sent one of his henchmen here to kill me. They called him Bulldog. No one knew his real name, and it's too late to ask now. A rancher and two of his wranglers were on his trail for stealing cattle in Texas and they had braced him. I could tell they weren't up to the task, so I stepped in and handled it for them. He was fast. His last shot hit the floor about two feet in front of me. I unbuttoned his buttons. I gave his belongings to the Texans.

This sort of catches you up on my summer. I miss you.

Love, Too

T. T. unfolded the newspaper article and held it up where the class could see it.

"This is the only letter I have received from my brother in a year. He seems to be so old to me. Shall we discuss his letter?"

Mrs. Newport approached the lectern. "I will lead the discussion. Someone tell me who the letter was from."

Connie spoke up, "it was from T. T.'s brother Too, and we know him from last year as Talon Too."

"Correct. Where was it from?"

The class answered, "La Junta, Colorado."

"What do we know about La Junta, Colorado?"

"One person by the name of Bulldog is buried there." The class laughed.

"Why was Talon there?" asked Mrs. Newport.

"He was on the trail of an outlaw by the name of Slager," another classmate answered.

"Why was he after Slager?"

"He is a Texas Ranger, and they sent him," said Ruth.

"I think it was more than that," said Beth. "He was there because Slager had killed Billie Jo, the girl he fell in love with. He's on a quest. How romantic."

"What else did we learn from this letter?" Mrs. Newport continued.

"He has killed several men and he has been wounded at least four times," said Margie. "I've heard of this Combine before, somewhere."

It dawned on T. T. that was the name Mister Braun used for Talbot's business. She wondered if the cattle coming from Kansas were stolen. Now, according to the letter and Mister Braun, The Combine was moving its operation to Wyoming.

"Very good, class, you were listening. Your next assignment is to tell about an act of compassion you have witnessed."

On the way home, Beth spoke, "T. T. your brother hasn't grown old. He's still the stuttering, shy, young cowboy you left in Wyoming. Billie Jo and Mimi showed you that, by the way he told you how he reacted to finding out they cared for him is such a personal way."

"Oh Beth, I love you for saying that." A tear came to her eye. "Remember, I told you I hoped no one would feel the pain of killing someone. Now that Talon has, it seemed as if he were getting used to it."

"But T. T., it was for the right reason, and I feel he has separated it from his true nature." Beth offered.

"Oh, I hope so."

The next day, T. T. started her new presentation, reading aloud from the paper, "An Act of Compassion, by T. T. Finley."

"In the winter 1867, the Sioux Indians were in a war with the settlers to protect their lands along the Powder River in north central Wyoming. It was a brutal war. Talon and I were eight at the time. We were snowed in at the Four T Ranch. Aunt Bertha had the hands move to the main ranch house because it was warmer than the bunk house. She was cooking our favorite stew, and the aroma filled the house and made our stomachs growl. Uncle Jim went out to fill one of the oaken water buckets with snow to melt for drinking water, when he noticed a light shining through the sideboards of the main barn. He thought one of the hands had left a lamp burning. So, he went to the barn to put it out. When he cracked the door open to slip into the barn, he was greeted by an Indian brave. The Indian's pony was dying. Uncle Jim approached the pony to see if there was anything he could for the animal. The brave didn't put up a fight because he appeared exhausted from his trek through the snowdrifts to get to our barn. Then a baby started to cry. Hunkered down in one of the stalls were an Indian squaw and two children. Uncle Jim walked over to the woman and picked up her baby. He motioned for the Indians to follow him. They followed him to the main cabin. Seeing how cold they were, Aunt Bertha went to work making a warm place for them, next to the open hearth. She found some of our old clothes and instructed Uncle Jim to get them onto the older child. She gave the Indian woman one of her wool dresses and helped her get into it. Then she placed some wool socks on her feet. She stripped the baby and got her wrapped in a wool blanket with a cotton lining. While she was handling the woman, Uncle Jim got a pair of his winter underwear for the brave. He found some old pants to give to him, along with a pair of wool socks.

"Aunt Bertha served the stew. She made sure the Indians were fed, along with us. The warmth of the fireplace and the food brought the Indians around to talking. They were almost in shock from their ordeal with the snowdrifts. The brave could speak English, although not well, Uncle Jim could understand him, though. His village had been attacked, and he had escaped with his family. His pony had carried them as far as it could go, with his final collapse in our barn. Uncle Jim sent two of the hands to see if they could do something for the pony. That was our introduction to Calling Eagle, his squaw Little Bear, his son Running Wolf, and baby daughter Little Feather. Aunt Bertha and Uncle Jim's compassion saved their lives and created a great friendship between our families. There were many unexpected, yet positive consequences. Little Bear gave Aunt Bertha an adult companion to share the lonely ranch life. Calling Eagle taught us to hunt and fish with Indian methods. He taught us how to trap the wild mustangs and to train them into working ponies. He came up with the idea to keep the breeding herd of cattle at the head waters of the streams running through the Four T Ranch. This allowed us to let the feeding herd move closer to our shipping point as they grew older, and from overgrazing our range. When Uncle Jim introduced the Churro Sheep on the Four T, Calling Eagle became the lead herdsman. Running Wolf and Little Feather went to school and learned how to read and write. All these things came from a single act of compassion."

T. T. collected her notes and returned to her seat.

"That was a very good essay, T. T." said Mrs. Newport. "Our next assignment is to stand and deliver a talk you have written—about what you have done to support your family."

T. T. agonized over what to write about. She finally plunged into a subject dear to her heart. When it came her time to present, she approached the lectern.

"The title of my essay is *What I Have Done to Support My Family*. From about ten years of age, Talon, Running Wolf, and I started to hunt, fish, and trap wild mustangs on our own. We had received expert guidance from Calling Eagle. He taught us to fish by using traps, and we managed to catch enough fish to have a good fish fry at least once a week. The method of trapping was simple. Using thick sticks, we would fence an area in deep water. This fence would form a large arc in the water which turned into a spiral in shallow water. As the fish swam along the fence they would find themselves in a shallow pool not knowing how to swim out. We would go to the shallow pools with a seine and pull them from the water. Large fish we kept, and small ones we released. The streams running through the Four T Ranch gave us plenty of spots to set our traps. Sometimes, we did it the sporting way with a line and a hook."

"We learned how to hunt with bows and arrows. About every two weeks one of us would get a deer. This we used for making our moccasins and feeding our families. Hunting with a bow took patience because you had to hide and hope prey would get close enough to use the bow. We didn't start to use firearms until we were 11. Occasionally we would bag a fish with an arrow, but only when we had given up on finding a deer.

"At 11 years old, we weren't allowed to venture too far from the homestead. This limited our endeavors to trap mustangs. Every once in a while, a herd of wild horses would stumble into our hunting and trapping domains. We had a small box canyon where we had built a barrier to hold wild horses. When a herd wandered into our area we would gently herd them into our trap. Our biggest haul was 12. When the horses were sold it brought revenue to the family. With Calling Eagle teaching us, we became very good horse trainers. When cowpokes found out who trained the horses for sale, they lined up for a chance to buy. Most of the time, our own hands wanted them. In that case, we were happy to supply the Four T Ranch with horses.

"As we grew older, we were allowed to venture further from home and use firearms. Then, we helped supply venison to the railroaders and horses to the army. I have often wondered how Calling Eagle felt about the horses going to the army. Someday, I'm going to ask him."

After the Christmas festivities, the dark days of winter seemed to drag on forever. One morning, as Beth and T. T. trudged up the steps of the school, Mrs. Ledbetter directed them to her office.

Beth asked T. T. "What have we done?"

T. T. shook her head, "I have no idea."

When they entered the office, Connie, Ruth and Margie were already there. They didn't have any idea why they were there, either.

A few minutes later Mrs. Ledbetter entered. She looked at the girls and asked, "What have you girls done now?"

They all looked at each other, not knowing what to say or what was coming.

"Well, Mrs. McIntosh is making arrangements for you to go on a trip to visit Vassar College in Poughkeepsie, New York. She feels all of you should try to continue your education. She has written Vassar about you and they want to interview you for possible admittance next fall. Each candidate must complete the interviewing process before being accepted into their program. Vassar is the women's equivalent to Harvard and Yale. She feels you five have the most potential of succeeding in the halls of higher learning. Before you leave school today, I want you to come by the my office and pick up the information for your parents to review, and next Monday I want you to let us know if you are interested."

Chapter Nine

March weather is unpredictable. One day spring, and the next there's winter snow. That day it looked as if it were going to snow. The cold wind already made it miserable. The travelers didn't care. They were filled with enthusiasm and with wonder about their trip. Ready to board a train to New York for a connection to Poughkeepsie, they were dancing with excitement. Mrs. McIntosh enjoyed seeing her blossoms with so much vigor. They were going to stay in New York overnight at one of the finer hotels and experience fine dining as a warm up for their visit to Vassar. One last adjustment to manners, if needed, would surely help their cause. For Mrs. McIntosh needed reassuring as to their readiness.

They boarded the train. The snow started as it pulled from the Philly station. Some passengers were warm at one end next to the stove, but the heat didn't reach the girls' seats. They shivered with cold, and excitement. Philly to New York wasn't far, but today the journey seemed endless. They rolled into New York just as it was getting dark. By the time they made it to the hotel, they were exhausted. After making it to their suite, they followed Mrs. McIntosh into the hotel's grand dining room. The guests were enjoying the falling snow scene, viewed through the grand windows of the room. They were shown to a round table that comfortably sat all six. The waiter gave each a menu, while asking them what they would like to drink. T. T. asked for coffee— hot, black and strong. Mrs. McIntosh didn't say anything about her ordering coffee, but T. T. felt like she would hear about it at some point. Another server poured each of them a glass of water. They properly placed their napkins in their laps. Then, the waiter asked for their orders. T. T. ordered a steak— pan fried and well done. The waiter gave her a funny look but went to the next person, without saying anything. Mrs. McIntosh stayed quiet.

"T. T., most people order their steaks cooked— at the most— medium rare. Why did you order yours well done and pan fried?"

"In the West, that's how you eat steak. On the trail, you don't have a lot of time to cook large meals, and it's easier to pan fry. You haven't the time to cook it any other way."

"I thought you roasted beef over a fire."

"You can, but it takes longer. You slice off a strip of beef and throw it into the frying pan. The pan is red hot and it sears the meat immediately, locking in the taste of the beef. When it is cooked, even though it's well done, the meat is still moist."

"T. T., about the coffee," Mrs. McIntosh changed the subject.

T. T. interrupted her in mid-sentence. "Oh, Mrs. McIntosh, I'm sorry. At Vassar, I'll drink tea."

The other girls laughed. They all enjoyed the dinner.

The late winter storm had dropped a pretty white blanket on New York, which made getting to the train station a challenge, but they made it in time. Leaving New York, they rode north through the Hudson River countryside. The whole area was covered with snow and the glare from the sunlight hurt their eyes. The scenery was beautifully filled with large country estates. Again, the train ride for a short distance seemed to take forever. When they left the train, there were two carriages waiting for them.

The carriage ride to Vassar offered more beautiful scenery, the least of which was the Vassar campus. *So this is what the higher halls of learning looks like*, thought T. T., as they were riding up the long approach to the main Vassar building. The drive was a long and circular paved trail through a huge garden. The main building was the largest building the girls had ever seen. They were greeted at the main door by a young lady named Lucinda Smith. She explained her job at Vassar was in the administration, along with being a corridor chaperone. She conducted a tour of the building, including the student rooms. The girls were impressed.

They were led to the admittance offices where the interviews would be conducted. There was a panel of five people there to complete the interviews. Three were faculty, one represented administration, and one man was from the financial board. The panel chairman was a man who appeared to be in his 60s. While the girls completed questionnaires, Mrs. McIntosh interviewed with the panel. Two girls were selected for interviewing first. The other three were taken to the dining room for tea. T. T. drank tea. When the first girl finished, she was escorted to the dining room and another was escorted back for interviewing.

T. T. was the last to be interviewed. She entered the room, not knowing what to expect. Immediately, the panel made her feel at ease. Then, they started asking questions.

"Please tell us your name."

"T. T. Finley."

"What does T. T. stand for?"

"Talon Two."

"That's an unusual name; tell us about it."

T. T. spent the next few minutes describing how she got her name.

"Where is your home?" one of the panelists asked.

"My home is a ranch called the Four T, located about 10 miles south of Medicine Bow, Wyoming."

"How did you get to Philadelphia?"

The interview went through the usual fact finding questions. Then the financial member of the panel asked, "How and who would be responsible for paying your tuition?"

"How much is it?" she asked.

"Around one thousand dollars a year is what it costs, as long as we can keep our expenses down."

"How long would I be here?"

"That depends on how well you are prepared to do the school-work. Now according to Mrs. McIntosh, you shouldn't have any problems in that area, so I would say three to four years."

"Oh, I'll pay for it myself. I have my own money," T. T. exclaimed.

"Where did you get that kind of money?"

"The two years before coming east I trained and sold enough horses to pay for Mrs. McIntosh's school, and I have more than enough left to pay here, too."

"Do you have any male visitors that would want to come and see you?"

"Only my twin brother."

The panel engaged in a lengthy conversation of what was expected of a student attending Vassar. The interview seemed to go longer than the others and it did. T. T. had several questions on what to expect from Vassar. The panel enjoyed the time because few applicants ever asked so many questions. It was as if T. T. wanted to begin her education right then. They enjoyed her comments. Then out of the clear blue sky, T. T. asked the question, "May I drink coffee here?"

The panel looked at each other. The chairperson looked at her, and replied, "You can, if that's what you want."

"Then I would like to come here to further my education."

"Would you be kind enough to leave the room for a few minutes?"

While she sat in the anteroom, her thoughts focused on what she had learned about Vassar. Soon she was invited back into the room.

The chairman spoke, "Miss Finley, we very seldom ever do what we are about to do. Generally, we write you a letter of acceptance, but in your case, we want you to know from us that we would like for you to attend Vassar. We will follow this invitation with a letter of acceptance. Will you join us at Vassar?"

"Yes, I would love to come here."

"Miss Finley, our thoughts were that a young lady who trains horses and drinks coffee would be a great influence on the well brought up young ladies of New England."

The panel escorted her to the dining room where the other girls were waiting.

"Now ladies, we'll have our corridor chaperone show you to your rooms for the evening. Then you'll join us for dinner in the best restaurant in Poughkeepsie," the chairman promised.

The girls settled into their rooms and congregated in a lounge at the end of the hall. They began to compare their interviews. They reported to each other that their interviews had gone well. T. T. kept to herself about the verbal invitation and her acceptance. Soon, they were bundled for the cold and off to dinner. The panel members intermingled with the girls and engaged them in conversation throughout dinner. The girls next to the corridor chaperone had a ton of questions for her. And their conversation seemed very lively. Mrs. McIntosh's demeanor showed the pride she had in her charges. Later, after they returned to Vassar, she cornered each to find out how things went. When she sat down next to T. T., Mrs. McIntosh said, while looking T. T. in the eye, and said, "I congratulate you, and thank you."

"For what, Mrs. McIntosh?"

"You're the only student that I have ever heard of who was accepted during the interview. And I thank you for not sharing it with the others, because they might not get accepted. You see, several hundred girls want to attend, but only a small percentage is accepted. The plain fact that you didn't share your success with the others shows your maturity and compassion."

T. T. cried.

The next morning they were at the train station to start the return trip. Today, however, they were not staying in New York but continuing on to Philadelphia. They would arrive early in the evening, without incident. When the girls got on the train, T. T. found a copy of the New York Times newspaper in her seat. The paper seemed to take a dim view of the Indians in the Dakota Territory. The Lakota Sioux Indians evidently had put together an alliance with the Cheyenne, with Chief Sitting Bull leading the alliance. They were allegedly creating havoc throughout Wyoming, Montana and the Dakotas. Editorial after editorial demanded that the government do something to protect the settlers in those territories. T. T. wondered how Calling Eagle viewed what was happening. The new flare-up came from reports of a gold find in the Dakota Territory. This started a rush to the area, causing the Indians to defend their lands. According to the news articles, the Indians were being dealt with harshly. It was at times like this that she missed Wyoming the most.

There was also an article on the free grazing issue in Wyoming. It seemed that large enterprises were moving into the territory, and by brute force were pushing out the small operations. Then she started to worry about the Four T Ranch. Uncle Jim had several good hands, but she and Talon were not there for support. *Were they being affected? Are they in danger from these outsiders?* She wondered. Then she remembered something about Mister Braun saying that Talbot was moving his operation to Wyoming. Could he be one of the big enterprises referred to in the article? If so, Aunt Bertha and Uncle Jim likely were in danger. Her Wyoming home was tugging at her and creating a war between home and Vassar, in her heart.

She had sent a letter last summer to Talon to warn him about Ben Iverson the cattle buyer. She failed to mention in the letter the Talbot plan of moving into Wyoming. *Oh, how I miss Talon,* she thought. It was becoming obvious she needed to go home before going to Vassar. She figured she would leave after school was out for the summer. If she found things in good shape, she would return to Vassar in the fall. The school year started the second week in September. That should give her enough time to go to Wyoming and make it back, if she didn't need to stay.

The once beautiful scenery of snow fields was turning into an ugly passage because of the soot from the engines. The settling of soot had turned areas along the tracks a dingy gray that permeated deep into the fields. She wondered how anything could grow under such a daily assault of spent coal. Then, as the train entered the more populated areas, the filth came from the human condition. *This is not very pretty,* she thought. *Seems a big price to pay for a little traveling convenience.*

In New York, the switch from one railroad to another consumed a lot of time, and the trip to Philly seemed to drag. While at the station, she had inquired on the costs of fares to Wyoming and found them reasonable even with the two-dollar-a-day extra charge for a sleeping car. When Margie saw her looking over a schedule, she asked T. T. if she was thinking about going home to Wyoming before starting at Vassar, if she was accepted.

"Why, yes, I am," said T. T.

"Would you like a traveling companion?" Margie asked.

"I haven't given it much thought."

"Beth, would you like to go to Wyoming this summer?" asked Margie.

"I don't know if my parents would let me go," Beth replied.

"I bet they will if we have a chaperone," Margie offered.

"You do know there is an Indian war going on in the Dakota Territory. Your parents may not think it safe for you to go," T. T. observed.

"With the right people going with us, they wouldn't care, and besides you can protect us."

"Now, that I don't know about."

"If you can do it, it ain't bragging," Beth said with a laugh, which the other girls repeated. She looked straight at T. T. "I guess the real question is, would you like for us to go?"

"I would love nothing more than to show you my home, but you do know it's not anything like how you live now," T. T. answered.

"I can't imagine being able to live like I do now in the future," said Margie. "I think it's time for some hardship."

"What do you mean?" asked Beth.

"Have you ever noticed how graceful T. T. is in everything she does? She's had to pull her fair share of the load at her home. Those kinds of demands have never been presented to us. Look at T. T.: she cooks, trains horses, and does all sorts of things we can't do or have never been allowed to do. We need a good taste of taking care of ourselves before going to Vassar."

T. T. laughed at them. "It won't be easy, but if you would like to go, I would love to have you with me. Maybe we could talk someone into going with us."

At the train station, Uncle John and Aunt Mary were waiting to pick up Beth and T. T. Mister Braun and Jonathan were waiting for Margie. The wind had picked up and the damp cold penetrated their clothing. Mrs. McIntosh hugged each of the girls before departing. She motioned for Uncle John and Mister Braun to talk with her. She warned them of the girls' pending plan to go to Wyoming when school finished the year. They thanked her for the warning. They looked at each other and said at the same time, "daughters." Then, they all laughed.

After they let Beth off at her home, T. T. started to tell her aunt and uncle about the trip. She related to them the articles she had read in the newspaper and wanted to know if Aunt Bertha or Uncle Jim had said anything about trouble. They assured her that her relatives were all right. Then, she told them about her interview at Vassar. She shared that to attend Vassar was something she really wanted to do. They agreed it would be great for her. Then, she told them how much more time she spent in her interview than the other girls had. Uncle John explained to her that the Vassar administrators were interested because they didn't get to interview girls with her background often; that they saw mostly girls from affluent New England families. She agreed. Then she told them she had been accepted to Vassar. They were shocked. They explained to T. T. how great an achievement it was to be accepted. Then, she told them the other girls didn't know, and that Mrs. McIntosh had thanked her for not sharing the news with the other girls. They understood why Mrs. McIntosh felt that way.

"I really want to go back to Wyoming after school is out and before I go to Vassar," T. T. announced.

Uncle John looked at her and said, "I think that's a good idea. Why don't you see if Beth or Margie would like to go with you?"

This startled Aunt Mary.

"Mary Grace, don't you think that would be a good trip for the girls?"

She didn't know what to say.

"Uncle John, I worry that it might be dangerous with the Indian war and the free range problems out west," T. T. said.

"Well, we need to plan for that," he said.

"How so?"

"Mary Grace and I will go with you, and we'll employ a Pinkerton agent or two to escort us. Maybe we can find out if your Texas Ranger brother could also meet us there."

"I'll write him tonight and tell what our plans are," T. T. brightened.

"John, are you saying we are going to Wyoming this summer?"

"Yes."

"I'll ask Beth and Margie's parents, and tell them I'll make all the arrangements."

At home, T. T. collapsed into her bed.

It snowed again and T. T. didn't attend school until the roads became passable for their carriage. On the first day back, she related to Margie and Beth that her Uncle was going to ask their parents about the trip to Wyoming. They were thrilled at the promising possibility that they may get to go.

A month later, she received the official acceptance letter to Vassar. When the girls met at school, Beth related to Margie and T. T. that she had gotten a letter from Vassar. Margie said she had received one, too. They looked at T. T. and she nodded she had received a letter. They all squealed with joy.

"One for all and all for one," Margie said. "Dumas needs to write a tale about the three women from Vassar."

At home that evening, Uncle John reported on how he did with the parents of the girls. They agreed to let them all go on the trip if John and Mary Grace were going. "The Pennsy railroad remembered you from two years ago and agreed to give us a special rate on three private cars, one for dining and sitting, and the other for sleeping," said her uncle. "They will supply the support people for our trip, and we are set to go the week after school is out."

BOOK
THREE

Chapter One

Gusty winds made the day unusually cold. The previous two days saw the area covered with heavy rains. Talon was at the depot awaiting the westbound train carrying Lowry and Cat. After his face off with Bulldog, the other hombres seen in town had disappeared to the north. He didn't give chase because he was ordered to wait for the other Rangers. It was late morning when the train arrived.

It pulled into a siding used for the loading of cattle. A boxcar door was opened and a ramp was placed from the door to the loading shoot. Lowry and Cat led all the horses from the car, and among them was Sally.

After their normal greetings, Talon asked, "how did you get Sally?'

Lowry answered, "Mimi brought her to us to deliver to you, when she traveled through San Antonio. Her parents were escorting her to Independence, Texas."

"What's in Independence?" Talon asked.

"She will be attending Baylor Female University. She started last fall with preparatory work to qualify her for the university next year. She said since she wouldn't be home to take care of Sally, she thought it better for us to care for her. We have, and Sally has repaid us by carrying our supplies."

"Did Mimi give you any message for me?" Talon asked.

"Only the details about where she was going to school and that you could write to her there if you wanted, or drop by to see her if you happen to be close by." Lowery replied with a wink.

"Her parents were happy to get her away from south of the Nueces. Things are still bad in the area, and I think they were moving her because of what happened to Billie Jo."

"Makes sense to me," Talon agreed.

"Your orders are simple, and that is to crush this cattle stealing ring who are supplying this eastern Combine. You are to follow the stolen herd and apprehend or kill the thieves. Your warrants are still good. They were happy to hear about Bulldog," Lowry reported.

"Let's get with it, then. I think the herd has been split. I'm way behind the eastern herd, but I think I'm ahead of the western herd. So we are going after the western herd first. What I had figured, and was confirmed by a west Texas rancher, they drive the herd through an area and mingle as many cattle with theirs as they can steal. The south Texas herd is moving north through New Mexico, I think. At least that's what I'm betting on."

"What's our first move?" Cat asked.

"We're going to follow the Arkansas River west to Pueblo, Colorado. Pueblo was an old trading post back when the Arkansas was the border between the United States and Mexico. If they drive the herd north of the Arkansas between here and Pueblo, then we'll pick up the trail. If we find no trail, that means, I think, they haven't made it this far north."

"Let's snap the head off a snake and get on the go." Lowry was eager.

While Talon was talking, he was giving Sally a nose rub. She was happy to see him. They mounted the horses and moved out of town to the west. They stayed south of the river, moving at a fast pace. Talon figured to camp somewhere along the Arkansas in the late afternoon. This way, they could build a fire and at least have hot coffee with their jerky, and have the fire out by nightfall. Then, they could climb to a higher vantage point and look for other campfires. The evening went exactly as planned, although they detected no other campfires. They spent the night peacefully.

Am I wrong? We'll know by tomorrow afternoon, he thought before drifting into a deep sleep. It felt good to have his trusted companions at his side again.

The ride into Pueblo didn't provide any answers. From what they could tell, no herds had crossed the river. If Talon was right, the herd must still be south of the river. He explained to Lowry and Cat that the Raton Pass route ran through Trinidad before bending due north toward Pueblo. He was gambling time as the eastern herd was steadily moving away from them. If he proved right, they would be able to eliminate part of the ring's operation. It was at dusk when they made the streets of Pueblo. They were still soft from the rains earlier in the week. They moved to the livery. As they were dismounting, Talon noticed a familiar sign: the tracks of the horse he had followed into New Mexico.

When the livery boy greeted them, Talon asked, "How long ago did the two cowpokes riding those ponies making these tracks arrive here?"

He answered, "About two hours ago."

"Do you have room for our four horses, where they can't be seen?" Talon asked.

"Yes, we do. There's another barn across the corral from this one, where we keep the draft horses. They'll be gone this week moving some mining equipment up to the coal mines. I can keep them there for you and no one will know."

"Good. Where did these two hombres go?"

"They said they were dying of thirst and headed to the first saloon on the south side of the street. I haven't seen them come out. They took their bedrolls with them. I figure if they are not in the saloon, then they've moved over to the Hotel on the next corner down."

"Is that the best Hotel?"

"It's the worst. The best is across the street on the next corner. They didn't look like they needed the best," the boy answered.

As they walked through the barn to the corral in back, Talon stopped at the stall containing the horse he had tracked. He asked, "The poke riding this horse, what did he look like?"

"He looked like a breed," said the boy.

"Did they mention any names?"

"The breed called the other one Tex."

"Thanks. Don't tell anyone about us asking questions, got it?"

"Yes sir."

They moved their horses into the draft horse barn. There, the livery boy put on the feed bags for the horses and promised to rub them down before closing for the evening.

"Well, I'm guessing we have just found Lightfoot Labo and Tex Ham. I trailed Labo on a wild goose chase into New Mexico and almost bought the ranch," Talon said.

"What happened?" asked Lowry.

Talon took several minutes describing the ordeal he had faced. "The way I figure it, they'll take some time in the saloon. We'll move over there and survey the place before we make our move. They may be meeting others and we need to see who they are. It just might save our lives. Lowry, chances are they won't recognize you. Cat and I are dead giveaways. You'll have to do the scouting."

"I agree, they don't know me. I can get it done quickly," Lowry responded.

They moved down the street with Lowry on the saloon side. Cat and Talon stayed in the shadows across from him. The wind picked up, and with temperatures dropping Cat began to shiver. Talon pulled him into a shadow that was sheltered from the wind.

"Cat, you cold?" he asked.

He nodded but claimed that he would be all right. They watched as Lowry entered the saloon. They would have to cross the street to peek through the doors. The windows to the street side were small and smoked over, not allowing a clear view of what was happening inside. They went to the corner of the saloon building and moved into the shadows and out of the wind. Cat continued to shiver. It took some time, but Lowry reemerged onto the boardwalk. Talon stepped out of the shadows and Lowry slowly meandered in his direction, rounding the corner into the shadows holding Cat and Talon.

"There are two of them. They are at the bar. The entire time I was there, they talked to no one, and not a soul tried to talk to them. I'm thinking they are either waiting on someone to contact them, or they don't know anyone is in the area," Lowry reported.

"Well they know *one* person and that's me. They trapped me in New Mexico. Now it's payback time." Talon promised.

Talon broke from the shadows heading for the door, when another stranger approached the door from across the street. Talon was already committed to moving through the door. When he entered the saloon he moved to a corner table to the left of the door next to the potbelly stove. The two at the bar didn't even notice he had entered. The stranger entered. Looking around the saloon he slowly walked over to the bar. The barkeep took a damp towel and wiped the bar in front of him. The breed looked at him as if he knew him. Then Tex said something to him. They left the bar for a table across the room from the stove. Lowry entered, surveyed the room, and approached the bar. The barkeep served him a beer.

Talon watched the three as they seemed to huddle close together talking in low murmurs. Tex waived at the barkeep and signaled for three drinks. The barkeep carried three shots of whiskey over to them. Talon could tell they were not very agile by the way they handled the drinks. They had had enough to drink to blur their thinking and slow their response time to danger. The third man had not touched a drink as yet, and was an unknown element in a shootout. In any fight he would have to be taken out first. He was carrying, and his holster was tied down which meant he had some experience when it came to guns. Could this be Jackson Slager, himself? Wasn't he with the eastern herd? There was only one way to find out. Talon moved out of his chair next to the stove and slowly moved toward their table.

"How are you doing, Lightfoot. Tex how about you? Who's your friend?" Talon asked.

Slowly the three looked up into the glare of the lamps at Talon.

Lightfoot Labo spoke, "Who are you?"

"You don't recognize me after you led me on a wild goose chase in New Mexico?"

Lightfoot Labo and Tex Ham shifted slightly in their chairs trying to get into a better position for what was coming.

"As I said before, who's your friend?"

"Marshal?" Ham said.

"Ah, you do know me. What took so long?"

The stranger spoke. "What kind of marshal are you?"

"Texas Ranger," Talon replied

"You are not in Texas now." The man said, emphatically.

"Well, stranger, let's explain it this way. I'm on the trail of seven yellow-bellied rats that kill women and children to rustle their cattle. And I've got warrants from the State of Texas. They have been upgraded to United States Government warrants that allow me to go anywhere to serve them. They're good for the named seven and any unknown associates that get in the way." Talon explained.

Lowry backed away from in front of the bar to the end. It looked that he was just getting out of the way of an ensuing fight. The barkeep reached under the bar to retrieve a double-barreled shotgun.

"Barkeep, put the palms of your hands on the bar," Lowry said.

The statement startled him. He turned and saw Lowry meant business, and complied with the order.

The three cowpokes over next to the stove got on their feet, but Cat, who had entered after Lowry, motioned for them to sit back down. They slid their chairs as far from the action as they could. All eyes were on Talon.

"Stranger, you are an unknown associate, and in Texas when serving a warrant we shoot first then bury. Who are you?"

"I'm a cattle buyer from Denver. My name is Ben Iverson."

The name rang a bell, Talon had just read about a Ben Iverson who had braced T. T. in a letter Lowry had given him yesterday. *So this is The Combine were fighting,* he thought. *How many men do they have with them?*

"So you're the dandy that my sister braced back east this summer."

The news startled Iverson. Talon could see in his eyes how uncomfortable he was hearing what he had to say.

"Ranger, there are three of us. You can't be serious about a play right now."

"Why don't you ask Labo and Ham? They and about 12 of their friends had me surrounded in New Mexico. I know I killed five of them and maybe one or two more when I broke out of their trap. You're playing a weak hand. They don't fight face to face. They're back shooters. Now the way I see this, we need to get this done. I haven't had my dinner yet, and I'm getting hungry."

Iverson held up his hands.

"That won't do Iverson. Since you braced my sister T. T. you're going to pay the piper now."

Labo flipped the table in the air in front of Talon, and all three went for their guns. Iverson was quick but dropped his gun when Talon's first shot slammed into his arm. His second caught Ham just below the rib cage on his right side swinging him to his right. His gun had cleared leather, but he didn't have time to get off a shot as Talon's third shot crushed his neck under his chin. He was dead before hitting the floor. The table had bounced into Talon's shin causing him to stumble backward while he was firing his fourth shot. It went wide of Labo. Labo's first shot was wild right of Talon and slammed into the bar between the barkeep and Lowry. His second shot hit the floor in front of Talon. Talon's fifth shot had hit Labo in the center of the chest a split second before he had fired his second. Talon holstered his first gun and drew his second and pointed it at Iverson.

"What's it going to be, Iverson? I can tell you prison time is not as bad as dying."

"I give."

"I figured that. Kick you gun over here and sit in the chair next to the wall."

Holding his bleeding arm, Iverson complied with Talon's orders.

Talon walked over to Iverson and slapped him upside the head with his pistol opening a gash under his left eye. "Now you're going to talk."

Talon was interrupted when the town marshal burst through the door with his two deputies.

"What's going on in here?"

Talon retrieved the warrants. "I'm a Texas Ranger," he said. "And these two dead hombres are Tex Ham and Lightfoot Labo. Here're the warrants for them, dead or alive. I'm Ranger Talon Finley, and these two gents at the bar are Rangers Lowry and Cat. They're with me.

The marshal took the paperwork from Talon and quickly read through it.

"Who's this other hombre?" the marshal asked.

"He started as an unknown associate, but we have identified him as a linchpin in a cattle-rustling outfit called The Combine operating throughout the west and on the east coast. This is Ben Iverson. He is a cattle buyer specializing in buying stolen cattle and shipping them to the east coast. Out of Texas, The Combine was running stolen cattle through Mexico and shipping them to Cuba. Now we are going to question this hombre and he's going to tell us everything we need to know about this operation."

"Let's take him over to the jailhouse."

Talon slapped Iverson across his right cheek with his pistol. "Get up and get moving."

"You can't do that," the marshal warned.

"This man is part of a group of hard cases that killed an entire family to steal their cattle. They raped the woman before they killed her. I'll never forget the scene. They also killed the love of my life because her family helped me after I was wounded in a gunfight with one of their gangs. The only way he stays alive is he talks."

Iverson, still holding his arm, was shoved toward the door of the saloon. When they hit the street, the cold wind chilled them to the bone. The jail was down the street to the east. It sat alone in a plaza across from the courthouse.

"Marshal, we haven't had our dinner is there somewhere we can get some grub?"

"Huey, run over to Molly's and get some grub for these boys. Tell her to make it special, since they're Texas Rangers."

The marshal looked at Talon and asked, "How old are you, son?"

"17," Talon spat out the now familiar lie.

Cat and Lowry shared a grin because they heard the same question everywhere their young Ranger friend went. Cat was still shivering as the brisk wind penetrated his thin southern Texas clothing. So was Lowry. Entering the jail, the marshal sent the remaining deputy to get the town barber. He was the closest thing to a doctor the town had, and he had seen a lot of gunshot wounds. It was just a matter of minutes and he was serving his guests hot coffee freshly brewed. There were three cells in the back of the jail, and they shoved Iverson in the middle one.

"Cat, hustle to the livery and get our rolls. Tell the livery boy that the cowpokes who came in earlier are dead and that the town now owns their horses and gear," Talon said.

It didn't take long for Cat to return. He was wearing a blanket around his shoulders for warmth. The small jail was sufficiently warm from the pot belly stove against the wall away from the cells. After Cat arrived a vivacious young girl escorted by the deputy bounced into the office carrying a tray and a basket full of eats for dinner. They were sitting around the marshal's desk eating when the barber came in carrying his supplies for treating a gun wound. Cat and Lowry helped him get Iverson's vest and shirt off to treat the wound. He also treated the gash under his left eye. Afterwards they fed Iverson.

Chapter Two

Iverson was sitting on his cot against the back wall of the cell. The marshal and the three Rangers entered the cell with chairs and started to question him.

"If you help us, we'll see the judge knows it. That means a reduced prison time. We'll have to take you back to Texas to control the proceedings, but in the long run, you'll benefit."

Iverson nodded his head.

"Tell us about The Combine."

"It was started by James Kincade and James Talbot out of Philadelphia. They were importing rum and molasses out of Cuba. In their business dealings there, they found that the Cubans needed beef. They were also importing small quantities of cochineal from Cortina out of Mexico. They mentioned to Cortina they needed cattle and he agreed to supply them. The price was very low, and they asked Cortina why the cattle were so cheap. He told them he would raid into Texas and rustle cattle from the gringos. That started the trade. When the railroad moved into western Kansas, they told Cortina they would buy more cattle for the east if he could get them to Dodge City. That's where I came into the deal. Jackson Slager knew my family and knew I was outside the law on several matters in Missouri. He told Cortina to have Talbot search for me. He did, and I became their cattle buyer. I would buy enough cattle to throw off suspicion of wrongdoing. We were buying cattle for cents on the dollar cheaper than other buyers. We were also accumulating free, unbranded cattle. By driving the stolen herds through the far reaches of a ranch, Slager and his crew would comingle the rancher's cattle with the herd. When they got to Dodge City, they would take the branded stolen cattle and load them for shipment east, as fast as they could. Any unbranded cattle they moved onto land north of Dodge City, branding them with The Combine brand.

"The idea was to let the herd increase naturally. Soon, they ran out of welcome in Kansas with this growing herd. They sent Kincade to Cheyenne, where he found out that a great portion of central Wyoming was free graze land. The new plan was to move The Combine herd to Wyoming, stealing as many cattle as we could along the way.

"The first stolen herd out of Texas went north just east of La Junta. You were sort of tracking it. If not, you had an inkling of a herd controlled by Slager moving north. We didn't figure anyone would catch on to our plan, but you did, Kid. We had to come up with something different. The new plan called for me to move to Pueblo. We would start moving the stolen cattle out of Texas through the Raton Pass and Trinidad to Pueblo. I would load the stolen branded cattle here, and send the unbranded cattle north to Wyoming. I was here to meet the first herd through the pass, and have them continue to Wyoming because the tracks have not reached here, as yet. They should be here sometime in January or February, or at the latest March. It's my understanding after asking around here that the trains will be running in March. I met Labo and Ham to find out about the herd. They had ridden in and left word where they would be at the hotel. The herd is about 20 miles south of here, but they decided to swing them east and bypass Pueblo. No one from here would know about the herd crossing the Arkansas moving north if they went far enough to the east. The herd is awaiting word to move, and guarded by several of the gang put together to kill you.

"The other plan was to encroach upon the legal owners of land in Wyoming by trying to cripple them by stealing their cattle and cutting them off from good water. We also can undercut their prices with our cheap stolen cattle. There is one large ranch southeast of Medicine Bow on the east side of the Medicine Bow Mountains owned by a man named Finley. His ranch was going to be the first target. He was running several head of cattle on that range branded with a wagon wheel of four T's. Funny thing to us was his headquarters was on the west side of the mountains. Slager figured it would be days before he realized his cattle were gone. They would be shipped from The Combine's private siding north and west of Laramie. The railroad was to start stacking cattle cars on the siding two weeks from now, to coincide with the herd's arrival. Every herd moving north was to take a few head from the Finley ranch'"

Iverson leaned back against the cell wall, his tale of well-organized criminal organization finished.

"I've got news for you, Iverson, that ranch is my family's ranch. To move us off of it you would have to kill me and my sister, and I haven't seen anyone with your outfit yet capable of that." Talon said, his face flushed with anger.

"I had no idea it was your family's ranch. I'm just relating to you the plan. I don't think they care who they steal from. Anyway, Kincade was playing cattle buyer in Laramie and Cheyenne, and I was playing cattle buyer here."

"Iverson, I'm still looking for Jackson Slager, Harry Simpson, Max Kelly and Clyde Hood, do you know where they are?"

"Jackson Slager is already in Laramie. The other three, plus about 10 others are driving the herd to Laramie."

"When do you think they'll get there?" Talon asked.

"They should roll into the Laramie area two or three weeks from now if they don't run into any weather delays," Iverson answered.

"Marshal, do you think you can hold on to this fellow until we get back from Wyoming?"

"It sounds like you made a good deal with him. I think with him wounded, he would be stupid to run. If he tries, we'll find him, and more than likely kill him," the marshal replied.

"He has given us the layout of the plan which means reduced prison time. He would be stupid to run, but if he does and you kill him, it saves us the bother," Talon said. "If you don't, I surely will."

Iverson was taking in the conversation with his head bowed—not saying a word. Finally, he lifted his eyes toward Talon and said, "Talon, I'm sorry about your sister, and I promise I won't run."

"You got off easy with T. T., Iverson; she would have killed you in a second. Most people think she has killed three men, one of which was your kin, but counting Indians, there are many more she has killed. We grew up tough, meaning it was kill or be killed. There wasn't any help on the Wyoming range in the '60s or early '70s. We had to protect ourselves, and help friends."

"I promise I won't run," Iverson repeated.

"I believe you, but believe this: if I have to chase you, you'll die."

"That, I do."

They spent the night in the jail, letting the deputies and the marshal take care of their business, while they guarded the prisoner. At dawn, the wind was still blowing — raw and cold. When the deputy arrived to take the morning watch, the three left to go to Molly's for breakfast. The short walk started Cat to shivering again and it wasn't unnoticed by Talon. Lowry fared better but not by much. After eggs, sausage, biscuits, and plenty of hot black coffee, they crossed the street to the mercantile store. There Talon introduced Cat and Lowry to long-handled underwear, wool shirts, and lamb's wool-lined winter coats. He bought Lowry some moccasins and Cat some winter riding boots, along with wool socks. He also picked up wool stocking caps for both of them to wear under their hats.

"Cat, you and Lowry go to the jail and change into these wintertime clothes, while I go check the horses. When you're finished, we'll go after the herd," Talon said.

"What are we going to do with it?" asked Lowry.

"The marshal told me the telegraph is working here. The railroad built it first, along the intended route for the tracks. That way they had communication to La Junta if they needed help. We're going to telegraph McNelly and ask him what to do with the herd. He'll probably tell us to sell it, knowing that we probably need the money."

"Then what are we going to do?" asked Lowry.

"Let's see if the captain has any orders for us first," Talon said.

They walked over to the future depot, where the telegraph office was located. They entered, hearing the greeting of the operator. Talon wrote out two messages, one for McNelly, and the other to Uncle Jim.

TO: CAPTAIN MCNELLY, TEXAS RANGERS SAN ANTONIO, TEXAS

FOUND LABO AND HAM. STOP. NO LONGER ALIVE. STOP. THEY HAD STOLEN CATTLE HERD. STOP.WHAT DO WE DO WITH IT? STOP. AWAIT YOUR ORDERS IN PUEBLO, COLORADO. STOP.

TALON

TO: JIM FINLEY, MEDICINE BOW, WYOMING

CATTLE RUSTLERS TO BE THERE TWO TO THREE WEEKS. STOP. IN PUEBLO, COLORADO NOW, WILL BE THERE AS SOON AS I CAN. STOP. MOVE CATTLE OFF EASTERN RANGE NOW. STOP. WIRE ME BACK. STOP.

TALON

Talon paid for the private messages and told the operator he would be waiting at the jail for the replies. They made their way to the livery to check on their horses before heading to Molly's for a sit down meal.

"We should get our replies in a day or two. In the meantime, we'll be on the lookout for any strange cowpokes coming into town looking for Labo or Ham. Cat, you hang around the livery. Lowry, watch the saloon, and I'll sit around Molly's. We'll meet at Molly's at dusk. After we eat, we'll retire to the jail and watch Iverson again tonight," Talon said.

The deputies were glad to see them when they walked into the jail because it meant another free night for them. The marshal said he could find some good men to help them drive the herd to Pueblo, adding that a couple of local businessmen had indicated interest in buying the herd for their ranches. Talon told him he needed to wait for McNelly's reply before selling any cattle. The marshal nodded that he understood. Lowry left to patrol the saloon for strangers and in a few minutes he was back. No strangers had appeared.

After two days, Cat approached Talon and thanked him for the warmer clothes. He told Cat that it would be a lot colder where they were going this winter and he would need the warmer clothes to survive. A youngster entered the jail and gave Talon a message. He gave him a nickel. The message was from Uncle Jim.

TO: TALON FINLEY, TEXAS RANGER, PUEBLO, COLORADO

MOVING CATTLE TO FREE RANGE ON OTHER SIDE OF WESTERN RANGE. STOP. CALLING EAGLE, GARY AND WOLF ARE WATCHING THEM. STOP. DID SEND THEM A MESSAGE TO WATCH FOR ANY CATTLE HERDS. STOP. NOT LIKELY THEY WILL BE FOUND THERE. STOP. SHEEP ARE ON EASTERN RANGE. STOP. NEW BREED OF SHEEP BERTHA BROUGHT BACK FROM EAST AROUND HOME. STOP. ALREADY SEEING SOME SIGNS OF ENCROACHMENT ONTO THE FOUR T AROUND DAMMED SPRINGS. STOP.

JIM

Within a few hours, the second reply came. The orders were simple.

SECURE THE HERD AND SELL. STOP. USE MONEY TO SUSTAIN YOUR EFFORT. STOP. KEEP TRACK ON HOW MONEY IS SPENT.

MCNELLY

"Deputy, where is the marshal?"

"Over at Molly's, drinking coffee with some good old boys."

They left the jail to find the marshal to ask his assistance in moving the herd. They told him to find the men willing to buy the herd, since they had would soon have one for sale. The marshal nodded and went to work rounding up some cowpokes to help with the move. He found six willing to do the work, and with a deputy, he sent them with Talon. They moved south on the trail to Trinidad. By midafternoon they had spotted the herd's dust cloud off to the west.

Talon told the hands to lay back a bit to avoid any gunplay that might erupt if the outlaws resisted. "This is our job, not yours," he said.

The three Rangers rode toward the dust as if they were traveling the trail. When they reached the herd, Talon rode up to of the outlaw wranglers and asked who was ramrodding his outfit. The wrangler pointed toward the front at the cowpoke riding the point. Talon rode up to the ramrod easily, as if he were going to ask for a job. He counted the outlaws while he rode to the point man and counted six by the time he reached the leader. The point man turned toward him. When he got over close to the outlaw, he pulled his gun and instructed the leader to have his men to converge on their position. As they started to assemble, Lowry and Cat joined Talon with their guns drawn but held low. When the six outriders assembled around their leader, the Rangers raised and cocked their guns.

"Men, we are Texas Rangers and you are cattle thieves," Talon said. "We're here to arrest or kill you, your choice. You should know that Labo and Ham chose to resist, and they are dead. Now make your choice; pull those pistols or unbuckle and drop your gun belts."

The ramrod gazed into Talon's eyes and saw the cold truth. He looked at the other two Rangers and saw the same truth. "Drop 'em, boys. We got no other choice."

One by one, seven belts with pistols holstered dropped to the ground.

"Wise choice, men," Talon said. He then motioned for the deputy to bring up the drovers and turned the herd over to them. "Drive it to Pueblo, men. We'll join you just as soon as we finish some Ranger business with these folks."

Lowry took down the outlaws' names while Talon sent the drovers on their way. Talon waited for Lowry to complete that task before dispatching the group with one last warming.

"Men, this is the way it's going to be. Once we telegraph this list of names to our captain in Austin, you will be listed as outlaws in Texas for cattle rustling. If you have done other crimes, we don't know about them. Our orders are to kill all associates of Lightfoot Labo and Tex Ham. We have already killed them, but we don't want to kill you. So we are going to put out posters for you dead or alive in Texas. If we ever see you again, we'll have to kill you. We're letting you go with a promise you stay out of Texas, Kansas, Colorado, Wyoming, Oklahoma, and New Mexico."

Then he named off the outlaws, one at a time, asking them if they wanted to die or take the deal. One at a time they took the deal and turned south.

"I've never seen anything like that in all my life," said the deputy, who had lingered to see how the Rangers did their business.

"If we would have had gun play, we would have scattered this herd all over southern Colorado," Talon explained. "Besides, when they found out their leaders were dead, we figured they'd have no will to continue. We were ready for a scrape but didn't really expect one."

"Do you think they'll really stay out of Texas, and the other areas you listed?"

"I really think they're headed home, wherever that might be. More than likely, home is Texas. If they lay low and stay clean, they should be okay. Texas is a big state."

"Why didn't you arrest them?" the deputy asked.

"For what? Being hired to drive a herd of cattle is not a crime. We didn't want to kill an innocent cowboy that needed to work. Most of them likely didn't realize they were dealing with criminals."

The deputy nodded and joined the others driving the herd. The Rangers did the same.

By sun down Talon could see the cowboys from Pueblo knew what they were doing. They probably worked for the men buying the cattle, he thought. About that time the marshal rode in with several more hands and the two potential buyers. He introduced the buyers to Talon.

One of the buyers asked the selling price.

Talon had asked Iverson what he would pay if he were buying the herd. Iverson said he would try to settle for eight dollars a head.

"I'm thinking 10 dollars a head," he said. "Looks like about five hundred out there."

"We were thinking six would be a good price."

"Don't know if the State of Texas would like six. Tell you what I'll do. I'll take nine and pay the cowpokes a dollar a head for driving them, say there are five hundred without counting them."

"Sounds like a good trade to us because it looks as if there are more than five hundred."

"Deputy, get the names of those who helped us where we can pay them. I assume these pokes work for you. Am I right?"

"Yes."

"Tell them the marshal will be holding their money."

The Rangers rode with the marshal and the buyers back to Pueblo. They left the deputy in charge of the herd while the wrangles split the herd for the buyers. The next morning the buyers showed at the jail with the money. They gave Talon 4,500 U.S. dollars and he gave them a bill of sale from the State of Texas. After paying the cowboys five hundred, he netted $4,000. Then he sent McNelly a wire telling him about the transaction and about the deal he made with Iverson.

"We'll need supplies for the trail. Lowry, you handle that for us. Get you and Cat some winter mittens, I forgot about getting those the other day. Cat and I will see to the horses and our gear, and we should be ready to ride as soon as you get finished. Marshal, we'll be back for Iverson. How much do you need for his upkeep?"

"How about paying 50 dollars a month?"

"Sounds good," Talon replied while he counted out 300 dollars. "Here's six months in advance. We'll be back to get him."

Chapter Three

The Rangers rode into Denver and found a hotel with its own livery. They took the time to rub down and feed their horses. Taking their bedrolls, they moved to the lobby to check in. They got a suite with two rooms and three beds. After they settled in, they went to the barber for shaves and baths. Properly cleaned and shaved, they found the recommended restaurant for a sit-down meal. The place was fancy, making them feel out of place. The girl serving them could see they were uncomfortable and she went out of her way to make them feel at home. In all, it was an enjoyable experience, but they were tired. Next was a good night's sleep.

They were off early the next morning. They needed to burn some miles because time wasn't on their side. It seemed that Sam and Sally knew they were going home. Their pace never faltered. It was fast and consistent, with heads down and driving. They made Fort Collins in just a few hours. As they moved north, the more they heard about Indian troubles. Fellow travelers warned about small bands of Indians attacking homesteads and other travelers. The stories didn't deter the Rangers. They made Cheyenne at sundown. The routine was the same. Take care of the horses, eat and sleep.

They headed due west out of Cheyenne to avoid Laramie. This trail allowed them to ride north through the eastern range of the Four T. By afternoon, they had made the Four T, Talon's home.

"We need to be careful along here, not because of Indians but because of outlaws encroaching on our ranch," Talon warned the others.

They slowed their pace and took the time to examine the trail ahead and behind from hidden vantage points. Finally, Talon found what he was looking for, a spring he and his gang of friends had dammed when they were kids. It supplied a cool fresh drinking place for cattle, sheep and wildlife. There was a camp there. They could see three cowpokes, but Talon didn't know any of them. He assumed they were some of the encroachers that Uncle Jim had mentioned in his wire.

"What's the best way to do this?" asked Talon.

"Why don't we go straight at them? They won't know who we are," said Cat.

"What do you think, Lowry?"

"I'm with Cat, let's go spoil their party," Lowry answered.

"Cat, you stay back in case there are others we don't see. Lowry and I will brace them, and move them out. You'll be our backup; if someone moves in behind us, take care of 'em."

Cat nodded.

Lowry and Talon slowly moved their horses toward the camp. When they got within a few yards, they hailed the camp.

"Hey the camp," Lowry yelled.

"Yo," came an answer.

"Mind if we water our horses?"

"Come on in."

They rode slowly into the light cast by the campfire. One of the encroachers sat on a log in front of the fire with a Winchester on his lap. The other two stood facing them as they rode into the camp. They dismounted and led their horses to the water.

"Didn't expect to see anyone on this range," said Talon.

"Yeah, well, we just moved in here to start setting up our cattle operation."

"How so?" asked Talon.

"This is free range territory and we're getting a head start for next spring. We expect our herd any day now."

Good intelligence, Talon thought. They were ahead of the herd from Texas.

"You know, I've always thought this range was owned by the Four T."

"Naw, it's free range."

Talon moved closer to the fire while the horses were drinking, drawing the attention of all three encroachers. "You got any coffee?"

The three encroachers were watching him closely and didn't see Lowry getting into position to flank them if there was trouble.

"Just threw the last cup away and haven't started a new pot yet."

"That's good. I'll tell you what you're going to do. You are going to saddle your ponies and move along off my range. I'm part owner of the Four T and you are on my land. It's important you go without a fuss so you can tell whoever you work for that the free range is north of Medicine Bow or the railroad. You need to stay away from here because our sheep will need this water during the winter."

"And if we don't?"

"First, you are surrounded. Second, any sudden move by you, you'll be killed." Talon gave his preplanned signal, and Cat splintered the log where the rifleman was sitting. "You will find out pretty quick just how much this 'free' range will cost you.

"Third, we don't really want to kill you because we need you to carry the message back to your boss. Now, I've got to ask you— how long will it be before your boss misses you?"

The rifleman leaned his rifle across the log and stood, "Mister, you got us this time, but you'll pay for it."

"Talk's cheap, buster. We'll see, what's it going to be?" Talon taunted.

Talon drew his pistol and shot the rifleman in the left leg so fast that the others didn't see it happen. They raised their hands.

"You move that Winchester again and you won't see tomorrow," Talon said. "All of you, drop your gun belts and mount up. Tell your boss I don't like being threatened. Tell him any cattle brought on the Four T becomes Four T property. Since you and I know each other so well, if I ever see you again anywhere, I'll kill you. Wyoming isn't safe for you. Tell him Finley sent you. He'll know."

They helped their wounded partner mount, jumped on theirs and moved off.

"We need to give them a few minutes head start and then we'll follow them," Talon said.

From a distance, Talon could see the encroachers heading directly toward Laramie.

"Cat, they haven't seen you. Follow them and see what you can learn. We'll be at the home place on the Medicine Bow River, south of Medicine Bow. You can't miss it if you ride the western bluff above the river."

Cat nodded, mounted and started following the three.

"Lowry, you and I will continue to look for other encroachers on our eastern range. Uncle Jim told me they were moving in around our dammed mountain springs. I know where they are, so if there are others we'll find them."

Late afternoon they found a second camp. Talon headed straight for them. This time, because there were four of them he didn't hail the camp. He and Lowry stealthily moved to the edge of their camp.

"Raise your hands!" he yelled. "Now!"

Startled, they turned toward Talon. Eying the two Colts pointed in their direction, the four pushed eights hands high into the night air.

"Throw your guns toward me with your left hands. Don't get cute; I'm pretty good with these, and I'm not alone."

They obeyed.

"You're on Four T land. Now that you and I have developed a close relationship, if I ever see you again I'll kill you."

"Are you Mister Talon?" the long, lanky cowpoke closest to the fire asked.

"Yes."

"Mister Jim said you would be along, we work for the Four T. We were cleaning out the springs. When we finished, we were to move the sheep into this area."

"I guess it's a good thing I didn't shoot you. We just had a run in with hard cases at spring six."

"We were told not to fight and to back off, if braced. Mister Jim said that strategy would change when you got here. Shall we go to the barn together?"

"Yep, but we'll keep the guns, just to be safe. I'll apologize later if needed."

It was well after dark when they rode into the barnyard. Two hands emerged from one of the barns with rifles in hand. Uncle Jim came out on the front porch.

"Talon! It's damn good to see you, son."

Talon dismounted and gave Jim a big hug.

"Do you know these hard cases?"

"They're not hard cases. They work for us."

"That's what they told me, but I wasn't taking any chances. Had to shoot an encroacher earlier today for threatening me. Sorry, fellas. Had to be sure."

"Don't mention it," the lanky leader said. "We'd do the same in your shoes."

"Uncle Jim, fellas, this is Lowry Cook, one of my fellow Texas Rangers. He and our scout, Cat, are with me to break up the cattle rustling ring called The Combine. They have a man named Kincade in the area, directing operations. Have you run across him?"

Lowry shook hands with all the hands. Then they heard a squeal. Aunt Bertha had come out on the porch and upon seeing Talon, she let go of her emotions. She raced to hug and kiss Talon. All the hands laughed. It was a great homecoming, under the circumstances. They all retired into the house, where Aunt Bertha started pulling out food to feed her lost son and his friend. The hands were enjoying the time as well, drinking hot black coffee and munching on Bertha's fried pies. While sitting and eating, Talon raised The Combine question again.

"What about this Kincade? Any of you run into him or heard anything about his operation?" Talon asked.

One of the hands spoke up, "I think I saw him at Mrs. Moore's place one morning after she had served the train passengers. He told her he was thinking about moving into the area east of Medicine Bow and asked her about the range south. She told him it was owned by the Four T since the early '60s."

"What's he look like?" Talon inquired.

"He dressed eastern, about six feet, ruddy complexion, and 180 pounds. He carried a Colt .38 in a shoulder holster, kinda hidden under his jacket and I think I picked up on a two-shot over under in his coat pocket."

"Was there anyone with him?"

"Not that I could tell. He did tell Mrs. Moore and Sally that he was expecting his herd to be delivered sometime in the next three weeks, and that he may want to go ahead and sell some of them. He wanted to know if he could use the siding west of town. She told him he would have to check with Jim Finley since it was the Four T's siding."

"That's how they work," Talon said. "They drive stolen cattle from Texas and comingle them with as many others as they can on the drive. They steal more as they move north. When they get here, their plan is to sell all the branded cattle and get rid of the evidence. They keep the unbranded ones for their own seed herd and set up on free graze land."

"Clever," said Jim. "What are you going to do?"

"Well, we have Federal Warrants for four of the men on the trail drive. We're going to take them— most likely dead. They are really bad people, Uncle Jim. Lowry, Cat and I will take care of them. We also have open warrants for any unknown associates, which covers Kincade and his partner back east."

"Now, who is Cat again, and where is he?" asked Uncle Jim.

"We had a run in with encroachers at spring six. I shot one in the leg to make a point and got them on their way. Cat is trailing them to see if they run to their boss. When he collects the intelligence we need, he is to meet us here. He's a Black Seminole Indian scout for the Texas Rangers. He's saved our bacon on several occasions. And he's my friend."

Aunt Bertha was in seventh heaven serving her men. She loved each, and truly loved to see them eat.

"Now I'm sure Kincade has amassed a good number of gun hands." Talon continued. "You and your men need to let us do the fighting. Don't be out on the range alone. Go about your daily work as if nothing has happened. When the herd gets here we'll take action. If they bring us the fight early, let us handle it. It's our job."

"Okay, Talon, it's your job. But remember it's *our* land," Uncle Jim answered. "If pressed, we know how to defend it."

Talon had to stifle a grin. Damn, he was proud to part of this family.

At noon Cat rode off the bluff overlooking the main headquarters of the Four T. By description the hands knew who he was and started to gather around the corral where Lowry, Talon and Jim were standing. Looking up they saw Cat ride into the yard.

Cat dismounted.

"Uncle Jim, this is Night Stalking Cat."

Jim shook hands with Cat. "Pleasure," he nodded.

"Same here," Cat replied.

"What did you find out?" Talon asked.

"I found Kincade in Laramie," Cat replied. "The three pokes we chased got their friend taken care of, then high tailed it out of town. I assume they took you for your word. I hung around to get a count on how many men he has working for him, and got an idea on who his leaders were. If I see them, I'll know them. They plan to hit the sheep and kill them off in the next day or two. We need the sheep in the best possible place to defend them. This afternoon can't be too early. If we can bloody them up some, they may lose their nerve. The hard cases he has around him won't stand and fight like the Greasers in Mexico. We have an advantage because we know they're coming."

"We're in luck," said Uncle Jim "The sheep are gathered in the canyon at the number one spring. That's where we would want them for our best defense."

"How many hands are with them?" asked Talon.

"Two."

"How many hands are here?"

"Eight."

"Send two or three hands to replace Calling Eagle, Wolf and Gary. That gets the paid cowboys out of harm's way."

"We can fight, Talon," one of the hands volunteered.

"I know you can, but they have a big stake in the Four T. I'm sorry, but they need to be here. You'll be doing us a favor by protecting the cattle herd, in case they have located them. You know, you could be attacked, too; nothing's completely safe with those people out there."

Jim selected three and sent them on their way. It would take the rest of the day for them to get there.

"Tell them to meet us at number one," Talon instructed as they rode out.

"Uncle Jim, I suggest you position the other hands around the home place, in case they come here instead of going after the sheep. Send one to take Aunt Bertha to Mrs. Moore's."

"I can't do that, Talon. When you were little she fought against Indians and bad men for her right to stay."

Talon conceded, knowing it would take a cavalry regiment to move his aunt if she wanted to stay. The Rangers mounted and headed for spring one. It was the closest to Medicine Bow and Talon knew how to cut through the ridges to shorten the trip. From what he could tell, things hadn't changed in the seven months of his absence. At dusk they arrived at the spring. They explained to the two hands what was happening. They agreed to stay and fight.

"No fire tonight. Cat, get high and look for campfires."

Cat moved back into camp about two hours after nightfall, reporting no fires were seen. He had found a good place to snipe with the Sharps. It was high and well covered. Early the next morning, Cat took Lowry and Talon to a spot deep in shadows, with a command of the surrounding area. They could protect the canyon with shots from 400 out to 600 yards. Talon pointed to a position lower on the slope where Lowry could protect the canyon with his Winchester. If he was in danger, Talon and Cat could get to his position quickly. The idea was to discourage the attackers before they got close. Talon thought, *Will it work? How many would have to die before it discouraged them? Would they bypass the sheep and attack the homestead? How long would it take before Calling Eagle would get there?* All these questions ran through his mind, as Cat used the glasses, looking for trouble.

It wasn't long in coming. Around midmorning Cat's glasses caught a flash of light in the distance. He focused in on the area and saw a group of about 10 men approaching their position. They weren't hiding their approach, flashing an arrogance that their numbers were sufficient to take on all comers. Talon readied himself to teach them different. Cat confirmed one of Kincade's leaders was out in front.

"Cat, I learned something about this when I was trapped in a desert in New Mexico. Killing a horse is as good as a man. Out here, there's little water unless you know where to go. And wherever it is, it's a long walk."

They watched as the men closed on their position. Talon's first shot would alert Lowry and the two hands. They were waiting for the sound to action.

"The next ridge they're about to ride over is right at 600 yards. When the last man crosses, they'll be in the open for about 200 yards, before gaining cover. That's when I'm going to start firing. Watch to see where the round hits to see if I'm leading them enough."

"The rider on the right is the leader," said Cat as the gang crossed the ridge.

Talon took aim, waiting for the last man to cross. When he did, Cat signaled him to fire. His first shot was lucky; it dropped a horse in the middle of the pack.

"Not enough lead," said Cat.

His second shot hit a rider, three behind the leader. They didn't seem to know they were being shot at. Talon's next two shots missed, and they started hearing the shots. It slowed them down for an instant, giving Talon time for a steadier aim. He knocked one out of the saddle. His horse kept running with the pack. The next shot missed, but the following shot hit a horse, knocking him down in front of two others, and all three horses and riders went down. Talon took aim and nailed one of the fallen riders. The 50 looked like it shattered his shoulder. They were getting close to making cover, when Talon drew a bead on the leader. When he came to the top of a small rise, he hammered him with a shot mid-body. He went down, pulling his horse with him. Four of the encroachers made the cover, and were not seen for several minutes. They had stayed low, walking their horses. Then they saddled and made a break to get out of range. Quickly, Talon and Cat gave up their position and moved into the canyon to get their horses. Lowry was waiting for them. They saddled and moved out of the canyon after the outlaws.

Talon had killed two. Four others had various wounds. They disarmed them and left them there "for the wolves," they told them. They were not going anywhere because of their injuries. The Rangers started after the four who got away. After they had gotten out of range they had slowed down, which gave the Rangers a chance to catch them quickly. The Rangers came over a ridge, and there they were meandering along. The Rangers were on them before they knew it. They surrendered. The Rangers stripped them of their gear and tied them to the horses, then linked the horses together in single file.

"This is how this works. We have federal warrants for your arrests dead or alive. If one of you tries to escape, we shoot all of you. If someone else tries to help you escape, we shoot all of you first and then go after your helpers. Cat, hang back and wait for Calling Eagle. When he shows, explain to him what has happened. Have him take care of the wounded souls we left back there. Then join us. We'll be at a walk. Feel like I'm walking Greasers into Brownsville."

They all laughed.

Chapter Four

The parade of prisoners drew a curious crowd as they entered, each onlooker throwing out a different theory on the strange scene. They slowly led the prisoners to the marshal's office. The marshal was Jessie Coglon, and he had known Talon since he was just a squirt of a kid. Jessie walked out on the porch of the jail.

"Well I'll be, Talon Finley. How you been doing, son?"

Talon swung out of the saddle and gave Jessie a big hug.

"I've been just great, marshal. It's good to see you."

Talon spent the next few minutes explaining what was going on with the prisoners. The marshal kept shaking his head and waved for Lowry to bring the prisoners into the jail. He used two separated cells.

"That's the best I can do to keep them apart."

"Bring one out here at a time for me to question, will you Jessie?"

"Sure. I want to see this."

Talon placed the first in a chair facing him.

"This is the way this goes. For you to have any chance to keep from hanging, you'll have to cooperate with me. If you don't, I'm going to take you all the way back to Texas like I brought you in here. If your pony were to spook and start to run it'll look like you're trying to escape, and I will kill you. What's it going to be?" Talon asked.

Jessie was flabbergasted at how tough Talon was talking, but not surprised. He had heard the talk of a young Ranger who shot straight and talked hard. This outlaw wasn't as hard as he pretended. He said he would talk pretty quick.

"Now, even if you talk, you are going to do prison time in Texas. Do you understand?"

The man nodded.

They all caved just as quickly, but Talon found that none knew who the ringleader was. They were kept in the dark and only had contact with their immediate leader. This displeased him but there was nothing he could do about it. Jessie promised to take care of the prisoners until Talon was ready to take them to Texas.

"Jessie, I need help. I'm on the trail of an outlaw by the name of Jackson Slager. He's driving a stolen herd of cattle up here for a man named Kincade. He's an Easterner. Have you run into this Kincade?" Talon asked.

"As a matter of fact I have. He's operating out of Medicine Bow. It's strange, because I saw him and a slick-looking gunslinger ride out of town late yesterday afternoon, heading south."

"Sounds like Slager."

With the new information, Lowry and Talon headed to the Four T Ranch. They were beginning to get worried since Cat had not shown up in Laramie. When they made it to the canyon, Cat was still there with the four wounded outlaws. He hadn't seen or heard from Calling Eagle. Talon made the decision for the sheep herders to move the sheep to the western range, south of the homestead. After he got them started, the Rangers mounted the four outlaws onto two horses, in typical Ranger style. They headed toward Medicine Bow. The wounded outlaws slowed their progress, and the trip took several hours more than it should. The long journey sapped their normal vigilance and dulled their senses, so they were shocked when just before entering Medicine Bow, a single gunshot knocked Talon out of the saddle. Cat and Lowry cut down the four prisoners and jumped off to tend to their friend as the prisoners' horses ran off, dangling their corpses. The slug had struck Talon in the back, just below his left shoulder blade. They quickly determined that the wound was painful but not lethal, helped along by Talon's cursing at his carelessness. Lowry got the young Ranger to his feet and they took defensive positions behind their horses.

They couldn't spot the shooter or shooters and no more shots came, so Talon insisted that they take him to Mrs. Moore's. Talon's throbbing shoulder made it difficult to move. Cat guarded their rear as Lowry practically carried his friend to Mrs. Moore's place, where they stretched him face-down across one of the tables and started cutting at his shirt to get at the wound. Mrs. Moore hurried in from the kitchen and at first saw nothing but an exposed and bleeding back. She didn't recognize that it was Talon, but went straight to work on someone in pain. She put pressure on the wound to stop the bleeding.

She could feel the bullet through the dish towel she used to stanch the blood. It wasn't very deep. She went into the kitchen and came back with a large bowl of hot water and more clean towels. She took a sharp paring knife and sliced the wound as gently as she could. She tried to pull the slug out with her fingers, and when that didn't work she sliced into the wound from a different angle and grabbed a nearby pair of cooking thongs to probe for the bullet. This time she latched onto the slug and probed it out of his back. She then cleaned the wound with warm soapy water. She soaked the wound in coal oil, then stitched the skin together with needle and thread. Throughout the ordeal, Lowry and Cat held Talon firmly against the table to keep him from moving. Mrs. Moore took a strip of cotton rag placed it over the wound and then bound it in place with another wrapped around his body.

"You sure were lucky, cowpoke," she said when she was finished. "The bullet didn't bury very deep. That back shooter must have been a good distance away, and your heavy coat and leather vest slowed the bullet some, too."

"Thanks, Mrs. Moore." Talon said.

When she heard the voice, it was the first time she realized it was Talon. She screamed, "Sally!"

Sally, dressed in flour up to the elbows from preparing doughnut dough, burst from the kitchen.

"It's Talon."

Sally screamed, too. She grabbed him, not thinking of the pain he was in at the time, and gave him a big welcome hug and kiss. "You've been shot," she observed.

"Yes, I know."

She kissed him again.

By this time, a small crowd had gathered outside on the porch. The small town didn't sport a marshal, so the citizens took care of themselves. The business leaders wanted to know what was happening. They had run down the horses with four dead men tied to them. They wanted to know who these men at Mrs. Moore's were. They came in asking questions. When they found out Talon had been ambushed and that they were Texas Rangers, their worries vanished.

Lowry looked at Talon and said, "You sure can ruin more clothes by being shot than anyone else I know." Talon managed to smile. By this time, Sally had cleaned the flour off herself and started cleaning it off Talon. When finished, she gave him another hug and kiss.

"Mrs. Moore, do have anything to eat, I'm hungry," Talon asked.

"Why am I not surprised?" she exclaimed.

"Lowry. Cat. Now, you are going to eat some *real* home cooking."

They all laughed. Sally hugged him again.

The townsmen said they would take care of the bodies, and said they were sorry he got shot in their town. Things settled down and then the pain struck. For such a small wound, the throbbing was just about unbearable.

"We need to get to the ranch." With that said, Talon got to his feet and made for the door.

"Oh Talon, you can't leave," said Sally.

"I've got to, sweets. Don't worry, though, I'll be back for another one of those kisses."

Sally blushed and thought, *what have I done?* She and T. T. had talked for years about how she should trap Talon, and she had just messed up the plan with her spontaneous emotions. *Or, maybe she hadn't*, she thought.

"Talon, you let your Aunt Bertha check that wound when you get to the ranch," Mrs. Moore said. "I figure you will be riding pretty hard, and we don't want those stitches to pull."

"Yes, Ma'am," Talon replied as the Rangers climbed back on their mounts. "Much obliged to you and Sally."

The Rangers rode out of Medicine Bow at a hot pace. They needed to get to the homestead, and it was getting late. They figured the shooter was long gone but not forgotten. His time would come. Riding through darkness didn't bother Talon, as he and Sam knew the way. When they got there, they hailed the home place and announced they were coming into the yard. Aunt Bertha met them.

"Oh, Talon, you were right," Aunt Bertha blurted. "They hit us this afternoon. We lost two hands and Uncle Jim has been wounded. If it hadn't been for Calling Eagle, we would have been doomed. He had decided to come by before going to the spring. He caught the raiders by surprise. Wolf and Gary killed three of them and they say they wounded one or two more before they pulled out of here."

Talon rushed in to see Uncle Jim. "What are the odds of us both being shot on the same day?" he asked.

Jim looked up and said, "It's not a bad wound, just a graze. Bertha fixed me up just like new. I hated we lost two fine hands, though. They fought with courage. They were not like the gunmen we faced."

"Uncle Jim, one of those gunslingers was waiting for us in Medicine Bow. He got me in the back. Mrs. Moore fixed me up," Talon said. "Aunt Bertha, Mrs. Moore said I should let you look at the bandage to make sure I didn't tear anything during our ride here."

The temperature was dropping and the wind was blowing in heavy gusts. By morning, the mountains were blanketed in the winter's first snowstorm. This would probably stop the range war. The outlaws fought like Indians—only in good weather.

Lowry and Cat went to Medicine Bow to send McNelly a wire telling what had happened. In the wire, they confessed they had lost the herd. It didn't make it to Wyoming, or at least not yet. They ate at Mrs. Moore's and Sally served them.

"So you're her," said Lowry.

Cat giggled.

256

"What do you mean?" Sally asked.

"You're the girl Talon named the 'prettiest strawberry roan I ever seen.' He told me every time he looks at Sally, he thinks of *Sally*."

She blushed. Her mother overheard the conversation and laughed. These Rangers were going to torment her, and she thought it was funny.

Lowry went on, "You do know he has a girl in every town in the Rio Grande valley both north and south of the border."

Sally caught on to what he was doing. "Did *you* shoot him in the back?"

Cat burst into laughter. He couldn't hold it any longer.

The weather turned even worse, and another winter storm blanketed the area. Lowry and Cat stayed in Medicine Bow waiting for a reply from McNelly— which they finally received, and it wasn't good news. The marshal at Pueblo had reported the escape of Ben Iverson. McNelly's wire indicated that Iverson had rejoined The Combine, ignoring Talon's warning of his fate if he did so. Also, McNelly said there were reports of a herd of cattle being shipped on the Kansas Pacific from Denver. Any cattle arriving in Wyoming will be without brands. Then he told them to continue to track down Slager and his men. The news of Ben Iverson's escape did not surprise Talon much. *I never was comfortable with the setup in that town. I'll stop and have a little talk with that marshal when we go back to Texas*, he thought.

The winter was extremely wet and cold and seemed to drag on and on. At least Talon had turned 17 and no longer had to lie about it. His shoulder was healing, too, with no apparent problems. His courtship of Sally was discreetly done, for fear she would become a target. He had not told her of Billie Jo or of Mimi, but the Moores becoming targets was a real concern. They were dealing with dangerous men. Lowry and Cat had spent many cold days exploring the Four T Ranch and reported new encroachers on the eastern range. They had set up several camps as if they owned the land.

Chapter Five

The decision was made to roust them out while the snow was still on the ground— to make them fight in the cold with the Rangers and the Four T hands fighting from an ambush. When the fight started, it would be impossible for any of them to go to Medicine Bow or Laramie because of the risk of being shot in the back.

Talon held a huge advantage over the encroachers; he knew how to work his way through the mountains. They didn't. This meant he could slip in on them without warning. For them to attack the home place, they could come over the western bluff overlooking the Medicine Bow River or up the river basin from the north or south. Any attempt would be quickly detected.

The Rangers closed in on the most isolated group of encroachers. They had the high ground overlooking the lean-to where the encroachers were living. They had built another to keep their horses out of the cold, with a small corral between. The idea of this attack was to destroy morale. They would burn the lean-tos and kill the horses and shoot at them, if given the chance. Cat and Calling Eagle took care of the burning part by firing flaming arrows into the structures. When the fire forced the horses into the corral, Talon shot them with the Sharps. The outlaws waited to the last possible moment to leave their lean-to. The four started taking immediate rifle fire from the Rangers. The attack was carried out in the late afternoon, so that when darkness fell the Rangers could slip away. It made for a long, cold day, but the first raid proved successful. The encroachers found themselves out in the open with no transportation— miles away from their nearest help. They would have to walk out in snow and ice to give any others a warning.

The next day the Rangers closed in on their second target. This time, they would attack at night, by first stealing the horses and then burning the structures. They were amazed how well organized the building of the camps had been and how fast they had been built in winter weather. Someone had planned this invasion of the Four T carefully.

The second raid went off without a hitch and had an added bonus. They captured these three occupants. They stripped them and rode them single file to the outskirts of Laramie, where they thought their ringleader was holed up. Riding these three freezing hard cases, tied to their ponies and helpless, straight into Laramie would cause a stir and hopefully send a message. Maybe Jessie would get involved by wanting to know what had happened to them. He would already know who did it and why, but hearing their side of the story would give the Rangers intelligence they didn't have before.

Their story was that they were just camping but they didn't have a reason for camping in the middle of winter, 20 miles from nowhere. They had no reasonable explanation for building a structure on some-one else's land. With the raids came retaliation, and the encroachers again tried to attack the home place. Running Wolf detected their plan early because they used the river basin as a conduit for the attack. They were easy to spot because they were operating in unfamiliar ter-ritory and the river's serpentine route through the basin slowed their "attack" to a crawl. The Rangers ambushed them when they got to a narrow, exposed area. Several men and horses were killed. Others got an unpleasant freezing bath by retreating through the river. Soaked and wounded, the attackers made their way out of the basin. Cat and Calling Eagle followed to find their base of operations.

Cat and Calling Eagle made it back home after sunrise, and they reported trailing the outlaws to a ranch headquarters north and west of Laramie. There were several new buildings and the range surrounding it had newly branded cattle. The brand was CWR with a bar under it. They also found several cattle with brands that looked as if they had tried to brand over the original brand. In the middle of the night com-ing back, they found two bodies of outlaws that had been wounded but didn't survive the trip to the headquarters. They salvaged the weapons and towed their horses back to the homestead.

"Obviously," Talon said, "they are raiding others, and they want our eastern range for their cattle. It also looks like the unbranded crit-ters from the missing herd made it to Wyoming. If they are not holed up in Medicine Bow or Laramie, they must be in Cheyenne. Their eastern tastes would be better served there."

Talon thanked them for the good intelligence, and after a good hot meal from Aunt Bertha, they went to the bunk house for some well-earned rest.

There were no more raids against the homestead, and a steady patrol of the eastern range found no new encroachers. Talon wondered what the opposition's next move would be. They didn't strike him as the type who would back off from their elaborate plan to dominate the Wyoming cattle industry. *What should we do before they make their next move?*

The spring thaw brought answers to this puzzle. They came in a message from Jessie. It simply stated the four hard cases the Rangers were looking for were in Laramie. They hadn't been disruptive, but he thought he could use some help. The messenger left, and after a few minutes Talon had Running Wolf trail him to see if he really came from Laramie.

The rider *did* take an eastern course, but Wolf stayed with him until he saw him break off to the north. Obviously, someone was setting a trap for the Rangers in Laramie. "Probably the back shooter," Talon said. "Question is, how do we break the trap?"

"They'll expect you to come into Laramie from the west," said Wolf. "We'll give them that idea by dressing three of our hands like you and sending them east. I'm guessing their spies will telegraph the word from Medicine Bow."

"Good thinking, Wolf. Let's place one of our men in Medicine Bow to look for the spies. That way we'll know who they are. If it's just one man, then we'll take him," responded Talon. "We'll slip out to the west and ride into Medicine Bow from the northwest and board the eastbound train. They won't be looking for us on the train. Wolf, you'll hang around town to nab the spy after he sends the message."

"One thing you haven't thought of, Talon," said Lowry.

"What's that?"

"What if the message is for drawing us off on a goose chase, and they raid here again? Our best guns will be miles away. And with guns gone, it makes us open here."

"You're right," Talon said. "We'll still use the feint, though. We'll first position Wolf in the mountain high ground to watch for the spies. Once he determines how many and which way they go, we'll have an idea of what they are planning. We'll start our men late afternoon, which would give them a midnight arrival in Laramie. Wolf, make sure our decoys ride as slow as they can without arousing suspicion. Don't want them taking any bullets meant for us."

"I see," Lowry replied, "That way, if the message is that they are on their way, we can board the train the next morning."

"Right."

Wolf spoke, "If the spies head toward their headquarters, then we'll know they are just drawing us out, and we can plan an ambush or maybe an attack on their headquarters early in the morning."

"We might as well put that into motion now," Talon agreed.

"Our three men need to circle to the south about halfway there and then come back here," said Lowry.

The three men were selected, and to give them an authentic look, Talon reluctantly allowed one of them to ride Sam. "Ride slow, big boy," Talon whispered in his horse's ear as the decoys set off. "And ride safe." They were off during the late afternoon. Wolf had moved to the south earlier, planning to double back into the mountains. It was going to take him a couple extra hours to get into position.

The three hands moved out, riding the Rangers' horses. At a distance, it was easier to identify the horses, particularly Talon's big blue roan. The Rangers followed later to an agreed staging area. Wolf rode in at dark. It was a plan to pull us away from home because the only spy headed northeast, toward the headquarters. Calling Eagle joined them after sundown and they started toward the headquarters.

"Eagle, you and Cat need to slip in on the guards and eliminate them. Then, we'll go after their horses and move them away as quietly as we can. After the horses are removed, I want you to use your magic and fire all the buildings. They'll have no horses to escape with and the fires will make them good targets. We'll spend a few minutes shooting at them, then we'll withdraw. They won't be able to a mount an attack against the home place for several days, which will give us Rangers a chance to appear in Laramie. The real hard cases will be there," Talon said.

It was an easy ride to The Combine Ranch under the full moon and clear skies. Their lights could be seen from miles away. Because of the moonlight, Eagle and Cat had to walk further than expected. The guards were not the most diligent of men and were taken easily. Then, they slipped into the corral holding most of the horses and gently moved them through a gap where they had removed the rails. They did this slowly. Opening the large stable barn, they led the horses out to follow the others. They rode two from the stable, herding all the horses away from the headquarters and out of sight. Afterward, they joined the group.

Talon, Lowry and Wolf positioned themselves in the best possible vantage points to fire on the headquarters. Cat and Eagle did their magic. They started with the outbuildings. Because of the hay in the large stable barn, it instantly burst into roaring flames. Then they fired up the main building with several flaming arrows. It wasn't long before they got a reaction from inside the building. The first outlaw opening the front door got a flaming arrow in the chest. He fell back inside as another arrow went through the door. You could hear screams from inside that they were being attacked by Indians. Cat and Eagle had retreated to their firing positions. The outlaws stayed inside as long as they could before bursting through any outlet they could find. The Rangers lit up the night firing at them. In the open, under an intense firelight, the hard cases were easy targets. The Rangers hammered them. Some were lucky, and they made it into the darkness away from the firing line. It was over. They had accomplished what they had come to do. The Rangers withdrew.

Wolf and Eagle headed toward the homestead. The Rangers headed to Laramie. They needed to show up there to give the leaders of The Combine a false sense of security that their plan had worked. They knew they were riding into a showdown, but was it going to be face to face or not?

They circled Laramie and came in from the east. They made their way to the marshal's office where they brought Jessie up to date on the events of the evening. He had not seen any of the suspected leaders and thought they had moved to Cheyenne to stay out of sight. He agreed with Talon that their cutthroat gang had to eliminate the Rangers and the Four T if The Combine was going to succeed in Wyoming.

Wolf, Eagle and Cat kept an eye on what was happening on the headquarters range. There wasn't much activity. They watched as some hands moved the cattle to a siding west of Laramie. The thought in Laramie was that they had been attacked by Indians wanting horses. The flaming arrows and running off the horses didn't fit the pattern of Texas Rangers.

The next time the Rangers slipped into Laramie, Jessie told Talon he had talked to Kincade the week after their raid. Kincade had asked specifically about Indian raids. Jessie said that he explained to Kincade that with the cavalry out chasing the Indians, they were subject to raids anywhere from the Powder River south to the railroad. So far, no trains had been raided, but other ranches had been hit in the same fashion as his. Kincade told Jessie that he had not figured on Indian trouble. But it was the main topic of conversation in the saloons and the newspapers. By all accounts, the summer of 1876 was going to be the great Indian war. The Cheyenne, Sioux and others were joining together for one last stand. Kincade thought that he was just unlucky.

As much as the Rangers searched, they couldn't find where Kincade and his friends were staying. It had to be Cheyenne. The cavalry hadn't been successful in finding the Indians, and until they were under control it looked like Kincade was going to stay hidden.

In mid-May, a rider from Medicine Bow showed up at the homestead. He was delivering a telegram, and Uncle Jim opened it.

"Oh my, Bertha, Mary Grace and John, along with T. T. and two of her friends will be arriving around the first week of June for a visit. What terrible timing. They say they'll be using private cars and the railroad will position them on a siding in Medicine Bow."

Chapter Six

They waved from the back of their sitting car as the train pulled out of Philadelphia. It was an afternoon start, which meant crossing the Appalachian Mountains during the first night out. Their train seemed to run into the usual delays because of the eastbound freight trains. It seemed as if they spent the whole night on a siding. T. T. was up early, wearing her western clothes. She spent the early morning with the valet and cook. Finally, she was in a position to order and receive a hot, black cup of coffee. The cook prepared for her breakfast sausages, eggs and toast with butter and jam. She felt so good she was going home. They had only made it through half of Pennsylvania during the night. This allowed for the viewing of breathtaking scenery of the western half of the state. Somewhere between here and Medicine Bow she was going to have to take the girls shopping for western duds. Her thought was to do it in Omaha. Without new clothes, they would be so out of place. The clothes they brought would cut down on their fun. Their riding clothes would be okay but not sturdy enough for the open range. She thought almost out loud, *I wonder how they are going to feel about bathing in the hot springs on the Four T. The hands are going to go goggle-eyed when they see them. I wonder how long it's going to take for one of the hands to do something really stupid.* It was hours before her friends awakened. They enjoyed their breakfasts while viewing the scenery. Uncle John and Aunt Mary enjoyed their breakfast in the sitting area of the car.

The girls had taken short train trips, but T. T. knew from experience that this was going to be a tiring ordeal. They spent their time asking T. T. all kinds of questions on what to expect. With so many articles in the newspapers about the Indian troubles in the northern plains, their conversations turned to Indians.

"Will we get to see Indians?" they asked.

"Well, we have an Indian family that is part owner of the Four T. You'll get to see them. They are Sioux and have been with us for years."

They arrived in Chicago the next day. It took an extraordinary amount of time to switch the cars from the Pennsy to the Rock Island Line. They left that night, being pulled by a westbound freight. They didn't know if they would be dropped somewhere along the way for a passenger train to pick up or not. Crossing the Mississippi was an event. The moonlight allowed the girls to get a good view of the river. They were amazed at how small it was. Throughout their school days all they ever heard was the mighty Mississippi, and they had expected a much larger river. They slept while moving through Iowa. It was late the next afternoon when they were switched to the Union Pacific at Omaha. T. T. asked when they would be leaving. The Union Pacific agent told her they were being added to the westbound freight in the morning. She took the girls shopping in Omaha. She got them out of their eastern dresses into western dress. Denim pants, cotton shirts, and western boots came first. Next, she got them bandannas and hats. Then, she bought for them some simple cotton dresses. Now they looked the part. T. T. asked Uncle John for her Colt, which he forked over to her.

Passenger service going west continued to be time consuming because of the eastbound freights. It was one siding to the next or one water stop to the next. It seemed to take forever. T. T. knew it wasn't going to get any better.

After two and a half days, they finally made it into Wyoming. The girls were becoming eager to get off the train. They could hardly contain their excitement. When they pulled into Cheyenne in the late evening, they were placed on a siding next to the depot. There, they spent the night. Their cars were attached to a passenger train leaving Cheyenne the next morning at 9 A.M. While sitting next to the depot, she was watching the passengers boarding the train. She noticed someone who looked familiar. It dawned on her it was Ben Iverson. Hastily, she jotted a message on a piece of stationary she found on the desk in the sitting car. She went to the back platform of the car and waved for a youngster to come over to her. She gave him 20 dollars and asked him to go send this message by telegraph, and he could keep the change. He bounded off in a flash. Within a few minutes he came running up to the car. She went to the back platform to meet him. He handed her 12 dollars and thanked her for the money.

"I said you could keep the change."

"Yes, Ma'am I know, but that would have been way too much."

She handed him the two dollars back. "At least keep this."

"Thanks."

He was off in a flash.

The train started to move. T. T. alerted one of the guards that Iverson was on the train and to be careful of anyone approaching the dedicated cars.

What was he doing here? It was strange to her that he would be in Wyoming. They were only a few miles away from Medicine Bow, and now she was getting excited about seeing Uncle Jim, Aunt Bertha and Talon, but worried about Iverson being on the train. It was going to be a great homecoming. She went into her sleeping compartment and practiced drawing her Colt. It didn't take long for her to get the feel of her weapon. She checked the loads. If there was any trouble, she was ready. The train took an unusually long time to get to Laramie, where she saw Iverson leave the train with two other men. She didn't have much time for thought as they were on their way in just minutes. Next stop would be Medicine Bow, unless they were sidelined for some reason.

On arrival in Medicine Bow, the train pulled onto a siding from the main track to drop the dedicated cars, then reentered the main track to back into the depot for the other passengers. In a few minutes, it moved away from Medicine Bow, leaving them abandoned on the siding. All of a sudden, there was a pounding on the back door of the sitting car. One of the guards went to investigate. It was Uncle Jim, and when he entered, T. T. greeted him with a squeal and ran to him. She gave him a big hug and a kiss.

"Okay, I've got transportation to the ranch. Are you folks ready?" asked Jim.

He had brought three ponies for the girls and a wagon for Uncle John and Aunt Mary. Wolf and Eagle had come with him and helped to get all their baggage onto the wagon. The sun was bright and the early summer afternoon was pleasant. The freshness of the air and the aromas of the wildflowers greeted the visitors. The wagon started, with Jim driving, and the girls —by now well-trained on how to ride western— easily mounted their horses and fell in behind.

Jim yelled at T. T. "Why don't you go ahead with the girls. They look like they can ride well enough and I know they need some excitement after that long train ride."

"Oh thank you, Uncle Jim, I'm sure they'll like the gallop."

Off they went and were soon out of sight of the wagon.

T. T. knew the way. After all, she had ridden it a thousand times. She put her friends to the test and they were keeping up. She could tell they were really enjoying the romp. It was the first time they had ever ridden in a wild environment, and they were getting the hang of the ups and downs of the trail. Everything T. T. had taught them about riding was coming into play on the ride to the ranch. T. T. took the western bluff trail which called for a steady climb for a few miles, but then the trail leveled out. She stopped.

"Smell the Medicine Bow river and its basin! Girls, this is where I grew up, the most wonderful place in the world." T. T. gushed.

"T. T., thanks for teaching me how to ride. This has been such a thrill, following you up this trail. Without your instructions I would have been in the wagon," said Beth.

Margie agreed.

They moved along several miles until they could see the buildings of the homestead. She took them down a steep trail, down into the river basin below, and then made a mad dash to home. As they were about to enter the yard, they were challenged by one of the hands. When he recognized T. T., he waved them on into the yard.

They came to a halt in front of the front porch. Aunt Bertha was the first out the door to greet them, and the hands started gathering around for the homecoming. Then Talon walked up behind T. T.

"Hello, sis," he said.

She screamed at the top of her voice when she heard his voice and turned to find a grown-up brother. She jumped on him and gave him a big hug. She had not seen him since she went east. He had grown into quite a man. He now stood at least six-feet tall, but still wiry in build.

When she grabbed him, he grimaced slightly, since his shoulder was still tender to the touch, on occasion.

"Oh, Talon, Ben Iverson got off the train with two other men at Laramie. I should have shot him right there." T. T. explained.

"You let *me* worry about that, sis." Talon replied.

"Sis, these are my partners and fellow Texas Rangers, Lowry Cook and Night Stalking Cat."

She greeted them in a gracious manner and then introduced her friends. "These are my very best friends from school, Elizabeth Mac-Dowell—call her Beth— and Margie Braun."

Aunt Bertha hugged each of the girls and invited them in. Everyone followed them into the house.

"Are you hungry?" asked Bertha. They nodded, saying they could eat something. Bertha served them beef stew with fresh made bread and coffee. Beth and Margie had never drank coffee before, but endured due to their finishing school training. T. T. got the sugar bowl and put two or three spoons of sugar into their coffee, and they were grateful. It did make it better for their tastes. T.T. loved hers hot and black.

Margie whispered something into T. T.'s ear, and she broke out in a laugh. T.T. thought, *I thought I would have to worry about the cowboys doing something stupid, but instead, now I have to worry about my girlfriends embarrassing me.* Margie remarked how handsome Talon and Lowry were. When T.T. looked again, she had to agree, but these were hardened men who had been put to many tests and had survived them all. Margie had never been around such in her life. *I'll have to lay down some rules when we get private,* she thought.

"Sis, I was sorry to hear about the train incident. It was no fun, for sure."

"Talon, how did you ever turn a horse delivery into being a Texas Ranger?" T.T. asked.

The girls were all ears. The only things they knew about Texas Rangers were written in the eastern newspapers and dime novels, and now they were meeting three.

About that time, Little Bear and Little Feather entered the front door. Again, T. T. screamed. She jumped and ran over to them and gave them both big hugs. Then she stepped back and commented on how much Little Feather had grown, and gave her another hug. Then, she introduced them to Beth and Margie.

The only people missing were Uncle Jim, Calling Eagle and Wolf, who were bringing her aunt and uncle in by wagon. Aunt Bertha had spent the day baking pies and she began to serve them. It was a real treat for the hands. Beth and Margie could see T. T.'s serving attitude came from her Aunt Bertha. These people really cared about each other, and it showed. It was a lesson they would take back east and carry with them forever. Bertha asked two of the hands to ride out and escort Jim. When they left, several of the other hands went with them.

"T. T., I've got you and the girls a place fixed in the loft. You may want to take some time and show them around," Aunt Bertha pointed upstairs.

T. T. took them around the grounds and showed them the barns, corrals, outhouses and other things.

Lowry looked at Talon and said, "What a mess, we're in the middle of a potential range war and these pretty young ladies show up."

"You're right. They are something to look at, and rich, too," Talon observed.

Cat spoke, "Keep your minds on Ranger business. We've got work to do and we now know where our wanted men are. They're in Laramie."

"Come on, Cat, don't be so hard on us. My eyes have been blistered by their beauty," said Lowry as he finished checking his saddle gear.

They all laughed.

The wagon finally rolled into the yard, and T. T. introduced Uncle John and Aunt Mary. Then, she introduced Calling Eagle and Running Wolf to the girls.

Everyone settled into conversations, and the hands left, along with Cat and Lowry. They were setting up their sentry duties, taking no chances on a surprise raid. It wouldn't take long before everyone in the area would know about the dedicated railcars on the siding at Medicine Bow, and whom the occupants had gone to visit.

Soon Talon left and joined the others.

"That was probably Kincade and Slager that got off the train with Iverson in Laramie. We need to go and check it out," Talon suggested.

They saddled their ponies and headed toward Laramie.

Chapter Seven

It was late afternoon when the Rangers crossed the ridge over-looking the eastern range of the Four T Ranch. To their surprise, in the distance to the south of where they were they could see a cattle herd grazing.

"Well, I'll be," said Talon. "They slipped this herd in on us during the last two days because we didn't patrol this range, and we didn't know it."

"We want to change our plans?" asked Cat.

"No, let's go cut off the head of the snake," replied Talon.

Moving off the ridge to the range below, they took their time to look for lookouts or guards for the herd. When they found the herd was unprotected this far north, they put their ponies into a fast pace. Their plan was to enter into Laramie by circling to the north. Stealthily walking the horses through the outskirts of town, they slipped behind the jail and hitched them. Surveying the area, and finding no prying eyes, they moved to the front and into the jail. Jessie and one of the deputies looked up at them with shock.

"Man, we didn't hear you coming," said Jessie.

"It's too late if you hear us," Talon replied.

They all chuckled.

"Three men got off the train today. One was Ben Iverson, an escaped prisoner from Pueblo, Colorado. Do you have a line on them?" Talon asked.

"That's what we have been doing, going through these wanted posters and trying to identify them. We've only found one of your Texas posters, Harry Simpson, and I think we've just found three more who are already here: Jackson Slager, Max Kelly and Clyde Hood. Nothing found so far on the other two. One of them left town on the afternoon eastbound passenger. I sent one of the deputies to find out where he was going. He found out that the destination was Philadelphia."

A deputy walked through the door. "Two are in the saloon. It looks like they are going to make a night of it. Three others just rode out of here, going west."

"Well, we missed the big cheese," said Talon. "But we have the little slices to go after. Which way to that saloon?"

"Can't let you do it now, Talon, too many people in the saloon for gun play. One of the deputies will keep his good eye on them while we wait. The more they drink, the easier it'll be to brace them."

"Jessie, how about keeping more than one good eye on them, it will take more than one." Talon proposed.

Jessie looked at the deputies and said, "You men know what needs to be done. No slip ups, understand?"

They both nodded.

Talon spoke up, "These men are killers and they're dead-on fast with a gun, so don't brace them under any circumstances. I've been after Jackson Slager for months. He has a bounty out on me dead which has given me several uncomfortable times in the last eight months. And I want him to know that *I* got him. Now, if that saloon clears out, come tell me"

Before they left, Jessie told them that he and the Rangers would be getting dinner and where to find them.

"Jessie, these deputies will follow orders, won't they?" asked Lowry.

"They're good men. They won't let you down."

Leaving the jail through the back door and taking the alleyways not to be seen, they entered the back of the eatery. They sat around a table in the kitchen and were served pan-fried steaks, well done, just as they liked them. Beans, sourdough biscuits, and coffee—hot and black, rounded out the fare. After eating, Talon checked the rounds in all his Colts. Lowry and Cat took the hint and did the same. They were ready, and just needed the word.

"Jessie, the hombre you couldn't identify has to be Ben Iverson, and I'm betting the other going to Philadelphia is one of the linchpins by the name of Kincade," Talon said.

"No, I know Kincade, and it wasn't him. Kincade has been putting on a show around here and in Cheyenne all winter. We know he has put out a lot of feelers about the Four T Ranch. Course everyone around here has told him the Four T has fought Indians and outlaws in the past, and it would take an army to move you out."

"Did any one come to you to tell you he had an interest in the Four T," asked Talon.

"Several did, and that's how I knew."

One of the deputies came into the back door and announced the activity was winding down, and that Slager and Hood were sitting at a table at the back left of the saloon. "It's not well lit where they are, he said, "As you move through the saloon doors, they're about 30 feet away."

The Rangers got to their feet. "Now, you deputies watch our backs because we really don't know if they have others with them. And please, let us call the dance. Cat, you and Lowry move toward the bar, and I'll try to slip in unnoticed."

They walked through the eatery and out the front door. As they walked into the street, Jessie and the deputies fanned out behind them. They surveyed the street for any suspicious characters. Finding none, they posted themselves in the dark shadows around the outside of the saloon.

The Rangers slipped through the batwings and headed to the bar. Their prey didn't make a move. Their heads were down and they were talking low, and studying a map rolled out on the table in front of them. Then Talon pushed through the swinging doors. It took a second for his eyes to adjust to the light. He spotted the outlaws, but they were Clyde Hood and Max Kelly, not Slager and Simpson. He walked over to where his shadow crossed the table in front of them.

"Hood, Kelly, I don't want to kill you, so why don't you carefully and slowly take out your guns and place them on the table, with their barrels facing you."

"Who in tarnation are you?" asked Hood.

"The Texas Ranger sent to kill you," Talon replied.

"Who might that be?" Hood asked.

"Talon Finley, or maybe you know me as the Wyoming Kid."

The color drained out of their faces. "You can't take both of us, we're too fast," Hood said.

"Don't want to kill you, but I can. Tell you what. I'll let you live and you give me Kincade's plan of action regarding the Four T Ranch. Then, I'll come back and take you to Texas for trial. What do you say?"

"You can't take both of us."

"Well you know that we've been told to kill first and don't worry about taking prisoners." Talon said.

Together, the outlaws flipped the table.

Talon's first shot cut through the edge of the table but still managed to hit Hood a passing blow to his left rib cage. It staggered him, destroying his timing enough for Talon's second shot to hit him high in the right shoulder. Hood's gun fired two quick rounds into the back of the table. Max Kelly had moved to his right and his gun was leveling off to a solid shooting position when Talon buttoned his shirt. Kelly never fired. His expression went blank, as if he was in shock, and he tumbled to the floor face down. In the instant it took to kill Kelly, Hood managed to pull himself together to make another attempt in fighting. Being right handed he was having trouble lifting his Colt high enough to make a clean shot. He fired twice more into the back of the table.

"Drop the gun, Hood," yelled Talon.

Hood ignored Talon. He used his left hand to support his right arm to take aim at him. Talon's final shot hit him below the chin knocking him into the back wall of the saloon. It was over: four shots, two dead.

Talon reached down and picked up the map they were looking at. It was of the Four T's eastern range, and showed a timetable for moving a herd of cattle to the Four T's loading pens at Medicine Bow. Talon handed the map to Lowry. The herd was to move in two days, according to the timetable of written instructions on the map.

"Well, that gives us time to destroy their plan," said Talon.

Cat was searching the outlaws for other information they may have been carrying. He came up empty. Jessie and the deputies were, by this time, standing in the saloon when Jessie said, and "I think you are faster than T. T."

Talon laughed and replied, "I hear she can hit five in five."

Jessie shook his head and muttered, "Five in five. It'll be the Fourth of July soon, maybe we'll get to see."

Other interested townsfolk were crowding into the saloon to see what had happened. Lowry noticed someone leaving the saloon and followed him out the door, but he was too late to stop him. He was already riding at a fast gallop to the west.

Reentering the saloon, he told Talon of the rider.

"I guess we'd better get going after him," said Talon.

Cat spoke up, "Let him get the message to them about Kelly and Hood. It will unnerve them and maybe a few of the soldiers will disappear."

"Good thought," replied Lowry. "Besides, by the time we get to our horses behind the jail he would be long gone and hard to track at night."

"Well, he is either going to the headquarters, the herd, or Medicine Bow, and I bet he doesn't make it tonight," said Jessie. "Talon, I have to tell you, I thought you weakened just before your last shot."

"I was trying to let him live to get information," replied Talon. "As it turned out the map had the written instructions on it. Let's get out of here. Is the telegraph still open?"

"Yes, but we'll have to hurry," replied Jessie. He took them straight to the telegraph office. The operator was going through his messages from the day when Talon asked him, "is there any message in the stack to Philadelphia?"

The operator looked up, and asked, "Who might you be?"

"Answer the man, Charlie," said Jessie.

"Sorry, marshal, I didn't see you."

"I think there was one sent this morning, let me see. Yep, here it is. It went to a James Talbot from someone signed Kincade." He handed it to Talon.

"He says arrangements have been made to ship the herd out of Medicine Bow in two days. That he is on his way to Chicago to collect when the herd gets to the buyer. Wow, they were paid 40 dollars a head, rail head delivered Chicago for steers 1,100 pounds or more. I can't wait to tell Uncle Jim about this."

Talon wired Captain McNelly about the deaths of Hood and Kelly and asking for warrants for Kincade and Talbot. Talon figured that Kincade would collect the money for the stolen cattle in Chicago and take it directly to Talbot in Philly. If necessary, Talon could travel to Philadelphia with his sister when she returned to school in two weeks. He ended the telegraph to McNelly by asking for instructions wired directly to him in Medicine Bow. Over the next two days he could serve the other two warrants and be ready to move east. He would send Cat to Texas with gear.

I want to take Lowry with me to bring them back to Texas. Could Texas Rangers arrange to have local authorities pick them up and hold them in Philadelphia until they arrived?

Chapter Eight

T. T. rousted her friends out of bed at dawn. "Come on, you have to see the sunrise!"

They rolled off their pads and climbed down from the loft. T. T. took them over to the wash basin and got their eyes open with a wet rag. Aunt Bertha had breakfast on the table: black coffee and toasted cheese on bread, a very simple fare. Beth and Margie both reached for the sugar and they didn't bother about measuring it. They just poured it into their coffee. They did take the time to stir. "Why are we up so early?" asked Beth.

"We have places to go, things to do, and people to see," replied T. T. "First, we are going to saddle our horses and ride to Medicine Bow and get Sally Moore, my very best girlfriend here, and then we are going to the hot springs for a soaking bath. After which, we are going to take Sally home and help her prepare the doughnut dough for to-morrow's doughnuts. Then we are going to hot trot it back home to help Aunt Bertha with the late afternoon chores. Doesn't that sound like a lot of fun?"

Beth and Margie looked at her through their sleepy eyes like she was a crazy woman.

"I had a long talk with Sam yesterday and he agreed to let me ride him. So I saddled Sam, Sally for Sally, and two much more spirited horses for you. You'll feel how much stronger they are when we climb the mountain trails today. Just remember what I've taught you. Now come on eat up and let's go!"

Beth and Margie did what they were told, as they were afraid not to be punctual. They quickly finished their meals and were out the door.

"T. T. don't we need towels if we are going to bathe?" asked Margie.

"Already in your saddlebags," replied T. T.

The girls checked their gear before getting on their horses. They both mounted and followed T. T. on Sam, towing Sally out the corral gate. Margie slowed to make sure the gate was securely closed. Then she quickly caught up with the others. Running Wolf was there to accompany them on their journey. T. T. was happy for the extra gun.

As they were told, Margie and Beth could feel the strength of their mounts as they climbed to the bluff trail to Medicine Bow. T. T. kept a much faster pace than before and they enjoyed the romp. The morning eastbound train had started to pull away from Medicine Bow when the girls hitched their horses to the rail outside Martha Moore's eatery. They bounded up the steps and through the door. T. T. was calling for Sally. Sally heard her voice and came out of the kitchen screaming. She couldn't believe it was her very best friend coming to see her. They hugged, kissed and danced with joy. The patrons got a kick out of seeing the reaction, since they all knew T. T., too.

Mrs. Moore came from the back to see what was happening. She also squealed and gave T. T. a hug and kiss. T. T. introduced Margie and Beth, and the Moores gave them hugs.

"Mrs. Moore, we came to take Sally away from you today. We're going to go to the hot springs for soakers."

Mrs. Moore answered, "Let me fix you girls an exciting picnic basket to take, but Sally, you need to be back no later than four to make the doughnut dough."

"Don't worry, Mrs. Moore, I've told Beth and Margie we're going to help her with it when we get back."

While Mrs. Moore was putting together the basket, T. T. told Sally, "I've brought your namesake to ride."

"You brought Sally for me to ride?" she said. "You're so thoughtful."

"You know, I took care of your brother after he was shot in the back. Oh, T. T. he's been wounded several times in gunfights, and his body is scarred from his head to his knees. It's just awful to see the scars."

"Why, Sally Moore, what were you doing looking at my brother's body?"

Sally turned crimson. All the girls laughed, and even Mrs. Moore and the patrons got a chuckle. The girls were out the door, mounted and gone in a flash. To keep up with T. T. you had to have a lot of energy. This went for horses, too. The girls could see why she had selected stronger mounts for them. They were getting used to the western style of riding at a gallop, with no time to waste in any one spot. This time they took a different trail, this one on the eastern side of the Medicine Bow River and into the mountains. When they crossed into the eastern range of the Four T Ranch, snuggled into a small canyon was the hot spring, which Talon had found years earlier. They had spent days carving a sitting pool so when they pulled a rock from the dam, gravity would feed the hot water into the sitting area. The water did have a slight mineral smell, but not too bad. And as far as they could tell, there wasn't any arsenic in the mix. Running Wolf said the water was good for mixing red war paint. It stayed on the skin longer. True to T. T.'s instructions, they were clad in cutoff long johns. They moved into the pool and did what they came to do— soak and talk about boys.

Running Wolf took a position above the springs, with his Winchester.

"What is Running Wolf doing?" asked Beth.

"He guarding us against unwanted guests," answered T. T.

"Like who?"

"Mister Mountain Lion has a family around here somewhere and they play in the pool occasionally. Sally and I were soaking one afternoon when one appeared on the ridge overlooking the spring. He stared at us for a short period and left. Since then we always bring someone to guard us."

"Is he a good shot?" asked Margie.

"He doesn't miss, but in this case, he would shoot to scare. The lions have as much claim to this area as we do, maybe more."

After soaking, the girls sat on the large rocks surrounding the spring and enjoyed the picnic lunch Mrs. Moore had packed.

Running Wolf joined them for the food. After they were finished eating, they were almost dry and they put their clothes on and prepared to leave. Soon, they were back on the trail to Medicine Bow. It was late afternoon when they hitched the horses out front. They bounded into the eatery, ready to plunge into the preparing of doughnut dough. They were all in the kitchen when they heard someone in the front yelling. T. T. went to check.

She found a foul-mouthed hard case ranting about something. T. T. asked if she could help. Sally was close to the door of the kitchen, listening to what was being said.

"I want the horse thief who stole my horse."

"About what horse are you talking?" asked T. T.

"Not one horse, but two."

"About which two are you talking?"

"They're the roans hitched out front; they were stolen from me."

"Oh, *I* own those horses," T. T. replied.

"They were stolen from me." He looked confused.

T. T. felt he wasn't ready for a female owner to pop out. "Yes, I bought those two horses from a Texas Ranger passing through. He said the horses were too easily marked it wasn't safe for him to ride them."

"I told you; those horses were stolen from me."

"Well they have been branded by the U.S. cavalry and he gave me the bill of sale the cavalry gave him, and on the back of it he wrote a bill of sale to me."

The hard case was stumped and he didn't know what to say. About that time, Ben Iverson entered the front door.

"What's taking so long, Simpson?" he asked.

"Well if it isn't that old coward, Ben Iverson," T. T. observed.

His eyes adjusted, he saw T. T. and went pale, slightly staggering into the hard case in front of him.

T. T. didn't hesitate. She drew and fired at Iverson. She hit him twice before he could adjust his stance. Simpson, realizing he was in a fight drew his gun, but missed T. T. as Iverson fell into him, knocking him off balance. T. T. laced him with three quick shots to the chest. They knocked them backwards over Iverson. She had again killed two men. This time, she had taken fire at close range and it unnerved her. She was shaking while she reloaded her Colt. Looking out the front window, she saw a slick looking man get on his horse and slowly ride out of town to the east. People were crowding into the eatery to find out who was doing the shooting. T. T. stood their trembling, and the girls surrounded her as she burst into tears.

"It was a great day up until now," T. T. said.

They continued to hug her and she began to settle down. Sally was nurturing her with hugs.

"Oh Beth and Margie, I surely didn't want to get you in harm's way. Please forgive me."

Margie looked at her and said with a smile, "You did it, it wasn't bragging."

T. T. seemed to come out of her mood with a smile, acknowledging Margie's comment.

"Mrs. Moore, is it all right if Sally comes to the ranch to be with us tonight?"

"I'll manage, it'll be okay."

The girls left, and on the way out of town they went by the rail cars to check on the help. They found them in good stead, and when T.T. told them Mrs. Moore would need help in the morning, they agreed to cover her needs.

Off to the ranch, the cool summer evening with the aromas of wildflowers and fresh air filled their lungs. Margie and Beth had fallen in love with the Four T Ranch. The bluff trail offered the quickest way home and the best viewpoints for the setting Wyoming sun. The atmosphere was stunning, as the stars filled the sky and they moved along the trail. Soon, they were challenged by one of the hands, but when recognized they were waved through. The girls gathered at the dinner table along with the hands, and they related to Aunt Bertha and Uncle Jim what went on during their day. When it got to the killing of the two hard cases, they were astonished by the story. All could tell T. T. was still shaken over the gunfight.

Chapter Nine

The Rangers had camped in the jail and were just getting awake when one of the deputies brought in a tray of bacon and biscuits from the eatery. Jessie walked in behind him.

"Just got this wire from Martha Moore to Talon," he said.

Talon reached up with his hand and took the message. He opened and took a minute to read it.

"T. T. killed Iverson and Simpson in a gunfight at Mrs. Moore's eatery in Medicine Bow. We'll need to telegraph McNelly — only one warrant left to serve."

Then another deputy entered the jail. "Talon, your Mister Slager just rode into town. He hitched up over at the hotel."

"Thanks. Let's go and get the hotel surrounded before he gets away. Now remember, this man is a deadly killer and faster than you'll ever imagine, so don't brace him. Kill him without warning, understood?"

They all nodded in agreement.

"Let's go out the back because I'm betting he has a front room in the hotel overlooking the main street. So you deputies go about your regular routine. He's been watching you and he'll know if you're on to him. Jessie will go out the back with us. Remember, go slowly and talk to people as you go," Talon suggested.

"Well, he saw me carrying the food tray, so we can't get out there too quick."

"That's a good idea. Let's eat. One of you go out still eating a biscuit and make your rounds. This way, we can watch his horse."

The deputy who had carried the tray left the jail, munching on a biscuit. The others stayed a few minutes before leaving. The Rangers and Jessie had one last cup of coffee each, and slipped out the back of the jail.

While Cat, Lowry and Jessie took positions around the back of the hotel, Talon made his way through its back door. Without disturbing anyone, he made his way into the lobby and eased over to a chair that was covered in shadows created by sunlight coming through the front window. He was going to wait for Slager. It wasn't long before he heard a stirring coming down the hall upstairs. When it hit the steps he thought his man was on the move and ready to run. It had to be Slager. He was carrying his gear with his left hand. This was the first time that Talon had laid eyes on him, but by description, he knew it was him.

Slager was slick and his Colt was tied down. He wore a white shirt and a cloth vest lined with a platoon of shiny silver buttons, neatly fastened from top to bottom. *Thanks for the nice targets,* Talon thought as he sized up his man.

He walked to the front desk, not bothering to look around the lobby, and was unaware that Talon was watching him. Talon slowly rose to his feet as Slager moved to the front desk to pay his bill. He stayed in the shadows so Slager would have to peer through the glaring sunlight to see him.

Slager turned to leave when Talon spoke, "Goin' somewhere, Slager?"

"Who's that?"

"Talon Finley, the Texas Ranger you put a bounty on, remember? Time to pay up."

He dropped his gear trying to find Talon in the shadows.

"It's like this, Slager, you can drop your gun and I'll take you back to Texas for trial or you can die right here. Make your move," Talon said calmly.

"Wait a minute, young man, my name is not Slager; it's Cliff Burns," the man replied.

"Cliff Burns?"

"Yes, I don't know anyone by the name of Slager. I was brought out here from Chicago by a fellow named Kincade. He was to meet me and take me to some loading pens west of here to look at a herd of cattle. I've been here three days and I haven't seen or heard from him."

"That's because he's on his way to Chicago or Philadelphia now, I don't know which."

"This has been a big waste of time for me," Burns said.

"Maybe we can do something for you. I can show you the herd and introduce you to the real cattlemen of south central Wyoming," Talon offered.

"That would be great. Did you say you were a Texas Ranger?"

"Yes, sir, I did."

"What is a Texas Ranger doing in Wyoming?" he asked.

"We're breaking up a cattle rustling ring out of Philadelphia and Texas. I may have just saved you some big trouble. Let's get you into the saddle to go see the herd."

Talon thought for a moment that was the closest he had ever come to drawing on an innocent man. It was due to the man's calm demeanor that he didn't draw. They walked out onto the front porch of the hotel and Cat, Lowry, the Marshal and his deputies met them.

"Slager is not here," said Talon. "This man is Cliff Burns, a cattle buyer from Chicago. Sorry, Mister Burns, we mistook you for a dangerous outlaw."

"That's okay, let's go see the herd."

The Rangers and Burns saddled and headed west. Burns didn't ride as well as the Rangers, so they set a moderate pace. By late afternoon, they approached the herd from the north and found it unguarded. Climbing onto higher ground, they surveyed the area and did see one campfire in the distance. When they approached, Talon hailed the camp, and got an immediate answer. They rode into the outlaw camp.

"Howdy, Mister," one of the cowpokes said.

"Howdy, stranger, what are you doing on the Four T range?" asked Talon.

"Well, we were hired to punch these cattle up here from Kansas. We've been here for a couple of days, but the fellow who hired us rode in here earlier, took four punchers with him and headed south."

"Did he say where he was going?" Talon asked.

"Nope, he didn't say."

"Did you pokes know you were driving stolen cattle?"

"Well, when we got here, we started to talk about that. Now, none of us want to be on the wrong side of the law. If they were stolen, we didn't do it. That's why we stayed, to make sure we didn't get ram-rodded into something we didn't do," the man answered.

"Good thinking. We are Texas Rangers and on the trail of the man that hired you. Which way did he go?"

"They headed south in a rush."

"Give me your names." Talon wrote them down in a small note-book he carried in his vest pocket. "Now you're working for me. Do you agree?"

"Yes, sir, we do," they answered.

"You cowpokes stay here until help arrives, and do what they tell you to do. And you're going to make it out of this without a black mark against your name. Do you understand?"

"Yes, sir."

"Cat, get on the trail. Lowry and I will catch up with you some-time tomorrow."

Without another word, Cat was on the move.

"Mister Burns, follow us."

Talon started moving into the mountains, finding his shortcut trail. It was dark when they rode into the homestead yard. Uncle Jim moved out of his rocker and greeted them.

"Uncle Jim, this is Cliff Burns, a cattle buyer from Chicago."

"Glad to meet you," replied Jim.

"We got a wire that T. T. shot and killed Iverson and Simpson. Is she okay?"

"It really shook her because Simpson got some shots off. I think it was the first time she found someone who could shoot back," Uncle Jim speculated.

"The only one left is Slager, and he headed south off our eastern range, abandoning the cattle herd he moved in there. Now there are four cowpokes staying with the herd tonight. I hired them and they expect to work for you when you get our gang there tomorrow morning. Uncle Jim, this is what I want you to do. Take the branded cattle and isolate them by the different brands. If you recognize the brands, notify the owners that you have some of their cattle. They can sell them or come get them. If you sell the cattle for them, have them pick up their money from you. Any unbranded cattle, split between the brands and the Four T equally. Mister Burns is going to buy the cattle at 45 dollars a head. Use the new pens Kincade and his friends built west of Laramie."

"We'll start on that first thing in the morning," said Jim.

"Where is T. T.?"

"She is in the house with the girls."

Talon and Lowry walked through the door, and found the girls surrounding T. T. He motioned for her to come to him. When she approached he told her, "I've got to leave and probably will not be back before you go back east. I want you to know that I love you and miss you when I'm away from you."

He hugged her. She hugged and kissed him. "Sis, try to stay out of gunfights. Please."

She wiped a tear from her cheek as he strolled out the door.

"T. T., please ask Sally to come out here for a minute, will you?"

Sally came through the door and Talon hugged her, and then gave her a kiss. "Will you wait for me, Sally?" asked Talon.

She hugged and kissed him. "Yes."

There were giggles from behind the door, and Talon turned Wyoming sunset red.

"Come on Lowry, we need to get going."

Talon left Sam and Sally in favor of the red he was riding. Sam marked him, and he didn't need to announce to everyone who he was. The trip to the eastern range took a little longer than usual because of the late arrival of the moon. Once they got to the slope above the cowpokes camp, they were able to pick up their pace. They hailed and slowly entered the camp. The four wranglers were happy to see them, reporting a calm night. Talon asked them in which direction Cat had disappeared. They pointed to a ridge to the south east. Cat had signaled them to start following him at that point and disappeared over the ridge. Talon knew how Cat moved; the trail would be marked by predesigned signals that only Lowry and he could understand. He hated leaving T. T. in such a short fashion, but he had unfinished Ranger business. Somehow he knew she would understand. Talon explained to the four cowboys what was going to happen over the next few days. If they performed, they would be given permanent jobs at the Four T. They showed their gratitude with solemn pledges to do their very best.

A crack of rose colored sky found the Rangers saddled and moving to the ridge where Cat had vanished. When they found the first sign, it signaled to them to make haste. The trail was obvious, so it didn't need a lot of tracking. It was straight south, without bend unless confronted by an obstacle. Their best guess was they were a half day behind. If they kept to a fast pace, they would close the distance. By noon they were getting close to Cat. By sundown, Cat had spotted them on his back trail and moved into a shadowy spot to wait for them. When they got close, he moved his pony from the shadows and gave a wave. Lowry picked it up and headed for him, with Talon behind.

"What do you think, Cat?" asked Talon.

"They're in a hurry and don't fear being followed," Cat responded. "This is way too easy."

"Lowry, what's your opinion?" asked Talon.

"I think they want us to think they're careless so they can ambush us if we slip up," he said.

"Just what I'm thinkin'," said Cat.

"That means they must have another herd coming this way and plenty of support to fight us. The question is, how far north is it?" said Talon.

"I've got a hunch about the route the herd is taking," said Cat.

"Give it to us," Talon replied.

"The second herd was moving north through Pueblo, and you messed up their plans. You captured Iverson and sold the herd for dollars on the head lower than it was worth. I'm thinking the marshal in Pueblo or someone in his office is in with them. Iverson got away pretty easy. What do you think?"

"Cat, I think you hit on it. Let's stop trailing and get ahead by making a beeline to Pueblo. We'll cut southwest here. They won't know we're not following them for a day or two. That will take them straight south and way east of where they want to go. We'll slip into Pueblo and wait," said Talon.

The Rangers were convinced they had made the right move. They kept an extra hard pace because there was still a chance the outlaws could change course and get to Pueblo before they did. That is, if that's where they were going. If not, then they would find them on the eastern route and time was all they would lose.

They approached the outskirts of Pueblo at dusk. The moon was near new, making it extremely dark as they passed through the shadows toward the livery. They rode to behind the draft horse barn and Cat went to the front, and cautiously slipped into the barn. He made his way to the back door and opened it for Lowry and Talon. They stalled the horses and in darkness, doing the best they could in feeding them. They rechecked their gear and their loads.

"It doesn't appear any of the draft horses are home, which means our being here won't be discovered right away," said Lowry.

"Let's move out. Cat, check the livery for any arrivals, and then move over to the marshal's office. Lowry and I will check the saloon and the hotel and wait for you," said Talon.

Cat was in and out of the livery, signaling there were no new horses. They stayed with the shadows and closed in on their objectives. It wasn't late, but activity around town seemed to be slow. The saloon was the most active place, but with only two patrons. After a few minutes, Talon and Lowry moved their way to the hotel. Peering through the window, they could see the night clerk asleep in his chair. They backtracked to the livery and soon Cat came through the back door. Only two deputies were at the jail. No lockups.

"Well, if we are right, we're here first," Talon said in a low tone. "Let's get some rest, I'll take first watch."

Lowry relieved Talon in the early morning hours. They decided to let Cat sleep because of his effort the days before in following the gang. They need him fresh for the coming scrape. Morning broke, and Pueblo got off to a lethargic beginning. A few dog barks, but not much stirring. Cat had positioned himself in the loft overlooking the front of the barn, with a view toward the saloon. The view was limited, but would suffice for now. He saw the livery boy scampering toward the livery. He motioned to Lowry and Talon of the boy's arrival. They took positions at the front door of the barn, peering through the cracks for his unwelcome arrival. Soon, Cat signaled all clear when he saw the boy moving away from the livery. The morning dragged along; they were in a waiting game.

Chapter Ten

When morning broke in Medicine Bow, T. T. was putting together a roundup plan with Uncle Jim. He just let her go on and on about
what they were to do. You could tell he was amused at her assertive-
ness. Because of the Indian troubles, Calling Eagle and his family
were to guard the homestead with three of the older hands. The young
hands were going to secure the herd on the eastern range to complete
what Talon had asked Uncle Jim to do. But T. T. felt it was a good
opportunity for the servants on the rail cars to enjoy seeing part of the
west. The girls were going to take horses to Medicine Bow for them
to ride and join the roundup. She thought it would something special
they could tell their children and grandchildren – 'We actually partic-
ipated in a roundup in Wyoming.' They were off early, with plans to
bring the six folks to the roundup camp on the eastern range. This
would probably take most of the day and she made arrangements with
the hands to have enough bedrolls and food for them to enjoy camping out. After a day or two of roundup she planned to take them to the
hot springs.

Climbing to the bluff trail while towing six ponies slowed their
progress, but the pace quickened after the climb. The girls were really
enjoying the riding and had mastered it better than T. T. thought possible. Sally, of course, was excellent at riding and was able to offer
Beth and Margie suggestions from time to time. When they rode into
Medicine Bow, Sally went home to tell her mother what their plans
were for the roundup. She came back with shocking news. Custer's
Seventh cavalry had been wiped out by the Sioux, Cheyenne and others at the battle of the Little Big Horn. The news disturbed T. T., but
she decided to go ahead with her plans. The Little Big Horn was miles
to the north, and she didn't feel there would be any Indian problems
this far south. It took some time to encourage the servants to go on the
roundup. T. T. adamantly insisted and they reluctantly agreed. She
knew she would have to lead them at a much slower pace than she
would prefer to travel. The men seemed better fitted for the riding,
while the women struggled. She had accomplished what she had set
out to do, and had her guests around a campfire for dinner. The wranglers had worked hard, and most of the herd had already been gathered. Sorting the gathered herd was going to take more time.

While the wranglers handled the sorting and driving toward the railhead, T. T. planned to take the guests to the hot springs. The men opted to stay with the herd, so the women started their trek to the springs. She spotted Gary Ogdalh and asked him to ride guard. He followed along for the safety of the group. It was a cool morning for the ride, and when they got to the springs, the sun was at midmorning. The girls wasted no time preparing the larger of the pools with the warm water. They soaked and frolicked as blue butterflies danced around them. At one time, they completely covered Beth— attracted to her red hair. Seeing her blanket of blue butterflies was worth the ride. About noon, they broke open their baskets for the day. Biscuits and sausages with jam, fried pies and doughnuts made the fare. The girls really enjoyed themselves, and T. T. and Sally enjoyed being with them.

It was obvious that T. T.'s kindness was for anyone to accept. She didn't think the worst of anyone, except those she had killed. It was a lesson that Beth and Margie cherished as they thought about times when they were awful toward their own servants. They made an agreement to change their attitudes toward all people, at least at first, to see if each person would respond. This trip into the wilderness of Wyoming was a once in a lifetime experience for the two chambermaids. They had never been treated like this, and one could tell they were astonished that such a young woman would make such an effort to be kind to them.

After they ate, they made their way to the eastern range and were soon up with the herd. The cowboys were pushing the segregated brands into different pens at the rail siding. There were two chuck wagons, setting up camp far away from the pens. Obviously, Uncle Jim was planning a feast. He had sent riders to the four brands to tell them what was going on and expected he would start to see a response to his messages by dusk. He knew he had better have plenty of vittles to feed his friends. Sure enough, the first to arrive was Nate Campbell, owner of the NC brand. He brought four riders with him entering the camp on a run.

"Nate, how you been?" shouted Jim.

"Sure was glad to hear from you. Tell me what's going on."

"Nate, this is Cliff Burns, a cattle buyer from Chicago."

"Mister Burns."

"Mister Campbell, please call me Cliff."

"What's this about my brand roaming your eastern range, Jim?"

"An organized band of rustlers moved into the area north of here and started rustling cattle. My son, Talon, a Texas Ranger, had trailed them from Texas and broke them up. He's off chasing the remaining lynchpin. They gathered the cattle on my eastern range, thinking I wasn't strong enough to ward them off. Cliff was summoned from Chicago to buy the herd by their eastern representative. So I decided to drive them up here and give you a chance to sell or take them home. For every steer with your brand there is an unbranded steer to go with him. Any unbranded steers left, I'm going to sell and pay the cowboys a reward for their hard work in getting them here."

"Cliff, what are you paying?" asked Nate.

"Since the cattle are ready to load, I'm paying $47 dollars a head where we stand, but you got to load them."

"Jim, are your men going to do the loading?"

"That's part of the deal."

"You just bought mine, then, Cliff," Nate said as the two shook hands.

T. T. rode her pony into the mix. "Hello, Mister Campbell."

"Well I'll be, T. T. you're all grown up. What a pretty lass you are."

"Thank you," she replied with a smile.

It wasn't long before the other three brands showed, and like Campbell, they sold their cattle on the spot. Burns asked Jim to send a messenger to alert the railroad that they needed to spot livestock cars at the siding. This was done. Medicine Bow was the closest, and the cowboy left in a hurry. He wanted to get back before the festivities were finished.

"Girls, you're going to be asked to dance, and you need to learn real quickly how to turn down proposals," said T. T.

She was right. When the campfire got to blazing, someone pulled out a fiddle and a guitar and they started playing their favorite ballads. The girls were asked to dance, and they did— all night. When the food was ready, they dined with cowboys all around them. Most of the cowpokes knew Sally and T. T., but these eastern girls talked so differently. To their credit, and T. T.'s training, they were the most gracious women on the frontier. The cowpokes asked all kinds of questions and finally got around to asking about riding horses.

Beth looked at one young cowpoke and pointed out the horse she was riding. They got interested in the horses because they were spirited mustangs.

"You've been riding that horse?" he asked.

"Why, yes, and Margie rides that one and Sally and T. T. ride the roans."

"Sure would like to see that."

"Well, when we leave in the morning you can ride along with us to Medicine Bow."

Beth had managed to pick up 12 riding companions for a morning ride. Sally and T. T. laughed because they knew they were going to see a riding show in the morning.

After hot coffee and biscuits for breakfast, the girls saddled their ponies. The cowboys were surprised they could do their own. Beth grabbed mane and rein and climbed into the saddle. They were ready. The cowboys seemed subdued, and the only reason T. T. could think of was, the girls were showing they knew how to ride. It didn't take long before some trick riding began to take shape. One after another the cowboys showed what they could do. T. T.'s guests were amazed at what a horse and a man could do together. The morning was cool for the season, and the ride along escort had plenty of energy. Soon, they were at Medicine Bow and the servants returned to their duties, after three days of wilderness. Time was fast running out on T. T.'s stay in Wyoming.

All the cowboys in the area knew T. T. There wasn't a one that hadn't been helped in some way by her. They also knew she could throw a gun faster than any of them. They knew of her exploits. She was so kind to everyone, but would take your head off if she had to defend herself.

The girls said goodbye to their new friends in what seemed to be an endless line. When it cleared, the girls climbed into the sitting car. They were exhausted from the three-day camping trip.

Uncle Jim and Cliff went through the process of counting the steers, while being watched by the different brands. They were satisfied with the count, and invited Cliff back in the fall when they would put together another roundup. He agreed to come. That afternoon, the railroad spotted the first of the cars and Jim's crew went to work loading them. That evening, an eastbound freight picked up the cars and dropped some more. By midmorning the cars were loaded and on their way. The process continued through the next day.

The next morning, Cliff and Jim caught the morning passenger train from Medicine Bow. Cliff had agreed to meet everyone at the Cattlemen's Association in Cheyenne to pay them. Jim's plan was to ride with him and catch the first train back. There were five smiling faces, when paid. An outlaw band had become a stroke of luck for these preyed upon ranchers.

The Four T hands had gathered around the depot waiting for the evening train from Cheyenne. There would be a lot of money on board. It was theirs and they wanted to protect it. The train rolled in slightly late. As Jim got off the train, the Four T cowboys gave him a cheer. He took them over to the dedicated cars, where they lined up and entered one at a time. The last four were the new cowboys Talon had hired.

The first one in, named Jack, asked, "Mister Finley, are we still going to have a job with you?"

"Son, you and your friends worked as hard as the rest, so if you want to stay, you'll have a job with me."

"I can't speak for the others, but I want to stay," Jack replied.

Jim handed him his money. His eyes got really big. "Mister Finley, thank you. I've never seen so much money in my life."

"You earned it, son."

After handing out the bonuses, Jim gathered the cowboys around him. "Men, we are going to make some changes to the Four T. The eastern range will be for sheep. We now have three kinds of sheep. We'll sell the mixed breed males as lambs to be slaughtered. We'll keep all mix breed females to increase our herd. We'll also have two purebred herds. They'll use the Medicine Bow basin around the homestead. We're going to move the cattle operation west of the Medicine Bow River, through a gap that offers a range along the Platte River. Our cattle are there now. Calling Eagle is in charge of the sheep, and we'll be in charge of the cattle. If I ask you to work cattle, I really need for you to work. You'll be further from any towns, and may get lonely. I'll rotate you so you won't have the same job all the time. Right now, I need those of you experienced in handling sheep here. I'm not trying to punish anyone, but until we get a better handle on our operation, this is the way it has to be. Any of you that want to move on, I certainly understand."

The girls were ready to move east. Their experience in the west was beyond what they thought it would be and now it was time to go home. The plan was to be picked up by the morning passenger train. A few of the hands were in town along with Gary to wave goodbye. They were all on the depot platform, mingling with the other passengers and eating a wonderful breakfast prepared by Martha and Sally. Uncle John and Aunt Mary, rested and relaxed after their days on the ranch and pleased that their charges would have stories to tell their children and their children's children, had already boarded, leaving the goodbyes to the youngsters. They had said theirs earlier to Jim, Bertha, Calling Eagle and Little Bear, They, too, would have some tales to relate to their society friends of the remarkable people building a world in the West where ability and hard work earned equal rewards for anyone willing to apply their assets.

"T. T., do you think that Ranger brother of yours will come back to me?" Sally asked.

"Why, Sally, he's been in love with you since he was 12. After what I saw this summer, there's no question that he thinks about you all the time."

"Oh T. T., I hope so, I love him."

"Since about 11 years old, I'd say."

They laughed.

The engine had pulled away from the passenger cars and was now backing onto the siding to connect with the dedicated cars. The girls, dressed in their western cotton dresses, were standing at the east end of the platform. Two down on their luck hard cases crossed the tracks in front of them and headed toward the platform. They passed five of the Four T hands, including Gary Ogdalhs. They rode right up to the platform where the girls were standing. One asked, "Do you know Talon Finley?"

The hands flinched when hearing the question.

T. T. answered, "Yes I do."

"Where can we find him?" the man asked.

"He's not here right now, and just exactly where he is, I don't know."

T. T. motioned for the girls to retreat from the edge of the platform. They casually took the hint and moved away from her. "What do you need him for?"

"That's none of your business."

"Oh, that's just a girl getting curious, that's all."

"There was a man killed here in the Medicine Bow about a month ago by the name of Iverson. He was our kin and we're here to get even."

"So you say," T.T. responded.

"We hear he was shot without warning."

"Oh, that's not true, he went for his gun," she said.

"How do you know?"

"I was there. Would you like for me to tell you what happened?" The man nodded and T.T. continued, "Finley was in Martha's eatery, when a man by the name of Simpson walked in claiming that the blue roan, hitched to the rail out front, was stolen from him. Why, everyone in town knew that Finley had captured and trained that horse. It had been sold to the cavalry and bought back. It had a U.S. Army brand on its left hip, and there was a bill of sale. When Finley told the man about the bill of sale, it flustered him. He didn't know what to say. Then, Iverson walked into the eatery. He saw Finley and went for his gun, which was a mistake. Finley killed them both."

"That's not what we heard," the man replied.

"It's true. You must accept it and move on. Oh, by the way it was T. T. Finley doing the shooting not Talon."

"Who's this T. T. Finley?"

"That's me. Your kin couldn't outdraw a girl. It was the second time that Iverson had braced me. I had told him if I ever saw him again I would kill him. And I did, along with Simpson."

The two started to make a move when four lassos jerked them out of their saddles and drug them away from the platform. The cowboys hogtied them and took their guns.

"Gary, I bet they have posters out on them. Why don't you and the boys take them to Laramie and see."

"You're amazing, T. T., bracing these fellows without even being armed."

"You think?" she asked, with a smile.

Gary chuckled. He helped the others get the two onto their horses, and headed toward Laramie. Then he looked at the hard cases and said, "Someday you'll thank me, because you almost died today."

"She had no gun," the man stammered.

"That you saw," Gary replied.

The engine made it back on the main line and was backing up to gather the passenger cars. The girls hopped onto the dedicated cars, waving their last goodbyes. The engine sounded its last alert for passengers, the conductor waved his flag and they were off. In just a few minutes, they passed the hands and waved as they moved on by. It didn't take long, with the excitement worn off and the clicking of the rails, to seduce the girls to sleep. Only T. T. remained awake, wondering when she would see Wyoming again.

Chapter Eleven

Cat was peering through a crack between the boards of the barn, when he saw the boy walking four horses into the livery. He didn't know for sure, but felt like it was the same four horses he had followed from Wyoming. He signaled to Lowry and Talon. Then, he saw the freight wagon coming down the street. He signaled this and dropped out of the loft. The Rangers gathered their horses and made their way out through the back door of the barn. Cat stayed behind to lock it from the inside. Then, he climbed back into the loft and made his way to the hay lift above the back door. Coming down the ropes, he joined the Rangers and slowly walked away from the barn. They were unnoticed and upon clearing the last structure on the alley, they mounted and headed to a small grove of trees just north of town. They weren't worried about water, since that had been taken care of early this morning.

"We'll wait for dark and move back into town. That way, we can get an ear on what they are doing. If the marshal is in with them, we'll find that out sometime tonight. Cat, is there a good place from which to listen close to the jail?" askcd Talon.

Cat nodded and said, "I think I can get on top."

"Good, we'll meet here after 2 A.M."

They each took a turn at lookout while the others slept. The afternoon finally gave way to sunset. Darkness settled around another moonless night. The three went into the town, taking their time not to be detected. Cat went to the jail, Talon to the hotel and Lowry to the saloon. The night wore on as few visitors entered the lobby of the hotel. Then, Talon got the confirmation he was looking for. One of the deputies came into the hotel and went up the stairs. A few minutes went by and the deputy came down the stairs followed by four hombres, one of whom was Jackson Slager. He was sure this time; Slager moved with the grace and confidence of a wild mountain cougar tracking a mule deer. He wasn't the tallest or heaviest of the group, but the others gave him extra space, even on the narrow staircase. He wore his gun tied down low, and the scabbard had obviously seen much use. His eyes never stopped scanning his surroundings. *This is a formidable man,* Talon thought, *a stone-cold killer who deserves no mercy. He won't get any from me when it's time.*

Talon watched from the shadows as they cleared the front porch of the hotel, heading for the eatery across the street. Talon changed his position, but stayed well-hidden by the darkest of shadows. He now watched the eatery. The second deputy arrived on the scene. After a few minutes, the first deputy left the eatery, heading out to do his rounds. Talon watched until the others left, heading toward the saloon. Talon followed in the shadows. From behind him a dog barked. He bounced between buildings and made the alley. The dog had been penned and could not trail, but did stoke enough concern that soon, three men came between the buildings. By this time, Talon had hidden. The men looked around a bit, and then moved back through the passageway from which they had appeared. Talon, knowing where they were heading, made his way to the saloon. He found Lowry or maybe Lowry found him, by signaling where he was hiding.

"We've got 'em," Talon whispered in a very low tone. "That dog back there almost fried my bacon."

Lowry nodded. "You sure it's really Slager this time?" he asked.

"It's him, Lowry, it's him. No mistake this time."

They waited in the shadows for their next move. About midnight, the men came out of the saloon and went to the hotel. The deputy went about his business of his rounds. Then he went to the jail. There had been no sign of the marshal, only the two deputies. They were the two that had helped the Rangers with the stolen cattle. Lowry and Talon made their way to the small grove of trees north of town. Sometime later, Cat made an appearance.

"How it go, Cat?" asked Lowry.

"I learned a lot. It's the two deputies, not the marshal. He did his job while I was there. He and his third deputy, the jailer, are not involved."

"How do you know?"

"When the jailer and the marshal went to dinner, the other two talked about what they were going to do with their money. They mentioned a herd that was to arrive soon through the Raton Pass. When the Marshal and the jailer got back, they shut up."

"Well, we found Slager and his crew, there are four of them. Now what do we do to trap them?"

"There's no herd yet, so let's watch them for the next couple of days and see if they have fallen into a routine. If they have, we can take them in the street on their nightly walk to the hotel from the saloon," suggested Cat. "It will give us time to make contact with the marshal. Three on four, out of the dark shadows, is pretty safe."

"Cat, I'm going to let you do the in-town watching, while Lowry and I go south to find the herd. There's a dog on the hotel side of the street. He's penned but not muzzled, and he likes to bark."

"So I heard."

Lowry and Talon saddled, checking their gear. They made a slow passage through Pueblo and headed south, bypassing Trinidad and into the pass. The darkness of the night had slowed them, but they picked up the pace at dawn. They stopped at dark, guessing they had covered two days of trail drive from Trinidad. They turned back the next day, at midafternoon. No herd had been seen.

"My guess is they are at least a week away. Driving a herd through this pass is not easy, and it must be taken slowly," said Lowry.

Talon agreed.

While they were resting, movement in the distance caught their eye: two riders moving south.

"It's a good thing they are not concerned with being seen," said Lowry.

"That's good for us. We'll duck into this shallow ravine, where they won't spot us."

They tethered their horses and made their way back to the top of the ridge. With his glasses, Lowry watched the riders approach. They were two of the men they saw with Slager in Pueblo.

"This is a break for us," said Talon. "We can handle them and Slager won't know it happened."

They mounted the horses and fell in behind the two outlaws. As the sun went down, the two stopped and made camp. The moon, being close to a quarter, made traveling in the pass risky to horses. As the night bore on, the Rangers watched as the two fell asleep. Slowly, they entered the camp. They identified the two as outlaws. They quickly disarmed the two without waking them. They were at least a week's walk from Trinidad, so they decided they would leave the men horseless and without supplies.

Talon woke them up. They started to go for their guns, but found them missing. Talon spoke, "This is how it's going to work. I have a federal warrant for Slager — dead or alive — and open warrants for any of his associates, known or unknown— also dead or alive. I don't want to kill you, so I'm going to give you a chance to disappear. If I ever see you again, I will kill you. In the meantime, you can run to where I'll never be and stay alive. What do you think?"

The two looked at each other and agreed they wanted to stay alive.

"Take off your boots. When you meet the herd coming up the pass, tell those hard cases if they come to Pueblo they will be killed— to the man. Since I don't know who they are, they have a chance to stay alive without a poster. Now, what are your names?"

He wrote them down in his notebook. "You now have posters on you in Texas, New Mexico, Oklahoma, and Kansas— dead or alive. If I ever see you again, you'll be dead."

The Rangers left the two without horses, supplies, arms or boots. Lowry dowsed their campfire with the last of their water, so they had no heat. "Have a good life, and here's to never seeing you again," said Talon.

They towed the horses and headed north. "That was tough way to handle them," said Lowry.

"Why waste two shells, when Mother Nature will do the job for free?" he replied. "They'll be mountain lion bait before the day is out.

If they get lucky, they may run into the herd and get help, but knowing that kind, they'll shoot them for us."

Dawn broke and the Rangers were tired, but they didn't change their torrid pace. They even slept in the saddle, one leading the other, the next night. They skirted Trinidad. By midday, they could see Pueblo in the distance. They stopped and rested. At midnight, they made their way across the river and to the small grove of trees north of town. Unsaddling their own mounts and the two extra horses, they took turns at lookout, and waited for Cat.

Cat came into camp just after one A.M.

Talon was in his bedroll, but not asleep, when Lowry nudged him. "Cat's here."

Cat began to go over what had happened the last few nights. The outlaws' routine was about the same, with one change. Slager had only one hard case with him now. "I don't know what happened to the other two, but did you find the herd?"

"We rode for two days south into the pass, and late afternoon on the third we took to the high ground. That's when we saw the two hombres you're missing, riding south through the pass. We fell in behind them and gave them the surprise of their lives." Lowry related.

"I see you have two new horses. What did you do, the mountain lion bait routine? All the draft horses left today. What do you say about moving into the barn tonight?" Cat asked.

Cat led the way. Moving to the front of the barn, he slipped through the door and opened the back door. The Rangers filed in and placed their horses in the two stalls closest to the back. Then they jumped into the loft. Cat stood first watch.

Morning broke on another sleepy day, and the Rangers slept through it. There were no encroachers into the draft horse barn, which made the day without incident.

"We need to slip out of here tonight and corral the marshal. He needs to know something is amiss with his deputies. They are usually eating dinner with Slager around 7 P.M. and don't make it back to the jail until after midnight."

"What about the jailer?"

"He comes in around eight."

"That means the marshal is there alone 'til about eight P.M."

"What do you think about moving in on him before the jailer gets there? We can have a heart-to-heart talk with him," said Lowry.

"We'll do it tonight," Talon answered.

The Rangers waited until after dark to leave the barn. They made their way to the jail through the back alleys. When they approached the front of the jail, they waited until there were no eyes to see them, and they crossed the porch and into the jail. A startled marshal looked to see them enter.

"Why, Rangers, I didn't think I would see you this soon." He reached under the desk mat and retrieved an envelope and placed on top of the desk.

"Here you are, Talon. I'm returning your money— $360. We didn't hold Iverson long enough to expect any pay. I still don't know how he got away, but I think I was sold out. I truly hope you nab him again."

"He's dead, marshal."

"How did it happen?"

"My sister shot him and another hard case by the name of Simpson, in Medicine Bow."

Talon took a few minutes to catch the marshal up on the story. He listened and then said, "I've got a problem here, don't I?"

"Yes you do. The outlaws have switched to Pueblo for shipping stolen cattle. They're driving a herd up through the pass as we speak. We have been here for several days and know your two outside deputies are in with the gang. What we don't know is if the jailer in with them."

The marshal got up and sat on the front of the desk. His eyes dropped to the floor as he said, "I have a suspicion about him being involved in the Iverson escape, but couldn't prove it."

"Let us help you by proving him guilty or not. He usually gets here at 8 P.M. Then you leave. The two outside deputies are eating dinner between seven and eight. When they finish dinner, they make their late night rounds and turn in. They never check on the jailer. You're the first to see him in the morning. He leaves and you take care of things until they show up later in the day. We'll work on him tonight. Don't tip him when he gets here, and we'll pretend we just got here."

The marshal agreed. When the jailer arrived, The Rangers were engaged in casual conversation. While the marshal introduced him to the Rangers he took an unusual stance. You could tell he was uncomfortable.

The marshal addressed the jailer, "I was telling them how their prisoner broke jail. Tell them your story."

"Well, I felt sorry for Iverson," the jailer started. "He was in pain, and hadn't been any trouble. So I let him out to exercise and someone knocked me out from behind. I never saw who they were."

"How did you know there was more than one?" Lowry asked.

The marshal got up and moved to the door, "I'll see you gents in the morning. They're spending the night in the jail to cut down on the expenses," he told the jailer.

After the marshal left, the real questioning began. The Rangers covered the whole day with the jailer. And when he finished, they started over with pointed questions. In the early morning hours, the jailer's story started to unravel. Each minute of questioning put more pressure on him and finally he broke. He confessed that the two deputies were in on the escape. There were other outlaws in town at the time and they wanted Iverson out and they paid for the escape. The marshal wasn't involved. That was good for the Rangers to hear.

"I knew your marshal wasn't involved when he gave the money back he charged us for keeping Iverson. That was the first thing he did when we walked into the office. That's a good sign he was honest. Now, we deal with lowlifes all the time. We can tell when you're lying. Knew it the minute you started to add to your story of what happened. If you had said I don't know what happened, you may have created enough doubt not to suspect you. But, you didn't," said Lowry.

"What are you going to do with me?"

"That'll be up to the marshal. Tonight we are going to tie you up and gag you," Lowry followed.

The Rangers left the jail and walked their prisoner to the draft horse barn. They continued to rest, taking turns on lookout. The marshal was earlier than usual, by a few minutes. He couldn't wait to hear the story. When he walked in, he saw a note in the middle of the desk. His face went to the floor when he read it. "I just can't believe it," he muttered to himself. "I really trusted him." He went about fixing a pot of coffee, slamming and pounding plates, pan and cups in the process. The more he thought about it, the madder he got. A few minutes later, there was a knocking at the back door of the jail. "Come on in, Ranger." The marshal had settled down, "We've got to nab the other two," he said.

"Here's our plan. You go about your business as usual today. The deputies will be with Slager eating dinner and you'll join us in the shadows around the eatery. When the first one come out and usually does a few minutes earlier than the other, we nab him. We'll tie, gag and take him to where we are holding the jailer. The two of us remaining will nab the second. Meet us in the shadows when you leave here."

After outlining the plan, Talon slipped out the back door. In a roundabout way, not to be seen, he made his way to the telegraph office. As quietly as he could, he entered the office. The operator was in his office, behind his public window. Talon gently rapped on the window. The operator recognized him.

"Let me in your office," Talon said quietly. "I need to talk to you about some things."

The operator complied.

Talon entered the office and sat in the corner where prying eyes couldn't see him.

"Here's the help I need from you. Any wires sent to or received from Philadelphia over the last two weeks."

"Just got one this morning from Philadelphia. The boy went to deliver it to a Jackson at the hotel."

The operator pulled it out of his stack of papers and handed it to Talon. Talon read the wire.

TO: MR. JACKSON, PUEBLO, COLORADO

WYOMING A BUST. STOP. SHIP CATTLE FROM PUEBLO. STOP. SENDING YOU A NEW BUYER. STOP. SHOULD BE THERE THIS WEEK. STOP.

TALBOT

He handed the wire back to the operator. "Any others?" he asked.

"I think there are, just let me check."

The operator took a few minutes to check the past days' traffic for other wires. He came up with three, all sent within the last week. Talon read them and they didn't provide any new information.

"Don't tell anyone I was here," he cautioned.

He left the office, heading for the livery.

It was getting dark, and Cat drew the short straw to stay with the prisoner. The Rangers moved out into the darkness and traversed through the shadows to their positions. It wasn't long before the marshal, doing the same, ran into Lowry. They waited outside the eatery for the first of their prey to fly into the trap. *Habits are fatal*, Talon thought to himself as the first deputy left the eatery. He was intercepted by Lowry and the marshal. It wasn't hard, because the marshal called to him out of the darkness. The unsuspecting deputy stepped right into the trap. They tied and gagged him. He sat motionless, behind where they were. The other deputy came out onto the porch with Slager and the other outlaw. They headed across the street to the saloon, where they parted ways. The outlaws went into the saloon and the deputy continued on his nightly rounds. This was a change from past evenings, because he usually parted ways at the eatery. The three pursuers adjusted and traversed along the other side of the street keeping out of sight. Finally, he crossed the street into the waiting hands of Talon. He stepped out of the shadows and dropped him with a blow to the side of his head with his pistol. Quickly he laced him tight with his rawhide lariat. Lowry and the marshal walked the two back to the jail. Talon went to the barn to help Cat move his prisoner to the jail.

They had three birds sitting in three separate cells, tied and gagged. Talon started to question the deputy he had banged in the head. The marshal had never seen anything like it. Talon started by banging him in the head a second time.

"Now, this is how it's going to go. You crossed the line— making yourself a hard case. Worse than being a regular hard case, you were the law when you turned. This makes you a dead man in Texas, where I'm going to take you for trial. Looking at you right now, I don't think you can make it."

The deputy squirmed, with his head throbbing. He was making out the message. The other two birds were looking at the scene.

"I've got a Texas and a federal warrant for Jackson Slager, dead or alive, and all known and unknown associates, which covers you. He and his gang have killed entire families to steal their cattle. He has himself killed women and children. This is who you decided to join with. When he was finished with you, he was likely going to kill you, too."

The man squirmed again, adjusting his sitting position.

"He put a bounty on my head because I was pursuing him. I mean to kill him. His men killed the love of my life in Texas, simply because she and her family took care of me after I was wounded in a shootout with one of his gangs. I vowed to kill him then, and anyone who helps him. You helped him."

As Talon finished talking, he slapped the deputy on the side of the head with his hand.

"You know I might just go ahead and kill you and question the others. The only way you can save your life is to talk to me. I want to know the plans for Pueblo and all involved who live here. That shouldn't be too hard. Marshal, get a pad and jot down the names of Slager's associates in and around the area. I think this man will cooperate now."

The marshal moved to the desk with paper and pen. He sat and listed the names of Slager's associates in the area. Well-known citizens were involved. It shook the marshal to see the depth of the corruption.

After the deputy spilled his guts, Talon gagged him again and tossed him into the jail cell like a ragdoll. The others witnessed the questioning with wide eyes, and when their turn came, they gave information even more willingly.

By the time Talon was finished with the other two, it was past 10 P. M.

"Marshal, you stay here. We're going after Slager."

The Rangers moved through the door onto the main street. It was the first time they didn't care if they were seen. Slager usually headed back to the hotel around 11. This night was no different. A few ticks past 11, he exited the saloon. He and his companion were two or three steps into the street when Talon stepped out of the shadows.

"Jackson Slager?" Talon called.

Slager froze, "Who is it?"

"Talon Finley, the Wyoming Kid, a Texas Ranger. You know. The one you have a bounty on."

"You mean Iverson and Simpson didn't kill you in Medicine Bow?" Slager asked.

"That wasn't me riding the blue roan. It was my sister and she killed Iverson and Simpson. She got Iverson with one shot and took three to kill Simpson."

"What do you want?" Slager asked.

"I want to kill you," Talon answered.

"There are two of us, and I'm a lot quicker and deadlier than anyone you have ever faced," Slager said as his slim right hand dropped closer to the Colt .45 on his hip.

Cat and Lowry stepped out of the shadows. "My friends will kill your hard case pal. I'm here for you alone. I'll give you a choice of coming back to Texas for trial or finishing it right now. It makes no difference to me. I'd just soon kill you. Before you decide though, think about how many drinks you've had tonight, and how it has slowed you down. Tell you what I'll do. I'll let you sleep it off and at noon tomorrow we'll go out back of the jail, and we'll see who is best?" Talon started to close the distance between them.

"Didn't anyone ever tell you that I don't drink, and I'm at my top now?" Slager asked.

Talon was still closing the distance. It seemed to unnerve Slager.

When Talon got to about 20 feet away, Slager drew.

Talon knew he was hit, he just couldn't identify where. Also, he knew he had made the smoothest draw he had ever made, and had fired what he thought were three shots when he heard the click on an empty chamber. Dropping the empty Colt, he drew his second. Slager was down, and Talon could see a flash of his gun in front of him, where he aimed and emptied another gun. Then the pain jolted him and he dropped to the dirt. He hurt all over. Soon, patrons of the saloon were in the middle of the street. One had brought a lamp.

"This one here is still alive, let's get him into the saloon," one of them suggested.

"These two over here are dead. These are the men who just left the saloon," another man said.

Talon, still awake, could feel he was being lifted by several hands. He was carried into the saloon.

"This man has been hit three times, but nothing serious. Send for the new doctor. Let's see what he does with gunshot wounds," the man ordered.

Talon put his hand up to block the light from his eyes, and there stood Cat and Lowry.

"Kid, didn't you check your loads before the fight? You only had three shells in the cylinder," said Cat shaking his head. "He hit you three times, a crease on the right rib cage under your armpit, your favorite knee, and a graze high on the left hip. You're not even bleeding badly. When you got hit in the knee, you went down.

"Where did I hit him?" Talon asked.

The marshal pushed through the patrons and said, "They have moved Slager's body out of the street onto a wagon. How many shots did you fire, Talon?"

"It must have been eight, I think."

"Kid, he outdrew you, but you waited 'til he made his move. In the dark, that gave him more of an edge. He hit you with his first shot. Then, you laced him up the middle. If you had had a loaded gun, he would have never hit you again. The next two times he hit you, he was going down. Flat on his back, his last shot went into the air over his head. Then you opened up with five more shots. If he had been standing, you would have riddled him."

"What happened to the other man?"

"He was at a disadvantage. He didn't get to draw first, and Cat and I killed him with one shot each. The Rangers are not going to be happy about you wasting ammo like that," Lowry chuckled.

Talon had recovered his energy and asked to be propped up. The doctor made it to the saloon just about that time. "Well, you're going to be the first gunshot victim of my new practice," he exclaimed.

"I hope I get a deal, I have three wounds."

Everyone chuckled.

"I've got to quit getting shot," Talon said.

"Maybe you should try staying further back," suggested Cat, winking.

"Next time, I will."

The wounds weren't serious. The new Doctor cleaned and bandaged them. "Try not to move around a lot the next few hours, and I'll bandage these again tomorrow."

"Lowry, Cat, marshal, I'm hungry as a bear out of hibernation. Is there any chance of getting fed?" Talon asked.

They slowly walked him over to the eatery, but it wasn't open. They went to the jail and waited for breakfast— the first sit down meal they had had in two weeks. After breakfast, they walked to the doctor's office where he had the bandages changed. From there, they went back to the jail.

As they entered, the marshal moved his chair to where Talon could comfortably sit.

"Marshal, if it's all right with you, Cat and Lowry are going to help you corral the men on the list. Do you think any of them will put up a fight?"

"Not after what happened yesterday, they won't. Rangers kill, and they'll not want any part of that. Besides, some may not be guilty yet. To *think* about handling stolen property is not same as *handling* it."

The Rangers spent the next two days rounding up the parties listed. The afternoon of the third day, the Rangers again met the last passenger train for the day. An easterner stepped from the train onto the platform, and the Rangers greeted him.

"Well, Mister Kincade, fancy meeting you here." Lowry said.

They took him to the jail.

Walking in, Lowry said, "Look who we have here."

"Kincade," said Talon. "At least we won't have to go to Philadelphia to get you. Does Talbot know you're here?"

He didn't answer.

"Just to catch you up, Slager is dead, and all his known associates in the area have been rounded up. We're going to take you all to Austin, and we're going to take our time doing it, so as to make it as uncomfortable for you as possible. We were waiting on you to leave," Talon offered.

Kincade gave no response.

"Marshal, you have a local mess to clean up. There's a herd in the pass headed this way. Contact this man, Cliff Burns, about buying the herd. My Uncle Jim Finley in Medicine Bow, Wyoming, can help you find him if necessary. List the brands and use the unbranded stock to find the owners of the branded stock. Any money left over goes to you and the citizens of Pueblo. You need to hire some new deputies and a jailer. We'll be through next year to check on how things went. Remember, any unknown associates of Slager are still wanted dead or alive. But some of the cowboys driving the herd may not know they're stolen. If you think them honest, let them go."

The marshal extended his hand, they shook.

In Ranger fashion, they tied Kincade to a horse, while Talon was explaining the rules about escaping. Kincade was white as a sheet when they left for Texas. Their last stop out of town was the telegraph office where Lowry sent wires to Captain McNelly in Texas and Jim Finley in Wyoming describing the shootout with Slager, Kincade's arrest and Talon's plan to take the easterner to Austin for trial. On a whim, he added to the bottom of the telegraph to Finley a single phrase: 'He wasn't bragging, 'cause he did it.'

Chapter Twelve

The Rangers had become accustomed to the cooler summer of Wyoming and Colorado. When they hit the arid Texas heat, they could feel the impact on their mounts and their bodies. They gave Kincade no quarter. The ride was hot, dusty and dry. They avoided most towns and encountered few travelers. Not being in a hurry, they didn't stress the mounts. Cutting across Texas, where they had never before traveled, added to the slowness of their journey. Cat scouted ahead and when camped, watched their back trail. Talon wanted to stop in Independence to see if he could find Mimi. This took them across Texas, north of where they had traveled in the past and further east than they needed to go. Soon, they were at the outskirts of the town.

"Camp here and I'll go and try to find Mimi."

They agreed to wait for him, explaining where they would be if not where he left them. He galloped into the town of Independence. Asking for directions on how to get to the school, he made his way across town. He found the school easily, but he had no idea of how he could find Mimi. He started asking people if they knew her and how to go about finding her. Eventually, he got lucky. A young lady knew her and where to find her. Following directions, he soon found her and her classmates in the cool afternoon shade of one of the University buildings. When Mimi saw him riding up, she jumped and ran to him. "Ranger!" she yelled. Dismounting, he hugged her. The embrace brought the memory of his recent wounds and registered on his face.

"Oh, Talon, you've been shot again."

He nodded yes. "I finished it. I killed Slager in a fight in Pueblo, Colorado. And I'm on my way to Austin with a prisoner, one of those who organized the whole sorry operation. I came by here to let you know that I got the man responsible for killing Billie Jo. I thought you would want to know."

"Thank you for letting me know," she responded.

One of her friends wanted to know who Talon was. She answered, "The bravest of all the Texas Rangers, the Wyoming Kid."

He hugged her again, turned and mounted. "Goodbye, Mimi, see you down the road, maybe."

"Oh, Talon, don't leave me."

"I've changed, Mimi. I'm a hardened killer and my love for you tells me you deserve much better."

He turned his mount and galloped off, not turning to wave good-bye.

Cat and Lowry hadn't made camp when Talon approached them. They could tell he wanted to move on, and they mounted their horses and started south. The next day, they arrived at Ranger headquarters in Austin. They walked their weary prisoner in and turned him over for trial. McNelly met with them after they refreshed themselves.

"Gentlemen, I'm glad you made it back," McNelly said. "You did a good job. Lowry, I'm promoting you to unit leader. Cat will re-main with you as a scout. Talon, I would like for you to be second in command, if Lowry will take you, and if you want the job."

"Of course I want the job, but I need to go to Brownsville to see Billie Jo's parents. I wanted to personally tell them I killed the man responsible for her death."

"Brownsville's where you'll be working. This is one of my last official acts as captain. I'm leaving the service. The lung disease is taking me and I need to be with my family. Thank you for doing the Rangers proud," the captain said.

"Do one more thing for me will you please, captain? Wire the marshal in Laramie and tell him what to do with the four prisoners he is holding for us. They were not a major part of the gang."

"Will do, Kid."

McNelly shook their hands and they left for Brownsville.

It was a hard ride because hot weather ruled south Texas in the dog days of summer. They spent the night at the Patterson ranch, which helped some. Talon had a long talk with Mister Patterson about abandoning Mimi in Independence. Mister Patterson assured him she would get over it. He rested better that night.

When they rode into Brownsville, their first stop was the mercantile. They tied their horses to the rail on the west side of the building and went in to find Mister Wise. Mrs. Wise greeted them first and called to her husband. He came out of the back and saw the Rangers. They shook hands. Talon began to speak, "I wanted you to know I killed the man responsible for Billie Jo's death. I also want you to know how sorry I am to have gotten you involved. If not for that, Billie Jo would be alive today. I am so truly, truly sorry. "

Tears flowed down his cheeks. He hugged Mrs. Wise. They thanked him for letting them know about the death of Slager. The Rangers turned and exited the store.

"Proud of you, Kid," said Cat.

"So am I," followed Lowry. "Let's go to camp and see what's waiting for us."

Coming Soon

THE HONEY HOLE

Book II of
The Four T Ranch Series

by O'Steve

"Angle the coach to the side of the road. Act like you're having trouble with the mules. When you are turned enough, I'll slip out the side," said Talon. "When they throw down their guns, drive the stage right through them. Help is on the way."

The driver gave an excellent performance. The mules cut into the guajillo scrubs on the right side of the road, and Talon disappeared behind them. The driver corrected the maneuver by straightening the mules back onto the road. In the process, he had advanced a few yards closer to the outlaws. The driver yelled, "What can I do for you hombres?"

They didn't answer. So he tried again. The second time they started walking their horses toward the stage. Their Colts were drawn and pointed at the driver and his shotgun. This time they spoke, "Up with your hands! Everybody get out of the coach!"

The driver whispered to the passengers to stay in the coach. They didn't move.

"Didn't you hear me? I said everybody out of the coach."

The driver again told them to stay put.

"There better be more than two of you," Talon said from a concealed position to their left. His voice unnerved them. "Throw your guns to the ground or die."

"We got you surrounded, mister," said the outlaw standing closest to Talon.

"I don't care, but *you* should," Talon said in a low voice.

"Why's that?" asked the outlaw.

"Because you're going to die if you don't throw down those Colts," Talon replied.

The coach was on them before their guns hit the ground. The driver was whipping the mules into a frenzied pace. The outlaws' horses reared in panic to move out of the way. After the coach passed, Talon grabbed the reins of one of the horses, and shot the outlaw riding it. While holding the reins of the horse, he knelt and shot the second outlaw before he could get control of his own horse. He mounted, and followed the stage.

He leaned into the saddle on one side of the horse to make a smaller target for any others who might be with the two hombres he had left dying in the road.

The driver slowed the mules after they had run a couple of miles. Talon caught them.

"Is everyone okay?" he asked.

"That was sure slick, Ranger," said the guard. "I've never seen anything like it."

Made in the USA
San Bernardino, CA
30 December 2013